Paul Thomas was born [...]
Welsh, his mother Irish.

His family emigrated to New Zealand in 1954 and he grew up in Timaru, Christchurch and Auckland. He studied English and History at the University of Auckland and upon graduating became a reporter with *The Auckland Star*.

Between 1980 and 1987 he lived in England and France, working as a travel writer and in public relations. During this period he travelled extensively, both within Europe and in Africa, Asia and the Americas.

He returned to New Zealand in 1987 to become features editor of *The Auckland Sun*, a new daily newspaper. After *The Sun* was closed in 1988 he worked in public relations, firstly in Auckland and then in Sydney.

His previous books, all of which were published by Moa Beckett, are *Christmas in Rarotonga* (with John Wright), *Running on Instinct* (with John Kirwan), and *Straight From the Hart* (with John Hart). *Old School Tie* is his first novel.

Paul Thomas is married to Jeni Porter, a business columnist with *The Sydney Morning Herald*, and is based in Sydney.

Previous books by Paul Thomas

Christmas in Rarotonga
Kirwan – Running on Instinct
Straight from the Hart

OLD SCHOOL TIE

PAUL THOMAS

Moa
Beckett

For Mum & Dad & Jeni

Acknowledgement

I would like to thank my friends
Steve Barter, for providing a piece of the jigsaw,
and Pam and Richard Thom for their boundless
hospitality during this and previous projects.

CHAPTER *1*

*I*t was entirely appropriate that Wallace Guttle, the private investigator, should have spent the last hour of his life looking at pictures of other people having sex.

Such pictures were both Guttle's stock-in-trade and the basis of what could be termed his sex life. As he studied these particular photographs for the first time, he congratulated himself on a job well done: the definition was superb given that they had been taken from a distance of 10 metres and through a window. The object of the exercise had been accomplished: there was absolutely no doubt as to the pair's identity nor the nature of their relationship.

Mingled with Guttle's self-satisfaction was disdain for the couple's carelessness in not bothering to draw the curtains; it offended his sense of professionalism when his quarry made things too easy. Not that it surprised him in the least. In the course of his long experience of such matters, Guttle had frequently observed that people engaged in illicit love affairs often took infinite pains to conceal the fact from those they lived and worked with in their day-to-day existences only to behave with a remarkable lack of caution as soon as they stepped outside that environment. He supposed it was the pent-up desire. Guttle was seldom affected by desire; for him sex was a solitary activity undertaken under controlled conditions.

He fanned the dozen large colour prints out on the desk in front of him. Six months they'd been at it the wife reckoned. She was probably right; Guttle had built up a very healthy respect for his female clients' ability to sense when their partners' libidos were focused elsewhere.

Guttle was one of those lucky people who love their work. He was a private investigator who specialised in personal and confidential enquiries. The changes in the laws relating to adultery, divorce and matrimonial settlements had driven some practitioners out of the industry and persuaded others to find new niches. Guttle, however, had stayed with what he knew and loved. As long as men and women lusted, lied, coveted, cheated, betrayed, suspected and succumbed to the green-eyed monster, he would make a living. In other words, he had a job for life. Guttle was aware that some of his acquaintances in the industry, particularly those involved in what could be broadly termed industrial espionage and counter-espionage, made more money than he did. But they were forever fiddling around with complicated and expensive equipment. Furthermore, their clients were often high-handed and demanding; those who employed Guttle's singular talents were generally prepared, in their consuming suspicion and fragility, to give him a free hand.

And the work itself! Guttle liked tracking people, spying on them, watching them in their most abandoned moments, figuring out their subterfuges, anticipating their moves, employing his ingenuity to obtain photographic evidence that could not be denied.

An aspect of his work which Guttle particularly enjoyed was reporting to the clients. Even clients who were unwaveringly convinced that their partners were having affairs reacted gratifyingly when presented with the photographic evidence. It tickled Guttle to hesitantly push the manila folder containing the photos towards the client then, leaving his hand on the folder and adopting an expression of solicitous concern, to say 'Maybe you shouldn't look at these.' He knew that once he'd said that, they'd no sooner follow his advice than run naked up Queen Street.

Guttle reshuffled the photos, noting what a fine physical specimen the female participant was. She was at least 20 years younger than his client, the betrayed wife. He thought, life's a bitch then your arse drops, your tits sag, and your husband starts bonking his secretary. When he showed his client the photos, first she'd get angry, then she'd cry; over what? The fact that her husband was porking a 23-year-old with a hot body and a dirty mind? Get real. Only the month before Guttle had handed a young and attractive woman a set of prints showing her husband performing oral sex on a male street kid in the back seat of his car. Now that, said Guttle to himself, is what I call a real kick in the guts.

The private investigator interrupted his reverie to glance at his watch; it was seven o'clock on a Friday evening. He knew he'd be the only person left in the three-storey Newmarket office block, just off Broadway. Under normal circumstances, he would have mixed himself a generous Scotch and water and reviewed the contents of the folder in his wall safe which contained the most salacious photos he'd accumulated in the course of his 20-year career. Tonight, though, he had an appointment with a client at 7.30.

The prospect left Guttle unenthused. It was not his usual type of case; it in no way catered to his perverse inclinations and was, in his opinion, essentially a waste of time. However the client had been insistent and, more to the point, prepared to pay the exorbitant rate Guttle had quoted with the aim of deterring him.

Guttle sighed, gathered up the photos and put them in his briefcase, turned off the lights, and locked his office. In the lift down to the basement carpark, he wondered how much longer this new client would be prepared to throw good money after bad. Not much longer, he supposed.

Guttle exited the lift and headed for his car, the only one

left in the dimly lit basement, mentally rehearsing the speech he would use to put the best gloss on his modest progress. As he fumbled to insert the key in the lock of his car, he was asked:

"Mr Guttle?"

Guttle, simultaneously, dropped the briefcase he was carrying in his left hand, jumped backwards a foot, and exclaimed "Suffering fuck!" in a voice several octaves above its usual timbre.

The speaker was standing in the shadows of a pillar half a dozen metres away, virtually invisible. Guttle was not a particularly brave man and had long feared that one day someone whose life had taken a turn for the worse as a result of his professional efforts would come seeking revenge. The speaker stepped out of the shadows and Guttle relaxed slightly; he'd never set eyes or trained a lens on him before.

"Jesus, I just about shat myself," he said.

The stranger chuckled, brought up his right arm, and shot Guttle three times through the head, which was twice more than was absolutely necessary.

Wallace Guttle had lived alone and, understandably, was largely shunned by his neighbours. Under normal circumstances, therefore, his body would have lain undiscovered in the basement carpark until the following Monday morning.

He was shot at 7.12pm. At 10.25pm Margo Dugdale, who worked as a receptionist for the law firm which occupied the second floor of the building containing Guttle's office, drove her 10-year-old yellow Datsun, at a speed several kilometres per hour above what was sensible, into the carpark and over the recently deceased private investigator.

Ms Dugdale had come from the Iguaçu bar and restaurant in Parnell where she'd just consumed three strawberry daiquiris in the space of 45 minutes. That was on top of the several beers she'd had at the regular Friday night office drinks

12

session, the two Bacardi and Cokes in the bar before dinner, and the half bottle of Hawkes Bay chardonnay with dinner which she'd eaten in the bar's restaurant with two colleagues from the secretarial pool. Back in the bar and halfway through her third daiquiri, she'd decided that the best possible way to complete these celebrations marking the arrival of the weekend was to engage in sexual intercourse, preferably several times.

By the time she drained her third daiquiri, she'd settled on a partner. The gentleman in question, a real estate salesman named Tony Rispoli, was quite amenable to her proposition which was worded in a manner precluding the remotest possibility of misunderstanding. Since he was married, chez Rispoli was out of the question as a venue for the assignation; since Ms Dugdale lived with her parents, staunch members of a particularly irrational branch of fundamentalist Christianity, her residence was equally unsuitable. They therefore settled on Ms Dugdale's office; she hoped that none of her colleagues had had the same idea.

Twenty-four hours after Margo Dugdale's stomach had spasmed horribly as she stepped out of her car into Wallace Guttle's brains, some 20,000 kilometres away in Toulouse, south-west France, Reggie Sparks, remittance man and failed gigolo, sat on the window sill of his sparsely furnished apartment and read the handwritten facsimile from his mother, Mareena. It was short and to the point:

Dear Reggie,
I was sorry to hear of your trouble with the police or whatever they were. I presume you and your friend Mr Khong were very drunk at the time. You were certainly very silly but that's no excuse for the way the police behaved. I hope Mr Khong's jaw is mending.
I am sending the money to pay your fine to your account with Banque Populaire and some extra to cover an air ticket home. Whether you decide to use it

13

for that purpose is up to you but I'm afraid to have to tell you there will be no more money from me should you decide to remain where you are. You've had a good run. How long have you been living in France – is it four years? Living rather well I might add. You seem no more able to pay your own way for any length of time than the day you left. As far as I'm concerned, this is the last straw – 20,000 francs is over 7,000 NZ dollars, which is hardly to be sniffed at.

Reggie, I'm sorry if this seems harsh but I really think it would be for the best if you came home. You can stay with me, just like old times.

Please let me know what you're going to do.

Your brother sends his regards.

Your loving mother.

Sparks re-read the fax, which had been sent to the cafe on the ground floor of his apartment building, with a mounting sense of resignation, grimacing at the reference to his brother. He folded it, slipped it into the back pocket of his jeans, stood up and stared out onto Place Wilson, a circular space in the centre of Toulouse, which is known as the Pink City on account of its ubiquitous rose-coloured terracotta walls and roof tiles. It was a glorious morning and already the outdoor cafes and the expensive boutiques were well patronised. Now that the gendarmes had dispersed the winos and beggars, old men sat reading their newspapers in the little park in the middle of the Place, which was full of life and bustle and steadily circulating traffic.

Goodbye to all this, thought Sparks. There was no question that he was going to have to do as his mother suggested and fly back to Auckland, which he'd left over a decade previously to wander the world. Despite his mother's wounding assertion, he had managed to support himself for the majority of that time; it was true, admittedly, that since settling in Toulouse his income had been a little irregular and had required topping up from time to time. But even leaving aside the ugly matter of money, it had been made abundantly clear to him that he was now a marked man as far as the French forces of law and order were concerned and he was well aware of what that meant. Look at poor old Khong.

The events to which his mother's fax referred, and which would precipitate Sparks' return to New Zealand, had occurred one month earlier. It had started when Sparks, out for a Sunday evening promenade, bumped into Larry Khong in Place du Capitole.

Khong, a fiftyish English-educated Lebanese, was a notorious figure among Toulouse's English-speaking community, virtually all of whom had some connection with the aircraft manufacturing consortium Airbus Industrie which was based on the outskirts of the city. Khong himself worked for Airbus as an aircraft salesman; his patch, broadly speaking, was the Arab world. He had several major deals to his credit which his numerous detractors, who habitually referred to him as "the filthy Arab", attributed to his alleged talent for bribery and corruption and the fact that he supposedly had every high-class call-girl from Paris to Monaco at his beck and call. They insisted that Khong's deals owed more to his willingness to bribe anything that moved when in the field and his ability to arrange the satisfaction of the depraved whims of Middle Eastern government and airline officials on their frequent visits to France, than to any aeronautical expertise or persistent salesmanship.

According to *Radio Couloir*, as the unofficial information system at Airbus headquarters was known, Khong was also in the habit of fiddling his expenses on a colossal scale, a cost ultimately borne by the taxpayers of France, Germany and the United Kingdom who funded Airbus. It was also whispered in the long corridors that he'd been caught red-handed by customs agents at Orly airport trying to smuggle diamonds into the country on his return from a trip to North Africa. In each instance, the gossip went, he had retained not only his freedom but also his job because of the intervention of some Arab princeling with a direct line to President Mitterand. Whereas many in the English-speaking community, whether out of jealousy or fastidiousness, detested Khong heartily, Sparks found him engaging company. Sparks was also intrigued by the talk of Khong's network of call-girls.

Sparks had never intended to stay long in Toulouse. It was a difficult place in which to scratch a living; he was a journalist by trade and, apart from a few pieces for the British rugby magazines, there was precious little scope for it. Eventually, in order to make a few francs before moving on, he'd undertaken some casual work as a translator and tour guide for the local tourism authority. It was there that he met and fell in love with Gisele Bacarat.

Gisele was a 30-year-old administrator in the tourism authority. She had short brown hair, big brown eyes, long brown legs and a slim, firm, flexible brown body. She was by a considerable margin the most uninhibited, inventive and energetic lover Sparks had ever had. She was also married.

That didn't seem to trouble her in the least. Sparks never ceased to be amazed at the way she'd sit up in his bed after a prolonged and fiercely passionate session of love-making and prattle on cheerfully and affectionately about her husband Pierre – what they did last weekend, where they were going for their summer holidays, what he'd given her for her birthday, what they'd had for dinner at her parents-in-law's place the night before and so on. One sultry late afternoon in July, as he lay naked on his back gazing in wonder at the bite marks and streaks of sweat on his torso, half-listening to Gisele complaining about how badly Pierre, who did something in a bank, was paid, he finally raised the subject.

"How do you do it?" he asked. "How can you spend the afternoon in bed with me then go home to Pierre as if nothing's happened?"

Gisele shrugged in that Gallic way which involves eyebrows, mouth, shoulders, arms and hands. "I don't understand. What do you mean, how can I go home to Pierre? He is my husband; it's completely normal that I go home to him, n'est-ce pas?"

"But how can you just switch from me to him? Doesn't what we've been doing affect you, you know, like the way you react to him?"

Gisele sat upright in the bed and waved a finger at Sparks. "Ah oui, now I understand. I didn't think you were so much the Anglo-Saxon, cherie. It is the English way that one has only so much love and to give it to a new man means taking away from the old. C'est vrai, non? You think that if I love you, I cannot love Pierre?"

"I was just asking," said Sparks. "Is that right? You really love me?"

Gisele's eyes flashed. "What do you think – I'd do this if I didn't?" she asked indignantly. "Of course I love you; I've loved every man I've had an affair with. But Pierre is the one I'll love always."

Sparks failed to grasp the significance of this remark and never really understood Gisele's ability to compartmentalise her life and control her emotions. Some 18 months later he discovered what it meant in practice. Early one evening after they'd made love, she got straight out of bed and went to the bathroom. That was unusual but Sparks assumed she was going out for dinner. When she reappeared, she began getting dressed.

Sparks propped himself up on an elbow. "Going out?"

She regarded Sparks solemnly. "Reggie, this was the last time. I can't see you any more. Pierre and I want to have a child so . . ." She shrugged as if further explanation was entirely unnecessary. As her words sunk in, Sparks' heart began thundering; a terrible feeling of nausea was spreading from the pit of his stomach. He vaulted off the bed and went to embrace her. She held up her hands to stop him.

"Please Reggie. You must understand. I must go now." She smiled a sweet, sad smile. He dropped his head, unable to look at her. She kissed him tenderly on his bowed forehead, whispered "Au revoir cherie", and was gone.

Sparks' recovery from heartbreak was slow and difficult. For several weeks he left his apartment only to go to the market or the laundromat; after five months he remained resolutely disinterested in any sort of relationship. The celibate life, however, was starting to make him fidgety. He found his thoughts turning in the direction of depersonalised sex. While the well-used ladies who patrolled certain side streets off Allees Jean Jaures held no appeal, the prospect of an encounter with one of Khong's exclusive stable – who were all stunning-looking and immensely skilled in his imagination, whatever they were like in fact – increasingly did.

He had attempted to broach the subject with Khong a few weeks before that fateful Sunday night, at a party in the English enclave of Pibrac, a village just outside the city. However Khong, a gregarious fellow at the best of times, was in social butterfly mode, flitting from one conversational cluster to another, quite unconcerned as to whether he was welcome or not. By the time Sparks was finally able to manoeuvre him far enough away from the other guests to feel comfortable discussing the topic of prostitution, Khong had consumed a stupendous quantity of armagnac. Sparks was still wallowing in euphemisms when Khong cut him short:

"Excuse me old boy, I must have a puke."

Two minutes later a hellish row broke out when the hostess discovered Khong, on his hands and knees, throwing up into the bottom of a wardrobe where she kept her considerable shoe collection. The hostess, a demure and retiring woman, began ranting obscenely at Khong, betraying a long-suppressed working-class accent and vocabulary; he affected not to notice the string of vile names he was being called, apologised fulsomely, presented her with a signed blank cheque,

18

and made as graceful an exit as was possible with a trail of richly-coloured vomit down the front of his cream cashmere jersey. The encounter in Place du Capitole was the first time Sparks had seen him since.

Khong, dapper as ever in a dark-blue silk shirt and cream chino trousers, had greeted Sparks warmly and insisted on buying him a drink. Once seated in a bar Sparks, conscious of Khong's unpredictability, wasted no time in getting to the point.

"Larry, I hear you're on good terms with some very classy, shall we say, ladies of the night?" he blurted.

The good cheer disappeared from Khong's black eyes.

"You've obviously been talking to some of my admirers," he said.

Sparks went a shade pink. "Shit, it doesn't bother me – in fact, I'd like to meet one."

Khong took a hard pull on his Glenfiddich and water and looked appraisingly at Sparks.

"I don't mean to pry Reggie, but are you liberally endowed with discretionary income?"

"Absolutely," said Sparks glumly. "Loaded."

"I can take that as a 'no'?"

Sparks nodded.

Khong pushed away his empty glass and leant back in his chair. "My dear chap, these ladies of the night, as you so delicately call them, are used to getting five thousand US and a Rolex for licking some sheik's backside. Now given that you're a white man with no visible diseases and" – he sniffed noisily – "no obvious stench, they might give you a discount; a tenner maybe."

Sparks started to protest but Khong gently but firmly interrupted.

"Reggie, even if you could afford it, why waste your money? These bitches are sharks – I'd rather spend the night with Yasser Arafat."

Sparks sipped his beer morosely. "It was a bit of a fantasy I suppose . . ."

Khong, restored to his customary joviality, clapped Sparks on the shoulder.

"Fantasies should remain fantasies Reggie," he boomed. "Reality is always a disappointment. Now where shall we eat?" It was clear that the subject was closed.

They bar-hopped for a while before deciding on L'Entrecote, on the corner of Allees President Roosevelt and Boulevard de Strasbourg where diners have only to decide how they'd like their steak cooked and which house wine they'll drink: red or rosé. Khong simplified things even further by ordering a bottle of each.

Afterwards Khong insisted that they went clubbing. He draped an arm over Sparks' shoulder: "Why a presentable chap like you should be contemplating going to a tart is beyond me. This town's awash with delicious soubrettes. We'll get you fixed up – just leave it to your Uncle Larry."

On the stroke of midnight, they were forcibly ejected from the Ubu Club in Rue Saint-Rome. Khong had taken his vow seriously despite Sparks' protestations. He approached a number of young women to ask, in his flawless French, if they'd like to meet Mickey Rourke, the film star. The offer was accompanied by eye movements and twitches of the head towards Sparks, by then too drunk to be embarrassed. Khong was rebuffed with varying degrees of brusqueness but remained unfazed until an outstandingly pert mademoiselle spat "Va te faire enculer" which amounts to an instruction to go away and submit to sodomy. Khong reacted to the implication by depositing a massive gob of mucus and saliva in her lemon cordial.

After being refused admittance to a couple of other nightclubs, they ended up drinking armagnac in Khong's apartment in an elegantly crumbling old building in Place des Jacobins. Shortly before two o'clock, when both were on the verge of falling asleep in their chairs, a savage catfight broke out in the courtyard below. Khong was galvanised. He sprang cursing from the sofa, rushed out of the room, and returned with a small black pistol. He flung open the double windows opening onto the courtyard and loosed off half a dozen shots. The caterwauling ended abruptly.

Khong returned to the sofa, giggling.

"Only blanks more's the pity," he said. "God, I hate cats."

There the matter may have ended had it not been for an unfortunate coincidence. Khong's apartment was on the third level; the apartment directly across the courtyard was occupied by a Palestinian surgeon, one Abu Fazali, and his family. Fazali periodically invited Khong over for a cous-cous but they were not intimate friends; Khong wasn't aware, for instance, that Fazali's brother, Naim, was a senior figure in the revolutionary council of the Palestine Liberation Organisation. Naim in fact happened to be visiting Abu from his base in Tunis that weekend and, Khong's gunplay notwithstanding, was at that moment sound sleep in his brother's spare bedroom.

There is a significant Arab community in Toulouse and most of the various strands of Arab radicalism are represented there. For reasons of protocol and security, given that several of the more extreme of these groups regarded the extermination of the leaders of the PLO as an absolute priority, Naim had quietly informed the French Foreign Ministry of his private visit to Toulouse.

The French Government regarded his visit as a major security issue; over the years it had been embarrassed more than once by Middle Eastern blood feuds spilling over onto French soil. As a result, stationed around Place des Jacobins that night were a dozen or so highly-trained killers from one of the various shadowy para-military outfits at the disposal of the French state.

Less than five minutes after the cat-scaring episode, the door to Khong's apartment was smashed off its hinges and in

21

stormed six heavily-armed, black-clad figures. Luckily for Khong, he had discarded the pistol; if he'd held on to it or kept it within reach, he almost certainly would have been machine-gunned into bloody shreds where he sat. As it was, he was struggling to his feet when the leader of the raiding party hurdled a low coffee table and kicked him with sickening force on the point of the jaw. Khong did a back-flip over the sofa and crashed to the floor where he lay very still. Paralysed by a combination of fear, fatigue and intoxication, Sparks remained sprawled in his armchair, which saved him from similar treatment. He suffered nothing more than a swollen upper lip when the muzzle of a sub-machine gun was rammed under his nose and held there while the intruders proceeded to lay waste to Khong's apartment.

Sparks was taken to an airforce base south of Toulouse and questioned for a day and a half. It was conducted with a minimum of brutality; Khong's firearm, it transpired, was a starting pistol. On the Wednesday morning Sparks was visited in his cell by an urbane civilian who appeared to know every detail of his life since he'd arrived in France. His visitor told him the affair had been "an unfortunate misunderstanding". It would already have been sorted out, he said, were it not for the fact that Monsieur Khong was proving difficult.

It turned out that Khong, speaking in a bubbling hiss through his wired-up jaw, was threatening, amidst repeated references to his friends in high places, to take the matter further. What eventually persuaded him to change his mind was a visit from a prosecuting magistrate who told him bluntly that unless he cooperated, he would be put on trial for firing on members of the security forces; exhibit A, he was promised, would not be his little starting pistol but a 9mm Beretta which ballistic tests showed had been used in the attempted assassination of an Israeli diplomat in Paris some months before. If it came to that, said the magistrate, Airbus would be building flying saucers by the time Khong got out of jail.

They were tried and convicted of unspecified anti-social behaviour and fined 20,000 francs. The day the money from his mother came through, Sparks paid his fine and bought an air ticket home. He then packed his bags, vacated his apartment and caught a train to Lyon where he spent his remaining funds on a gastronomic binge in that city's famed grand restaurants. At the end of a week of relentless self-indulgence and suffering the worst hangover of his life, Reggie Sparks took the fast train to Paris where he boarded a 747 bound for Singapore.

CHAPTER 2

*T*he police investigation which commenced upon the discovery of Wallace Guttle's body was initially complicated by confusion over the precise cause of death. That he'd been run over was clear; how he came to be lying on the floor of the carpark and what state he was in when Margo Dugdale's Datsun trundled over him were, for the time being, matters of conjecture. Having rung the police from her office, Ms Dugdale was of little assistance to them on their arrival; befuddled by alcohol and convinced that she'd done terminal damage to her employment, her right to drive a car, and whoever it was down below with his head squashed beyond recognition, she was reduced to tearful incoherence.

Tony Rispoli was no help at all since, having assessed the situation as being fraught with the potential to ruin virtually every aspect of his life, he'd departed the scene even before Ms Dugdale had dialled the emergency number. Taking advantage of Ms Dugdale's disorientation, Rispoli slipped quietly away, thanking his lucky stars that the lady had been more interested in exchanging bodily fluids than life stories or even names for that matter.

Constables Crane and Drinkwater from the Newmarket police station responded to Ms Dugdale's call. Their first thought was that the deceased had passed out, either drunk or ill, and, in doing so, had by pure bad luck positioned his head in the spot which Ms Dugdale's front right wheel would later also occupy. A swift perusal of the photographs in Guttle's briefcase suggested other possibilities and persuaded them that the safest and most sensible course of action was to alert higher authority. That arrived on the scene shortly after midnight in the forms of Detective Inspector Finbar McGrail and Detective Sergeant Tito Ihaka.

Constable Crane had been put through to Ihaka when he'd rung Auckland's Central Police Station to report a suspicious death. He informed Ihaka that the contents of the briefcase indicated that the deceased was Wallace Guttle, a licensed private investigator; that said briefcase contained photographs of a highly personal if not scandalous nature; and that a second and closer inspection of the deceased revealed what could be entry wounds. A quick search of the area had failed to turn up any firm evidence of foul play, such as ejected shell casings.

Ihaka listened with growing perplexity. He'd been on the point of going home where he planned to have several beers with his takeaway dinner and, in the unlikely event that he'd managed to programme his VCR correctly, watch a rugby league match. He thought about what Crane had told him for several seconds, then snapped: "Was the fucker shot or not?"

Ihaka considered Constable Crane's answer to be less than satisfactorily concise covering, as it did, an hysterical woman, the partially crushed head, and a mysterious male companion who'd vanished from the scene. He cut Crane short, hung up, alerted forensic, then walked down the corridor to McGrail's office.

Finbar McGrail, 44, had grown up in Belfast, Northern Ireland, and joined the Royal Ulster Constabulary straight from school. By the age of 30 he was regarded as one of the RUC's rising stars. At least that was how he was described in a front-page lead story in *The Belfast Telegraph* relating how he'd led a team of detectives which had tracked down an Irish Republican Army hit squad. All four members of the hit squad had died the previous day in a British Army ambush involving careful planning, clinical execution, and sufficient firepower to have sunk the royal yacht Britannia. As he read the article, McGrail reached two conclusions: firstly, that the so-called troubles in Northern Ireland would more than likely continue for the rest of his career; secondly, that being the case, the odds on his reaching retirement age were no better than even. Finbar McGrail put down the newspaper and rang directory service to obtain the telephone number of the New Zealand High Commission in London. When he got through to the immigration department, he asked whether they were interested in acquiring the services of a trained detective and devout Presbyterian whose hobbies were jogging and military history.

Tito Ihaka was well aware that McGrail was a lay preacher, that he'd run a dozen or so marathons, and that he needed very little encouragement to talk at length about war in general or his favourite practitioner, Field Marshal Montgomery of El Alamein, in particular. In Ihaka's view, none of these things were as close to the Ulsterman's heart as a good murder.

He knocked on McGrail's door and went in; McGrail looked up from his paperwork, his thin, dark face expressionless. McGrail's dourness was a byword among his colleagues; a bold constable had once slipped a tape of the children's song *The Laughing Policeman* into a tape deck when McGrail was expecting to hear the confession of a housewife who'd beaten a vagrant to death with a hockey stick for trampling her daffodils. McGrail had maintained a poker face as the song, punctuated by frequent bursts of braying laughter, filled his office. Those who witnessed it swore that a flicker of a smile did cross his face when he told the constable in question that he was being transferred to Otara, or "Jungleland" as it was known to those who worked there.

This ought to cheer you up, you gloomy prick, thought

Ihaka: "Sir, Newmarket just reported a guy run over in a basement carpark. Looks like it's a private investigator, fella called Wallace Guttle. The boys on the scene think he might've been dead already."

McGrail took off his glasses. "I know of Guttle," he said. "He takes dirty pictures."

"That fits," said Ihaka. "He had a briefcase full of fuck photos – not porn, more like shots of someone caught doing a bit of sly rooting by the sound of it." Most junior officers watched their language around McGrail in deference to his churchiness; Ihaka made no effort to temper either the foulness of his speech or the crudity of his observations. He lived in hope of provoking a reaction but thus far not even his most imaginative clusters of obscenity had ruffled McGrail's *sang-froid*.

McGrail's thin-lipped mouth twitched; there was a perceptible stirring of interest in the dark-brown eyes. He stood up, six foot tall and lean as a lifeguard, carefully rolled down his shirtsleeves, and reached for his jacket.

"It looks like we'll be working this weekend, Sergeant," he said, leading the way out of his office.

Yes Deacon, thought Ihaka. Sex, murder, perversion – beats the shit out of family service any day.

Reggie Sparks' usual policy when flying was to drink steadily from take-off to touchdown. He did so not because he was a nervous flyer or found air travel too disagreeable to be undertaken sober. It was simply that he was temperamentally almost incapable of declining free drinks. This time though, to his mild surprise, he found himself sipping his vodka and tonic disinterestedly, having to make a conscious decision to accept the offer of a glass of wine with dinner, and allowing the liqueur trolley to proceed down the aisle. Sparks was preoccupied; he knew he'd reached a watershed and the realisation had prompted some soul-searching, although reviewing his

27

achievements required only a few of the 28 hours it took Singapore Airlines to transport him from Paris to Auckland.

Sparks had been born in Auckland 39 and a half years before, the son of Stanley and Mareena Sparks, née Hazard. His father owned a scrap metal business, the earnings from which he supplemented with income derived from a black market meat racket. Every Thursday night he'd drive an old Bedford van into the carpark at a South Auckland freezing works; his accomplices would then transfer fresh meat, which they'd smuggled out of the works, from the boots of their cars to the van. In the evening Sparks would tour the rugby and rugby league clubs selling the meat at a carefully calculated discount to butcher shops' prices.

The management of the freezing works knew all about the meat smuggling ring. Seeing that it comprised the site representative of the freezing workers' trade union and his entourage of enforcers, management felt that the weekly theft of a few hundred pounds worth of meat was an acceptable price to pay for a quiet life: it ensured comparative industrial relations stability and meant the bosses could stroll around the works without worrying about the possibility of having a meat hook embedded between their shoulder blades. One Thursday night however, Stanley drove his meat-laden van out of the freezing works car park and into a police road block.

By that stage Stanley had profitably off-loaded his scrap metal business so the two years he spent in Mt Eden prison were not a great hardship for his family, although Mareena had to put up with regular unannounced visits from male admirers keen to capitalise on her husband's absence. On his release, Stanley bought into a milk run. The 5am starts left him with plenty of spare time in the afternoons, which he spent fishing, doing odd jobs, and stalking his former accomplice in the meat racket.

He'd learned, via the highly effective intelligence network in Mt Eden Prison, that he'd been sold out by the union representative, who'd since become a Labour Party member of parliament. Although now based in Wellington, the MP returned frequently to Auckland to – in ascending order of priority – see his family, consult with his trade union masters, and visit his mistress who resided in a small block of flats in Epsom.

While in prison Stanley had also learned about the mistress and where she lived. He often spent an hour or two of an afternoon parked across the road from the block of flats in the hope of encountering his betrayer. Eventually his patience was rewarded.

When Stanley saw the MP and his girlfriend pull up in front of the block of flats, he slid out from behind the steering wheel and walked round to the rear of the van, in the back of which his carpentry tools and gardening implements were arranged on a blanket. He selected a mini-crowbar, about a metre long. Head down and holding the crowbar down his leg, he crossed the road and approached the couple. He walked straight up to them and, without a word of warning or introduction, took a good backswing and cracked the man on his right knee. He collapsed on the grass verge, moaning loudly. The woman squealed. Stanley told her to clear off.

Stanley was contemplating where to strike next when the MP spoke urgently through gritted teeth: "Leave it mate, leave it. I'll make it worth your while."

Stanley rapped him crisply on the left ankle. The MP switched his grip from his right knee to the new source of pain and swore feebly.

"No bullshit," he gasped. "Lay off and I'll give you some red-hot bully. Deal?"

Stanley nodded. He fully intended to carry on until he'd broken several bones but thought he might as well hear what the man had to say.

"They're going to build a harbour bridge," groaned the MP. "It'll be announced next month."

Stanley bashed him once more then walked back to his van, threw the crowbar in the back and drove off.

Despite Mareena's protestations, Stanley sold the milk run and sank the receipts, plus most of their savings, ill-gotten and otherwise, into North Shore real estate. The Harbour Bridge was opened in 1959. In mid-1962 Stanley sold one of his several Takapuna Beach waterfront properties at a handsome profit and bought himself a second-hand Jaguar. He sold two more 18 months later and moved the family into a two-storey house with a swimming pool in Victoria Avenue, Remuera, which he regarded as the poshest street in the poshest suburb. They moved in on the hottest day of that summer. After he'd mowed the large front and back lawns, Stanley stood in the shallow end of the pool with a beer in one hand and a cigarette in the other and told his wife he'd never mow another bloody lawn as long as he lived. The following day he rang the headmaster of Prince Albert College to discuss the enrolment of his two sons.

As an ex-jailbird, it tickled Stanley's fancy to send his boys to the most exclusive school in town. Prince Albert College had been founded in Meadowbank 100 years earlier by a group of God-fearing Auckland merchants who profoundly admired Queen Victoria and her German consort. The school had promoted the values associated with their reign – religiosity of the Anglican persuasion, hard work, puritanism, and conformity – ever since.

Despite the pleasure it gave Stanley, the decision to send Reggie and his older – by 18 months – brother Gavin to Prince Albert was not a complete success. Gavin – conscientious, obedient, eager to please – was highly regarded in the college's staff common room. He passed through in the top form and was made head of his house.

If Gavin inherited his mother's social ambitions, Reggie was very much his father's son. He was a schoolmaster's nightmare – lazy, disruptive, always looking for the short cut and, most disconcertingly, apparently blessed with a cast-iron bottom which made him impervious to the threat of the cane, even when wielded by the headmaster, Dr Foster Hogbin. A towering, angular figure who only removed his mortarboard to eat, sleep and worship and who was prone to mood swings of unnerving suddenness, Dr Hogbin could go from a state of beatific serenity into a paroxysm of frothing rage in the blinking of an eye. If he considered the boys were making too much noise as they changed classrooms between periods, he was likely to gallop down corridors with a cane in each hand and his university cloak billowing behind him, howling "Scoundrels! scoundrels!" at the top of his lungs, and flailing indiscriminately at those too slow to take refuge.

At the end of Reggie's fifth form year, Dr Hogbin wrote on his end-of-year report: "To say that Reginald is a disappointment would be an understatement of grotesque proportions. The consensus among those unfortunate enough to teach him is that he is a shiftless lout, devoid of even the slightest redeeming feature. I urge you to consider whether he would be better suited to the state system where, for all I know, those tendencies of his which to us seem thoroughly anti-social might scarcely attract notice."

When Dr Hogbin was in an implacable frame of mind, his comments in reports could be brutally frank. But even by those standards, these were harsh words. They were written in the hope of shaming the Sparks into withdrawing Reggie from the college since he hadn't actually done anything which in itself justified expulsion. Such subtlety was wasted on Stanley. Before long however, the Doctor's prayers were answered.

Early the following year, a few of Reggie's classmates organised a party. Reggie wasn't invited since the venue was the home of a boy who regarded him as insufficiently house-trained. The snub rankled because the boys' parents were overseas and parties without parental supervision were rare events promising unimaginable decadence. In retaliation Reggie anonymously tipped off a gang, the Boot Hill Mob, which drew its membership from the Glen Innes state housing area, about the party. He'd expected that a few gang members would crash the party, swagger about threateningly, commandeer whatever booze they could find, and then go on to something more their speed than a bunch of private school kids playing Beatles records and postman's knock. He seriously underestimated the surge of class resentment felt by the Boot Hill Mob when they barged into what was indeed one of the grander properties in the eastern suburbs.

Things got rapidly out of hand: a motorbike was ridden through the house and out onto the grass tennis court where a series of high-speed manoeuvres involving violent braking were performed; a piano was pushed into the swimming pool; a double bed was heaved through a first floor window onto the street; girls were pawed; boys were punched; a great deal of methodical damage was done.

The anonymous tip-off came to light when the police rounded up the Boot Hill Mob later that night. Under pressure from the owners of the sacked mansion, Dr Hogbin launched a witchhunt to find the culprit; Reggie was a prime suspect. As the enormity of the situation dawned on Reggie, so did the realisation that if he wavered for one second in his denials, he was doomed. Even when Dr Hogbin's interrogation went well outside the most broad-minded view of what constituted acceptable headmasterly behaviour, Reggie stuck to his guns. He was not believed of course and even Stanley accepted that his son's position at Prince Albert had become untenable. It was not to be the last time that Reggie Sparks failed to last the course.

Sparks completed a relatively incident-free schooling in the state system and astonished all who knew him, even given the accreditation system's lack of rigour, by gaining university entrance. He then passed an undistinguished year and a half at Auckland University before being cast out of the grove of academe.

It was not so much his failure to pass any units which annoyed the authorities as his habit of producing ever more elaborate and heart-rending excuses for failing to hand in assignments. In order to mollify and disarm his various tutors, Sparks invented the comprehensive maiming or deaths – lingering in some cases, traumatically unexpected in others – of grandparents, aunts, uncles, sisters and brothers. The hospitalisations, touch-and-go fights for life, or funerals inevitably took place in the remotest parts of the country necessitating his absence from Auckland for periods of a week or more.

Sensing that his English tutor was becoming suspicious, Sparks produced the excuse that brooked no scepticism. He wrote off his parents, claiming they'd been obliterated when their hired car had been crushed like a bug by a 10-ton truck somewhere on the endless highway which crosses the Nullabor Plain from Adelaide to Perth. At a film society wine and cheese that evening, the English tutor mentioned Reggie's orphan-hood to a colleague in the history department. The historian was surprised to hear of Mr and Mrs Sparks' fate since Reggie had told him only the week before that they were indefinitely confined to a decompression chamber in Honolulu, having suffered serious attacks of the bends in a diving accident. The English tutor then surveyed Sparks' other tutors and pieced together a chronicle of carnage involving car crashes, plane crashes, rare diseases, hunting accidents, shark attacks, botched operations and acts of God. It was clear that either Reggie was a compulsive, shameless and sick-minded liar or, that when it came to ill-starred families, the Kennedys had had a dream run compared to the Sparks.

Reggie then startled his parents by announcing that he wanted to become a journalist; he subsequently amazed them

33

by gaining a cadetship at *The Auckland Evening Standard* and making of a success of it. He endured the abject existence of a cadet reporter without complaint; he dutifully covered numbingly boring local body meetings; he did little to antagonise his superiors and even managed to ingratiate himself with the chief reporter by happily running down to the TAB to place his bets. Reggie, it seemed, had found his vocation.

By the time he reached his mid-20s and after six years at *The Standard*, Sparks had become a valued member of staff, regarded as a young man with a real future in the game. While his lifestyle was messy, it was quite unremarkable by the standards of the newsroom. His writing, excitable at first, had adapted to the narrow discipline of the news story – the one sentence intro; what, when, where, why and how; arrange the facts in descending order of importance. Hard news was really his forte – no one chased an ambulance with greater zeal or gathered facts more single-mindedly – but his mentor, the chief reporter, decided he should gain experience of politics. Few had attained a senior editorial position at *The Standard* without a stint in the parliamentary press gallery in Wellington, an experience which supposedly imbued one with the wisdom and gravitas to pen weighty leaders on subjects ranging from the crushing of the Prague Spring uprising to the meaning of Easter. To groom Sparks for the gallery, he was promoted over the heads of more senior reporters to cover the Auckland City Council.

At this pivotal point in his career, Sparks discovered the work of the American journalist Dr Hunter S. Thompson. Thompson scorned the principles of detached observation and impartial reporting by which news journalism traditionally operated. He became part of the story; he was aggressively partisan; he frequently attacked those with whom he disagreed in savagely abusive language. He also celebrated in his writings a wild and bohemian lifestyle fuelled by relentless consumption of alcohol and drugs.

Sparks was captivated by Thompson's rebellion, his flouting of convention, his zany insights, his roaring outlaw behaviour, his twisted humour, his thundering, exhilarating, Biblically uncompromising prose. However, New Zealand journalism in the late 1970s was not ready for Hunter Thompson imitators, no matter how pale.

Warning bells sounded when Sparks submitted a feature about the deputy mayor, a large man of forthrightly conservative views, whom he described as being "as piggishly greedy as King Farouk and also sharing the late Egyptian monarch's absolute indifference to the plight of the dispossessed and disadvantaged". The line was sub-edited out. Subsequent stories from the city council roundsman needed pruning to delete unsubstantiated allegations of graft and gratuitous denigration of council officers. The mounting concern about Sparks' copy coincided with a barrage of complaints from councillors and council officials about Sparks' behaviour which had changed from not unpleasant directness to crusading abrasiveness in the space of a few weeks. Within a month of embracing gonzo journalism, Sparks had been removed from the city council round.

He was transferred to a new section of the paper called *City Beat* which had been launched with the aim of attracting a youth readership. Perhaps it was felt that his newly truculent attitude would strike a chord with alienated teenagers but, after a series of corrosive record reviews peppered with comments like "if pus made a noise, this would be it", the feedback from readers indicated that they would prefer a less trenchant approach. His career as a reviewer was terminated when a record distributor filed a writ against the paper claiming damages for loss of sales after Sparks had written that "clinical tests at Harvard University have established that listening to disco music can cause rectal cancer".

By that stage Sparks had precious little support among the paper's hierarchy. He was put on final notice and transferred to the sub-editors' desk where he was kept under constant supervision. Unable to imitate Dr Thompson in his work, Sparks sought to do so in his lifestyle. He stepped up his alcohol intake and began taking whatever drugs he could lay his hands on. However, among the attributes which Thompson possessed but Sparks did not was the Doctor's self-proclaimed "mule shark" constitution. After a month-long spree of whisky, marijuana and LSD, Sparks threw the newsroom into uproar by stabbing the shipping reporter with a copy spike, apparently in the conviction that he was a giant lizard. After being subdued, Sparks lost consciousness for 36 hours; when he woke up, he was unemployed.

CHAPTER 3

Wallace Guttle was shot on Friday, August 13. Seeing no more than a second separated Guttle's realisation that he was about to die and his demise, he didn't have a chance to reflect on the significance of the date. On the Wednesday of the fifth week after that event, Constable Jarrad Renshaw was working the midnight to 8am shift at the Harbour Bridge police station. It turned out to be an eventful night.

There was the usual paperwork, the distasteful task of cleaning up after an incontinent drunk who'd staggered in looking for somewhere warm to spend the night, and a barney in one of the Fort Street knock shops between an Estonian seaman and the manager over whether the "hostess" or the client bore ultimate responsibility for the achievement of an erection. Then just after 4 o'clock a mate who was working the same shift at the Papatoetoe station rang to tell him about something which had happened on his patch. Renshaw understood why his friend wasn't wasting any time spreading the news. The incident had the two hallmarks of your classic on-the-job story; it was bizarre, even by cops' standards, and it reinforced their basic working premise that most people out there are pretty fucked up: a man who'd been woken up by the barking of the dog next door had beheaded the canine with a chainsaw and flung the severed head through his neighbour's bedroom window. His neighbours' reaction was vociferous rather than violent; although they were mightily upset at having their three-year-old Alsatian's head and a fair amount of broken glass land on their bed in the early hours of the morning, they also had enough sense to keep their distance from someone wielding a blood-stained chainsaw.

What with one thing and another, the duty constable didn't notice the car on the monitor screen until 4.27am. Even as he picked up the phone, the presence of a stationary car on the Auckland Harbour Bridge was being reported by Beryl Baptist, a 20-year-old welfare beneficiary of Whangarei.

When she'd awoken at 1.35am that morning to discover that her live-in boyfriend of two weeks' standing hadn't returned from what he'd promised would be "a quick beer with the boys", Ms Baptist had made a snap decision. She threw some clothes into an overnight bag, strapped her year-old son Axl into the baby chair in the back seat of her heavily rusted Honda, and drove south with the intention of spending a few days in Auckland with her sister Eve.

Driving south across the Harbour Bridge at 4.18am, Beryl noticed the stationary car in the far left north-bound lane at the bridge's highest point. She found it ominous that the driver's door was open but there was no sign of the driver. When Beryl arrived at her sister's flat in Grey Lynn, and following their short but vicious exchange, she rang the emergency number and reported what she'd seen.

At 4.21am Fred "The Freckle" Freckleton left his villa in Herne Bay to drive to the studio in Takapuna from which, each weekday morning, he broadcast the mixture of semi-hysterical gibberish, juvenile smut and pop music which had made him the undisputed king of Auckland's early morning air waves. At 4.28 The Freckle stopped his Porsche behind the newish Saab 9000 parked on the crest of the bridge blocking the far left-hand lane. He peered in the windows, front and back; the car was empty. Shivering a little from the early morning chill and a vague sense of apprehension, he peeped tentatively over the railing; in the darkness, he would have been lucky to spot a school of whales frolicking in the sea 43 metres below. The Freckle was on his car phone explaining to his producer why he was going to be late when the police car arrived.

The Saab belonged to Victor Appleyard. Three hours after Eve Baptist had called her younger sister a "bludging slut" and three and a quarter hours after he'd plummeted into the still, grey waters of Waitemata Harbour at a speed approaching 100 kilometres per hour, Victor Appleyard's body bumped ashore at the Chelsea sugar refinery in Birkenhead.

In the following 48 hours policemen and women shuffled, for the most part apologetically, through the existence out of which Victor Appleyard had, seemingly, opted although neglecting to formally announce the fact in a farewell note.

Appleyard had been the 41-year-old director of sales and business development for Berkeley Enterprises, a substantial property and construction company. The small police team which arrived at Berkeley's five-storey Onehunga headquarters at 11am was led by Senior Sergeant Ted Worsp who, over the course of his three decades in the police force, had gained a reputation for sensitive handling of such situations.

Worsp's experience had taught him that when men like Appleyard went off the rails in some shape or form, their secretaries were invariably excellent sources of information and insight. The late sales director's secretary was Janet Gabites, 49. On meeting her, Worsp noted her age, homeliness and the absence of a wedding ring. When she volunteered that she'd served Appleyard for eight years, his satisfaction was complete. He dispatched his underlings to interview Appleyard's fellow executives and settled down with Miss Gabites and a cup of tea.

After half an hour of Miss Gabites, who turned out to be every bit as infatuated with her ex-boss as he'd guessed, Worsp felt he knew as much about the saintly Appleyard as he wanted to know.

"You know what it's like Sergeant," said Miss Gabites, dabbing away with what Worsp estimated was the tenth tissue she'd immersed in her moist eyes since the interview began. "I'm sure it's the same in the police; the people who care, who can't simply shrug their shoulders and switch off, just get taken advantage of. As if Victor didn't have enough on his plate, they" – her eyes swivelled like anti-aircraft guns across the office to the boardroom – "dumped Australia in his lap, so he was spending a lot of his time over there trying to sort out the mess they've got themselves into. No wonder the poor man hadn't been on top of the world lately – he was working himself into the ground."

Miss Gabites nudged her chair slightly closer to Worsp's, lowered her voice, and continued: "I'm not a gossip Sergeant – I'd like to think I haven't got a malicious bone in my body – but I have to say that Victor could've done with more support at home. Maybe I'm speaking out of turn but Louise – that's Mrs Appleyard – never seemed to accept the hours Victor had to work, the travel, the stress, or the importance of being the corporate wife from time to time. Mind you, on the other hand, she certainly gave the impression that she was only too happy to have the rewards – the lovely house, the skiing holidays, the clothes. It's not for me to say so but there are people here who'd tell you that she enjoyed the benefits of being Mrs Victor Appleyard but resented the sacrifices and, as you know Sergeant, you don't have one without the other."

The picture of Victor Appleyard which emerged when the police team held their de-briefing session late that afternoon was of a good bloke, solid citizen and dedicated company man. Some of his colleagues had commented that he'd seemed preoccupied and somewhat withdrawn in recent weeks but put it down to the extra pressure that went with being given responsibility for Berkeley's troubled Australian subsidiary. There were hints of tensions on the home front. A check of his diary had revealed nothing untoward. He'd appeared to be okay the previous evening, ruefully resigned to working until past midnight. No one at Berkeley had ever entertained the idea of him committing suicide.

"That proves bugger all," pronounced Worsp. "People who go round saying they're going to top themselves either end up in loony bins or dying in bed at the age of 90."

Louise Appleyard did not conform to Senior Sergeant Worsp's expectations or experience of widows.

Slim, elegant, darkly attractive, and seven years younger than her late husband, she sat at the jarrah table on the deck overlooking Lake Pupuke smoking a Dunhill and drinking coffee. There was a mobile phone on the table. Every few minutes it would ring and Mrs Appleyard would pick it up and listen for a while. Then she'd murmur a thank you and say she'd better go, she was being interviewed by the police and no doubt they were anxious to get back to catching criminals.

Constable Beth Greendale admired the fact that little more than 24 hours after learning of her husband's death, Louise Appleyard's only visible concession to the situation was dark glasses, which were really unnecessary in the weak early spring sunshine. Senior Sergeant Worsp felt otherwise. Sure it's black he thought, but the skirt could be a bit longer, for Christ's sake. It wasn't that Worsp was averse to long legs in black stockings but he was used to grieving women responding more favourably to his snowy hair and breezy personality and what, in his frequent moments of conceit, he thought of as his reassuring, even comforting manner. When, on their way out to the deck, Worsp had laid a solicitous hand on Mrs Appleyard's elbow, she'd reacted with a slight but perceptible recoil and a tense little smile which together amounted to an injunction to keep his hands to himself.

Constable Greendale who, after a day's exposure, was starting to tire of Senior Sergeant Worsp, had picked up on the body language immediately. She was looking forward to the interview.

Worsp began by asking Louise Appleyard if her marriage had been a happy one. She lit another cigarette and exhaled luxuriantly causing the sergeant, a reformed smoker, a moment of acute discomfort.

"Is that a polite way of asking if I drove him to despair?" she replied with another tightly controlled smile. "I'd say we were at least as happy as most couples that I know. If you ask me 'was I in love with Vic?', the honest answer is 'no' but then I can't imagine anyone still being in love – in the giddy, head-over-heels sense – with their partner after 10 years. That's not to say I didn't love him because I did. I take it the distinction's not lost on you Sergeant?"

She looked at Worsp curiously. He has no idea what I'm talking about, she thought.

"If you ask me did Vic and I still make love," she continued coolly, "then the answer would be 'occasionally', certainly not as often as I would've liked. But then 14-hour days don't do much for the libido. If you ask me whether I made up the shortfall elsewhere, then the answer's 'no' but, in the spirit of candour you've so skilfully encouraged, Sergeant, I'll admit that it crossed my mind from time to time. I doubt that makes me much different from most wives – and certainly not from most husbands."

What a bitch, thought Worsp. He cleared his throat and said, "One or two people at the office had the idea you didn't go much for his job and the company scene generally."

Mrs Appleyard traced her right eyebrow with a bright red fingernail. Constable Greendale got the impression that she'd already decided that talking to Worsp was a pointless exercise.

"You've obviously been talking to Janet – my number one fan," she said off-handedly. "The company's okay as companies go but it forces people into a very narrow existence.

Some of them probably don't have to be forced – as far as they're concerned, the world outside Berkeley and their areas of business may as well not exist – but there was a lot more to Vic than that. I thought they were using Vic, just dumping more and more on him. I suppose he could've said 'no' but that wasn't Vic's way; he'd just take a deep breath, square his shoulders, and carry on. Lately though, I think he'd started to question whether he wanted to spend the rest of his working life in such an environment."

"So you think this questioning process led to him . . ." Worsp left the question hanging in the air.

Louise Appleyard looked at Worsp with almost clinical interest. Constable Greendale caught the look. Here it comes, she said to herself.

"Oh that?" said Louise. "For a while I thought we were going to sit here and talk about my sex life all morning." Worsp squirmed on his substantial buttocks thinking, no wonder the poor cunt jumped.

Louise Appleyard re-crossed her legs and leaned forward. "Let me spell it out for you Sergeant, as plainly as possible," she said. "Vic did not kill himself. Let's say for the sake of argument that it all got too much for him – the pressure, the disillusionment, wondering what it's all about, the fact that I wouldn't give up smoking, that I didn't want babies, all my other failings that Janet would've filled you in on. The point is that if Vic was anything, he was considerate and he was also insured for well over half a million dollars. So if he was going to commit suicide, he wouldn't have done it like this – he would've made it look like an accident."

Worsp and Greendale made a no more than cursory inspection of Victor Appleyard's study on the basis that if he was going to leave a suicide note, he wouldn't leave it in the bottom drawer under the manuals explaining how to programme auto-dial into his telephone. Worsp lapsed into sullen silence on the drive back to town. The fact that Louise Appleyard had treated him with such transparent disdain was bad enough; what was much worse was that it had been witnessed by a 22-year-old female constable.

"What about the insurance thing then?" asked Constable Greendale as she piloted the police car past Westhaven at 20 kph above the speed limit.

Worsp perked up: "Love, the hardest thing for a suicide's family to accept is that they were the last thing on his mind. You see, suicide is the ultimate act of selfishness," he said, grateful that the phrase he'd heard or read somewhere had popped back into his mind when it was needed. "If Appleyard had really cared about her, he wouldn't have jumped off the Bridge would he, so why the hell should he worry about stuffing up her insurance? Believe me love, I've heard that line before today. The way I see it, the pressure and that got too much for him. Now ask yourself: is he really going to spend his last hours on earth trying to come up with some tricky way of doing it so his missus – who he probably couldn't stand anyway and who'd blame him? – gets her hands on the insurance? Do me a favour. And of course it might've been done on the spur of the moment – you know, he's been thinking about it for a while, then one night coming home across the Bridge, he decides tonight's the night.

"See, the other thing you've got to remember when you're talking about making it look like an accident as if it's the easiest thing in the world, is that it's not that easy. There aren't an unlimited number of ways you can kill yourself, you know. It's a question of what means are available. Plus, of course, for most suicides, there's only one or maybe two ways that they can actually bring themselves to do it. Just because a bloke might be quite prepared to poke a gun in his mouth and pull the trigger doesn't mean he could face slashing his wrists; a lot of people are just too bloody scared of heights to jump off a bridge. You know what I mean? It's illogical, sure, but that's

44

the way it is. So it's not like they've got 101 ways to choose from and can pick the one most likely to fool us and the insurance company."

"I'm not sure that's quite what she meant," said Constable Greendale but she didn't pursue the discussion. She'd heard enough of the wit and wisdom of Ted Worsp for one day.

The contents of Victor Appleyard's Saab were spread out on a desk. Worsp poked disinterestedly through the contents of the black airline pilot's briefcase; others had already done so without finding anything of interest. There was a fat hardback book about Japanese management techniques. As Worsp idly flipped through it, a folded card, slightly smaller than the normal-sized Christmas card, fell out. Worsp examined it. It was white with decal edging; on the front was a rather florid crest and the words "Prince Albert College Ball, 1970".

Something stirred deep in Worsp's memory. He opened the card. Printed on the top of the inside left-hand page were the words "Dance Card"; written on the dotted line below in a loopy, girlish hand was "Bronwen Ticehurst". Worsp, feeling slightly dizzy, put the card down and sat back in his chair.

After a few seconds he picked up the card again. Below her own name and on the facing page, the long-dead Bronwen Ticehurst had written the names of her partners for the various dances at the 1970 Prince Albert College Ball. One of them was that of the just-dead Victor Appleyard.

Worsp put the card down again and stood up. "The suicide note," he said to no one in particular. "He left one after all."

CHAPTER 4

*D*espite his almost cherubic appearance, Jackson Pike competed with the Prime Minister, the Minister of Finance, and one or two of the more nauseating television personalities for the unofficial title of the most hated person in New Zealand.

Pike was rarely troubled by this. Whenever he felt particularly put-upon, he consoled himself with the knowledge that, as the editor and joint proprietor of the monthly magazine *New Nation*, his unpopularity was more than matched by his influence.

As a young and dedicated journalist, Pike had often worried about the future of print journalism. One Sunday morning, in the course of a two-hour run along the waterfront, he realised that the remorseless decline in the quality, quantity and readership of the nation's newspapers presented a golden opportunity. Within six months he had secured backing for his venture; a further six months later the first issue of *New Nation* appeared. The print run of 15,000 copies sold out within 72 hours.

New Nation set out to be all things to all people. It combined news and lifestyle, weightiness and frivolity, hard-hitting investigative journalism and racy and irreverent celebrity profiles. Determined to avoid the fence-sitting blandness of most newspapers, Pike had launched his organ vowing that, whether the subject was restaurants, rugby or race relations, *New Nation* would leave its readers in no doubt where it stood. He further vowed that the magazine's stance would be determined by the merits of the case rather than prevailing orthodoxy or current fashion: one month a sacred tenet of political correctness would be ridiculed, the next the outcome of yet another experiment in economic rationalism would be subjected to equally scathing scrutiny.

While this broadened the magazine's appeal, it also meant that, over time, it had offended virtually every shade of political opinion and special interest group. Very early on, Pike had decided that if he was going to give offence, he might as well be hung for a sheep as a lamb. Therefore when *New Nation* took aim at someone, it did so not with a popgun but with an artillery piece.

Even though Pike was widely loathed, his magazine's popularity meant that he could not be ignored by those who wished to influence public opinion, whatever their particular brand of snake oil. After more than a decade of being paid grudging tribute, Pike had become as selective as a diva about whom he hob-nobbed with. Cabinet ministers could bombard his secretary in vain with luncheon invitations; tycoons could spend months trying to entice him to a weekend at their rural retreats. The exception was a man who was so old, he was widely assumed to be dead; in 13 years Pike had never missed his monthly lunch with Garth Grimes.

Pike and Grimes had instituted their monthly lunch when Grimes retired. There had been a period, after *New Nation* had really taken off and when Grimes still ventured out, during which the lunches would take place at one of the few and invariably very expensive restaurants in Auckland which found favour with both of them. But since reaching the age of 90, Grimes' excursions had been limited to his twice-daily shuffles along Takapuna beach.

From then on Pike would arrive at the old man's seafront bungalow with a hamper of food, a month's supply of overseas magazines, and a very good bottle of wine. He would make Grimes his first gin and tonic of the day and himself a Campari and soda. They would discuss current events, both domestic and international, and Grimes would give a brisk analysis of them which Pike usually found more illuminating than anything he'd come across in the seven daily newspapers and 15 periodicals which he made it his business to read. Grimes would then deliver a detailed critique of the last issue of *New Nation* while Pike took notes. They would then have lunch, either at the table by the full-length window or on the deck overlooking the beach, depending on the weather. Over lunch Pike would pass on all the unprintable gossip which he and his team of writers had picked in the preceding four weeks.

When Pike ran out of gossip, they would reminisce about the defunct *Auckland Evening Standard* where they'd both worked in the 1970s, Pike as a feature writer and Grimes, as he had been since returning to New Zealand in 1952 after 32 years overseas, as the star columnist. Occasionally, when Grimes was feeling particularly frisky, his reminiscences would include the unusual, even bizarre, sexual fantasies he had entertained about some of the *Standard's* female reporters. As he listened to Grimes' mellifluous purr, Pike would reflect that he was in the presence of almost certainly the dirtiest-minded nonagenarian in New Zealand and possibly in the world.

After lunch, Pike would make coffee and take notes as Grimes proferred story ideas and any leads or tidbits he'd picked up from the surviving members of what had been a legendary network of contacts. Thus it was that on one of the few rainless days of that spring, Pike and Grimes sat on the deck and discussed the strange death of Victor Appleyard which had occurred four weeks previously.

Garth Grimes regarded himself as fortunate to have been born in 1900. It meant that he was too young for the First World War and too old for the Second. He'd enjoyed what he referred to as "the last fluttering heartbeat of civilisation" – the 1920s – and the post-1945 boom during which he'd managed to position himself for a comfortable retirement. Now and again, when he was advancing this view, someone would ask "What about the Depression?" Grimes would reply that he'd spent most of the 1930s in Shanghai smoking opium and hadn't noticed. This was something of an embellishment of the truth which was that, during his time in Shanghai, he'd never been so short of funds that he couldn't afford both "a fine meal and an evening with the innkeeper's daughter".

Grimes had left New Zealand in 1920 and spent the next three decades roaming the world as a foreign correspondent, mostly for Reuters. Being inclined to pessimism, he'd concluded in the late 1930s that only the United States was likely to be spared the chaos that he foresaw engulfing the world and accordingly had taken steps to secure himself a posting in Washington. When the threat of nuclear war between the USA and the USSR emerged in the early 1950s, Grimes decided that, in the event of hostilities, his apartment building less than a mile as the crow flew from the White House would be vaporised by the first Soviet missile. It was time, he felt, to go home. In 1965 Grimes' American wife died suddenly. Virtually overnight he ceased to care a great deal either way about his and the human race's continued existence; ever since he had maintained a sunny, untroubled disposition which was the envy of all who knew him.

Grimes had always assumed that the rather self-indulgent, at times debauched, life he'd led and the fact that the only exercise he'd ever done was ascending stairs two at a time would ensure he was spared the indignities of extreme old age. It came as something of a surprise therefore when, on reaching 70 and on the brink of retirement, he underwent a thorough medical examination and was pronounced to be in rude health and good for a couple more decades.

Taking the doctor at his word, Grimes, to the

consternation of those journalists at *The Standard* who'd been jockeying to take over his thrice-weekly column, announced that he wouldn't be retiring after all. For another decade he continued to produce his urbane columns, melanges of opinion, gossip and arcane knowledge, and to supplement his income with what he called his "letters to friends".

To the rest of the trade, this was known as "ratting" – writing, usually on the sly, for other publications. The fundamental principle of ratting was maximum income for minimum output; the ideal rat was done during work time and involved only the most superficial changes to a story which had already been written for the newspaper which paid one's wages.

Grimes was King Rat. Each afternoon he methodically went through the tray on the news editor's desk containing copies of all stories filed that day, tut-tutting gently over grammatical imperfections, stylistic gaucheries and inept intros. Selecting any stories that might be of interest to his paymasters on four continents, Grimes would re-nose and re-angle them where necessary then stroll down to the main post office to arrange for their transmission to various overseas newspapers and magazines. Their voraciousness for New Zealand news never ceased to amaze him.

Under normal circumstances, the fact that the highest-paid journalist on the paper was at least doubling his income through the labours of others could have caused resentment in the newsroom. However Grimes, as well as being regarded with something approaching awe because of his age, reputation, and exemplary professionalism, played the role of mentor to many *Standard* journalists. Any reporter, no matter how lowly, could go to him for general guidance or help on a story in the knowledge that it would be provided with the utmost affability. The young Jackson Pike, despite his burgeoning reputation as a feature writer, never filed anything until it had been given Grimes' seal of approval.

Grimes finally retired on his 80th birthday. After long and careful calculations based on the assumption that he would live to the age of 95, he established that he'd accumulated sufficient wealth to afford his daily intake of a quarter of a bottle of gin, a bottle of decent wine, a glass of cognac and 10 cigarettes for the rest of his life without having to sell his house for which in 1979 he'd been offered just over $1 million. He had absolutely no desire to live anywhere else.

In retirement he'd settled into a routine from which he seldom deviated. He rose at 8am and made himself a cup of tea and a boiled egg, read the paper, and smoked two cigarettes. Regardless of the weather he would then go for a walk on the beach. Several of the organisations for which he'd ratted had neglected to take him off their mailing lists when he'd retired so each day's post brought newspapers airmailed from Hong Kong, London and New York. On his return from the beach, he would sit at the table by the big window which looked out to where sea met sky and read them with care. At midday he'd mix himself a gin and tonic; at 12.30 he'd have lunch, usually cold meat and salad, and a glass of wine from the bottle he'd finish with his evening meal.

After lunch he'd walk on the beach again, then take a nap from which he'd be roused by his middle-aged daughter who did his shopping and some cooking and often daydreamed of the house she and her husband would build on the site when Grimes died. She was sometimes troubled by her inability to suppress a twinge of resentment whenever anyone remarked on her father's durability.

Before dinner, which was always unfashionably rich when his daughter cooked, Grimes would drink two gin and tonics while reading a book or one of the magazines supplied by Pike. Sometimes he would watch the news on television although doing so usually caused a deterioration in his mood. After a leisurely dinner he would retire to bed with a book, perhaps something by P.G. Wodehouse – he re-read all the *Blandings Castle* and *Jeeves* novels each year – and a digestive. After reading for an hour or so, he would turn off the bedside light and lay his head on the pillow. As he lay in the darkness, he'd wonder if this would be the sleep from which he'd never wake up. Just in case, he'd select one incident from his extensive and varied sexual experience and recollect it in every detail. Garth Grimes did not believe in an afterlife.

"This might make something for you," said Grimes stirring his coffee. "Remember that Appleyard business?"

· "The Berkeley guy?" said Pike. "Goodbye cruel world off the Harbour Bridge?"

Grimes, who remembered Pike when he'd been less callous about such matters, nodded. "That's the fellow. I seem to remember the coroner hedged his bets somewhat."

"Had to; Appleyard didn't leave a note. What about him?"

"Had a ring the other day from my man Worsp," said Grimes. "The sergeant at Central. The man's as vain as an archbishop; I mentioned him in a few columns 20 years ago and he's been ringing me ever since, mostly to tell me how clever he is. For once he had a rather interesting tale to tell. I don't suppose the Prince Albert College hanging means anything to you?"

Pike shook his head.

"It happened in 1970. I made a few bob out of it as it happens – *The Daily Mail* couldn't get enough of it although they kept asking me to get some sex into it. What happened was that a girl named Bronwen Ticehurst, who'd been at the college's annual ball, was found dead in the bell tower. She'd hung herself using a school tie."

Pike nodded. "Yeah, it rings a bell."

Grimes smiled thinly at Pike's unintentional joke. He tended to think that all that held Pike back from being a great editor was that he took everything, himself included, a shade too seriously. He continued: "Well as you can imagine there was a tremendous palaver. By all accounts she was a radiant little creature from a nice home; in those days, parents who allowed their daughters to go to private school balls rather expected them to come back alive. It was all too much for the headmaster, a very queer fish called Hogbin; he took to barking like a half-witted sheepdog in the middle of communion and had to be confined to a padded cell."

Pike pushed aside his notebook. "This is absolutely riveting Grimy but what's it got to do with Appleyard?"

Grimes regarded Pike placidly over his half-moon glasses. Perhaps, he thought, he could do with a little more patience as well. "Is my narrative too discursive? I hope not; one associates long-windedness with senility. The connection is that the police found Bronwen Ticehurst's dance card from the ball in Appleyard's briefcase; his name was on it."

Pike had a quick mind and Grimes enjoyed watching him use it. Pike put his elbows on the table, pressed his folded hands to his mouth, and looked intently at Grimes for half a minute. "He was with the girl that night, kept the card ever since, then bales out," he said slowly. "So what's the theory – he killed her and then went through 20-odd years of torment till he couldn't bear it any more?"

"That seems to be the sergeant's theory which in itself is cause for scepticism. The coroner made no mention of it; couldn't really I suppose – it does involve a couple of hefty assumptions and I don't suppose there's much inclination to re-visit the girl's death." Grimes took a piece of notepaper from his cardigan pocket and spread it on the table in front of him. "I persuaded the sergeant to give me all the names on the card; you might find a couple of them interesting."

Pike's eyes narrowed and he reached for his notebook.

Grimes read the names slowly: "Appleyard of course; Dermot Looms – he must've been her partner because he was

53

down for several dances; Maurice Trousdale; Basil Batrouney; Caspar Quedley and Trevor Lydiate."

Fuck me gently with a chainsaw, thought Pike. Baz Batrouney had been a big name on the local rock music scene in the 1970s; at the height of his fame and amidst suggestions that he was severely drug-addled, he'd abruptly retired to Waiheke Island and become a recluse. Quedley was a high-powered public relations man, while Lydiate was a debarred lawyer who'd been imprisoned for embezzling a couple of million dollars from a client.

He reached across and picked up the list. "What about these two characters, Looms and Trousdale – they mean anything to you?"

"Looms no," said Grimes. "I suspect Trousdale's one of the carpet Trousdales."

"Perfect," said Pike. If Grimes was right, that made him a member of one of Auckland's wealthiest families. "This could be a beauty. It'll take a bit of work though – we're bloody stretched at the moment. I might have to put a freelancer on it. Any suggestions?"

"As a matter of fact I have," said Grimes. Pike noticed a glint of amusement in Grimes' watery eyes; look out, he thought, the old trickster's up to something. "Guess who I heard on the radio the other day talking about being run out of France? Our old chum Reggie Sparks."

Pike's smile vanished. He pushed his chair back hard, stood up and began pacing around the deck. "Grimy, this is a brilliant story idea and I'm extremely grateful and all that, but Sparks? You've got to be joking. He's a fucking psycho – remember the time he stabbed Col Dumpley?"

Grimes chuckled. "How could anyone forget? A great day for journalism. Surely you're not going to hold that against him? The boy was on drugs at the time. Good Lord, I remember when I ate magic mushrooms in Mexico – the very last thing you'd want in that state is to be confronted with a sight as horrible as the Dump. I'd have gone for him with whatever I could lay my hands on too."

Pike continued to pace. "Grimy, you know I normally follow your advice without question but not this time; I'm not having that maniac running round town representing my magazine."

"Well it was just a thought," said Grimes imperturbably. "It simply occurred to me that since Reggie would've gone to Prince Albert with these fellows" – he waved the list – "he might have a bit of a head start so to speak."

Pike stopped pacing and stared at Grimes. He came back to the table and sat down heavily.

"If you change your mind," said Grimes selecting a cigarette, "you should be able to get in touch with him through his mother; she lives somewhere in St Heliers. I think you're being harsh on Reggie, Jackson – I always found him a pleasant young man. By no means the worst reporter either. Not a lot of flair, I grant you, but quite a toughie behind that dishevelled exterior. I knew his father Stanley you know – the original likeable rogue. He bought property over here around the same time as I did; we probably got advice from the same source."

CHAPTER 5

*C*ontrary to his and Detective Sergeant Ihaka's expectations, Detective Inspector Finbar McGrail was not enjoying the Wallace Guttle investigation.

The post-mortem had established that the private investigator's death had been caused, not by Margo Dugdale's well-worn Goodyear, but by the three .32 calibre bullets which had penetrated his forehead in close formation. The fact that the killer, using a handgun in poor light, had been able to place three rounds into such a small target – Wallace Guttle's forehead had been more simian than professorial – strongly suggested that he, or conceivably she, was a professional.

Getting to grips with Guttle's shambolic files had been a major undertaking in itself. McGrail's preliminary review of their contents had been conducted with the grim fastidiousness of a man who doesn't own a dog removing dogshit from his front lawn. His distaste for the whole exercise was in sharp contrast to Ihaka's lip-smacking enthusiasm which extended to marking the subjects of Guttle's photos out of 10 for appearance and technique. After three painstaking weeks, they'd compiled a list of people who might have held a grudge against Guttle. It was a long one. They and their team then embarked on the slow, often embarrassing and ultimately fruitless process of checking out everyone on the list. After more than a month of interviewing, there was only one name left.

McGrail paused outside the half-open door of the small meeting room at Central Police Station from which the Guttle investigation was being coordinated. He listened to the guffaws from within with disbelief tinged with irritation. Wouldn't he ever get bored with those damned photos?

He went in. Ihaka was flourishing a photograph of a man performing cunnilingus and telling a pair of constables: "I didn't recognise this bloke when I went to see him – I was expecting someone with a moustache."

The constables tittered nervously. McGrail said, "May I interrupt the gynaecology lecture?" The constables slipped out of the room, closing the door behind them. Ihaka sipped his tea.

McGrail looked at the photo. Extraordinary, he thought; Guttle must've been close enough to smell them.

"Well Sergeant, what can you report?"

"I'm seeing Mrs Broome, the one who's been overseas, at 11 this morning. She's the last."

"We haven't got a lot to show for six weeks' work, have we?"

Ihaka shrugged. "We got fuck all."

McGrail sat down opposite Ihaka. The desk between them was piled high with files, photographs and transcripts of interviews.

"We had to go through this process of course but if it was a hit – and I'm sure of that – the answer isn't in there," he said, pushing a pile of folders a centimetre or two.

Ihaka nodded. He and the inspector had had this conversation before.

"All anyone in here," said McGrail giving the stack another nudge, "would've got from killing Guttle is satisfaction. For them the damage had been done – getting rid of him wouldn't repair their relationships. You've got to feel pretty strongly to kill someone just for revenge – it's got to be churning your guts day and night. And when you hate that much, you're more likely to do it yourself than hire someone."

Ihaka knew McGrail didn't expect an answer so he didn't give him one.

McGrail opened a manila folder and began sifting through it. "You've talked to them, sergeant, you've read the transcripts. Most of these people are well off, professional types. How many of them would know where to find an assassin?"

Assassin, said Ihaka to himself. He thinks he's back on the Bogside. "Very few sir," he said. "I don't suppose there's a lot of call for assassins in Remuera."

From the start of the investigation, McGrail had urged Ihaka and his team to look beyond Guttle's files and photos. "Nine out of 10 times," he told them, "hiring a killer is a business decision rather than an emotional act."

McGrail's theory was that Guttle hadn't been killed because of something he'd done; he'd been killed to stop him going any further with something he was working on or to stop him acting on something he'd found out. Ihaka thought the theory made sense the first time he'd heard it; he still tended to think so even after hearing it repeated twice a week for six weeks. The problem was that Guttle enjoyed his secrets too much to share them with anyone. No one knew what he'd been working on when he was killed; he hadn't kept a diary or notes of work in progress. Plus, he was a one-man band; he'd had a woman who came in for a couple of afternoons a week but only to do administrative chores.

They'd wasted a week tracking down Tony Rispoli, Margo Dugdale's mystery companion. Rispoli had been subjected to one of McGrail's legendary interrogations – dispassionate, detailed and demoralising – at his home in front of his wife. Ihaka had gained the impression that Rispoli would have the distinction of being Guttle's last victim. Even in death it seemed, Wallace Guttle was able to put asunder those whom God had joined together.

McGrail stood up. "Okay, see this woman then give me a

progress report. When I've seen that, I'll review this whole investigation. Doesn't look like either of us are going to make our names on this one sergeant."

Ihaka met McGrail's expressionless gaze then reached for his favourite file. "A pain in the bum sir," he said, "in every respect."

If the cigarettes and whisky had caught up with Stanley Sparks a month earlier, he would have died a very rich man. Not that the September 1987 crash reduced him to penury; it simply restored the status quo by wiping out the gains he'd made riding the stockmarket in the mid-1980s. As it was, Stanley had left his widow with more-than-adequate capital and a large and comfortable freehold house in one of St Heliers' nicer streets. It was there that Reggie Sparks had taken up residence on his return from France.

Reggie's major achievement since his homecoming had been to persuade his mother to subscribe to Sky Television. As time passed, he strayed less and less from the sofa in front of the television set in the downstairs den. He'd seen a lot of movies and gained what he felt was a reasonable grasp of the situation in the Balkans. Mostly though he watched sport. South African rugby featured prominently on the sports channel and Sparks had watched enough of it to recognise the players' names, most of which, at first hearing, sounded like someone clearing their throat prior to spitting.

Although Sparks didn't realise it, the phone call from Jackson Pike was ideally timed. His mother Mareena was a patient and tolerant woman but didn't possess inexhaustible supplies of either quality. She'd accepted that Reggie would need a period of readjustment and if that meant lying on a sofa watching television for up to 15 hours a day, so be it. Reggie had made some contribution to the household, revealing a hitherto unsuspected interest in cookery. His specialities were the traditional French casserole dishes like *boeuf bourgignon*, *navarin de mouton* and *coq au vin*. But the sense of well-being induced by *etuvee de veau au vin rouge* and a few glasses of South Australian shiraz only lasts for so long; in Mareena's case, it tended to evaporate almost completely by midday the following day, particularly if the cook was still in bed.

It was nine weeks to the day since Reggie's return. That was as much readjustment as Mareena was prepared to countenance; it was time, she felt, for Reggie to get off his backside, find a job, and either move out or start paying rent. So Mareena stood in the doorway to the den, arms folded, regarding her unkempt son without affection and steeling herself for confrontation when the phone rang. She answered it; it was Mr Jackson Pike of *New Nation* magazine calling for Reggie Sparks.

The previous night, Reggie had stayed up till four in the morning watching caribou racing live from Lapland and drinking malt whisky. Three aspirins and two glasses of Berocca had had no discernible anaesthetising effect on the starbursts of pain behind his eyes. Neither Jackson Pike nor *New Nation* meant a thing to him but even with his perceptive faculties dimmed to a level barely above sleepwalking, he'd sensed that his mother was on a mission. That could only mean one thing and it was a thing he would take every opportunity to postpone. He hauled himself off the couch and picked up the phone.

"Hello."

"Sparks? It's Jackson Pike here. We worked together on *The Standard* a long time ago."

Sparks closed his eyes and made a superhuman mental effort – Pike: short, dark, wrote features, up himself.

"Yeah. How are you?"

The half-hearted note of familiarity disappeared from Pike's voice altogether. He was all business.

"Listen, what are you up to these days? You still a hack?" He didn't wait for Sparks to respond. "I run a magazine called

New Nation and I need someone to chase down a story. Could be a good yarn. You interested?"

Sparks listened to Pike with mounting unease. The feature story the editor outlined sounded like an extremely tricky and demanding assignment and it was a long time since Sparks had attempted serious journalism. Given the state of his morale and assuming his firestorm of a hangover ever abated, he reckoned he could just about process a press release into a 10-paragraph news story. Pike was talking about something else altogether. Christ, listen to him.

". . . okay, the basic story is these six guys who were involved with this girl who died 20-odd years ago, how it affected them, and what's become of them since. But I see it as, like, an extended metaphor for the way the country's changed in that time: you know Lydiate, the lawyer who's inside, could symbolise the collapse of ethics in business, the way greed and corruption have taken over; Batrouney, the musician, he stands for the dark side of sex, drugs and rock 'n' roll, the end of seventies innocence; Quedley, the PR man, symbolises the rise of the image maker, the manipulator, that whole image industry – advertising and PR – and the way it's been able to suck money out of the taxpayer by advising government departments and all that shit. Appleyard's obviously the starting point and you're going to have to get a handle on what the hell was going on inside his head – could he have killed the girl? Was he haunted by her death all this time? I don't know about the other guys but I'll bet they're good stories too. I mean, Trousdale's apparently the heir to a massive fortune. What d'you say? If it comes off, it'll be a cover story and a bloody good way for you to get back into it and get some profile."

What's this fucking maniac talking about? Sparks wondered. He desperately wanted to hang up and lie down in a dark room. He couldn't do that, not with Mareena standing right next to him looking expectant. He muttered his acceptance and half-listened as Pike jabbered about money, deadlines, photographs and posting him out the newspaper clippings on Appleyard.

"Okay, all set," said Pike. "Keep me posted on how you get on."

"Hang on," said Sparks. "Where do I find these guys?"

"You ever heard of the phone book?" said Pike testily after a meaningful pause. "You went to school with these wankers, Sparks; if you can't even find them by yourself, what sort of crap are you going to come up with?"

Sparks said "Yeah, okay" and put the phone down. He smiled weakly at his mother.

"Well Mum, back to work."

He told her about the assignment. She was doubly pleased because it meant the moment of reckoning could be postponed, perhaps indefinitely. Who knew where this might lead? As she headed upstairs to make lunch, she called over her shoulder: "I'm sure Gavin can help you get in touch with those people; he's got a couple of friends in the Prince Albert Old Boys' Association."

Sparks slumped on the sofa. There were three thoughts running through his head and he wasn't sure which was the most depressing.

There was the fact that his mother's mind had moved much faster than his when it came to tracking down the dead girl's dancing partners; there was the prospect of having to spend time with his brother and, worse, ask him for help; and there was Pike, the hotshot magazine editor – another contemporary who'd outstripped him.

In the first few weeks after his return, Sparks had made an effort to get in touch with old friends but the reunions had proved dispiriting experiences. Even those who'd been just as directionless and irresponsible as him now seemed to have something for themselves. They had homes, families, jobs that they actually seemed interested in, reputations, even a little fame in one or two cases; they had something to show for being

40-odd. What did he have? Big fat zero. Sure, some of them had changed for the worse; some of them had become conventional and boring and smug. But they had a focus and, for better or worse, seemed happy about it.

He'd come to dread the questions that invariably followed the greetings and nostalgia: So what've you been up to, Reg? What are your plans? You going to buy a place? Better move fast, the market's heating up. Don't tell me you didn't bring a little mademoiselle back with you? When do you hit the big four-O Reg – or is that a rude question? Reggie, one word of advice – superannuation; we've got to look after ourselves now, mate, because the government sure as hell won't.

All of them growing up, settling down, making it, going places, carving out their little niches, finding a meaning in their existences to sustain them through the home stretch, the hard stretch, the real thing.

Starting to feel like the train's left the station boy and you ain't on it.

Tito Ihaka parked in front of Priscilla Broome's smart Mairangi Bay townhouse with a view. He wondered where the ex-husband was living now and decided it would be somewhere just as good if not better. Despite everything you heard about blokes being taken to the cleaners in divorce settlements, it was Ihaka's experience that the legal system was piss-poor when it came to separating rich men from their money.

You sound just like your old man he thought, smiling at the idea. Ihaka doubted that his late father, despite the firebrand rhetoric, had ever laid a finger on a genuine class enemy. By all accounts though, he'd thrown his considerable weight about very effectively in the murky and often violent factional disputes in which he and his fellow communists often engaged. In fact, continually engaged; they just never seemed to find the time to overthrow the system.

His father had been something of a maverick: a fervent

admirer of the politically unsound – in Moscow-aligned circles – Josef Broz Tito, hence Ihaka's christian name. Had he lived to see it, the gory dismantling of Tito's legacy would have been the second great disappointment of Jimmy Ihaka's life; the first had been his only son's decision to become a policeman. Although a heretic on some issues, Ihaka senior held straight-down-the-line Marxist views on the police's role in the class struggle.

Priscilla Broome had overdone the sun-bathing during her six weeks in Noosa. In Ihaka's opinion, one of the few direct benefits of being born brown was that one felt little compulsion to waste summer lying in the sun cultivating skin cancers, as Mrs Broome, whose complexion bore a resemblance to the skin of a passionfruit, obviously did.

Mrs Broome was unable to contribute much to the investigation. Her attitude to violent death was essentially that she'd like to rule it out of her life altogether but if it had to happen to someone she knew, who better than Wallace Guttle? It was a sentiment Ihaka found difficult to fault.

Ushering Ihaka to the door, Mrs Broome decided to give him the benefit of her thoughts on the subject of death.

"I'd never known anyone who's died mysteriously or violently and then all of a sudden, it happens to two people I know within a few weeks. When I say that, I didn't really know Guttle and quite frankly wouldn't have wanted to, but I knew poor Victor Appleyard quite well. And even more of a coincidence, not long before he died, Victor rang me to ask about Guttle and get his phone number."

Like most policemen, Ihaka was not a great believer in coincidence.

"Appleyard – he was the bloke who went off the Harbour Bridge? Bit of a high flier? Hang on, let me re-phrase that – a big-time businessman?" She nodded. "What did he want Guttle for?"

"He didn't say." Mrs Broome looked slightly embarrassed.

"I'm more a friend of Louise, Victor's wife – widow I should say. I suppose she must've told him that I'd used a private detective to . . . when my marriage got into trouble. Victor must've told me three or four times that it was nothing to do with him and Louise; he said it was a business matter that he wanted Guttle for. Between you and me sergeant, I wasn't sure I believed him. I wondered if I should tell Louise – I thought my loyalty was really to her but you've got to be so careful when you get involved in other people's relationships; you can do more harm than good. Then of course when Victor . . . well, it's the last subject you're going to bring up, isn't it?"

"I guess so," said Tito Ihaka thinking, is this a clue? Did Rose Kennedy own a black dress?

CHAPTER 6

*G*avin Sparks, the accountant, checked the time on his assertive sports watch again. It was a nervous reflex – so Reggie was late, so what else was new? The second pre-dinner Scotch was also a sign of nerves; Gavin drank, as he did most things, in moderation – two snorts before dinner on a week night was loose behaviour by his standards.

It was all of 30 years since Gavin had felt entirely comfortable in his brother's company so it was par for the course that he wasn't looking forward to the evening. To make matters worse, their mother had got it into her head that this story for *New Nation* was make or break for Reggie and was expecting – no, demanding – Gavin's cooperation and encouragement.

Gavin was profoundly unenthusiastic about the whole project. The thought of his erratic and disaster-prone brother and that scandal rag *New Nation* combining forces to rattle the skeletons in Prince Albert College's cupboard was gravely disturbing. It could have professional ramifications; the old boy network was good for business. Besides, his son James was due to start there the following year.

Despite his reservations, Gavin would do what he could for his brother because Mareena had asked him to and Gavin was as good and dutiful a son as he was a father, a husband, and an accountant. Gavin Sparks took his obligations seriously and took pride in performing well in his various roles. He saw himself as a contributor, a good citizen. Of course he earned a good living, but that didn't mean he thought money was the be-all and end-all; he just wanted to do the best he could for his family. If everyone had Reggie's attitude, where the hell would we be?

The prickly defensiveness of this train of thought was prompted by Gavin's certainty that, in the course of the evening, he and everything he stood for would be subjected to mockery: mocked for being an accountant, a suit, for making money, for taking life seriously – mocked for not having failed! Of all the things about his brother which irritated Gavin Sparks, the most grating by far was Reggie's assumption of superiority. What in God's name did he have to feel superior about? He took a deep breath. Tonight was another night; whatever the provocation, cordiality must be maintained. Reggie, according to their mother, was taking a tentative step in the right direction and nothing could be done to derail his comeback from semi-retirement.

The doorbell chimed. Gavin let in his brother. As they shook hands, he registered that Reggie hadn't shaved, needed a haircut, and was wearing their late father's favourite sports jacket. That jacket's at least 15 years old, thought Gavin, and it's in a hell of a sight better condition than anything else he's got on.

"G'day Gav," said Reggie handing over a brown paper bag containing a $12 bottle of red wine. "Nice jeans. Iron them yourself?"

Heather Sparks stood, unnoticed, in the doorway to the lounge and observed her husband and brother-in-law. Gavin stood straight-backed to the left of the fireplace; Reggie was half-sitting, half-lying in the armchair, his legs splayed out in front of him.

The odd couple, she thought; nothing in common except their name and their noses. Start at the top: Gav's hair's still black; looks a lot better since he started going to that new place too. Maybe a lighter touch with the blowdrier my darling – it's just a tad too neat. Reggie boy, do my eyes deceive me or do I see a few grey hairs? God, you'd think he didn't own a comb, the way it sticks out all over the place. I bet Gav walks into one before the night's out; he'll recommend the guy who does his hair and Reg'll have that crooked grin on his face and say something like "Why the fuck would I want hair like yours?" So sweet to each other. Gavin, why are you wearing those designer jeans I got you? You don't like the damn things, you're always saying you're not built for jeans. He's trying to avoid – what was it Reggie used to say? – looking like he's cracking walnuts in his arse. Same reason he's put on that Country Road shirt. The sweater with the diamond pattern's not quite right though; you can never avoid the golf club look entirely, can you my dear? Reg, Jesus, where'd you get that disgusting jacket? Otherwise the old uniform, old being the operative word: old jeans, old sneakers, old shirt. More to the point, what's underneath? Gav keeps fit but he was skinny to start with; all the jogging gives him that stringy look. Reggie's got more meat on him, but the sort of life he leads, maybe it's gone soft and flabby? Oh I don't know – there's nothing hanging over his belt and that backside still looks nice and firm. Get that shirt off Reggie; let's have a good look at you. That'd really make Gav's night.

Instead she said, "Which one of you boys is going to carve?"

Although Reg Sparks liked to think he didn't envy his brother one iota, it wasn't true. He envied him Heather. Watching them during dinner, he thought, as he always did, how did a quince like him get a woman like her?

Afterwards, back in the lounge with a glass of port, Gavin gave voice to his concerns.

"Do you really think this is such a good idea? I mean, dragging up all this stuff is going to upset a few people."

"Christ, the story's going to get done whether I do it or

not. You should've heard Pike on the phone – the guy was raving."

"But do you have to do it? I can tell you, it's not going to make my life any easier."

It wasn't the smartest thing Gavin could've come out with. Reggie had never seen his role in life as making his brother's life easier and wasn't about to start.

"Well, it's up to you," he said. "I mean, this wasn't my idea. Mum just thought you could give me a hand getting hold of these guys but if you're not happy about it . . ."

That had Gavin protesting that he'd never said he wouldn't help and all right, let's have a look at the list, most of them would be his year so he'd probably know himself. Reggie thinking, Jesus Gav, you're such a pushover.

Darkness rolled across Gavin's face as he read the list. His brother sat in silence thinking, what's the bet one of them's his biggest client?

When Gavin finally spoke, his voice was flat and lifeless.

"Looms, he was off a farm up north. He's probably still there; the Old Boys' Association's bound to have an address. Batrouney was the pop star, wasn't he? Wouldn't have a clue where he got to. Trousdale's family used to own Fabrice Carpets; they sold it for a fortune. Maurice hasn't done a stroke of work in his life – as far as I know, he sits around in his apartment in Herne Bay waiting for his mother to die. Trevor Lydiate stole a couple of million off a client and blew the lot; he's in some minimum security prison. The client was actually Barry Plugge, the strip club king, so they say Lydiate's better off inside where Plugge can't get at him. And Quedley – well, just look in the phone book."

Gavin handed back the list, gulped the rest of his port, and leaned back in his chair staring at the ceiling.

"What's up with you?" said Reggie.

"Quedley hasn't changed. He's still the golden boy, too much charm for his own good. We bumped into him a couple of years ago. It was one of those nights when Heather overdid it . . ."

Over the years Reggie had heard the odd story about what his mother referred to as "Heather's problem". As far as he could tell, it boiled down to the fact that when she'd had a few, she became a bit of a flirt – pinched a bum or two, turned the New Year's Eve kiss into a tongue wrestle; the same sort of stuff most men do given half a chance. If Gavin's stricken look was anything to go by, she'd given Quedley a lot more than a cheap thrill.

"We went to a party on the Shore somewhere. A client of mine was there and baled me up in a corner; I just couldn't get away from him. When I finally managed to escape, I couldn't find Heather anywhere so I went looking for her."

Reggie knew what was coming; it was just a matter of how bad. He felt slightly queasy. He was also very curious.

"I found them – Heather and Quedley – in the spare bedroom, down to their underwear. Heather had played up a few times before – you know, embarrassing stuff but nothing to get too worked up over. She never took any of it seriously, you know? This time though, she was . . . gone – way gone."

Gavin was still staring at the ceiling, replaying the scene in his mind as he'd done a thousand times. Reggie wasn't sure what he felt for him; eventually he decided it was respect. You're a tougher man than me pal, he thought.

There was one question he had to ask: "What did Quedley do when you walked in?"

Gavin shook his head slowly. "Didn't turn a hair. He just said '*C'est la vie*', picked up his clothes, walked out and left us to it. He was just the same at school – had a nerve you wouldn't believe."

On his way out, Reggie stopped by the living room where Heather was playing scrabble with James. Saying his goodbyes, he was unusually attentive to his nephew. That's nice, thought Heather. Normally he acts like Jamie doesn't exist.

Tito Ihaka had expected more of a reaction when he broke the news to Louise Appleyard that her late husband had hired a private investigator specialising in confidential enquiries. What he got was "Really?" accompanied by expectantly arched eyebrows. The tone and expression implied that Ihaka would have to come up with something better to justify his visit.

"You don't believe it?"

"If you say it's so Sergeant, I believe you."

"But?"

"Look, I think we're at cross-purposes. I'm prepared to believe Vic hired this character but it wasn't to check on me."

"How do you know?"

"Because there was nothing to check," she said with the diminishing patience of a teacher explaining something glaringly obvious to a backward child. "Vic knew that so why would he waste money confirming what he already knew?"

"So why did he hire the bloke?"

"Obviously to find out something that he didn't know," she said in an even sharper tone.

Ihaka had checked the Appleyard file beforehand. "Could it have had something to do with the girl's dance card that was in his briefcase?" he asked.

Louise Appleyard knew all about the dance card too. Its discovery had led to another trying session with Senior Sergeant Ted Worsp.

"Possibly," she said reflectively. "The thing had stayed with him, no doubt about that. It seemed a little morbid to me although it was never the sort of fixation that that buffoon Worsp made it out to be – all that drivel about Vic brooding on it for 20 years. If you want my opinion, Vic hadn't had the card for long; if he had, he would've shown it to me at some stage. I suggest it would be a more productive use of your time, Sergeant, trying to find out where the card came from than worrying about whether I was a naughty girl."

If you had been a naughty girl, thought Ihaka as he drove away, I sure as hell wouldn't have minded seeing the pictures.

About the time Tito Ihaka was trying to visualise Louise Appleyard in the throes of passion, Reggie Sparks was speaking to her on the phone seeking an interview. An hour earlier, the approach would have been unceremoniously rebuffed. However Ihaka's visit had given Louise pause for thought. This had been her first exposure to the police mentality and it had left her unimpressed: their matter-of-course assumption of sexual shenanigans on her part; their apparently unshakeable determination to view Victor as a suicide; their breathtaking leap of logic to link her husband with the Ticehurst girl's death. There was something to this Guttle connection but the police would just sit on their fat collective arse . . . unless she could find some way of pressuring them to pursue it. Like a story in *New Nation*.

So at 11.05 the following morning Reg Sparks, wearing a new pair of Levis, an ironed shirt and his late father's jacket, knocked on Louise Appleyard's front door. A minute went by then the door was jerked open. There was a gust of perfume, a swirl of black hair and a female voice saying very quickly, "Come in Mr Sparks, make yourself comfortable. I'm just on the phone but I'll be with you in two ticks."

She led Sparks through to the large kitchen, which opened out onto the deck, then disappeared. Sparks looked out through the condensation on the sliding glass doors at the rain which was coming down in a silver sheet. Spring wasn't like this when we were kids, he thought. It was dry and crisp and at morning break there was a race to get the best positions to bask in the sun for a quarter of an hour. Now it's always grey and gloomy and pissing down with rain. Must be the greenhouse effect – all that spray-on shit.

There was music coming from a ghetto blaster on the kitchen bench. It sounded like Lloyd Cole. He listened to the

72

words: "Now when you're puttin' on your face/Guess that you feel kinda low/Knowin' that you're past your best/And you got nothin' to show." Sounds familiar, he thought. Then the chorus: "Only this time round you might have to . . . pay for it."

It was not a good moment to be reminded of his short and ignominious career as a gigolo but the memory flash was so vivid that Sparks felt his cheeks burning. It was all that fucking German's fault, what was his name? Klaus something. Standing there in that bar in Toulouse, about seven foot tall, checking his biceps and his profile in the mirror, looking like the prototype for the master race, bullshitting about the money he'd made as a gigolo on the Cote d'Azur, finally coming out with why didn't Sparks go down there and try it? Sparks, ordering two more beers, saying "All very well for you mate, but I don't look like some genetic engineer's wet dream."

"Not at all, not at all," said Klaus vehemently. "The most important things are that you can be very charming and you can get hard at the right time, even if the ladies are a little old and not so beautiful. Okay? It is not necessary that you are handsome, just that you are not ugly. Also you must not be short, you must not be fat, you must have all the hair. So you are fine. Of course" – he looked Sparks up and down – "you must dress in the correct way."

If Sparks had dispassionately assessed himself in terms of Klaus' specifications, he would have had to acknowledge that he was not renowned for his devilish charm. Furthermore, his ability to stand and deliver on demand was untested. However, it was late at night and he was drunk, a combination conducive to the formulation of hare-brained schemes. Two days later he was in the bar of the Hotel Negresco on Nice's Promenade des Anglais, dressed in a pale green linen suit he'd bought in Bangkok and casting meaningful glances at any woman of mature years who entered.

His first assignation was with a 50-year-old spinster from

Somerset. When he discovered that she was staying not at the Negresco but at a much more modest establishment several blocks back from the beach, Sparks began to wonder whether they were thinking in similar ballparks with regard to his fee. As it turned out, she had no figure in mind; indeed she was quite oblivious to the fact that she was party to a commercial transaction. He discovered how it was done on his second attempt when the lady, an Austrian, demanded payment from him before she'd removed a single garment. Sparks fled with guttural oaths ringing in his ears, caught the next train back to Toulouse, and avoided the company of women for several weeks.

The traumatic recollections left him ill-prepared for his interview with Louise Appleyard. After she'd spent 15 minutes explaining why she was sure her husband hadn't committed suicide and urging him to follow up the Guttle connection, she felt compelled to ask Sparks if he possessed the memory of a chess grandmaster since he was neither using a tape-recorder nor taking notes. Half an hour later she watched Sparks trudge through the rain towards his mother's car. If that's an ace newshound, she thought, I'm Opo the dolphin.

CHAPTER 7

While the meeting with Reggie Sparks did little for Louise Appleyard's spirits, it had quite the opposite effect on him. He sensed that she hadn't been overly impressed with him and was determined to give her cause to revise her opinion. It had been some time since he'd had a goal in life.

Gavin had supplied phone numbers and addresses for Looms, Trousdale and Quedley. Directory service provided the phone number of the prison one hour's drive south of Auckland where Lydiate was incarcerated and Jackson Pike's secretary had rung with Batrouney's address on Waiheke Island. If Batrouney was on the phone, he had an unlisted number.

Dermot Looms was indeed still on the farm. He responded with the no-nonsense gruffness one associates with the rural sector: "If you want to come all the way up here, that's up to you. Sounds like a waste of time to me." *New Nation* seemed to carry more weight in Quedley's office; his secretary arranged an appointment for the following Monday morning on the spot. Trousdale had his answering machine on so Sparks left a message.

When Trevor Lydiate, the disgraced lawyer, got the message left by Sparks, he swore under his breath and requested permission to make an immediate phone call. He rang a South Auckland car dealer, one of the few people in what had been his social circle who would still take his calls, and told him to drop what he was doing and get down to the prison that afternoon.

When the car dealer got back to Auckland after visiting Lydiate, he followed to the letter the procedure the lawyer had laid down before entering prison. He stopped at the first public phone he saw and dialled the number he'd memorised. The man who answered the phone said: "Service department."

"Is Danny there?"

"Yeah, speaking."

The car dealer said, "A journalist from *New Nation* magazine, called Reggie Sparks, wants to talk to Mr Brown," then hung up.

The car dealer got back into his car, his mind abuzz. He wondered who Danny was; he wondered what Lydiate was up to; he wondered if he'd been wise to agree to help Lydiate on a no-questions-asked basis. He also wondered how long Reggie Sparks had left to live. Some two months before, the car dealer had relayed another message from Lydiate to the taciturn Danny, that "a private investigator called Wallace Guttle is sniffing around Mr Brown". A week later he read in his morning paper that Guttle had been shot dead in a Newmarket carpark.

Most of all the car dealer wondered if being Lydiate's go-between made him an accessory to murder.

After the call from the car dealer, the man named Danny, who repaired electrical appliances, left his workshop and walked across the road to a phonebox. He dialled a number that he'd known off by heart since long before Lydiate had become a guest of the Crown. After two rings the receiver at the other end of the line was picked up. There was no greeting or acknowledgement. Danny repeated the message that the car dealer had given him and hung up. Unlike the car dealer, he neither reflected on the consequences of his action nor was he curious as to the identity of the silent party at the other end of the line. As long as his unknown benefactors continued to pay $50 into his TAB account each week, Danny was quite happy to go on being a link in the mysterious chain.

His call had gone to a red telephone, one of three on a large and tidy mahogany desk in an office above The Blue Angel strip club in Auckland's Karangahape Road. The man behind the desk groaned when the red phone emitted its distinctive ring; lately that sound had heralded nothing but bad news. After he'd heard Danny's message, the man planted his elbows on the desk, put his head in his hands, and said in a loud and troubled voice: "Just one motherfucking thing after another."

The man was Barry Plugge. Gavin Sparks had described him as "the strip club king"; a Sunday tabloid had once dubbed him "Auckland's Sultan of Sleaze"; Plugge saw himself simply as a businessman, someone who identified a need and catered to it.

At the peak of his fortunes in the late 1970s, Plugge had earned close to $1 million a year from a dozen flourishing strip joints and massage parlours around Auckland. However the 1980s had been a difficult decade: first came the relaxation of the censorship laws which resulted in pornographic videos becoming freely available; then came AIDS; then came some serious competition.

Plugge took a dim view of all three. He considered sex should stay in the strip clubs and massage parlours where it belonged, not on the shelves of neighbourhood video rental shops. Porn videos, he felt, simply encouraged masturbation, a practice of which he disapproved as unyieldingly as did the Vatican. Plugge, who'd been happily married for 27 years, could think of nothing more demeaning for a grown man than masturbating in front of a television set. However, there was also a commercial dimension to his disapproval: masturbation was bad for business. "Wank, wank, money in the bank," he would say. "A bloke's not going to go to a massage parlour if he's just jerked off."

AIDS, he insisted, was something which happened to male homosexuals and drug addicts and his girls were neither; a few of them were undoubtedly lesbians but, to quote another of his aphorisms, "no one ever caught AIDS off a dildo".

Plugge, an ardent nationalist, was proud to be a New Zealander who employed New Zealanders and who provided entertainment for New Zealanders while performing a useful social service in the process. It infuriated him the way offshore operators had tried to muscle in on his patch in recent times – the Italians from Sydney and, even worse, the Asians who flew in "students" from Thailand and Hong Kong, girls who'd work for next to nothing and were often prepared to dispense with a condom for a few extra dollars. And when Plugge, having seen his revenues decline precipitously, swallowed his pride and his principles and brought in his own Asian girls, what did those little yellow animals do? They put a fucking contract out on him!

These negative trends had forced Plugge both to look around for opportunities to diversify and to consider resorting to the sort of strong-arm methods he had always shied away from. And it was the combination of the two which had reduced him to sitting at his fine desk with his head in his hands, feeling sorry for himself.

Throughout his career, Plugge had followed three basic rules: never a borrower or a lender be; never take commercial advice from a lawyer; and never make decisions when in the grip of emotion, whether the extreme of mood was up or down. Brooding on his problems, Plugge reflected bitterly that he was now paying the price for having broken two of these rules. At the time though, it had seemed too good to be true; ever since he'd been in business, he'd been ripped off by lawyers. Then, right when his cash flow was being squeezed, he'd been presented with a scheme for getting it back with interest.

It all began with an invitation to lunch. It came from Trevor Lydiate, a partner at Trubshaw Trimble & Partners, a law firm whose exorbitant fees matched the plushness of its downtown offices and the self-esteem of its principals. Plugge had had little to do with Lydiate, indeed regarded him as just another of the supercilious nancy boys with limp handshakes of whom there were plenty at Trubshaw Trimble. But Plugge, who wouldn't shout his best friend a meat pie if he could possibly avoid it, would put up with a lot for a free lunch anywhere, let alone at Antoine's. Obviously Lydiate would want something but he was too well-bred to raise it until after the food and drink had been ordered. And then . . . well, thought Plugge, I've told much more intimidating characters than Mr Trevor Lydiate to get fucked before today.

They lunched well. Lydiate proved to be an excellent host, avoiding any mention of business until the dessert plates had been removed and the neighbouring tables vacated.

Then Lydiate made his pitch: "Barry, I'm leaving Trubshaw Trimble to set up my own practice and I have a proposition for you."

The liqueur trolley arrived. Plugge chose the oldest and most expensive cognac on offer and was impressed when Lydiate nodded his approval and followed suit.

"You've got $200,000 in our trust account," continued Lydiate. "Off the top of your head, how much would you have invested in the share market, sitting in bank accounts, that sort of thing – I'm talking about money which could be redirected at short notice?"

Plugge didn't need to think about it. "Nine hundred grand give or take a few bucks."

Lydiate whistled softly. "Now I gather the business is currently making around $300,000 a year after tax. You don't have to answer this but I shouldn't imagine you declare every single dollar that comes in the door?"

Plugge swilled his brandy and felt the heat rise to his face. The lawyer interpreted his smug expression as agreement.

"For the purposes of this discussion, we'll assume that's the case. Okay, here's my proposal: you clean out your bank accounts, cash in your shares, and get your money out of Trubshaw Trimble. Then you hide it offshore – I don't know, stick it away in the Cayman Islands or something; we can work that out later. To all intents and purposes though – and there'll be all the paperwork to verify it – you will've given me that money to use through my trust accounts. All right? Then for a couple of years, you take as much as possible out of the business and do the same thing – hide it offshore and pretend I've got it. When we've built the amount up to, say, two million, I own up that I've stolen it and blown the lot. You get reimbursed the full amount from the lawyers' fidelity fund and I go to jail. While I'm doing time, you put my share into an offshore account so that it's waiting for me when I come out. That's basically it."

Lydiate leant back in his chair and sipped his drink. Plugge, his large ears by now bright pink, stared at him with newfound respect.

"That easy huh?"

"Yep, that easy. Believe me, I didn't dream this up last week; I've been thinking about it for years."

"Say we get two mill – how'd we divide it?"

"Well I'm the one who's taking the fall – I get disbarred and sent to the slammer – so I reckon that entitles me to a round million."

"A mill for you, a mill for me – that seems reasonable."

"Not quite. We'll need a partner, an accountant. The books are going to have to be absolutely shipshape."

"You got someone in mind I suppose?"

Lydiate smiled cheerfully. "He gets $200,000. Of course on top of that, I'll need play money."

Plugge's eyes narrowed. "What the fuck do you mean, play money?"

"I'm meant to've blown two million right? That means gambling, high living, conspicuous consumption. If it's going to stack up, I'll need to've established a pattern of behaviour – you know, overseas trips, first-class travel, five-star hotels, spending sprees, and so forth."

"How much are we talking about?"

"I'd say another $200,000 should do it."

"Jesus wept. What does that bring my cut down to?"

"Six hundred thousand – but remember that's pure cream. And you don't have to do a bloody thing for it."

The lunch had taken place almost four years previously and since then events had unfolded very much as Lydiate had outlined as they worked their way through most of a bottle of 1951 cognac. It all went without a hitch; at least, it had done until the day his red phone rang and Danny relayed the message that a private investigator was asking questions about Lydiate.

Plugge was not by nature or inclination a violent man. The types of characters his industry attracted meant that now and again one had to deal with people who responded more readily to a fist in the face or a boot in the groin than to reason. When such measures had been required in the past, they'd been satisfactorily performed by the large and stupid men whom Plugge employed as bouncers. But earlier that year, when Plugge found himself under siege from the Italians on one side and the Asians on the other, both groups having abandoned any inclination to peaceful co-existence and now clearly hell-bent on driving him out of business, he'd had to rethink his attitude.

In the space of three weeks, one of Plugge's clubs was firebombed, the word went out that there was $25,000 to be earned by putting him on a slab, and the head of his "security" team was dragged into an alley where his left achilles tendon and right thumb were severed. The other bouncers decided that Plugge's wages and the occasional free blowjob were not worth the risk of being subjected to this sort of fiendish oriental cruelty and took to their heels. In fact the knifework had been performed by a 49-year-old Henderson grandfather of Croatian descent who'd just returned from doing a spot of ethnic cleansing in Bosnia. It was done on behalf of the Italians from Sydney for $2,000 and the promise of tickets to see his favourite soccer team, AC Milan, next time he was in Europe.

Desperate times require desperate measures and Herman Pickrang, whom Plugge recruited on the advice of one of his heavier underworld connections, certainly qualified under that heading. Pickrang took the fight to the enemy; on his first day on the job, he walked into an Italian restaurant, seized one of the trouble-makers from across the Tasman, pushed him head first into a pizza oven, and held him there until his eyeballs crackled and popped like frying eggs.

Then he accosted the wife of the Hong Kong gentleman who'd put the bounty on Plugge's head, surprising her while she was walking her prize Pekinese. Pickrang snatched up the dog by its hind legs and flailed it against a concrete telephone pole, reducing the beast to hairy jelly. As the horrified woman tried to flee, he seized a large handful of her hair and yanked it out by the roots leaving her with a monk-like bald patch. The contract was cancelled the following day.

Plugge was not comfortable with such methods but told himself he had to fight fire with fire. The Guttle business, however, was another story; that was overkill. It was partly his fault: that was the second time he'd broken one of his rules. He'd just heard that his two best strippers had found God and were retiring to devote themselves to His service when the call came through on the red phone. Plugge didn't lose his composure very often but when he did, a search party had to be sent out to get it back. He'd rampaged round his office, throwing things, bellowing that no snotbag snoop was going to poke his nose into his affairs and get away with it, and demanding of Pickrang was he going to stand around scratching his arse or do something about it, the long streak of piss? Pickrang did something about it all right; the fucking madman went out and blew Guttle away. Hadn't he ever heard of breaking a guy's legs, for crying out loud?

CHAPTER *8*

*R*ummaging through the accumulated flotsam and jetsam in his mother's basement, Reggie Sparks found his old record collection which included Basil Batrouney's farewell album, *Going Mad in Public*.

The cover photo showed Batrouney standing in the middle of a downtown intersection wearing only a Napoleonic hat, gumboots and a pair of underpants the waistband of which had been hitched up well above his navel, accentuating his genital bulge. Beneath the flamboyant headgear and framed by lank black hair was a pale, oval face dominated by a pair of bulging, frog-like eyes. All in all, Batrouney looked thoroughly deranged.

Mad as a snake, thought Sparks.

The only track off the album which Sparks could remember was the notorious *Smack gets in your Eyes*, a paean to drug use which had goaded several parliamentarians into demanding Batrouney's imprisonment. These calls were resisted although the song was banned from the state-controlled airwaves. The album's ability to offend the establishment more than compensated for its total lack of musical or lyrical merit and ensured its commercial success.

Sparks caught the Quickcat to Waiheke Island and took a taxi from the wharf to the township of Onetangi. The address he'd been given turned out to be a nondescript weatherboard house a block back from the waterfront. Sparks mounted the steps to the veranda and knocked on the front door. It was opened by a stout man of early middle age. His receding wiry grey-black hair was pulled back into what Sparks assumed was a bun or a ponytail and bushy white muttonchop sidewhiskers emphasised the pumpkin-like shape of his face. He peered benevolently through large round spectacles with lenses like the reinforced windows on a despot's limousine.

"Does Basil Batrouney live here?"

"That's me."

It hadn't for a moment occurred to Sparks that this portly Dickensian figure was the former wild child of New Zealand rock music. He was so thrown by the admission that all he could think of to say was, "We went to the same school."

Batrouney stared at him blankly for 20 seconds.

"School," he said eventually. It was neither a statement nor a question. It reminded Sparks of the way little children utter words because they like the sound.

Off to a promising start, thought Sparks. "Yeah, Prince Albert College."

There was another long silence. "Groovy. But as my old amigo Bobby Zimmerman said, 'that was in another lifetime'."

Jesus, what a fruitcake, thought Sparks. "Look, I'm a journalist," he said doggedly, "and I'm doing this story for *New Nation* about a group of guys – including you – who were at Prince Albert College together . . ."

"A journalist, eh? Thought I'd finished with them."

Batrouney shrugged, turned and walked down the hallway. "If you want to rap, come in," he called over his shoulder. Sparks followed. Batrouney had a bald crown and a pony tail which hung like a dead animal between his shoulder blades.

He led Sparks into a room set up as a study. There was a large desk with a computer, a printer and a fax machine, an old kitchen table covered in files, magazines and drawings, and a draughtsman's board. Batrouney sat on the swivel chair at the desk and pointed Sparks to an old sofa against the wall.

"You still in the music game at all?" asked Sparks trying to get the conversation going.

"Man, I don't even have a transistor." Batrouney got heavily out of the chair and went to the table. "These days, I draw comic strips; just call me the Walt Disney of Waiheke." He picked a comic from a pile on the table and tossed it to Sparks. It was called *Grub* and subtitled *The Kiwi Lavatory Humour Comic*. On the cover was a cartoon of a hugely fat man sitting on the toilet. Underneath it said: "In this issue – how to leave giant skidmarks every time. Plus! Ron's Runs, Wendy's Wide-On, Perry and his Poo-Ring and much, much more!"

Sparks glanced up at Batrouney who was swinging to and fro in the swivel chair, humming tunelessly. "It's not everybody's bag," he said. Sparks put the comic down on the arm of the sofa.

"You do it all yourself?"

"No, no, a bunch of us put it together." Batrouney giggled. "I've just invented a new character – 'Jack Stack and his Magic Crack'."

I don't believe this, thought Sparks. He tried to look interested. "Yeah? What's that about?"

"Jack's a super-hero, kind of like Batman, except what he does is suck bad guys up his arse. Like a black hole out in space." He giggled again.

"Can't see it ever being made into a movie," said Sparks, "but I've been wrong before. So how many copies do you sell?"

"You'd be surprised," said Batrouney primly. "We did our homework. Scatological humour – that's like to do with arseholes and farting and stuff – is the big growth area in comics. So," he beamed at Sparks, "can I put you down for a subscription?"

"No thanks. I'm more your *Doonesbury*, that sort of thing."

Batrouney looked a little miffed. "Suit yourself."

He lapsed into silence. Christ, thought Sparks, now I've upset him. However after a minute or two, Batrouney came abruptly back to life: "Now this school thing: fact is, there's nothing I can tell you. All I remember from those days is this stuff." He waved the comic. "You know, schoolboy humour. See, I divide my life into BD and AD – before drugs and after drugs. What I remember from the BD period doesn't amount to shit."

Sparks was curious. "What about the bit in between, when you were actually on drugs?"

"It was a big bit. They really are missing years, man – just a blur."

"So all the fun, the groupies . . ."

Batrouney shook his head slowly. "You tell me. I might as well have been a clerk."

"That's tough," said Sparks sincerely. "But getting back to BD, to your Prince Albert days – surely you remember Bronwen Ticehurst, the girl who hanged herself? You danced with her at the ball."

Batrouney blinked rapidly behind his thick glasses. "Man, all I remember is it was a heavy scene. What did we used to say – bad karma? Yeah, that was it – it was bad karma."

Sparks sighed and closed his notebook. He suspected that what Jackson Pike had in mind went a little deeper than bad karma.

The class of '70 isn't holding up too well in the hair department, thought Sparks as he watched Dermot Looms, the farmer from up north, coming down the steps towards him. That was where any likeness to Batrouney began and ended: whereas the creator of *Grub* had the flab and pallor of a sedentary recluse, Looms was every inch the outdoorsman – tall and rawboned, his face and exposed scalp weathered the colour of varnished wood.

"Sparks is it?"

"Yes."

"You Gavin's brother?"

"Yes."

"You got kicked out, right?"

"Well, technically speaking I wasn't expelled . . ."

"Doesn't matter a bugger now. Let's go round the back."

Looms lived in an old colonial-style farmhouse, white-painted timber with a grey slate roof, at Tapora on the Okahukura Peninsula which juts out into Kaipara Harbour. To the right of the house was a double garage; behind it was a rose garden and a lawn which sloped away to some farm buildings. Beyond them, the paddocks rolled down to the sea. They sat in the sun on white wrought-iron garden furniture. Sparks explained his assignment.

Looms rubbed his forehead. "Christ, what a terrible thing that was. I hardly knew Bronwen, you know. Mum was friendly with her mother and they jacked it up between them, for me to take Bronwen to the ball. I was so bloody socially backward I wouldn't have had a partner otherwise but it was hard lines for Bronwen; she wasn't short of admirers. Trouble was, she wanted the one bloke who could take her or leave her. I suppose that's what it boiled down to in the end, the whole sorry business."

"Who was that?"

"The Ghost – Cas Quedley. You'd remember him?"

Sparks nodded.

"We called him the Ghost after the cartoon – Caspar the friendly ghost? Good name for him too."

"What was the story between him and Bronwen then?"

"They went out a couple of times. She was pretty rapt in him; so were half the girls in town for that matter. Anyway Cas gave her the flick – I mean, she wasn't the only one that happened to; he was a terrible bugger with the birds. At the ball I had a couple of dances with Bronwen, then she says she's

88

got to talk to Cas, she'll be back in a minute. Off she went and that was the last I saw of her. Apparently she fronted Cas and he told her look, it's all over, don't be a pain in the arse, so she shot through. At least that's what I thought – that she'd just buggered off home. Her folks' place wasn't that far from the college. Of course, what she did was go up to the belltower and – well, you know the rest."

"What about Victor Appleyard? How did he fit in?"

"Oh Christ, poor old Vic. Well he was one of the bunch panting after Bronwen – in fact he was pretty stuck on her. He took it real hard."

"So he had the hots for her but she wasn't interested?"

Looms shook his head stiffly. "She wasn't interested in him or me or anyone but Quedley. It was Cas or no one."

"I've heard the cops think Appleyard might've jumped off the Bridge because he had a guilty conscience. Is it possible he could've killed Bronwen in a jealous rage, you know, just couldn't handle being rejected?"

Looms let out his breath explosively. "Whew, that's a bit of a shocker. Let's put it this way, Vic was just about the last bloke you could imagine doing something like that . . ."

"That's what the friends and neighbours always say, isn't it? 'He was such a nice, polite man, I'd never have picked him as an axe murderer'."

"Yeah, I guess so."

"How about Quedley? How did he take it?"

Looms sat back and folded his arms. "Well as I said, the Ghost was a good name for Cas. You never knew what was going on there. I mean, he wasn't what you'd call sentimental. His mother died when we were at school and no one knew till weeks later. But sure, it must've upset him. I wouldn't have liked to've been in his shoes."

"Why, did people blame him?"

Looms waved a hand at an invisible fly. "Oh you know, there was whispering behind his back. I think a few doors were shut on him, he wasn't welcome in some quarters anymore. But you couldn't really blame him. For a start, the birds knew where they stood with him – shit, he went through them like it was a race. And you know what it's like at that age – kids put each other through the emotional hoops all the bloody time."

They walked back to Mrs Sparks' Peugeot. Looms looked in the driver's window: "You know, after you rang the other day, I got to thinking about that year. When you think about it, two suicides within a few weeks – it's a bloody wonder parents weren't pulling their kids out of the place."

"I left at the beginning of that year and I sort of lost touch," said Sparks. "Who was the other one?"

"The chaplain, Padre Swindell. He drove his Morrie 1100 straight into a wall – couldn't have been more than a few weeks before the other business. They tried to make out it was an accident but apparently there was nothing wrong with the car, the weather was okay, and the old bloke never touched the piss. It looked like he just pointed the car at the bloody wall and put his foot down."

Sparks sat in the reception area of Quedley Communications (Counsel, Strategy, Crisis Management) trying to differentiate between the various attractive young women flitting to and fro. It was no easy task; there seemed to be a distinct Quedley Communications look – long hair, short skirts, high heels. After a 10-minute wait, a statuesque brunette swayed into his line of sight, breathed, "Mr Sparks? CQ will see you now," and escorted him down a corridor to Quedley's office.

It was a huge office, big enough to house a large desk in front of which were positioned three high-backed chairs, an eight-seat meeting table, a couple of long sofas arranged around a low coffee table, a small bar and assorted foliage. There's still enough room to land a helicopter, thought Sparks.

Caspar Quedley, wearing a beautifully cut dark double-breasted suit and displaying a very deep tan and very white teeth, rose from behind the desk and advanced on Sparks, hand outstretched. The handshake he administered was impressively muscular and of precisely calculated duration: sufficiently protracted to convey an enthusiastic welcome without suggesting freemasonry or arousal. The tan, the firm grip, the erect posture, the wide shoulders and the flat stomach all proclaimed that here was a man who sprang from his bed at 6am and ran 10 kilometres before breakfast, a man who pumped iron, a man who played a rip-roaring game of squash, skied like a daredevil and liked the sting of salt spray in his face. What an arsewipe, thought Sparks. He sourly noted that, unlike his contemporaries, not a square centimetre of scalp peeped through the glossy black curls which tumbled onto Quedley's forehead and lent a touch of boyishness to his slightly unreal good looks.

"Thanks for seeing me Mr Quedley," said Sparks. "Or should I call you CQ?"

Quedley grinned disarmingly. "You can call me Caspar or you can call me Shitface – it's entirely up to you. Take a seat."

As he poured the coffee, Quedley made small talk about *New Nation* and Jackson Pike – "We've all got to strive to stay on side with young Master Pike."

Sparks interrupted him. "Mr Quedley, I couldn't help but notice, you seem to've surrounded yourself with bimbos. Any particular reason for that?"

Quedley put down his cup and leant forward, half-smiling. "Well Reggie, bimbo is a somewhat judgemental term implying that these young women perform no function save the decorative. That isn't entirely the case. To answer your question: yes, there is a reason for it. The fact is that, despite everything one hears and reads about women in the workplace, 90 per cent of the time in corporate public relations we're dealing with men. And the simple truth of the matter is that on the day-to-day stuff, most men, whether they admit it or not, would rather deal with an attractive woman than a man. The reality is that a lot of executives look upon dealing with PR issues as almost light relief, a bit of a break from the real work. So I've always had the view that it's important to ensure that there's an enjoyment factor – if you like, it's a case of giving 'em what they want, not what they necessarily need."

Sparks raised his eyebrows. "It makes it all sound pretty . . . superficial."

Quedley leaned further forward, looking thoroughly earnest. "Abso-fucking-lutely. If I can go off the record for a moment: this is a superficial industry for superficial people. If public relations ceased to exist tomorrow, it wouldn't detract in the slightest from the sum of human happiness; in fact, you could argue that mankind would be better off. Imagine a world in which companies and governments and institutions were judged purely and simply on their merits rather than all the outrageous bullshit they spread around – on what they do rather than what they say they do. But I put it to you, it requires a certain wit and cunning to make a good living out of something so fundamentally artificial and to do so, what's more, by gouging money out of the supposedly canniest, most hard-nosed, most financially literate sector of society – big business. Which brings us back to my bimbos, God bless each and every one of 'em."

Quedley paused from his dissertation and looked at Sparks appraisingly. "So you're Gavin's brother?"

"Yes."

"I believe I've met your sister-in-law. A delightful creature – what's her name?"

"Heather."

"By God Heather, that's right," said Quedley slapping his thigh. "How could I forget? Been quite some time since I've seen either of them."

Sparks glowered at him. "You married Mr Quedley?"

"No sir. Haven't got the temperament for it."

"I suppose it's difficult for a man about town like yourself to settle down?"

If Quedley sensed the hostility radiating from Sparks, he gave no sign of it. He regarded Sparks amiably. "Man about town – haven't heard that term for a while. If you mean that I like to do a bit of rootin' from time to time, well I'll own up to that. Don't you?"

Sparks ignored him. "I guess that was the problem with Bronwen Ticehurst – she just didn't understand your temperament?"

Quedley held Sparks' stare. "I don't know why Bronwen killed herself. That night at the ball she asked me if we could have a relationship and I said no. I heard afterwards from a couple of her friends that it hurt her – apparently she believed she was in love with me – so maybe you could argue I drove her to it. If so, it was by being honest. Obviously, if I'd thought for one second she was going to do what she did, I would've handled it differently although if you follow that line to its absolute logical conclusion, I couldn't ever have broken up with her – I'd have had to have married her to keep her alive. But who the hell knows? Maybe there were other things in Bronwen's life that made her unhappy, things that none of us knew about, and me giving her the elbow was simply the straw that broke the camel's back. Now personally, you or anybody else can write whatever the fuck you want about me – I've got a fairly thick skin and I'm pretty much beyond caring what people think about me – but don't you reckon Bronwen's family could do without *New Nation* raking over it after all these years?"

"Well I suppose that's the difference between journalism and PR; as they say, news is what someone, somewhere wants to suppress."

Quedley sniggered derisively. "Pomposity doesn't become you Reg. Besides, you know who said that? Some Fleet Street press baron, no doubt trying to justify running a 'what the butler saw'-type story. That's the sort of self-serving sound bite I'd be proud to come up with."

Sparks shrugged. "So who did you take to the ball? She must've been special – sounds like most of the other guys would've crawled over broken glass for Bronwen."

Quedley pursed his lips. "I wouldn't want this to be taken the wrong way but I don't remember. She was new, that was all."

"She was a challenge, was she? Yeah, I hear you like challenges." Quedley started to say something but Sparks pressed on. "What you were saying about *New Nation* raking over Bronwen's death, as if we're doing it just for the hell of it; that's crap. We've got something to hang it on – the Victor Appleyard connection."

Quedley sat up. "You know about that?"

"About what?"

Quedley's genial poise had slipped. "Well I'm not sure I want to . . ."

"If you mean, have we heard that Appleyard might've had some sort of fixation about Bronwen Ticehurst, the answer is 'yes'."

Quedley slumped back on the sofa. "Well I'm sorry to hear that but at least it didn't come from me."

"Well was it true?"

Quedley stood up and walked round in a little circle. "Look, Victor was a nice guy and I really don't want to go on the record about this but I guess you'd have to say that he seemed to have a bee in his bonnet about it. He came round and talked to me about it a couple of times."

"Where was he coming from?"

"Well that's it, I couldn't really work it out. He just seemed to want to go over and over the same old ground. You know, no one's ever accused me of being the most sensitive soul on the block and I make no apology for not accepting responsibility for Bronwen's death, but going through it all chapter and verse wasn't exactly my idea of a good time."

"Would you say he was obsessed with it?"

Quedley grimaced. "Obsessed is an ugly word. I don't know I'd say that. But he certainly had an itch he couldn't scratch."

On his way out, Sparks asked Quedley about the chaplain.

"Old Pard Swindell? Yeah well, there you go. Who knows what that was all about? Far be it from me to speak ill of the dead but I suspect he was well and truly screwed up. I mean, a clergyman, a bachelor, a boys' boarding school – nod, nod, wink, wink, know what I mean? He was probably a bit of a tortured soul and was punishing himself for some trivial lapse that you or I wouldn't lose a moment's sleep over."

They shook hands. Quedley's smile was full of sly humour. "Terrible things, consciences. We're much better off without them, eh Reggie?"

I can't help it, thought Sparks going down in the lift. I really ought to detest that man – but I don't.

CHAPTER 9

When Maurice Trousdale, the heir to the carpet fortune, returned to his multi-million dollar Herne Bay apartment after his four-day, eight-restaurant trip to Sydney, he stood in front of the big window in his upstairs living room and looked out across Westhaven marina to Waitemata Harbour, the North Shore and the Harbour Bridge. After contemplating this scene for several minutes, he turned away sighing. Even the view no longer worked. There'd been a time when, on his return from overseas, he'd stand at the window thinking it was good to be back, good to be home. Now even that sense of belonging failed to uplift him. He could feel a blue period coming on.

Trousdale's occasional spells of gloomy introspection resulted from his dwelling on the fact that his only role in life – that of heir – essentially involved outlasting his mother. Given that his mother was almost twice his age, it was not a lot to ask and Trousdale felt that he'd pretty much got the hang of it. He felt ready for something a little more demanding, something that would stretch him.

Trousdale spent a quarter of an hour musing on his dilemma. Having failed to come up with any stimulating projects which didn't require high intelligence or physical courage or drive and energy – none of which he possessed – he played back the messages on his answering machine. Among the invitations to weekends at Pauanui, cocktail parties and gallery openings was a message which at first gave him a nasty jolt, then triggered some furious thinking. The conclusion he eventually reached transformed his mood like a blaze of sunshine after a summer shower.

The message was from Reggie Sparks and was a request for an interview in connection with an article he was preparing for *New Nation* magazine. The message concluded with a volley of names, some familiar – Victor Appleyard, Caspar Quedley – some all but forgotten – Bronwen Ticehurst, Basil Batrouney. The common thread seemed to be Prince Albert College.

Trousdale's initial alarm was caused by the mention of *New Nation*. The magazine had a gossip column, *Aucklander's Diary*, in which Trousdale featured from time to time. There'd been a reference several years previously which he could still recite from memory. It had read thus:

"A pall of gloom descends on the festive season! It is one's melancholy duty to report that yet another year has passed in which Maurice Trousdale, globetrotter, patron of the arts, *bon vivant* and heir to the Fabrice Carpet fortune, made no discernible progress towards finding a consort.

"It defies belief that, in this savagely materialistic age, a man who stands to inherit around $200 million when Mater, the doughty Lydia, turns up her toes, can be entering his 40th summer still a bachelor. It's hardly as if Auckland is devoid of women intent on marrying money; in the salons of Parnell and Remuera, the smart restaurants, the yacht clubs, the member's stand at Ellerslie, in fact everywhere the voluptuaries, phonies and *nouveau riche* white trash who make up what passes for Auckland society gather, one is in constant danger of being trampled underfoot by hordes of debs, 'models' and assorted bimbos flashing thigh and breast at anything they suspect is male, single and rich. So frenzied has the hunt become that even being of dusky hue is no longer unacceptable providing the tinted gentleman's net wealth is in the right ballpark.

"So how come, I hear you cry, Maurice is still fancy-free? Your diarist's theory is that for even the most single-minded gold-diggers, the thought of having to submit to the pudding-like albino's clammy caresses on a nightly basis is too horrific to contemplate. *Plus ça change, plus la meme chose* . . . as a lad at Prince Albert poor Maurice was dubbed 'The Troll' because of his general unsightliness and shunned by the smart set."

Trousdale and his lawyers had debated whether or not to sue. The hawks among his legal advisers had argued that the item was so malicious, so gratuitously offensive, that no court in the land would have an ounce of sympathy for *New Nation*. The doves cautioned that defamation cases could be brutal and demeaning affairs; the defendant could be expected to leave no stone unturned in exposing every unsavoury aspect of the plaintiff's character and the resultant humiliation could far exceed that caused by the original libel. In the end Trousdale decided to turn the other cheek, swayed by the unthinkable prospect that *New Nation* might produce as witnesses the women who'd participated in his rare and uniformly gruesome sexual experiences.

Forbearance had its price. From then on, the editor of *Aucklander's Diary* felt sufficiently emboldened to preface any reference to Trousdale with the label "pudding-like albino".

What galled Trousdale most of all though was the realisation that the diary item was another sally in the campaign of denigration and humiliation which had been mounted against him, intermittently, for almost 30 years. He'd suspected it straight away – "Pudding Bum", "Slimefingers", "the Albino" and "the Troll" were all lampoons invented at Prince Albert College by his once and future persecutor, the diabolical Caspar Quedley. Trousdale's suspicions had been confirmed by Quedley himself when they'd met shortly after the item appeared. Not that Quedley had owned up to planting it in *Aucklander's Diary*; he hadn't needed to. The malicious gleam in his eyes, the predatory grin, the greeting – "Bugger me blue

Trousers, you get paler every time I see you; you must live under a fucking bridge" – were all intended to let Trousdale know that the Ghost had struck again.

So while the very name *New Nation* had caused Trousdale to flush to the roots of his thinning hair, the remainder of Sparks' message prompted some careful thought. He'd often yearned to revenge himself on his tormentor but Quedley had seemed unassailable. If I handle this right, thought the carpet heir, I can get back at that swine through the very vehicle he used to ridicule me. Trousdale sat down at his antique writing desk, took a clean sheet of paper, unscrewed his red lacquer fountain pen and started making notes of what he would tell the man from *New Nation* about Caspar Quedley.

Sparks had two messages when he checked in at *New Nation*: the first was an invitation to join Maurice Trousdale for lunch at Le Brie restaurant the following day. The second was an instruction to call the supplied telephone number at exactly 2 o'clock that afternoon if he wanted to know the real story about Trevor Lydiate. He did so.

The call was answered on the fourth ring.

"Who's that?" said a deep male voice.

"Reggie Sparks. Who am I talking to?"

"Never mind that, pal. You want to know about Lydiate or not?"

"Sure."

"Okay, you know Potter's Park on the corner of Dominion and Balmoral? There's a kids' playground, right? Behind it, just up the rise, there's one of those round things that bands play in."

"A rotunda."

"What?"

"That's what it's called, the round thing – a rotunda."

There was a short silence. "Sparks?"

"Yep."

"Shut your hole. You want to know about Lydiate or not?"

"Yeah, I want to hear about Lydiate."

"Okay, be at that whatever the fuck it's called in Potter's Park in one hour. How old are you?"

"Thirty-nine."

"What are you wearing?"

"Jeans, blue shirt, brown jacket. How will I recognise you?"

"I'll be the one in the hotpants."

The anonymous caller hung up.

Sparks sat in the rotunda in Potter's Park for half an hour. He would have waited a little longer, even though by then he was pretty sure that he was wasting his time, but it started to rain and the temperature dropped appreciably. He ran back to his mother's car.

Herman Pickrang, who'd been observing Sparks through a pair of binoculars from his car parked in the car park of the Kentucky Fried Chicken outlet on the other side of Dominion Road and wondering how long it would take the dumb shit to figure out he'd been jerked, said "About fucking time" and started his car. Pickrang had set himself two objectives for the afternoon – to find out what Sparks looked like and where he lived. Neither proved difficult. Having paraded himself for identification purposes, Sparks continued to oblige, driving straight to a house in St Heliers where he put his car in the garage and went inside. After following him there, Pickrang, who felt rather pleased with himself, decided he'd go home and play with his electric train set.

Sparks rang Jackson Pike and gave him a brief and uninformative account of his progress. Pike was unconcerned by the lack of detail: the mere fact that Sparks had found and interviewed some of the dead girl's dancing partners meant that he'd already surpassed Pike's expectations. Sparks asked Pike if he had a means of putting a name and address to the phone number he'd been given by the no-show. He hung on while Pike called a contact in Telecom who reported that the number was that of a public phone box in New North Road. Sparks had expected something of the sort. He found it interesting, in a detached sort of a way, that expecting such an answer did absolutely nothing to allay the unease it caused.

When Sparks was ushered to the table, Trousdale took a hurried slurp of his dry martini, brushed some flakes of crust from the corners of his mouth, hauled himself to his feet and extended a pudgy hand.

Like the man who doesn't know much about art but knows what he likes, Reggie Sparks had no particular notion of what the heir to a fortune should look like but his luncheon companion certainly wasn't it. Trousdale was short – no more than five feet five – and plump. In the exact centre of his fat, pink face was an incongruously babyish button nose. Occasionally women, feeling obliged to find a redeeming feature in the swollen expanse of Trousdale's face, professed to find his nose cute. Trousdale himself considered it a damn nuisance since it failed to provide satisfactory support for his spectacles. Trousdale's hair was bone-white and very fine and, beneath it, countless tiny beads of perspiration glistened on his pink scalp. Trousdale sweated a great deal. Some of his acquaintances, who considered him close to being a glutton, assumed it was excitement which made him sweat so much in restaurants.

They ordered. Sparks, recently health-conscious, chose soup and grilled snapper with a green salad; Trousdale, for whom meals were an important filler of the all-too-many hours which make up an empty life, nominated garlic snails followed by venison casserole and vegetables du jour. Suspecting that his guest might decline the offer of wine, he called for a bottle of pinot noir without consulting him.

As they waited for the food, Sparks outlined his brief from *New Nation*.

Trousdale swallowed the last mouthful of his martini. "So what did you make of the exquisite Caspar?" he asked.

"Quedley? He struck me as a pretty smooth operator."

"A smooth operator?" Trousdale arched his almost invisible eyebrows and turned down the corners of his prim mouth. "I must say that if describing Caspar as a smooth operator is any indication of the level of insight and originality we can expect in this article, I don't think I'll bother to read it."

Only the brief flaring of his nostrils betrayed Sparks' urge to reach across the table and prong Trousdale's jaunty little nose with his fork.

"Well to be absolutely candid, my dear old sausage," he said calmly, "I don't give a rat's arse whether you read it or not."

Trousdale dabbed his forehead with a napkin, his other hand fluttering in appeasement.

"I do beg your pardon – that sounded rather impertinent. No, what I really meant to say was that describing Caspar as a smooth operator seems rather an understatement."

Sparks' gaze remained indifferent. "Well I get the impression that you're just itching to tell me about him so why don't you?"

Trousdale, hot and flustered, wriggled on his seat; his armpits were positively frothing. This was not how it had been meant to go at all: he'd planned to manipulate Sparks like a puppeteer, have him dancing his tune without even knowing it. Still, there was the opening. He took a deep breath.

"Well, I think one must always remember that Caspar's family was of comparatively modest means and at school he was very, very conscious of the fact. You know, see him swanning around town today as to the manner born and it's easy to forget his rather humble origins. His father was a vicar, you see, and the only reason Caspar went to Prince Albert was because of the clergy's discount on school fees – they only paid 50 per cent from memory. As I say, he was very aware, was Caspar, that he was something of a have-not compared to most of his schoolmates. I remember going to the movies with him and a few others during the school holidays, in our fifth form year I think, and someone commented on the fact that wherever we saw Caspar out of school – at a party, at the football, in town, whatever – he seemed to be wearing exactly the same clothes. I'm sure it was said in all innocence – just one of those thoughtless, flippant things teenagers say – but Caspar was quite hurt by it."

Trousdale felt a fresh outbreak of sweat on his forehead and applied the napkin. The fact of the matter was that he himself had drawn attention to the pathetic paucity of Quedley's wardrobe. It had been a put-down worthy of Quedley himself in its calculated nastiness, a moment to savour. Quedley had blushed absolutely crimson and the others, sensing his vulnerability like sharks scenting blood, had gleefully twisted the knife in the wound.

"Anyway, Caspar became terribly money-conscious. He always had some sort of little money-making scheme on the go. Believe it or not – and this is strictly off-the-record by the way – in our last year he somehow got hold of an advance copy of an exam paper, university entrance history I think it was, and sold sneak previews."

"What, to a public exam? How the hell could he do that?"

"No, no, no. It was the internal school exam but he sold it to all the fellows who failed UE the year before and were trying to get it accredited on internal assessment."

"Even so, how'd he get hold of it?"

"God only knows. Maybe he sneaked into the masters' common room one night and made a copy of it. As I said, he always had something on the go, he was always hatching a plot."

Trousdale attacked his food, noting with approval that

Sparks was scribbling furiously in his notebook. I just hope he's up to the task, thought Trousdale. God, Quedley will hate this stuff coming out.

Sparks put his pen down and took a hurried mouthful of fish.

"What about Appleyard? Anything you can tell me about him?"

"Nothing much really – we weren't close either at school or subsequently. Although funnily enough, I did see Appleyard not that long ago – no more than a few weeks before he died, I guess – over in Sydney. I bumped into him in the lobby of the Regent Hotel and he insisted on having a drink. Now you're interested in that Ticehurst girl aren't you? Well, I swear, that was the only subject he could talk about. He was awfully het-up about it, asking me all these questions about her and the ball. What could I say? Without wishing to appear callous, I had one rather off-hand waltz with the poor thing; it was hardly worth committing the details to memory."

"What did he say about it?"

Trousdale arranged his knife and fork on a spotless plate. He was more interested in dessert than the subject of Victor Appleyard.

"Oh, I don't know. To be frank, it was going in one ear and out the other. All I can remember was him rabbiting on that he'd come across someone in Sydney who'd shed some light on it all."

Sparks had a moment of genuine excitement. "Who? Did he say who it was?"

"Oh no. I actually asked, out of politeness rather than curiosity, but he said he'd been sworn to confidentiality or some such. I must say, I found his behaviour rather extraordinary; it did occur to me that he might've been slightly off his head and what do you know? Next thing, he's jumped off the Bridge."

CHAPTER 10

Reggie Sparks had virtually no interest in clothes. As far as he was concerned, one wore clothes to avoid pneumonia and arrest. In France he'd had two comparatively expensive items in his wardrobe: a linen suit and a Burberry raincoat. After the ignominious gigolo episode, he'd given the linen suit to the tramp who sometimes slept in the doorway of his apartment building, on the condition that, in future, he would urinate somewhere else. He'd kept the raincoat, wisely as it turned out, since in Auckland that spring fine weather, like the ideal guests, came rarely and didn't stay for long. Sparks was wearing the raincoat when he called on the widow Appleyard for the second time. She opened her front door, looked him up and down, and checked her watch.

"Is school out already?"

"What?"

"The coat, Mr Sparks. You look like every parent's nightmare."

Since their first meeting, Louise Appleyard had seldom been far from Sparks' thoughts. He'd been keenly anticipating her instant, unguarded reaction to his unannounced visit, thinking that it would be a pointer, at least, to whether her attitude towards him was essentially positive or negative. He'd envisaged a range of responses, some of them wildly optimistic, some, on the basis of being prepared for a let-down, less so; being likened to a child molester had not been among them.

He forced a stiff grin. "Thanks for reminding me; I'm almost out of boiled lollies." She acknowledged his re-bound with a slight incline of the head and half-smile. He moved rapidly to the matter at hand.

"I just thought I'd drop round and let you know where I've got to. I've talked to all but one of the guys on the dance card. A couple of interesting things have come up."

He was admitted. They went into the kitchen where he sat on a bar stool at the bench while she made coffee.

Sparks began his report: "The first guy I saw, Batrouney, the ex-rock singer who lives on Waiheke, he was basically a waste of time. Guy's as crazy as a shithouse rat."

Louise raised an eyebrow.

Sparks misread her reaction. "Sorry, pardon the French. Thing is, the guy admits he gave himself one hell of a hammering with the drugs. He's only half here. You know what he does with himself these days? Draws dirty comic strips."

"What sort of dirty?"

"Stuff for grubby-minded kids."

She looked at him expectantly. "Give me an example."

"You know, it's full of . . . bodily functions," he said, stirring his coffee. "The stories are like 'Ron's Runs' and 'Wendy's Wide On'."

Louise giggled. "'Wendy's Wide On'? You're kidding."

"Absolutely not. You wouldn't believe some of this stuff. Jesus, I thought I had a pretty basic sense of humour." He shook his head. "Anyway, as I say, old Basil's out there on his own private planet. More to the point, his memory's completely shot – he'd have trouble remembering how to get to the bathroom let alone what happened at that ball in 1970."

"Oh well, strike one. Who was next?"

"Dermot Looms. He's a farmer up near Wellsford, one of your good, keen men. He was Bronwen's partner at the ball but reckons that didn't mean much because their mothers jacked it up for him to take her. He did point out something

106

interesting though: a few weeks before the ball, the college chaplain also killed himself."

"What's interesting about that?"

He shrugged. "I suppose interesting's the wrong word – strange maybe. Don't you think two suicides at the same school within a few weeks is a bit of a coincidence?"

She took a thoughtful drag on her cigarette. "Hmm. What else did he say, the farmer?"

"Nothing much. He said your husband and a few others were pretty keen on Bronwen."

"Oh I knew that," she said smiling. "Under that earnest exterior, there was a genuine romantic. Vic used to say he was hopeless when he was young, falling in love at the drop of a hat. But that one was strictly one-way traffic, wasn't it?"

"Yeah, well she had the same problem with Caspar Quedley. He was my third call."

"Oh yes, I've met him. He's rather gorgeous-looking, works in advertising or something like that? I'm thinking of the right one, aren't I?"

"I don't know," lied Sparks. "Quedley's a public relations man."

"It's not exactly a common name. What does he look like?"

Sparks shrugged, frowning. "I guess . . . smooth."

Louise Appleyard smiled enigmatically. "Okay, so what did Mr Smoothiechops have to say for himself?"

"Well, Quedley said your husband went round to see him about Bronwen Ticehurst. He said he wouldn't say he was exactly obsessed about her but he wasn't that far off. Then I talked to this strange little bloke Trousdale who said pretty much the same. Trousdale ran into Victor in Sydney just before he died and reckoned he really got into his ear about the girl and the ball and whatnot. Anyway, this is what I wanted to ask you about: Trousdale was saying your husband had met someone in Sydney who'd shed some light – those were his

107

words – on the Ticehurst business; said he was quite worked up about it. Any idea who it was?"

She shook her head. "No. He never said anything to me."

"Did he have a diary or something, maybe an address book, that he put phone numbers in?"

"He kept a desk diary at Berkeley. I doubt if that'd tell us much – he wouldn't have taken it away with him." Her hand holding the cigarette stopped in mid-arc, halfway to her mouth. "Christ, of course – the electronic organiser." She ground the just-lit cigarette in an ashtray and hurried from the kitchen, returning a minute later with the biggest briefcase Sparks had ever seen. She laid the briefcase on the kitchen table, clicked it open, rummaged inside for a moment and produced a flat black rectangular object, slightly smaller than a paperback book. To Sparks it looked like a calculator.

"The police went through his briefcase," she said. "They probably thought this was a calculator."

Sparks said nothing. She opened it out, revealing a keyboard and screen.

"Lucky I'd forgotten about this otherwise I might've wiped all Vic's stuff and used it myself, to keep track of my frenetic social life. Now let's see, when was Vic's last trip to Sydney?" She pulled a calendar off the wall and flipped through the pages, then began jabbing the small keyboard.

She peered at the instrument's small screen. "Okay, he went over on the 20th of July and had dinner that night with TR – that'd be Toby Redsell who runs Berkeley in Australia. Wouldn't you know it, it's all bloody initials." She punched another button. "Hang on, here we go – on the 25th he had an appointment with Lloyd Chennell and on the 27th with Julian Gage. I can't remember Vic talking about either of them. They mean anything to you?"

Sparks nodded, trying hard not to look pleased with himself. "I'm pretty sure there was a teacher at Prince Albert called Chennell. Gage rings a bell too. Can I use your phone? I know someone who'll know for sure."

Herman Pickrang sat in his car parked 50 metres down the road from Louise Appleyard's house and watched the rivulets of rain run down the windscreen. He'd followed Sparks there and now he was going to have to wait for him to emerge. Although he didn't particularly enjoy sitting in a car watching the rain, he would do it for as long as he had to. Among the many things Pickrang had learned during his 25 years in the army was the art of waiting for something to happen.

Pickrang was 49 years old. On his tax return and for similar official purposes, he described himself as a security consultant. In fact he earned his living by scaring, hurting, and occasionally even killing people. Pickrang sometimes wondered if he was what the newspapers called a psychopath. He'd tell himself that he couldn't be a psycho because he did what he did for money rather than for pleasure. Every now and again though, a voice from deep inside his head would point out that that really didn't prove much because he enjoyed doing it anyway. Pickrang would bring these interior debates to a close by deciding that it made very little difference to his victims whether he was a psychopath or not.

Pickrang was highly qualified for his work on several counts. In the first place, he had a frightening appearance. He was the son of Janey Wang, a Chinese/Samoan whore who'd worked the logging camps of the mid-North Island, and one of her customers. Watching Herman grow, Janey decided that his father must have been a tall pakeha which narrowed the possibilities down but not enough to point the finger with any real conviction. Not long after she became pregnant, Janey had set up home with a Maori logger named Joe Pickrang. Janey gave her son Joe's surname and the Christian name of her very first customer, the scion of a wealthy German family with large land-holdings in Samoa.

Pickrang had inherited his mother's tiny cat-like head

and slightly slanted eyes. These attributes gave Janey, who was barely five foot tall, an exotic look. However on Pickrang, who had also inherited his unknown father's long and sinewy frame and who at 19 was six feet five inches tall, the effect was quite unearthly and had earned him the nickname "Pimplehead" when he joined the army. The unusual pattern of his hair loss over the following 30 years had heightened his menacingly alien appearance: he was completely bald except for a swathe of black fuzz which swung across the back of his head from ear to ear like a hammock and a greying V-shaped clump, all that remained of what had once been a widow's peak, which sat in splendid isolation high on his forehead. People noticing Pickrang walking towards them in the street would often wonder why he didn't wipe the bird shit off his head.

As a youth, Pickrang had been a keen and promising rugby player, his height, spring and athleticism making him an adept lineout forward. At first his brutal inclinations helped rather than hindered his career, selectors in country areas having traditionally valued "a bit of mongrel" in their forwards. One chilly afternoon in Tokoroa however, Herman Pickrang discovered the old adage that those who live by the sword sometimes perish by it. Before the game was quarter of an hour old, he'd delivered carefully targeted kicks to the heads of three members of the opposition and left livid sprig scrapes on the back and buttocks of several others. It was proving a most enjoyable afternoon until, returning to earth after a mistimed lineout jump, he was struck just below his right ear by a fist the approximate size and consistency of a cannonball which has been gathering barnacles on the seabed for several centuries. His head exploded in a flash of white light and the crackle of splintering bones. By the time he came off his liquid diet 10 weeks later, Pickrang had decided to quit rugby and join the army.

While Pickrang doubted, on balance, that he was a psychopath, most who crossed his path felt strongly to the contrary. In the army, an institution which has long valued psychopathic tendencies provided they are accompanied by a readiness to follow orders and a tolerance for uncomfortable uniforms and for being shouted at from close range, Pickrang found his natural home. He rose to become a sergeant-major in the SAS where his apparent relish for enduring extreme discomfort and eating disgusting things during survival exercises, coupled with his unflagging enthusiasm for making life hell for those under his command, made him a highly-regarded figure.

After 25 years in the army, Pickrang retired reluctantly into civilian life. It was a source of aggravation to him that, having spent two-and-a-half decades mastering numerous ways to kill people, he'd never actually had the opportunity to put this knowledge into practice. Just as disturbing was the dreary prospect of no more of the unarmed combat sessions at which he'd routinely exceeded the parameters of pain and punishment which instructors were permitted to inflict. What, he wondered, does a highly-trained fighting man with powerful if controllable sadistic urges do when he can no longer serve his country? After much thought, Pickrang reached the obvious conclusion: he became a thug-for-hire.

Pickrang's second career had gone swimmingly until the mix-up over the private investigator Wallace Guttle. The whole business still gnawed at him. Not only had Plugge refused to pay for what had been an outstandingly executed job but he'd had to stand there and take some of the ripest, crudest abuse he'd received since he'd been a raw private. For a man with 20 years' experience of screaming elaborately filthy insults at others, it had been an unsettling experience. Now he was having to traipse around after this clown of a journalist hamstrung by humiliatingly restrictive rules of engagement. It was an insult to his professionalism.

If Pickrang had been less engrossed in revisiting Plugge's irrational and unjust reaction to Guttle's flawless assassination, he might have noticed Detective Sergeant Tito Ihaka driving past in an unmarked car. Ihaka, on his way to call on Louise Appleyard, recognised Pickrang's distinctive features from one swift sideways glance. Ihaka drove on past the Appleyard house and pulled to the side of the road.

Pickrang had never actually been convicted of a criminal offence although he'd been interviewed by the police in relation to a number. Those of his victims who'd lived to tell the tale preferred not to. Ihaka wondered what a fully-fledged criminal monster like Herman Pickrang was doing in this pleasant and peaceful street on the shores of Lake Pupuke and whether it had anything to do with Louise Appleyard and her dead husband who had hired the also dead private investigator.

Reggie Sparks rang his brother Gavin.

"Got a couple of names for you; I think there's a Prince Albert connection."

"Fire away."

"Lloyd Chennell."

"Yep, he was a teacher there back in our time. He taught arts subjects, English, history, that sort of thing. He was quite good."

"Do you know where he is now?"

"He went to Australia. Last I heard, he'd done all right, got himself appointed headmaster of one of the top schools – I can't remember if it was Sydney or Melbourne. I could find out for you."

"Okay, second name – Julian Gage."

Gavin groaned. "Shit, I knew it. I won't be able to set foot in the place after this story comes out."

"Why, what'd he do?"

"Oh, even you'd remember Gage, surely? He was the character who everyone reckoned was gay. With good reason too from what I've heard of him since. I think he went to Aussie as well."

CHAPTER *11*

*I*haka waited in his car across the road from the Appleyard residence. Eventually the front door opened and a man he didn't know came out. The man turned to Louise Appleyard, who was standing in the doorway, and went to shake hands. The gesture seemed to surprise and amuse her but she carried it off gracefully. The visitor then walked down the path, got into a Peugeot, and drove away. Ihaka watched in his rear view mirror as Pickrang did a U-turn and drove off after him.

Louise Appleyard thought the knock on her front door meant that Reggie Sparks had found an excuse to return and found herself smiling as she went to answer it. However it wasn't the journalist; it was the large Maori policeman whose name she couldn't remember and whom she suspected of being smarter than he pretended to be. Louise did what she always did when caught slightly off-guard, which seldom happened; she stood there saying nothing and looking good.

"Detective Sergeant Ihaka, Mrs Appleyard. How are you?"

"I'm well, thank you Sergeant. Do come in. Two visitors in one day – it's bordering on hectic."

Following her down the corridor to the kitchen, Ihaka said: "Yeah, I saw the bloke who just left. Who was he, if you don't mind me asking?"

"I'm sure you have a reason other than nosiness for

wanting to know so I'll tell you: his name's Sparks, Reggie Sparks. He's a journalist."

"A journalist eh? Now why would Herman Pickrang be tailing a journalist?"

"I'm sorry?"

"While you and Sparks were in here talking about whatever it was you were talking about, a fella called Herman Pickrang was sitting in his car just down the street. When Sparks left, Pickrang followed him. Who's Pickrang? He's probably the nastiest thing on two legs in this town. In fact, that's being unfair to rottweilers. He's a hood, a heavy, someone who earns a crust by bashing people up – or worse."

Ihaka had been looking forward to testing the thickness of Louise Appleyard's coolly ironic exterior. He was glad to find that it wasn't double-glazed. Her hand jumped to her mouth: "Good God. Is Reggie in some sort of danger?"

Ihaka nodded slowly. "If Pickrang was stalking me, I wouldn't be laughing about it."

"We've got to warn him," she said, pawing through the bits and pieces on the kitchen bench. "He left me his phone number – it's here somewhere."

"If you don't mind Mrs Appleyard, I'll do that – I'd like to talk to Mr Sparks. So he's working on a story, is he?"

Louise, disoriented, rubbed her forehead. "Yes he is, for *New Nation* magazine. I suppose in a way it's what we were talking about last time you were here – the Ticehurst girl's dance card. He's talking to the men on the card, I think to do a story on what's happened to them since. It was Vic's death that gave them the idea."

"Yeah, well that's the press for you. To be honest, I'm surprised you're helping them."

Louise brought her chin up. "They didn't get the names from me, Sergeant. Mr Sparks had them already. And as for helping him, why shouldn't I? At least he's going about it with an open mind; you people seem to have taken the view from

114

the very beginning that my husband committed suicide and probably murder to boot. I can't see that I've got much to lose."

It took Ihaka less than five seconds to work out how *New Nation* had obtained the names on the dance card. Ted Worsp, he thought; that sack of shit could talk under wet concrete.

He said, "Where do I find Sparks?"

When the *New Nation* editor Jackson Pike was told by his secretary that there was a Mr Sparks wanting to see him, he half-expected that Sparks had come in to admit defeat. However the Reggie Sparks who entered his office was not the twisted substance abuser who'd lunged at Col Dumpley with a copy spike all those years before, nor the clueless wimp to whom he'd given the assignment. While Sparks didn't look like a convert to temperance, clean living and early nights, he was by no means the burnt-out shell Pike had expected. What surprised Pike even more was that, far from weasling on the story, Sparks clearly had the bit between his teeth.

He went straight into his pitch: "Mate, I wouldn't try to tell you how to do your job but I reckon we might be coming at this thing from the wrong angle. The sort of story you were talking about, using these guys as symbols of what's happened to the place over the past 20 years – well, let's face it, you can do that state of the nation stuff any time. I mean, how interesting are these turkeys anyway? Batrouney's a rock 'n' roll casualty – what would that make him? Number 900 in an unlimited series? Quedley's a slick PR man; well aren't they all? At the end of the day, he's a bit of a show pony. Looms is just down on the farm minding his own business and Trousdale's a pathetic little blob who's only interested in his next feed."

Pike leaned back in his excessively large chair and gave Sparks what he thought of as his "first base" look. It was intended to be both encouraging and challenging, to say "Okay, you've got my attention, now let's see if you can convince me".

Sparks, who assumed the editor was holding in a fart, was mildly flattered. Realising that the look hadn't conveyed the message, Pike spread his hands and said, "I'm listening."

"I think Appleyard found out something about the death of Bronwen Ticehurst – maybe that it didn't happen the way they said it did or that there was a lot more to it. To me, that's the story – what did Appleyard find out? Because whatever it was, it was enough to make him jump off the Bridge – or enough to make someone throw him off."

Pike lurched forward and planted his elbows on his desk. "Hang on, I must've missed something. How did we get to that?"

"You know the cops' theory is that he had something to do with the girl's death and was driven to suicide by guilt. I don't think that stands up. Mrs Appleyard's absolutely convinced he didn't kill himself. I know that in itself doesn't prove a thing, but surely to Christ she and others would've noticed something if the guy had been dragging this terrible secret around with him all these years. That's the first thing. Second, if he'd known all along what really happened to her, why does he suddenly get a bee in his bonnet and go round quizzing people about it? As far as him being murdered: well, if he didn't jump, what did happen? Either he stopped his car on the Bridge to sniff the sea air and fell – and both parts of that proposition are hard to believe – or someone shoved him. There's one other thing: Appleyard had hired a private detective."

"What for?"

"Well we don't know, do we, because a couple of weeks later someone blew the guy's brains out."

Pike's eyes widened.

"It was a guy called Guttle. Mrs Appleyard says he definitely wasn't hired to check up on her. Okay, again you can take that with a grain of salt. All I can say is, I've talked to her and I'd be surprised if it turns out she's bullshitting."

Pike thought about it for a minute or two. No matter how much Sparks had cleaned up his act, it went against the editor's usual practice and instincts to let a freelancer, particularly such an unknown quantity, drive the story. On the other hand, sometimes the best stories, the real ball grabbers, came when a journalist got this sort of gut feeling. And Sparks did seem to have a reasonable grasp of it.

"All right Reggie, we'll do it your way for the time being. So what's the next step?"

Sparks grinned. "I'm glad you raised that."

After Ihaka had left with a promise that he, personally, would alert Sparks to the Pickrang menace, Louise Appleyard made herself her fifth cup of coffee and lit her tenth cigarette of the day and sat down to review recent events. Pickrang's sudden materialisation was genuinely alarming but at least the police were aware of it. On the subject of the police, Ihaka was certainly a vast improvement on Worsp. There definitely was, she'd decided, a shrewd mind behind the immobile brown face. Under the circumstances, his sheer bulk was quite reassuring as well. Her thoughts didn't dwell on Ihaka and Pickrang for long; there was another, more diverting, development to consider.

By and large Louise Appleyard didn't care what other people thought of her; she considered it one of her few strengths. Even so, there was one reputation she was reluctant to risk gaining – that of merry widow. Hence she'd resisted all attempts to draw her back into the social swing. These attempts had begun in earnest the previous week, exactly four weeks after her husband's funeral. Four weeks seemed to be regarded as the appropriate period of mourning and self-denial. She hadn't known whether to laugh or cry when she received that first dinner party invitation accompanied with a delicately worded rider to the effect that there'd be an unattached male of suitable age and social status among the guests for her to cast an eye over.

All the same, her own instinctive responses were now telling her it was time to get on with life. She suspected that Reggie Sparks fancied her and far from being offended or unnerved, she'd quite enjoyed the faint buzz of the electricity of attraction which flowed between them, albeit predominantly in one direction. I'm not quite sure where I stand on that one, she thought. He's not exactly every maiden's dream but then again, he's not the tongue-tied scruff and all-round no-hoper I took him for at first.

Somewhat more tantalising than the rumpled and awkward Sparks was the prospect held out by Audrey Benn, the wife of one of Victor's colleagues at Berkeley Enterprises. While other would-be hostesses had been euphemistic, in some cases to the point of inscrutability, Audrey had been refreshingly direct when she'd called that morning.

"My dear," Audrey had said briskly, "it's time to throw off the widow's weeds. I know you've been knocking back invites right, left and centre but be warned – there'll be high dudgeon if you don't take your place at the dinner table here next Saturday night. I've moved heaven and earth to snare Auckland's most eligible bachelor for the occasion. I'm sure you know to whom I'm referring – Caspar Quedley."

Louise had said she'd think about it. It wouldn't do to appear too eager.

Ihaka had checked Sparks' phone number against his mother's listing in the phone directory and then driven to St Heliers. There was no sign of the Peugeot or of Pickrang. He rang the doorbell. After identifying himself and assuring Mareena that her son was not about to be led away in handcuffs, he was invited in for a cup of tea and a peanut brownie.

After two cups of tea and three peanut brownies and a discussion about race relations, a subject on which Mrs Sparks proved to be surprisingly well-informed and enlightened by what he assumed were the standards of St Heliers matrons, Ihaka, sitting by the window, observed Sparks pulling into the drive. He was closely followed by Herman Pickrang.

During the afternoon Pickrang's frustrations had finally boiled over. Fuck this, he thought. Any prick with a car and a pair of eyes could do this job. First chance I get, I'm going to scare the living shit out of Sparks and if Plugge doesn't like it, he can blow it out his arse.

Pickrang didn't decide to flout Plugge's express instructions solely because of his resentment at being treated as just another hired hand rather than as a highly qualified specialist. During the hours he'd spent dogging Sparks, it had occurred to Pickrang that he'd effectively rendered himself obsolete as far as Plugge was concerned. Since his retaliatory missions against Plugge's Asian and Australian rivals, peace had returned to Karangahape Road; Plugge was treating him in this demeaning fashion because he'd outlived his usefulness. If Plugge's going to give me the flick, thought Pickrang, why the hell should I worry about pissing him off?

Sparks hadn't noticed Pickrang's red Mitsubishi, which had been parked just down the road from his mother's house all morning and had followed him around town for most of the afternoon, so he was only mildly curious when it pulled up behind him. Curiosity turned to amazement when Pickrang got out of his car. Fucking hell, he thought, what sort of a mutant is that? Amazement turned to bowel-activating fear when the creature spoke.

"Hey cuntbag," it said. "I'm going to rip your fucking ears off."

Ihaka came out of the house and strolled down the drive to join them. For a couple of sickening seconds, Sparks thought he was pincered. However when the newcomer spoke, it was apparent that he and the ear removalist were not working as a team.

"G'day Herman," said Ihaka. "Eaten any babies lately?"

Pickrang checked his inclination to fling the insolent intruder to the ground and stomp his testicles into powder. The fact that this big buck knew his name and felt bold enough to insult him could only mean one thing.

"You're a cop."

"I'm a cop and you're a headcase – that's why we're here. Whose dirty work are you doing today, Herman? Who told you to lean on Mr Sparks?"

Pickrang took a couple of paces backwards and opened his car door. He gestured rudely, got into the car, reversed out of the drive, and sped off amidst the thump and whine of violent gear changes.

"He said he was going to rip my ears off," said Sparks. "Would he really do that?"

"Herman must like you," said Ihaka. "He usually goes straight for the nuts. So what did you do to upset him?"

Sparks noticed he was trembling slightly. He put his hands in his pockets. "I'm not sure. I guess it must be something to do with Trevor Lydiate."

"Who?"

"I'm doing this story for *New Nation* magazine . . ."

"I know about your story," said Ihaka. "I've been talking to Mrs Appleyard."

"You know about the dance card?"

Ihaka nodded.

"Lydiate's one of the names on it. He's a lawyer who's doing time for embezzlement. The other day I got this anonymous phone call from a guy saying to met him in Potter's Park if I wanted the oil on Lydiate. Well I went but no one turned up. The guy on the phone was your Herman whatsisname – the thing that time forgot. I recognised the voice as soon as he opened his mouth."

CHAPTER *12*

*C*aspar Quedley, the public relations wizard, lived in a smart new townhouse in Mission Bay. It had two bedrooms, a study, a living room with a fine view of Rangitoto Island, a heavily marbled bathroom with a large spa in which Quedley now and again stage-managed romps involving sufficient quantities of champagne, cocaine and partner swapping to constitute an orgy in these austere and unspontaneous times, a wine cellar, a dining room and state-of-the-art kitchen neither of which were often used, and a two-car garage which housed his Lexus and four-wheel drive. He also owned a hideaway, which he liked to think of as spartan, at one of Coromandel Peninsula's more spectacular and inaccessible beaches. Despite the various attractions of his two homes, Quedley was happiest in his office.

As he'd indicated to Reggie Sparks, Quedley was unreservedly cynical about the public relations industry. In fact, in his case public relations was just a conveniently vague term for a range of shadowy activities.

Quedley's office was the hub of a far-flung network of friends, acquaintances, contacts and informants who were constantly feeding in information, speculation, rumour and gossip. This Quedley filtered, processed and distributed in whichever direction best served the agenda he happened to be pushing at the time. His network extended across most sectors of business, through the media, and to the uppermost reaches of the major political parties. Quedley's clients paid handsomely for his information, analysis, advice, and, they mistakenly believed, loyalty. Most of those who dealt with him, whether as client or contact, underestimated the extensiveness of his network, his access to the highest offices and biggest boardrooms in the land and his capacity for manipulation: many would have scoffed at the notion that his influence matched their own; only the very well-connected, the real insiders, understood that Caspar Quedley was one of the two or three dozen most powerful people in the country.

Quedley also enjoyed the interaction of office life. Although he chose to live alone, he enjoyed having people around him, especially if they were young, bright, attractive and female, as most of his staff were. It was often whispered where PR people gathered that Quedley conducted staff recruitment interviews on the casting couch; he'd heard the stories and found them highly offensive. To Quedley, seduction was sport. In sport there was little or no satisfaction in gaining victory over a handicapped or disadvantaged opponent; likewise where was the challenge, where was the achievement, in getting a woman into bed through the use of pressure or inducements? It was one step up from paying for it.

He had, it was true, slept with a number of his employees, but always at their instigation and after exhorting them to look upon it as nothing more than a short-lived exercise in mutual physical gratification; it would not, he would warn, lead to a deeper relationship nor to advancement within the Quedley organisation. Sometimes these warnings went unheeded and the liaison's aftermath would be an embarrassing scene. When that happened, Quedley, who detested emotionalism, would vow never again. These vows were seldom observed for long; Quedley was no more capable of adhering to his own rules than to anyone else's.

However, this particular Thursday morning in late October, office affairs were far from Caspar Quedley's mind.

In his morning mail was a hand-addressed letter, postmarked Sydney and labelled "Private and Confidential". Quedley opened the envelope; it contained a single sheet of unfamiliar handwriting which read:

'Clifftops'
Ocean View Road
Palm Beach NSW 2108

Caspar,

I am at my beachhouse for what is almost certainly the last time. Although my doctor still can't bring himself to state the obvious, he no longer bothers with the customary encouraging platitudes. I can almost read my death certificate in his eyes. I can hardly do anything for myself now; even the simple act of writing is beyond me and I'm having to dictate this to my friend Dean Delamore, whose unstinting care and support has been all that has sustained me of late.

By contrast, your support has been conspicuous by its absence. I see from my diary that it is nine months to the day since I told you of my condition. When we spoke then, you promised to visit me at the first opportunity. Not only have you not come to see me but you haven't even bothered to pick up the phone and give me a single, solitary call. Surely you were well aware how much a visit from you would have meant to me and, conversely, how wounding your indifference has been. I'm deeply shocked that, after all we went through together, you could turn your back on me at this time.

No doubt a religious person – someone like poor Chaplain Swindell for example – would say that someone in my position should feel forgiveness rather than bitterness. Personally, I've always thought deathbed conversions or transformations were cowardly. So I'm going to behave bitterly but in a way which should appeal to your finely-developed sense of malice. A few weeks ago, before I became a real cot-case, I sat down and wrote a little memoir of those strange days at our dear old alma mater. It's a rather riveting read, if I say so myself. If you don't put in an appearance before I go, Dean will send it to an appropriate and interested party.

I'd better stop there and get this in the post. Time is short.

Julian

After he'd read the letter, Quedley said "Fuckfire" in a hoarse whisper. He checked the postmark; it had been posted four days earlier. Christ, he thought, I hope the little queer hasn't croaked already. He leant back in his chair and thought furiously for a couple of minutes. Then he flipped through his address book, found a number and dialled it. The phone rang three times then there was a click and a recorded message came on:

"Hello, this is Julian Gage. I can't come to the phone right now but if you leave a message after the beep, I'll get back to you as soon as I can."

The beep sounded. Quedley put the phone down. Would it be a good idea to leave a message, he wondered? What the fuck, the sooner you make contact, the better.

He rang the number again. When the beep sounded, he put every ounce of shame, regret and wheedling salesmanship he could muster into his voice and blurted, "Julian, it's Caspar. Please forgive me. I'm absolutely ashamed of myself. I've been unbelievably busy but there's no excuse for it. I'll come over as soon as I can – this weekend. In the meantime, don't . . . do anything hasty."

Quedley hung up. That's a holding action at best, he told

himself. The question is, how am I really going to deal with this? Of course, Bill Tench. If it wasn't for me, Tench and that trash he employs would be breaking rocks in Mt Eden jail rather than getting fat on some of the plummest security contracts in town.

Quedley went to his address book again, dialled the number and was put through.

"Bill, it's Caspar Quedley. I need you to do me a favour old chief, bit of a delicate one. I need someone to go to Sydney straight away, like this afternoon, and perform a little task for me. It could be quite tricky – not exactly by the book, shall we say? I'll pay top dollar."

"We talking about the sort of bloke who won't take 'no' for an answer here?"

"Exactly. That's precisely the sort of operator I'm after."

"There's one bloke who comes to mind," said Tench. "Leave it with me. I'll see if he's available and ring you back. If he's on, how do you want to play it?"

"I'd much prefer to stay at arm's length. How about if I brief you and you brief him?"

Quedley ordered coffee and waited for Tench to call back. Yes, he thought, that's the way to handle it. Get someone over there pronto to intercept Julian's poison arrow.

His private phone rang.

"All set," said Tench. "This bloke's a starter."

"Billy my boy, you've surpassed yourself. Let's meet for a sandwich in Cornwall Park in an hour's time and I'll tell you all about it."

Caspar Quedley wasn't the only prominent Auckland identity to be rattled that morning.

Unease descended on Barry Plugge, the striptease impresario, as soon as Detective Sergeant Ihaka entered his office. It was the grin, Plugge decided. When a cop wore that sort of big, friendly grin, it meant he was about to shove it up you in a major way.

Plugge's secretary brought in coffee and biscuits and set the tray down on the low table separating her employer and the policeman.

"Mallow puffs," exclaimed Ihaka. "That just about amounts to bribery."

He picked up a mallow puff between thumb and forefinger, studied it fondly, and popped it in his mouth. He thought about having another then dragged his eyes away from the tray and looked at Plugge.

"Barry, they tell me you've got Herman Pickrang on your payroll these days. He's a bit heavy-duty for you isn't he?"

"Give us a break, Sergeant," said Plugge indignantly. "You know the ructions we had around here. When it reached the stage I had a fucking contract put out on me, I decided well shit, I better get myself some protection. You can't blame me for that."

"I don't think the journalist that Pickrang's been heavying is trying to put you away Barry."

Plugge frowned. "A journalist you say? Don't know anything about that; it can't have been on my account. Don't forget, Herman's a free agent, he doesn't just work for me."

Ihaka was grinning again. "Yeah Barry but the word is, he's been pretty much your man full-time since you pooed your pants over that contract. What I can't figure out though is why you of all people should care if a journo wanted to talk to Trevor Lydiate?"

Plugge's expression froze and he made a low grunting sound. Ihaka gulped another biscuit.

"Isn't it unbelievable these lawyers ripping off their clients?" said Ihaka shaking his head. "So many of 'em, you can't keep track. Anyway, the point is, here's your boy Pickrang following this journo all round town and threatening to do Christ knows what to him – well shit, I don't mind admitting, it made no sense to me. I asked myself, 'Why should Plugge give a flying fuck if every man and his dog want to talk to Lydiate?' So I had a chat to a mate of mine in the Fraud Squad; he thought it was pretty strange, too. He said it almost made him wonder if there wasn't more to Lydiate's little number than meets the eye. Anyway, he and his boys are going to talk to the Law Society and have a good long look at the whole thing. I just thought you'd like to know."

Ihaka wolfed a final mallow puff and stood up. Plugge sat in silence, looking as if he'd swallowed something vile and was waiting for his system to reject it.

Ihaka paused with his hand on the doorknob. "Speaking of Lydiate – you remember a private investigator called Guttle who got smoked a while back? He was working for a bloke – who's also dead now, by the way – who was poking around in something where Lydiate's name came up. I guess we're going to have to have another look at that too."

Louise Appleyard had found phone numbers for Lloyd Chennell and Julian Gage in the directory section of her late husband's electronic diary. Sparks rang them from Auckland to try to set things up in advance. Chennell was wary; to secure the interview Sparks had had to feed him a long and inventive spiel, claiming he was doing a story, using Prince Albert College as a case study, about whether private schools should be responsive to social change or maintain their traditions at all costs. The call to Gage got an answering machine. He didn't leave a message.

Sparks caught the mid-afternoon Air New Zealand flight to Sydney and took a cab from the airport to his Kings Cross hotel. There was a fax from Gavin waiting for him. It read: "LC was deputy head of history at PAC from 1968 to 1974. The head of department supervised the teaching of history at scholarship and bursary level while LC did so at UE and school certificate level. His responsibilities included setting internal exam papers."

Just after seven o'clock Sparks went out for a stroll and something to eat. He walked through the Cross, running the gauntlet of pimps, whores and hustlers, towards Potts Point. He crossed the street to avoid a melee involving a trio of skeletal hookers, their skimpy outfits revealing decaying blue-tinged flesh, and a ragged wino whose eyes rolled comically in his plum-coloured face. Sparks didn't see Herman Pickrang in the rear seat of the taxi which halted for him at the pedestrian crossing, and Herman Pickrang was having too much fun observing the dementia of the street people to notice Sparks.

CHAPTER *13*

*A*dversity, it is often said, brings out the best in people. It was a moot point whether there was any "best" in Barry Plugge to be brought out but once he'd recovered from the shock of Ihaka's bombshells, the Sultan of Sleaze surprised himself with his self-possession, decisiveness, and ruthless cunning.

Admittedly the lack of histrionics once the policeman had departed was mainly due to the fact that the gravity of the situation had stunned him into a state bordering on catalepsy. After sitting virtually motionless for 25 minutes, Plugge cleared his mind of nightmarish visions of penury, imprisonment, and being sodomised by large, brutal men with tattoos and dreadlocks, and forced himself to think.

Of the two related crises, the Guttle matter required the more urgent attention. Despite Ihaka's needling, it would take the Fraud Squad some time to get around to reviewing Lydiate's scam given the apparent epidemic of white collar crime and the fact that they already had a conviction. But murder was murder. What linked him to Guttle was Pickrang – Pickrang whose unbelievable incompetence, whose chronic inability to follow instructions, whose savage impulses had got him into this mess. Pickrang's job had been to discourage interest in Lydiate and thereby ensure that the Plugge-Lydiate connection remained hidden from view. He had achieved the exact opposite. And what, Plugge asked himself, would the useless turd do when the cops got their hands on him, which wouldn't take long? Save his own hairy arse, more than likely. There was no dodging the fact that Herman Pickrang had become a liability.

Pickrang hadn't been heard from for a couple of days which, in the light of Ihaka's visit, was in itself disturbing. First thing the next morning, Plugge dispatched his new chief bouncer to establish Pickrang's whereabouts. Just before midday the bouncer reported that Pickrang was not answering his home or mobile phone and hadn't been sighted in any of his usual haunts.

"Get out to his place and have a look," Plugge told him. "Break in if you have to."

"What if he's there?"

"If he's there, you won't have to break in will you?" said Plugge in an eerily calm voice. He put the phone down thinking, the bastard knows he's fucked up so he's gone to ground; maybe that'll take the heat off. Even as he permitted himself that glimmer of hope, it occurred to Plugge that if Pickrang wanted to melt into a crowd, he'd have to hide out in a leper colony.

Half an hour later the bouncer rang again.

"Boss, I'm out at Herman's place – I kicked the door in like you said – and I reckon he's gone to Sydney."

"Sydney?" yelped Plugge. "What the fuck would he be doing there?"

"Well I wouldn't know. It's just that I found this thing from a travel agent on his kitchen table. It's got Herman's name on it and it's a sort of schedule, all typed up, saying when he's got to be at the airport, what flight he's on, where he's staying and all that. According to this, he went over to Sydney yesterday afternoon."

"When's he meant to be coming back?"

"Doesn't say. It says 'open return'."

"Okay. Get back here and bring that schedule thing with you."

Plugge hung up and stared at the wall. A plan was taking shape in his mind. The more Plugge thought about it, the more he liked it. It was simple, easily executed and would solve the Pickrang problem at a stroke. It was one thing to identify Pickrang as a threat which had to be neutralised; it was quite another to actually do the neutralising. Plugge was well aware that his other employees would sooner rub themselves down with raw offal and jump into the shark tank at Kelly Tarlton's Underwater World than tangle with Pickrang; his plan overcame that problem. He went into his private bathroom and splashed some cold water on his face. As he looked at himself in the mirror above the handbasin, he said out loud, "Herman, you're about to find out the hard way that it doesn't pay to screw around with Barry Plugge."

Rocco Perfumo was just seeing out the last of the lunch customers at the inner-city pizzeria restaurant which doubled as the headquarters of his family's New Zealand business interests when a waiter told him he was wanted on the phone. He walked to the far end of the restaurant and picked up the receiver.

"Yeah?"

"Is that Rocco Perfumo?"

The caller sounded like he had a mouthful of industrial strength glue. Perfumo wondered why he was going to such lengths to disguise his voice; all New Zealanders sounded the same to him.

"Yeah. What do you want?"

"Remember Herman Pickrang?"

Remember Herman Pickrang? Was this arsehole some kind of comedian? What does he think – that every second day some fucking gorilla who looks like Doctor No on steroids comes in here and shoves my brother head-first into the pizza oven?

Rocco's brother Martino had suffered impaired eyesight and severe facial scorching as a result of his insertion in the wood-fired oven, the virtues of which were extolled in the restaurant's advertising. He was now convalescing back in Sydney. His sight was nearly back to normal but it would require costly plastic surgery to repair his complexion. Without it, he faced the prospect of going through life looking like a sand-blasted beetroot. The brothers had demanded revenge but their uncle, the head of the family, had ruled that an escalation of the dispute might draw unwanted attention to the family's presence in New Zealand. Rocco had chafed under the veto, convinced his uncle would have put family pride ahead of profits had it been his son whose head had been baked.

"Course I remember him, the cunt," snapped Rocco. "What about him?"

"I just thought you'd like to know – he's in Sydney right now, staying at the Grosvenor serviced apartments in Potts Point."

The caller hung up. Perfumo looked at his watch. He had time to get the late afternoon flight to Sydney. He rang his mother's apartment in Sydney's inner west. His brother answered.

"Marty, it's Rocco. I'm coming over for the weekend. We got some business to take care of."

Lloyd Chennell, the headmaster of St Bartholomew's College, a private boys' school in the posh Sydney suburb of Bellevue Hill, looked at the antique clock on his antique desk. It was 4.15 on a Friday afternoon; another week over. It had been a testing week: a cache of the drug Ecstasy had been found in a stationery cupboard; persons unknown had released a cage of laboratory mice in the head of maths' new car; and a Taiwanese multi-millionaire had removed his son from the school after the lad had been left traumatised by a bullying campaign culminating in a mock lynching, dealing a severe setback to

Chennell's strategy of cultivating the Asian community to make up for the fall-off in enrolments from hard-pressed country folk.

On the positive side of the ledger, the senior tennis team had won its rubber against traditional rivals, Marsden Grammar. In his eight years as headmaster of St Bartholomew's, Chennell had learned that the Friends of St Bart's, the all-powerful grouping of old boys and parents which dominated the board of governors, would turn a blind eye to pure heroin being sold from the tuck shop as long as victory was achieved in the various sporting tussles with Marsden.

Chennell was spending the weekend in the Blue Mountains and was anxious to be on his way. First though, he had to do this bloody interview. He cursed the conceit which had caused him to agree to the thing in the first place. He had done so for one reason only: being written up in New Zealand's leading magazine as the headmaster of one of the southern hemisphere's most prestigious schools would be an unwelcome reminder for his former colleagues at Prince Albert College – those patronising oafs now washing down the bitter taste of failure with cheap sherry in the staff reading room or languishing in their dim provincial colleges and second-rate prep schools – that he'd gone on to far greater things.

He vaguely remembered this journalist fellow Sparks droning on about the theme of his article, some idiotic guff about whether private schools should respond to social change. As if I bloody care, he thought. To Chennell, a private school was a meal ticket, a way to make a living without having to endure the nameless horrors of the state system. He would spend another cloistered decade at St Bart's and then take a comfortable retirement; after that, it was all the same to him whether they outlawed private schools, burnt them to the ground or turned them into loony bins. A career of dealing with the children of privilege had left Lloyd Chennell with an outlook which verged on nihilism.

At 4.30 Reggie Sparks, wearing a respectable pair of corduroy trousers, a new sports jacket and his late father's lawn bowls club tie, was shown into Chennell's office. The gloom created by the dark wood panelling and the heavy drapes, illuminated only by the single lamp on the large desk in the corner gave Sparks a nasty moment of *deja vu*. However the figure who rose to greet him bore no resemblance to the schizoid colossus Dr Foster Hogbin.

Sparks had only the haziest recollection of Chennell; he'd put it down to his indifferent memory but the fact of the matter was that Lloyd Chennell was rather forgettable. He was of medium height, slim and moved with a loose-limbed, boneless slither. He had sandy hair, spectacles, a high, brainy forehead, a loose, wet mouth and wore a tweedy brown suit and brown brogues which gave him the appearance of a boffin masquerading as a squire. Sparks was intrigued by his ears which were bright red, almost crimson, and unusually fleshy; they looked as if the slightest perforation would unleash spouts of blood of the sort one associated with decapitation. Chennell's pallor also made Sparks wonder if this build-up of blood at the extremities was depriving other organs.

For half an hour, they addressed the ostensible subject of the interview. If Chennell had been more experienced in dealing with the press, it might have occurred to him that Sparks, having opened proceedings with the broadest of catch-all questions, made no effort to shepherd the discussion in any particular direction with more specific follow-ups. Chennell accepted the opportunity to blow his own trumpet and was doing so tunefully, to his ears anyway, when Sparks brought the recital to an abrupt halt.

"When you think about it, some pretty strange things went on at Prince Albert back in 1970. I mean, first the chaplain steered his car into a brick wall; then the girl hanged herself at the ball; now I hear there was a black market in exam papers."

Chennell stared at Sparks, his ears glowing like horseshoes fresh from the furnace.

"You have the advantage on me there," he said finally.

"You'd remember a bloke called Caspar Quedley?" Chennell nodded. "Apparently, before the exams, he was flogging the UE history paper around the place. You were in charge of setting that paper; how do you think he got hold of it?"

Chennell rose. Something was terribly wrong here. How it had come about could be established in due course; the immediate priority was to terminate the interview.

"Mr Sparks, I have no idea what you're talking about so there's little point in pursuing this discussion. I'm going away for the weekend and I've delayed my departure on your account but I'm not prepared to do so a minute longer for this sort of scurrilous nonsense."

Sparks seemed quite unflustered by the headmaster's indignation. He flipped his notebook shut and put his pen in a jacket pocket. He looked up at Chennell who was now standing next to him.

"What about Victor Appleyard – had you come across him lately?"

Chennell decided not to wait for Sparks to get to his feet. He walked to the study door and held it open. "Appleyard? I heard he died, that's all."

Sparks stopped at the door and extended his hand to Chennell. As Chennell withdrew his hand after a fleeting touch, Sparks looked at him quizzically and said, "That's odd because I know for a fact that Appleyard had an appointment with you the last time he was over here. I suppose you're going to tell me you haven't clapped eyes on Julian Gage for 20 years either?"

The reference to Gage was a stab in the dark but the effect was spectacular: Chennell recoiled as if Sparks had requested one of his choirboys for use in a satanic rite.

135

"Get out of here this minute," he hissed. "And rest assured your editor will be hearing about this."

Sparks nodded. "You bet."

Herman Pickrang walked down the avenue in Potts Point checking the street numbers, enjoying the warm afternoon sun and congratulating himself on his good fortune. This Sydney job couldn't have been better timed. Even before Ihaka's appearance, Pickrang had been well aware that he was losing ground with Plugge; Plugge would've gone apeshit if he'd found out the cops had somehow got involved. All in all, it was better for everybody if he spent a bit of time out of Auckland. Maybe he should've let Plugge know about his run-in with the cop but he could talk his way out of that if he had to – I figured the best bet was to lay low for a while, keep my head down blah, blah. Not that he particularly gave a shit about Plugge except he could do without the guy going round town badmouthing him; it wouldn't do his reputation any good. In the meantime, he was going to make sure he did the business on this job; whoever he was working for was paying bloody well and there might be more down the track – providing he didn't fuck it up.

Pickrang stopped outside a handsome three-storey terrace and checked the number against the address Tench had given him. He opened the cast-iron gate, walked up three steps to the tiny porch and rang the bell. The door was opened by a young woman whose pale face contrasted with her uniformly black colour scheme: she had black hair cut page-boy style, a black dress, black stockings, black shoes and black rings under her eyes. Pickrang leered down at her thinking, I'd give you one love if you asked me nicely.

"I'm looking for Julian Gage," he announced. "Is he in?"

The woman half-closed the door and moved nervously behind it shaking her head. "No," she said huskily. "He's gone away – overseas."

Pickrang consulted his piece of paper.

"What about Dean Delamore?"

"He's gone too."

"Who are you?"

"Miranda. I'm house-sitting for Julian. He should be back in a week or so." She started to close the door. "Maybe you could come back then . . ."

Pickrang dropped his shoulder and rammed it hard against the door. It flew open, knocking the woman backwards. She began to protest.

"Shut your gob," snarled Pickrang. He entered the house shutting the door behind him. "Gage's got something that belongs to a friend of mine and he wants it back. I'm going to find it so if you want to stay in one piece, just keep quiet and stay out of my way."

Pickrang searched the terrace literally from top to bottom, beginning on the third floor and working his way down. It was not a difficult task – the house was immaculately tidy and there were few obvious hiding places – but his search proved fruitless. By the time he reached the last room, the kitchen, he was in a foul mood which wasn't improved when he found there was no beer in the fridge. He summoned the woman. She came hesitantly, hands clasped in front of her.

"I'm looking for something like a letter, you know, a few pages with writing on them. It might be in an envelope or some sort of package or maybe a folder or notebook. Have you seen it?"

The woman shook her head.

Pickrang said "Fucking shit" then brushed past her and stalked down the corridor. He stood in the doorway and said, "I'll be back," then left, slamming the door behind him.

Miranda, whose real name was Dean Delamore, stood in front of the large mirror in the hallway and removed the wig. He ruffled his hair which had been plastered to his scalp, then took a tissue from his handbag and wiped off his lipstick. He wondered what the frightening stranger would've done if he'd

137

told the truth: that Julian Gage had been dead for two days and that the previous day, he'd dropped a letter from Gage to Victor Appleyard into the airmail slot at the Potts Point post office.

Dean Delamore was pretty sure lying had been the sensible course of action. He decided he wouldn't tax his already fragile state of mind by contemplating what the frightening stranger would do when he found out he'd been lied to.

14

*C*aspar Quedley had woken up with a hangover too often to bother berating himself for having less sense than one of Pavlov's dogs. Similarly, he had given up making pointless and self-deceiving resolutions to stay off the booze for a week, a month or a year. Even the soreness at the back of his throat and the foul taste in his mouth, the residue of one of his occasional cigarette binges, didn't cause a twinge of self-disgust. Caspar Quedley had long ago accepted himself for what he was and looked upon the various facets of his nature – the admirable and the unattractive, the healthy and the perverse – with equanimity. The simple fact was that he was going to get shit-faced from time to time; it was as inevitable as death, taxes and flatulence. Yes, he felt dreadful but experience suggested it was nothing that a 10km run, a gargantuan break-fast, and a contemplative and productive 20 minutes on the toilet couldn't fix.

Quedley checked his watch – it was 9.30 – threw back the duvet, rolled out of bed, stretched, scratched, and pulled on a white towelling robe. On his way downstairs he checked the answer phone in the study; the flickering light showed he had two messages. He pressed the playback and was assailed by the strident and slightly hectoring tones of Audrey Benn.

"Caspar, Audrey Benn. It's 9.30 on Friday night and this is just a little reminder that you have a dinner engagement here tomorrow evening. I'm absolutely counting on you so don't let me down."

"Slutfire," said Quedley. "What in the world possessed me to agree to that?" Before he could grapple with that mystery, he found himself being harangued by a frantic Lloyd Chennell.

"Caspar, it's Lloyd Chennell. I've just had this journalist from *New Nation* magazine in to see me – an insolent shit called Sparks who was at Prince Albert. He made out he was doing a story on private schools but that was just a pretence to get in the door. Caspar, he brought up the exam paper; he brought up Julian. How much does he know, for God's sake? What sort of story are they going to do? Call me as soon as you can – I'll be in the Blue Mountains."

This is starting to give me a monumental slack, thought Quedley sourly as he erased the messages. *New Nation* must be taking this bloody thing seriously if they've sent Sparks over to Sydney. And how the Christ had he got onto Chennell and Gage? First things first. Quedley retrieved his address book from his briefcase, found the number for Chennell's cottage in the Blue Mountains, and dialled. Chennell answered, sounding peevish, after a dozen rings.

"Caspar here."

"Dammit Caspar, what time is it? I was sound asleep."

"Don't whine please Lloyd. The first sound I heard this morning was that of you wetting your panties, which is an extremely fucking disagreeable way to start the weekend, especially when one has a severe headache. I'm in no mood to be grizzled at."

"All right, okay. Anyway, what about this blasted journalist?"

"Exactly what did he say?"

"He said he'd heard that in 1970 you got an advance copy of the UE history exam paper and sold it to your pals; he wanted to know how you'd got hold of it. Then he threw Julian at me."

"In what context?"

"He asked if I'd seen him."

"What'd you say?"

"I refused to discuss it. I ejected him from my study."

Oh yes, thought Quedley, I can just imagine that. I bet Sparks is still shaking.

"Caspar, did you know Sparks was doing this story?"

"Yeah I did. He came to see me a couple of days ago."

Chennell, the quaver back in his voice, began demanding to know why he hadn't been alerted but Quedley cut him off.

"Stop bleating," he snapped in a voice without a trace of its customary banter. "I didn't take him seriously; obviously that was a mistake which now has to be rectified. Is Sparks still in Sydney?"

"I've no idea. He came to see me late yesterday afternoon."

"Assuming he's still there – any idea where I can get in touch with him? I mean, did he leave you a contact number or anything?"

"He did as a matter of fact. When we arranged the interview, he told me to leave a message for him at his hotel if I needed to change the time. It was the Plaza, I think. Yes, the Plaza. I believe it's in Kings Cross."

"Okay, leave it with me. I'll take care of it. If you hear from him again, find out where he is and let me know straight away."

"Thank you Caspar. I needed some reassurance. I really couldn't bear the thought of that business seeing the light of day."

Quedley put the phone down. What an old woman Chennell was. The generalised throbbing in his skull had centralised to a pinprick of intense pain high in his frontal lobe; he was in dire need of a fresh orange juice and a strong cup of coffee. As he made his way downstairs, he thought of something which perked him up enormously. He remembered why he'd accepted Audrey Benn's dinner invitation: because the extremely fuckable – and now fancy-free – Louise Appleyard would be there.

Caspar Quedley was an expert and dispassionate analyst of the various forms of communication, spoken and unspoken, used in social conduct. He employed this expertise in various ways, one of which was to assess the attitudes of attractive women towards sex in general and sex with Caspar Quedley in particular. They were categorised under various headings ranging from "mattress crusher" to "convent fodder". In almost two decades of employing his system, he had only once been dangerously underprepared for an encounter. He'd made a point of avoiding politicians' wives ever since. He'd met Louise Appleyard a few times over the years and was sure he'd detected a spark of interest in her dark eyes. She was by no means a flirt: she'd simply held his look for that extra second or two; when he'd try to catch her eye again, she'd flick him a slightly mocking smile and look away. But back then, he told himself, her husband was always lurking around, boring someone shitless on the subject of interest rates or CBD rents or something equally fascinating. After allowing for the husband factor, Quedley had categorised Louise Appleyard as a "slow burner", one of those cool, self-contained types who like to be in control of themselves and the situation; they didn't let go often or easily but when they did, it paid to be in racing condition because one was in for a wild ride.

In the course of these musings, it occurred to Quedley that there was a second very good reason for devoting close attention to Mrs Appleyard. He hadn't really thought about it in all the excitement but the "appropriate and interested party" to whom Julian Gage was threatening to send his odious little memoir could well be the late Victor Appleyard. It makes sense, he thought: Appleyard could've seen Julian on one of his trips to Sydney and Julian's probably been too busy dying to have caught up with the fact that virtuous Victor is no longer with us.

Quedley squeezed three oranges, drank the juice, made himself a cup of coffee and returned to the study. Before I do anything else, he thought, I need to get a message to my man in Sydney on the subject of Reggie Sparks, who's becoming tiresome.

The army had eradicated any inclination in Herman Pickrang to lie abed; regardless of the day of the week or the state of his health, he liked to be up and doing by eight o'clock. So when the go-between Bill Tench tried to get hold of him to pass on Quedley's message, Pickrang was in downtown Sydney doing some shopping. He bought himself a baseball cap to protect his scalp and a diver's knife. He then followed the advice of his next-door neighbour and visited the Queen Victoria Building, Darling Harbour and the Opera House. Just before midday he picked up a hire car and drove out to Watson's Bay where, once again on his neighbour's advice, he ate fish and chips at Doyle's restaurant. When he received the bill, he made a mental note to do something moderately painful to his neighbour when he got home. After lunch, he went for a leisurely drive through the eastern suburbs. The more mansions he passed, the more resentful Pickrang became; he was so preoccupied with envy that he didn't notice the dark green Ford which had followed him since he'd picked up the hire car.

When Pickrang returned to his serviced apartment in the early afternoon, there was a message to ring Tench. He did so, reporting on his lack of progress and receiving his instructions with regard to Reggie Sparks. He had mixed feelings about this new assignment: while he was pleased that someone was prepared to pay him handsomely to have a second crack at the journalist, he was puzzled as to how it had come about. Was there any connection with Plugge and Lydiate? After a few minutes of unproductive mental effort, he reached his usual conclusion – who gives a fuck? What mattered was getting the job done.

Pickrang had planned to use the afternoon to check out Gage's place at Palm Beach but that could wait. Instead he walked over to Sparks' hotel and sat in the lobby. Watching the comings and goings, he observed that when guests left their keys at reception, they were put in cubby holes marked with their room numbers. Eventually he walked over to the desk and told the receptionist he wanted to leave a message for a guest, Mr Reggie Sparks. The young woman handed him a small notepad and a biro. Pickrang wrote "Meet me in the bar at 6pm, Bert", folded the piece of paper, and handed it to her. He watched her put the message in the cubby hole, noting the room number. There was a key in the cubby hole so Sparks had gone out. Pickrang selected a chair on the far side of the hotel lobby well away from the main entrance and sat down to await the journalist's return.

This time when the doorbell rang Dean Delamore looked through the peephole. He didn't know the man standing on the doorstep; he also looked too straight – with his sports jacket and his uncool hair, neither short enough nor long enough – to be a friend of Julian Gage's. On the other hand, he looked a lot less threatening than the gatecrasher of the previous day. Delamore opened the door as far as the security chain would allow.

"Yes?"

"Oh hi," said the stranger. "Does Julian Gage live here?"

"Julian's not here at the moment."

The stranger gnawed his lower lip. "My name's Reggie Sparks; I'm a journalist from New Zealand. I was really hoping to talk to Julian – are you expecting him back shortly?"

"No. He's gone away for quite a while."

"Bugger," said Sparks, grimacing. "Look, you're obviously a friend of his, you might be able to help. Did Julian ever mention a guy called Victor Appleyard?"

"I've heard Julian talk about him. What's your connection with Appleyard?"

"Before he died . . ."

"Appleyard's dead?" exclaimed Delamore. Sparks nodded. Delamore unhooked the security chain and opened the door.

"You'd better come in."

Sparks entered.

"We'll sit outside in the courtyard," said his host. "Down the corridor and through the kitchen."

Sparks walked through to the courtyard which was bathed in afternoon sun and sat down at the wooden table.

"I'm Dean Delamore by the way. Can I get you something – coffee or a juice?"

Sparks declined. Delamore was in his mid-20s with short dyed blond hair cut Roman style, troubled brown eyes, and a slim, wiry build. He wore an unbuttoned check shirt over a snug-fitting white singlet, black stovepipe jeans, Doc Martens and gold earrings. Sparks assumed he was gay.

Sparks told Delamore about Appleyard's interest in the events of 1970 and his meetings in Sydney with Gage and Chennell: "Whatever he found out, he went back to Auckland all fired up about it. Then he died and now I'm sort of trying to piece it together. Appleyard's wife's – widow's – helping," he added, as if it gave the enterprise legitimacy.

Delamore came and sat down opposite Sparks.

"Julian's dead. He died on Wednesday."

"Jesus Christ. How'd he die?"

Delamore lowered his eyes and fiddled with one of his earrings, then looked defiantly at Sparks. "He had AIDS."

Sparks, expressionless, held Delamore's gaze for a few seconds then looked away.

"I'm sorry."

Delamore nodded. "So am I."

He went into the kitchen and came back with an apple. As he ate it, he told Sparks about the threatening note Gage

145

had sent Caspar Quedley and how, two days previously and according to his instructions, he'd posted Gage's letter to Victor Appleyard.

Sparks whistled softly. "What did it say?"

"No idea. I just dropped it in the post."

"Had he ever talked to you about any of this stuff?"

Delamore shook his head.

"Well I guess we'll know soon enough. I'll ring Louise and let her know it's coming."

"There's another thing," said Delamore. "Quedley must've got a big shock when he got Julian's letter. He left this smarmy message on the answering machine – you know, please forgive me, I'll come over and see you as soon as I can. I think he sent someone over here to find what Julian wrote. This guy barged in here yesterday, really rude, and searched the place. You should've seen him – he was unreal, like maybe two metres tall and kind of Asian-looking. And he was bald except for this chunk of hair right here," he said pointing to the middle of his fringe.

Holy shit, it can't be, thought Sparks. "How big was his head?" he asked.

Delamore looked puzzled. "What do you mean?"

"Did he have a really small head?" asked Sparks, making a shape with his hands.

"Right, yes he did, a tiny little head, like really out of proportion with the rest of him. Do you know him?"

It must be, thought Sparks. The sort of biological quirk which results in a Herman Pickrang happens once a generation at the most. But if Pickrang works for Quedley, where does Lydiate come into it? Maybe it was Quedley all along who was trying to scare me off and the Lydiate stuff was just a smokescreen.

"I'm pretty sure I do and if it's who I think it is, just stay well out of his way. The guy's an animal."

Delamore shrugged. "Tell me about it. I'm not going to

146

hang around here. I've got to do a show tonight, then I'm spending a couple of days up at Julian's place at Palm Beach. It's my last chance; they're putting it on the market."

On the way out Sparks asked Delamore what sort of show he was in.

"A drag show," said Delamore brightening up. "It's a hoot. If you've got nothing on tonight, you should come and see it – Oscar's in Oxford Street. It'll broaden your horizons."

Sparks paused at the bottom of the steps down to the street. "What makes you think my horizons need broadening?"

Delamore looked down at him gravely. "You might be different but I find most people's do."

Herman Pickrang's failure to intercept Reggie Sparks that Saturday afternoon was due more to nature than dereliction of duty. After Pickrang had sat in the lobby for two hours monitoring every arrival, the several beers he'd had at lunch began to make their presence felt. Stoically, he remained at his post for a further 30 minutes until the pressure from his bladder became unbearable. The sight of Herman Pickrang mincing at high speed through the lobby with his thighs clamped together and his bottom protruding in the manner of a female baboon in mating season attracted the attention of most people in the area. No one eyed him more intently than Sparks, who was about to enter the hotel through the large glass doors. Instead he spun on his heel and walked quickly away.

So what do I do now, he wondered. I'm being pursued by a violent maniac who appears to have taken up residence in my hotel; my credit card is in a safety deposit box in the hotel and I have exactly $70 on me; I don't know a single person in this entire city. Except Dean Delamore.

Sparks walked back to Gage's terrace and rang the bell. There was no answer. His mind was racing. That club, what the hell was it called? Oscar's. Sparks looked at his watch: 5.15pm. He found a public phone box, inserted a handful of coins and dialled Louise Appleyard's number. It was, he reflected, the only phone number he knew off by heart. She answered on the seventh ring.

"It's Reggie Sparks."

"Reggie, sorry to do this but I was literally on my way out the door; I've got a taxi waiting."

"Not to worry. I just wanted to let you know you'll get something in the post in a day or two addressed to your husband. It might explain quite a lot. It's from Julian Gage, one of those guys Victor saw over here. Gage died a few days ago – it's a long story. I'll let you go – have a nice night. I'll tell you all about it when I get back."

Sparks replaced the handset wishing he'd never made the call. Now he was going to feel low all weekend; it sounded like she had a big evening lined up. Later Sparks would wonder about that call and whether things would have turned out much differently if Louise Appleyard had either let the telephone ring or been in less of a rush to get to her dinner party.

CHAPTER *15*

*I*n the large mirror above the fireplace, Louise Appleyard watched the two men eyeing her, or to be precise, eyeing her legs which were displayed to advantage in the black lycra bodysuit she was wearing under a boldly embroidered jacket. They'd been eyeing her on and off from the moment she'd arrived; she wondered how long it would be before their wives noticed. She also wondered when the fat man, whose name she'd forgotten and to whom she was pretending to listen, would finish eulogising her late husband and release her hand from his moist grip. Not till we're called to the table, she guessed.

The drawing room in which Audrey Benn's guests were having pre-dinner drinks was at the front of the house, close to the front door, so the words with which Caspar Quedley greeted his hostess carried clearly: "Audrey, you appalling old gargoyle, what's for dinner?"

The eyes of all the guests, even of the pair who'd been admiring what was visible of the curve of Louise Appleyard's buttocks below the hem of her jacket, swivelled to the doorway. Quedley sauntered into the room with a simpering Audrey Benn on his arm. He wore a rumpled, navy blue suit with loose-fitting jacket and baggy trousers and a black polo-neck sweater. He surveyed the gathering, inclined his head grandly, and said, "Greetings earthlings."

Audrey steered him straight over to Louise. He shot a

suspicious glance at her companion, who had at last let go of her hand, and asked: "Is this man bothering you?"

"Not at all," she said, faintly embarrassed by the lack of conviction in her voice.

Quedley looked dubious. "I'm not sure I believe you. You do realise Harvey here's a well-known snowdropper?"

"A what?"

"A snowdropper. You know, a person, usually of the male persuasion, who steals ladies' undergarments off clotheslines. Lord knows what he does with them – chews the crotches out of 'em more than likely."

Louise, struggling to keep a straight face, turned to Harvey, who'd gone crimson and started to pant. "Harvey, can this be true?"

Before he could reply, Audrey cut in to ask Quedley what he'd like to drink. Harvey used the diversion to beat a retreat.

"I thought you'd never ask," replied Quedley. "I'll have bourbon, thanks Aud, providing you serve an acceptable brand. Wild Turkey or Maker's Mark would be the shot; if I must, I'll settle for Jack Daniel's. Three fingers with plenty of ice if you'd be so kind."

Audrey raised her eyebrows at Louise. "I'll see what I can do."

As Audrey Benn departed on her mission, Quedley smiled benignly down at Louise. "Alone at last. Long time, no ogle. So how the hell are you, old girl?"

She shrugged. "Oh pretty good."

"I'm sorry as hell about Vic. He was a good lad."

"He was that."

He nodded. "Managing okay?"

"Yes, I'm fine."

"Not sitting around moping I hope. You get out much?"

"As a matter of fact, this is my social comeback."

He whistled. "Strewth, you picked a beaut. Why this show? You'd have more fun at the dentist."

"Well if I read Audrey right, she's rather relying on you to provide the sparkle."

"She's a devious critter, isn't she? She used the fact that you were coming to get me along; wild horses couldn't get me here otherwise."

Louise, wide-eyed: "And to think little old me did the trick – flattered I'm sure."

"Now Louise," said Quedley, mock-serious, "you know bloody well I've been slobbering over you from a discreet distance for years. If it wasn't for the fact that the very thought of adultery is deeply abhorrent to me, I'd . . ."

Louise, looking over his shoulder, saw Audrey Benn coming and interrupted him. "Ah here we are – here's your drink."

Audrey belligerently thrust a heavy crystal tumbler at Quedley. "All I can say Caspar is you damn well better enjoy this. I had to send my son next door for it and he wasn't impressed."

Quedley sipped and smacked his lips. "Dashed decent of him. Sorry to be a pest Aud but, as I was saying to Louise, this is no mere whim – this is a deep and enduring yearning."

They were placed next to one another at the table. As they sat down Quedley said quietly, "By the way, have you heard about the story *New Nation* are doing?"

"Yes I have," said Louise. "In fact, I've talked to the journalist a couple of times."

"That doyen of journalism, Reggie Sparks? I shudder to think what sort of dog's breakfast he'll come up with."

"Oh I don't know, I suspect Reggie's a bit more capable than he sometimes appears. He rang me tonight actually – from Sydney. He went over to see a couple of people that Vic had talked to about . . . well you know what it was about; he came to see you, didn't he? Anyway, Reggie said one of them – Julian someone . . ."

"That'd be Julian Gage," cut in Quedley. "I heard he was at death's door?"

"I'm afraid he's knocked, entered and shut the door behind him – just this week. But Reggie was saying that, before he died, Gage wrote to Vic all about that business at Prince Albert. Apparently his letter's in the mail."

Quedley shook his head. "I could probably tell you right now what it'll say." He lowered his voice. "Listen, why don't we leave the living dead to it as soon as we decently can and have a drink somewhere? I'll tell you all about little Julian. You should know the whole background before you read it – and definitely before you even consider passing it on to *New Nation*." His concerned expression lifted, replaced by a lop-sided grin. "It won't take long. Then we can talk about you and me."

At 8pm Sydney time, an hour after Audrey Benn's guests had taken their first sip of toheroa soup, Herman Pickrang left Sparks' hotel. His quarry had not appeared and the long and fruitless stake-out had left Pickrang ravenous and in a volcanically bad mood. He found a McDonalds where he ate three hamburgers, three helpings of chips and an apple pie. He then bought two six-packs of beer and returned to his serviced apartment.

At 9.30pm Pickrang came out of the apartment building with a six-pack under his arm and got into his hire car. He switched on the interior light and spread out a map of greater Sydney. When he eventually located Palm Beach, he swore foully; it looked a good distance away. However, as the hours had crawled past in the lobby of the Plaza Hotel, Pickrang had become increasingly convinced that Julian Gage and the item he'd been sent over to secure were out at Palm Beach, at the address Tench had given him. Besides, he thought, what else is there to do: sit in that shoebox watching TV or go back up the Cross and buy himself a root. Fuck that. Pickrang had decided that the prostitutes in Kings Cross were the most repulsive representatives of the oldest profession he'd ever come across. And you've blocked some shockers in your time, he said to himself, smiling grimly at the memories.

By 10.30pm Pickrang was in the northern suburb of French's Forest, pulled over on the side of the road studying the map for the third time since leaving Potts Point. Fifty metres back down the road Rocco Perfumo cursed, flicked off his headlights and swerved in behind a parked car.

"I'm telling you, the cunt's lost," repeated his brother Martino.

Rocco looked across at his brother. Martino's face was starting to flake again.

"Course he's fucking lost. Question is, where the fuck's he trying to get to?"

Martino opened the glovebox and brought out a .38 calibre revolver.

"Why don't we do the fucker here and now, just pull up beside him and blow him away?" He extended his arm and sighted down the gun barrel just as a man out walking his dog strolled past their car.

"That's why, for fuck's sake," said Rocco heatedly. "Put that fucking thing away." He cuffed his brother affectionately on the shoulder. "This is great, man – the longer he fucks around out here, the better for us. We'll just wait a bit longer, till no one's around, then do it. He's dead meat, mate – no worries."

It was between the rack of lamb with rosemary and the caramelised pear tart that Louise Appleyard decided in principle that she would go to bed with Caspar Quedley. It briefly occurred to her that perhaps she should send him a signal that she was thus disposed; if he carries on knocking back the red wine at this rate, she thought, sleeping with him might turn out to be exactly that. However as she shrank from unambiguous gestures such as casually dropping a hand on his inner thigh, she was forced to pin her faith on Quedley's constitution and to hope that he could see some benefit in stopping short of intoxication.

It had been more than a decade since Louise Appleyard had seriously contemplated having sex with anyone other than her late husband so she was understandably nervous. Apart from anything else, she was not entirely sure of Quedley's aspirations. He was not the easiest person to read: he paid attention to her in short bursts, radiating charm like heat off a bonfire; in between times he had fierce discussions on sport with the other men, once even threatening, when chided by Audrey Benn for antisocial behaviour, to lead a breakaway male group into the kitchen.

The other diners hung on his every word, solicited his opinions and sought his approval of theirs, cackled at his witticisms, and cooed like pigeons at his revelations of political and commercial intrigue. They were, by and large, a staid and conventional crew, middle-aged-going-on-old in attitude if not in fact. In their company, Quedley stood out like a black panther in a pet shop. Every now and again, he bared his teeth as if to remind them that suburban dinner parties were not his natural habitat.

Harvey's wife Eleanor, a permed and powdered supporter of worthy causes, was defending the Aotea Centre, Auckland's star-crossed performing arts centre, against well-rehearsed charges of being a white elephant when Quedley intervened.

"Personally I don't give a toss whether it makes money or not. I mean, it's there so surely to God it's only common sense to use it? Whether or not the events they stage make a profit says a lot more about the management and the Auckland public than about the building. If we're going to debate the merits of the building itself, we should be concentrating on the aesthetics of it: is it pleasing to behold? Is it beautiful? Eleanor?"

"Well yes, I happen to think it is rather . . ."

"Fine. Eleanor, I take it you subscribe to the view that

architecture is an artistic medium and therefore that a building can be a work of art?"

"Of course."

"Okay. I submit that the defining quality of art is poetry. Poetry has two meanings: in the specific sense, it's a composition usually involving rhyme and metre, the stuff we were taught at school. In the wider sense, poetry is that quality in a work of art – be it a piece of music, or drama, or a novel or a building – which engages our emotions, uplifts our spirits, puts us in touch with our higher selves. It's what separates art from entertainment. Now I've got a place down at Coromandel. It's pretty rough and ready: instead of a proper toilet, I've got an outhouse, a long-drop – your basic little wooden sentry box built over a bloody great hole in the ground. In summer, believe me, she gets ripe in there. You get these bluebottles – they're as big as hummingbirds but their radar's not as good so they keep flying into your mouth. Anyway, the point I wanted to make Eleanor, with all due respect, is that there's a thousand times more poetry in my nasty, smelly, flyblown little outside shithouse than in the Aotea Centre."

Throats were cleared around the table; there were a few nervous chuckles. Louise looked at Quedley expecting to see his usual ivory grin. He was looking at Eleanor with an almost quizzical expression, head slightly tilted and smiling pleasantly but without showing his teeth; the smile hadn't reached his eyes which gleamed coldly. It reminded Louise of the way her brother would look at her when they were children playing Monopoly, when he'd put a hotel on Park Lane and she'd landed on it.

By the time coffee and liqueurs arrived, most of the men were the worse for drink. Quedley though, who'd had as much as anyone, seemed quite unaffected. Someone proposed that everyone should tell a joke and the motion was carried by acclaim. Once again Louise was reminded of her childhood; the jokes were the sort of dismal, sanitised little yarns her parents and their friends used to tell when they'd had a sherry or two and shed some of their excessive decorum. The men hooted and the ladies made indulgent, boys-will-be-boys faces at one another when Harvey told the story of an engineer who came up with a new method for getting rid of the stench from the local abattoir: he suggested running pipes from the killing chain into a gigantic tank so that the odours would dissipate in water. The mayor derided his theory saying, "Come off it mate; haven't you ever farted in the bath?"

When it was Quedley's turn, Audrey Benn instructed him, "Now Caspar, no filth thank you very much."

Quedley shrugged. "I'll have to pass then. I don't know any clean jokes."

The other men, none of whom had had the nerve to tell a proper dirty joke, set up a chorus at this, demanding that Quedley should have his turn.

Quedley held up his hands in a gesture of surrender. "If you insist but don't say I didn't warn you. It's actually a salutary little tale this: a woman gets a part-time job as a barmaid at the local pub. So on her first day, a Saturday, she kisses her husband on the cheek and heads off full of enthusiasm. Everything's going well until a couple of hard cases wander in. They swagger up to the bar and she goes over to serve them, putting on her brightest smile. 'And what would you like, sir?' she says to the first hard case. He looks her up and down and says, 'I'd like to smear raspberry jam all over your tits – and then lick it off'."

There were a few snorts of suppressed laughter. Audrey Benn peered closely at something in her coffee cup.

"Well as you can imagine, the woman's a bit thrown but the boss had warned her she'd have to put up with a certain amount of crude and uncouth behaviour. So she keeps her smile in place and turns to the second guy. 'And how about you sir: what would you like?' 'I would like'", said Quedley speaking very deliberately, "'to fill your vagina' – he didn't use that word but in deference to Audrey's sensibilities I shall – 'I would like to fill your vagina with ice cream and then eat it all out'."

Eleanor, her cheeks flushed, got to her feet. "If you'll excuse me, I'm just going to powder my nose."

"If I was you, old thing, I'd have a widdle while you're there," said Quedley. "Save having to make another trip. Where was I? Yes, so this is all too much for the poor woman. She bursts into tears, dashes out of the pub, jumps in her car, and hightails it. She's still distressed when she gets home where her husband's got his feet up watching television. He leaps up when he sees her: 'Darling, what's happened?' So she tells him about the two hard cases and how the first one wanted to smear raspberry jam all over her breasts et cetera. The husband's outraged. 'No one talks to my wife like that,' he declares. 'I'm going down there to have a piece of these bastards.' He puts on his jacket and as he's going out the door he says, 'By the way, what'd the other one say?' 'He said he wanted to fill my vagina with ice cream, slurp, slurp, yum, yum.' The husband stops in his tracks, turns around, takes off his jacket, goes back to his chair, sits down and turns on the TV. 'What are you doing?' asks his wife. 'I thought you were going to sort those horrible men out.' The husband looks at her and says, 'Anyone who can eat that much ice cream is too big for me'."

Louise Appleyard had felt the tension build in the room as Quedley told his joke. She knew that, whatever the outcome, she wouldn't be able to stop herself laughing. The gross and unexpected punchline came as a release; she threw her head back and roared with laughter. Some of the men joined in while the other women exchanged dazed shakes of the head. When the laughter died down, Audrey refilled Louise's coffee cup and said: "You two obviously have something in common."

"Grubby minds," said Eleanor, pinch-faced, from the doorway.

Louise, still laughing, looked at Quedley thinking, well that's not a bad start.

CHAPTER *16*

*T*he ambiance at Oscar's Night Club turned out to be less confrontational than Sparks had anticipated. Earlier in the evening, over several espressos in a Darlinghurst coffee bar and when not brooding about Louise Appleyard, he'd given some idle thought to what he might encounter there. His speculations were largely populated by the stereotypes of gay subculture: musclemen with shaven heads, self-mutilators with metallic items embedded in every appendage, deviants using colour coding to advertise their readiness to indulge in various unthinkable sexual practises. However, at first sight the clientele resembled a gathering of ardent young Christians although Sparks couldn't remember whether the Mormon missionaries who'd doorknocked around Auckland during his childhood had been permitted to cultivate hair on their upper lips. Most of the moustaches sported by Oscar's patrons were under-stated if not apologetic affairs even when accompanied by Vandyke beards; there were no cow-puncher handlebars or walrusy tea-strainers. Nor were there peaked caps, chains, or leather trousers customised to expose the buttocks. Oscar's, it seemed, was not the favoured haunt of the flamboyant and exhibitionist among Sydney's gay community but more of a rendezvous for those who only fully emerged from the closet at weekends and even then preferred not to make a fuss about it.

The club itself was long and narrow, on three levels. At

one end was a raised stage, at the other a long bar with stools and an open kitchen. In front of the stage was a small dance floor with most of the remaining floor space given over to tables and chairs and more seating along the walls. Sparks watched the show – a series of impersonations of Hollywood's *grandes dames* – from the bar. He thought he spotted Delamore as Carmen Miranda but it was hard to tell under the fruit. In between the acts a disc jockey played dance music. Sparks, mooching at the bar, received only one invitation to dance. Taken by surprise, he declined the invitation more emphatically than was called for. The rejected party, a well-built young man, shrugged his impressive shoulders and muttered something to his two companions which caused them to shoot oblique accusatory glances in Sparks' direction.

Shortly before 11pm the MC announced the last live act of the evening. The Rexettes performed in the style of the all-girl groups of the 1960s, their repertoire including *He's a Rebel* and *Big Girls Don't Cry* which was particularly well-received. Delamore, in a black wig and abbreviated body-hugging white dress, wiggled becomingly and emitted a piercing falsetto. After six energetic numbers, the Rexettes waved and blew kisses to the audience and tripped girlishly off the stage to the accompaniment of whoops, whistles and wild applause.

Sparks decided he needed another beer before he was ready to venture backstage. He was sipping it morosely when Dean Delamore, still in full Rexette costume, tapped him on the shoulder.

"I thought it was you – it's hard to tell with the lights," he said. "I didn't expect to see you here. So – what'd you think?"

"It's good," said Sparks nodding. "Especially the Rexettes."

"Yeah, everyone likes them. I tell you, it's hard work doing that Frankie Valli falsetto though; I start running out of breath towards the end." He patted his cheeks. "Are my cheeks red? I feel like I've got a real glow on."

Sparks shook his head. "No, they're fine. Would you like a drink?"

"Yes please, a Coke."

Sparks turned round to attract the barman's attention asking himself, what are you doing? That's a bloke, remember? You're carrying on as if he's Sharon Stone. He ordered the drink then turned back to Delamore.

"To be honest, I didn't really come to see the show," said Sparks. "I'm in a bit of strife. You know the gorilla who turned up at your place? I didn't tell you this but I had a run-in with him in Auckland a few days ago – he was all set to give me a hiding to make me drop the story. Anyway, right now he's camped out in the lobby of my hotel. My credit card and cash are in the safety deposit box and I don't know another soul in Sydney. I was wondering if I could crash at your place tonight?"

"Well sure, except remember I said I'm going out to Palm Beach tonight?"

"How far's that?"

"About an hour or so."

"Well, if it's not a hassle. I can get a bus back tomorrow."

"It's no problem at all. I'll just get my stuff and we'll get going. It'll be nice to have someone to talk to on the way."

Delamore was back in a couple of minutes, wearing a faded denim jacket over the white dress.

"I can't be bothered getting changed. You right? My car's just outside."

Sparks finished his beer as Delamore started for the exit. As he passed the group at the other end of the bar, Sparks noticed him exchanging words with his would-be dancing partner. Outside the club he caught up with Delamore and asked what the conversation had been about.

Delamore looked at him curiously. "Nothing."

"No come on, what'd that guy say? I'm only interested because he asked me to dance before."

160

Delamore put the key in the car door and looked at Sparks over the roof of the car.

"If you really want to know, what he said was, 'Do you get off going with straights?' "

They got into the car.

"What'd you say?"

Delamore started the car and steered it out into the traffic. Without looking at Sparks he said, "I said it depends on the straight."

In the end it had all been resolved with a minimum of fuss: as the dinner party began to break up, Louise Appleyard had murmured that she'd better order a taxi; Caspar Quedley had offered her a lift home; she'd replied, expressionless, "Whose?"

When they got to Quedley's place, they decided, without actually discussing the matter, to postpone both the drink and the discussion about Julian Gage and his letter. Instead, after some imperfectly coordinated kissing and urgent thrustings against one another and without shedding any more clothing than was absolutely necessary, they fornicated on the long leather couch in the living room which looked out to Rangitoto Island. The spontaneity suited Louise Appleyard who'd been looking forward, albeit nervously, to the sex but slightly dreading the preliminaries. Afterwards, as they sprawled on the couch breathing heavily, she reflected that, all in all, the exercise had gone better than could have been expected apart from a slight hiccup when the image of her late husband had flashed into her mind.

Quedley, noticing her pensive expression, reached over to brush the hair off her face.

"Post coitum omne animal triste est," he said.

"What?"

"It's Latin. Roughly translated it means that all creatures feel a bit down in the dumps after a legover."

"A legover?" she said. "How romantic."

He kissed her on the nose and stood up. "My dear, there was nothing romantic about what just took place. Not to put too fine a point on it, we coupled like beasts. Now if you'd care to hop into the spa, I'll fetch the champagne."

Quedley also fetched some cocaine which he deployed in rows on a silver tray. Louise thought about declining but decided it was a little early in her new career as a born-again party girl to start applying the brakes. After trying a couple of lines she concluded that cocaine was over-rated. Caspar Quedley, on the other hand, wasn't.

When the champagne and the cocaine were finished and their skins began to wrinkle, they got out of the spa and into Quedley's large bed where they made love again, this time in a more excursive manner, deriving as much enjoyment from the journey as the arrival. Insufficient clothing had been discarded during their first engagement to permit a thorough review of the other's physique; in the course of the leisurely repeat, neither suffered the disappointment which often attends the sexual experiences of the no-longer young: the discovery that artful outfitting and tailoring have concealed slackening muscles, subsiding flesh and coarsened skin.

They talked about Julian Gage on the way out to Palm Beach. According to Delamore, he'd owned a couple of wildly expensive light fitting shops which had done very well during the mid-1980s when money was no object for those who overnight conjured fortunes from their computer screens. Then, as the end of the decade approached, he'd been diagnosed HIV positive.

"He used to say he was lucky," said Delamore. "As soon as he knew, he sold his shops for a good price. Six months later the party was well and truly over – after the economy had gone south, there weren't many people still willing or able to shell out 10 grand for a lamp. He reckoned if he'd sold a year later,

162

he would've been lucky to cover his loans. He sold the terrace in Potts Point too and rented it back so he had enough money to make the most of the time he had left. He bought his place at Palm Beach and did a lot of travelling. I was lucky too – I came on the scene just at the right time and he took me with him. It was wonderful – we always flew first class and stayed in the best hotels. You name it, we went there – Paris, Venice, New York, New Orleans, Rio. We went on the Orient Express and the QE2 and cruising in the Caribbean; we even went on safari in Africa although a person less keen on roughing it than Julian would be hard to find." Delamore stared ahead dreamily. "It was like a fairy story. I said that once and he said, 'Yes and we're the fairies'." Delamore smiled for a few seconds, then the smile faded and he continued in a voice which resonated with loss and bewilderment: "About a year ago, the symptoms started to appear. In a few months he went from being a normal, healthy person – as far as the outside world knew – to an invalid. A few more months and he looked like something out of a concentration camp, a skeleton with skin. At the end he was just a shell. It was like he'd been eaten by termites – you thought one tap and he'd crumble into dust and blow away."

They drove across the Spit Bridge in silence and headed out through Manly to the northern beaches.

Sparks eventually broke the silence: "So he never said a word about what happened at school?"

"Nothing specific. But seeing Appleyard definitely unsettled him. He said afterwards that he had a big decision to make because he had something on his conscience which he wanted to resolve before he died. I asked him what the decision was and he said it wasn't just him who'd be affected."

"He didn't say who else?"

"No."

"But that letter to Quedley sort of speaks for itself, doesn't it?"

"I guess so."

163

"Did he ever talk about Quedley?"

"Oh God yes, all the time. Once he even called him 'the love of my life'."

Sparks stared at Delamore for a moment then he noticed how far the hem of his dress had ridden up his slim thighs and hurriedly looked away. "You telling me Quedley's gay?"

Delamore looked at him coldly. "You make it sound like being a necrophiliac or something."

Sparks waved a hand apologetically. "No, no, I didn't mean that. It's just that the guy's got a reputation for being a big-time womaniser."

Delamore shrugged. "I never said he was gay; what I said was Julian adored him."

"What, you think it was all one way – what's that word . . . ?"

"Unrequited."

"Yeah, unrequited. You think it was like that?"

Delamore's mouth twisted. "It's hard to say. I suppose that was my basic impression but Julian could be coy and drop these little hints . . . I'd say it was probably one-sided, kind of a hopeless infatuation rather than a relationship, certainly as adults. But who knows what happened at that school? It was a boarding school after all. Didn't you say you went there too?"

"I was a day boy."

After that Delamore put on a tape and they listened to Edith Piaf for the rest of the way.

As forecast, a cold front had rolled through Sydney early that evening bringing steady rain and driving the temperature down. Even allowing for the hour, Palm Beach seemed abandoned; few lights showed as they drove along the sea front. Clifftops was perched right on the edge of the hill overlooking the far end of the beach. It was down a drive at the end of a no-exit road; the nearest house was about 50 metres away.

Delamore stopped in front of the white-washed wooden house and slumped back in his seat.

"I've just thought of something," he said. "We're assuming that Quedley sent that guy – what's his name, Pickrang? – over here, right?"

"It looks that way, doesn't it?"

"Julian was a bit of a show-off; he couldn't help himself. When he bought this place, he had some personalised stationery done with the address on it, you know? That letter he sent to Quedley, the one he dictated to me, was on that letterhead. What I'm saying is, Pickrang could know about this place."

"Yeah, that's a point but I wouldn't worry about it tonight," said Sparks after a few moments. "For a start, we know where Pickrang is – he's parked in the lobby of my hotel waiting for me. And even if he got sick of that, he's hardly going to drive all the way out here at this time of night and in this weather, is he?"

CHAPTER *17*

*D*espite having set out for Palm Beach more than two hours before Delamore and Sparks, Herman Pickrang got there five minutes after they did. Peering through the half-moons of visibility created by his windscreen wipers, Pickrang was frequently tempted to abandon his circuitous expedition to try again in daylight and, hopefully, more favourable weather the following day. Each time he'd remind himself that both the hour and the foul weather were ideal for his purpose. When he finally found his way to Palm Beach, he then faced the problem of locating 5 Ocean View Road. He briefly toyed with the idea of knocking on the door of one of the few houses from which lights glowed behind curtains before deciding that it would be unwise to ask directions to an address at which one intended to commit one and possibly several crimes. There was nothing else for it but to start at one end of the small community and work methodically across it, checking the street signs. Fortunately for Pickrang, he chose to start at the right end.

To ensure that Pickrang didn't notice he was being followed, Rocco Perfumo had taken to switching off his headlights for minutes at a time. There was hardly any other traffic on the roads so it was easy enough to follow Pickrang by his tail lights.

Pickrang found Ocean View Road at exactly one o'clock that Sunday morning. He drove slowly to its dead end and pulled over to the side of the road. When Perfumo saw Pickrang's lights go off, he cut the engine and drifted to a halt at the top of the street. Pickrang got out of the car. He could see lights through the trees and made his way carefully down the drive towards them. A car was parked outside the compact wooden bungalow. Staying in the shadows, Pickrang approached the house and went silently up the stairs to the veranda. The rain was easing and he could hear music over the dwindling hiss. He flattened himself against the side of the house, inched up to a window and peered in.

Pickrang was not greatly prone to self-pity. Even so, his recent string of reversals had left him in a put-upon and resentful frame of mind; he'd been feeling that it was about time he got a break. One peep through the window convinced him that, at long last, his luck had changed. In the foreground was the woman from Gage's house. She was wearing a sexy little white dress and wriggling around the room in time to the music with a glass in her hand. Over in the corner, slumped in an armchair and watching the woman with an odd sort of half-smile on his face, was the journalist Reggie Sparks. Pickrang leaned against the wall and breathed deeply. His nostrils flared. He grinned horribly, the rapacious, age-old grin of the predator in the night. He took three long strides along the veranda, threw open the door, and stepped inside.

"Howdy," he said.

Pickrang closed the door behind him and looked from Delamore to Sparks. Both of them stared at him in dumbstruck horror. He unzipped his light windcheater, reached inside and, with a slow flourish, produced the diver's knife with the thick eight-inch blade. He dropped into a half-crouch holding the knife extended in his right hand and crabbed towards Sparks, who sprang to his feet and looked wildly around for something with which to defend himself. When he'd closed to about a metre, Pickrang switched the knife to his left hand and feinted a thrust to Sparks' belly. Sparks bleated like a dying sheep and dropped his hands, his eyes bulging in agonised anticipation of the knife's cold plunge. With a snap of his hips, Pickrang came out of his crouch and slung a whiplash right hook to the side of Sparks' jaw. Sparks jitterbugged backwards, his legs splaying like a new-born foal, and spilled over the armchair he'd recently occupied onto the floor where he lay face down and utterly motionless.

Pickrang slowly straightened up and turned to Delamore who was clutching the wine glass in front of him in both hands.

"Wouldn't mind a drink myself," he said. "What've you got there?"

"White wine," said Delamore in a near-whisper.

"Cat's piss," said Pickrang. "Where's Gage?"

"He's dead. You're too late – that thing you're looking for is gone too. I posted it myself."

Pickrang's brow furrowed. "Posted it – where to?"

"Auckland. I didn't notice who it was addressed to; I just stuck it in the mail like Julian told me."

"You didn't notice who it was addressed to eh? Course you didn't." Pickrang grinned playfully. "We can talk about that later – after I've shagged the arse off you." He put the knife down on the arm of the sofa, unzipped his jacket and laid it on top.

Delamore wished to God he hadn't spent so much time cultivating a girlie voice. He tried to speak in a timbre redolent of pendulous testicles and jutting Adam's apples but all that emerged was a reedy squeak.

"Look there's something you should know . . ."

Pickrang chuckled, shaking his head. "Let me guess, it's that time of the month? I think you've got me mixed up with someone who gives a fuck."

Delamore pulled off the black wig revealing his short, slicked-down blond hair. "I'm not a woman."

Pickrang's amiable expression disappeared. He regarded Delamore through slitted eyes. "What the fuck is this?"

"I told you, I'm not a woman. I'm in a drag show – this is one of my costumes."

"What are you talking about?" snarled Pickrang. "You got tits."

"That's part of the costume too. Look." Delamore reached behind him, undid a couple of buttons on his dress and slipped it off his shoulders. He shrugged out of the padded brassiere and dangled it in one hand; with the other he pulled down the front of his dress to expose a flat, lightly tanned chest dotted with a few clumps of downy golden hair.

"You're a fucking transvestite," said Pickrang hoarsely.

Delamore shook his head. "No I'm not, I'm a performer, a singer. I only wear women's clothes in the show."

"Bullfuck. You had 'em on the other day."

"It was a new outfit," said Delamore wearily. "I was just trying it on."

"Don't shit me." A foxy glint came into Pickrang's eyes. "I got a blowjob from a trannie once – up in Singapore. I bet you've blown the old meat trombone plenty of times."

"I'm not touching you, you animal," said Delamore, eyes blazing.

"Oh we're choosy are we? Don't tell me you haven't gobbled matey here," he said with a jerk of his head towards the recumbent Sparks. Pickrang advanced on Delamore and was unzipping his fly when the door opened and the Perfumo Brothers walked in. Rocco shut the door and leaned against it with his arms folded; Martino pointed the revolver at Pickrang's chest.

Rocco, his lip curling with disgust, took in the scene. "Well wouldn't you know it?" he said. "Big, bad Herman turned out to be a screaming fag."

There was a long silence. Pickrang stood with his hands on his hips looking from brother to brother. Finally he said, "Who the fuck are you?"

"So you don't remember us, huh?" said Rocco as Sparks

169

groaned and sat up. "Take a geek at him. That's what happens to your face when it gets shoved in a pizza oven."

Pickrang nodded his understanding. He'd taken it for granted that this pair intended to kill him; now he knew why. There was one other thing he needed to know.

"How'd you know I was here?"

Rocco smiled maliciously. "I'm glad you asked that. You're on someone's shit list, mate. A little bird told us you were coming to Sydney, where you'd be staying, the works. We've had you in our sights since you got here, just waiting for the right moment. Now here we are – I mean, this is perfect."

Pickrang's curiosity was satisfied. He'd work out who'd tipped them off in due course. First things first. These guys are a couple of fucking clowns, he thought. One gun between the two of them; following me around waiting for the right time to do it. Jesus, talk about amateurs. You want to shoot someone, you walk up, no warning, no big speeches, no nothing; you point the fucking gun at them and pull the trigger. End of story.

Rocco Perfumo was talking to Delamore and Sparks, asking them if they were in some sort of three-way homo thing with Pickrang. Delamore was embarking on a laboured explanation when Rocco interrupted.

"Forget it, I don't want to know. It's got nothing to do with what we're here for so why don't you just fuck off back to New Zealand? Sounds like you got no reason to care what happens to this cunt and if you want to stay in one piece, you'll forget you ever saw us."

Delamore picked up his overnight bag and helped Sparks to his feet. "Of course," he said. "Thank you. Thank you very much. We're out of here right now."

Neither spoke till they were out of Palm Beach and back on the main road.

"You all right?" asked Delamore.

"Yeah," said Sparks thickly. He flexed his jaw. "Nothing broken anyway."

Delamore began shaking violently, causing the car to wobble. "Oh God," he said, "I was absolutely terrified. Pickrang thought I was a she and wanted to have his wicked way with me. They turned up just in time, those two."

Sparks stared at Delamore for a few moments then leaned back with his head on the headrest. "Jesus, no wonder you're still shaking."

"What do you think they'll do to him?"

"I don't know and I don't care – the worse the better far as I'm concerned. I just wonder if they know what they're up against." Sparks rubbed his stomach gently. "Jesus, I really thought it was all over when Pickrang went for me with that knife. I could almost feel it going in."

"I wonder what happened to the knife," said Delamore. "He didn't have it when they came in." He smiled wanly. "Maybe he thought it spoiled the romantic atmosphere."

Pickrang was propped against the back of the sofa, quite relaxed. "So what now?" he asked.

"What happens now," said Rocco, "is that we shoot you and you die. Then we'll go back into town, go to a nightclub, and have a bottle of champagne to celebrate. How does that sound?"

Pickrang looked thoughtful. "I don't know about the champagne; that shit gives me a hangover."

Rocco looked at Pickrang incredulously.

"Shall I shoot him now, Rock?" said Martino.

"Hang on, why don't we just see if there's an oven in this place?" said Rocco.

Martino nodded, giggling happily. His brother's path to the kitchen brought him within two metres of Pickrang. As Rocco walked past, Pickrang, in one swift, fluid motion, pushed off the sofa, effortlessly dragged him in with his left arm and wrapped him to his chest. He clamped Rocco to him with one arm, reached under his windcheater which was draped over the arm of the sofa and brought out the diver's knife which he held across Rocco's throat.

"Drop the gun," he said to Martino, who held the .38 at arm's length, unsure of where to point it, "or I'll cut his head off."

"Shoot him Marty," screamed Rocco. Pickrang clamped his left hand over Rocco's jaw to silence him and jabbed the index finger into his right eye for emphasis. He threaded his right arm under Rocco's armpit. With the knifepoint pricking Rocco under the chin, Pickrang hoisted him a few inches off the ground, effectively denying Martino a clear target.

"Put it on the sofa now," snapped Pickrang.

Martino lowered his arm. "I have to Rock," he wailed. "I have to."

He put the pistol on the arm of the sofa.

"Now back off. Stand over by the doorway."

Martino did so. Pickrang lowered Rocco to the floor. He retracted his right arm and positioned the knife point just below Rocco's right ear. He grinned and raised his eyebrows at Martino then, with a grunt of effort, forced the knife inwards and upwards. Two-thirds of the blade disappeared. Martino screamed and darted towards the sofa but Pickrang flung Rocco aside and swooped on the pistol. Martino turned and lunged for the door but Pickrang caught him by the back of the shirt, jerked him up short, then rammed him face first into the wall. He whirled Martino around and flung him onto his back on the sofa.

Pickrang placed his left knee on Martino's chest and loomed over him.

"If I wasn't in a hurry," he said conversationally, "I'd stick your head in the oven till it melts."

He picked up a cushion with his left hand and placed it over Martino's face. Perfumo flailed his legs unavailingly, like a beetle flipped on its back. Pickrang thumbed back the hammer and pressed the muzzle against the cushion. He fired three times, moving the muzzle slightly each time. The first shot missed altogether; the second clipped the point of Perfumo's cheekbone and ploughed a furrow up the side of his head, removing part of his left ear; the third entered his face just below his nose, precisely where previously the left and right halves of his mustache had met. After the pizza oven incident, Martino had found it difficult to cultivate hair on his upper lip; eventually he'd decided that a moustache which sprouted unevenly in the style of a moulting chicken's neck was worse than no moustache at all. Thus he died clean shaven, breaking a family tradition, by no means confined to the menfolk, that went back many generations.

CHAPTER 18

*C*aspar Quedley lay on his back, snoring faintly. At intervals of approximately 90 seconds his mouth fell open and a fresh globule of saliva emerged to join the thin trail of dribble running down his chin, under his ear, and into the little pond of drool which had formed on his pillow. There was a whitish wedge of coagulated spittle in the other corner of his mouth and the inner corners of his eyes, on either side of the bridge of his nose, were likewise gummed with nocturnal emissions. All in all a big night for discharges, thought Louise Appleyard.

Having completed her slightly disillusioning inspection, Louise got out of bed. She paused to look at herself in the mirror above the chest of drawers. Satisfied that she could withstand early morning scrutiny at least as well as her bedmate, she put on Quedley's towelling robe, and went downstairs. She was sitting at the kitchen table drinking her second cup of tea when Quedley appeared half an hour later. He wore jeans and an old sweatshirt; his hair was damp and his collection of encrustations had been rinsed away.

He halted in the doorway and studied Louise warily.

"Hello," she said.

Quedley's expression grew even more dubious. Finally he asked, "Do I know you?"

Louise sipped her tea. "I think I come under the heading of a barge that passed in the night," she said. "Give it a little

174

while, it'll probably all come back to you – the tedious dinner party, too much to drink, latching onto a bit of stray. Perhaps you should keep a visitor's book by the front door and get your pick-ups to sign in as they enter. Might help you to keep track."

Quedley nodded gravely. "Not a bad idea."

He switched on the coffee machine and took a packet of coffee out of the freezer then sat down opposite Louise.

"So how'd you be?"

Louise smiled back. She hadn't been sure what to expect from Quedley in terms of his morning-after manner although a marriage proposal would have surprised her. Above all she'd dreaded a review of the events of the night before or even, God forbid, an appraisal of her performance.

Quedley insisted on cooking breakfast. Louise estimated it had been at least five years since she'd eaten bacon and eggs; she'd forgotten what a satisfying meal it could be.

As she cleared away the plates, Louise said: "I seem to remember you were going to tell me about this communication from beyond the grave? Or was that just part of the seduction process?"

Quedley raised his eyebrows. "Excuse me? I seduced you?" He sat back in his chair and assumed the air of a raconteur. "Yes, I was going to tell you about poor Julian. You've heard the line about the practising homosexual who believed that practise makes perfect? That could be Julian's epitaph. You know they're always arguing about whether someone is born gay or goes that way because his mother made him play with dolls or because he was groped in the pup tent by a scoutmaster? If ever anyone was born bent, it was Julian Gage. By the time I got to know him – he would've been 15 I guess – he knew he was gay; what's more, he was pretty open about it which took a bit of nerve in those days."

"I'm trying to picture him," said Louise. "What did he look like?"

"Oh he was a handsome youth, all right – good looking,

olive skin, big brown eyes – and promiscuous. It turned out to be a fatal combination – he ended up getting AIDS."

"Oh no. The poor, poor man." After a pause, she said: "Some might find the accusation of promiscuity a bit rich coming from you, in view of your reputation." Quedley started to protest but she continued: "So Caspar, is all this leading up to a confession; did you fall victim to his charms?"

"I didn't as a matter of fact but not for lack of effort on Julian's part. Despite that – or maybe because of it – we ended up being quite good friends. I saw a lot of him after we left school and even after he moved over to Sydney, we kept in pretty close touch. Then, a few years ago, he was diagnosed HIV positive. I did what I could: went over and saw him, lent him – gave him – some money so he could do a bit of travelling and whatnot. But it wasn't enough. He became more and more demanding; he'd want me to drop everything at a moment's notice to spend time with him or shell out a small fortune so he could get the miracle cure at some clinic in Bermuda or Turkey or somewhere. Eventually I drew the line, I said 'Sorry Julian, that's it pal, no more'. Well fuck, overnight" – Quedley snapped his fingers – "I became the Anti-Christ. He accused me of abandoning him and started making these threats – he was going to expose me, destroy my reputation, God knows what. I didn't take too much notice, I just thought the poor bastard's going a little crazy. Jesus, I could understand that; who wouldn't? And he might've had a point – maybe I should've done more for him; I'm not one of nature's good Samaritans, I'd have to admit. But you know, I don't have unlimited funds plus I had a business to run. The way my business works, if I'm not there, the revenue dries up pretty quickly. My staff can handle the day-to-day stuff but the key relationships are between me and the top people in the client companies. And what they're paying for is seven days a week, 24 hours a day access to me.

"So anyway, just before he died, Julian sent me this letter

176

saying he'd make me pay for turning my back on him by exposing all the terrible things I'd done at school – cheating, blackmail, driving people round the bend, you name it." Quedley shook his head wearily. "He said he'd written it all out and was going to send it to an interested party – enter, stage right, your late husband."

"Yes, Vic saw him in Sydney."

"Oh well, there you go – perfect timing."

"Are you really worried about it? I mean, who would believe it?"

Quedley shrugged gloomily. "I guess it depends what he's said but people love scuttlebutt don't they? The thing is, reputation counts for a hell of a lot in the PR game but there are a few people out there who'd just love to see me on the back foot and would be only too happy to spread the dirt around. What really scares the shit out of me is the thought of *New Nation* getting hold of it – that bloody Jackson Pike would have a field day."

Louise walked round the table and stood behind Quedley, brushing the hair off his forehead. "Don't worry your little head about it, sugar. Whatever he's said about you, no one's going to see it. It'll go straight into the fire."

That Sunday morning Reggie Sparks and Dean Delamore caught the 10.25am Air New Zealand flight to Auckland. Delamore had announced during the drive in from Palm Beach that he'd also be going to Auckland; he said he'd been planning a trip for a while and now seemed like a good time to get out of Sydney. That suited Sparks. Delamore, he felt, could contribute a lot to his story.

They boarded the aircraft at 9.50am. At 9.55am Herman Pickrang entered a departure lounge elsewhere in the terminal where passengers on the 10.40am Qantas flight to Auckland were waiting to board. At 10am, when the business class passengers on his flight were called, Pickrang went over to a bank of pay phones. He inserted a few coins and dialled the number for the Ristorante Vesuvio in Leichhardt which he'd got off a card in the late Martino Perfumo's wallet. Pickrang had simply been helping himself to the dead man's cash but the card, which identified Martino Perfumo as the manager of the Ristorante Vesuvio, had given him an idea.

A woman answered the phone.

"Martino Perfumo's the manager of your joint, right?"

"Yes he is. He's not here at the moment though. He should be in around 11."

"No he fucking won't because he's dead; dead as a dodo. So's his brother."

"There must be some mistake . . ."

"How about I talk, you listen? You got a pen? You'll want to write this down. The pair of them are in the boot of a green Ford parked in the garage of number 14 Clifftops Road out at Palm Beach. Right? The garage door's down but it ain't locked. Now this bit's really fucking important. They're dead because this Kiwi guy Barry Plugge put a contract out on them – that's P,L,U,G,G,E. He's over in Auckland. You pass this on to the right person, he'll know who Plugge is. You got all that?"

"I think so."

"What's the guy's name?"

"Plugge. Barry Plugge."

"Good on you."

Pickrang replaced the handset and strolled back to the lounge. Most of the other passengers had boarded which suited him down to the ground because he was not fond of queuing.

Steven Perfumo, the lawyer, sneaked another furtive glance at his watch. It showed the time as just after 1pm. Perfumo was fretful because he had planned to have lunch with his third best friend's wife with whom he very much wanted to go to bed. Her husband was due back from Ho Chi Minh City, where he'd been setting up a pet food business, early the following morning. After that, such an illicit liaison became an undertaking requiring more boldness than Perfumo possessed.

The lunch was to be the final move in a delicate and patiently conducted campaign and Perfumo had been confident of success. It was, he felt, unbelievably if characteristically inconsiderate of his clownish cousins to get themselves murdered on this particular day; it was always on the cards that they'd end up full of holes and stuffed in the boot of a car but why the fuck did it have to be today? Not that he dared give voice to these thoughts in the presence of his father, the head of the Perfumo family, who sat on the other side of the desk, his face twisted with grief and remorse.

"This is my fault," said his father for the fourth or fifth time. "I should've acted when Martino's face was burned. I should've allowed Rocco to take revenge."

He would've only fucked it up, thought Steven, staring at the ceiling. He decided to make one last effort to bring the discussion to some sort of conclusion. "Dad, we went through all this at the time," he said, leaning forward, elbows on the desk. "You know why we didn't respond and you know it was the right decision. The strategy was to set Plugge and the Asians at each others' throats and to stand on the sidelines looking good by comparison while they fought it out. We talked about how it was different over there and that we simply couldn't afford headlines about the Italians coming in; it was a sound business decision. The real question is, how do we deal with this?"

His father ran his fingers through his silver-streaked hair then shrugged and gestured in the Latin manner to indicate that he was unconvinced by his son's argument. Not for the first time it occurred to Steven Perfumo that perhaps his father watched too many gangster movies.

"Explain it to me," said the old man. "How did this terrible thing happen?"

Steven breathed deeply. Maybe they were finally getting

somewhere. "As I was trying to say, it looks like a payback that went wrong. I've just been on the phone to Gino over in Auckland; Rocco told him he was coming here for some unfinished business. Gino made a couple of calls and it turns out that Pickrang – the guy who shoved Marty's head in the oven – was in Sydney this weekend, right? So it's pretty obvious what the unfinished business was. Secondly, Pickrang was working for Plugge – he's the established operator in the Auckland market – but Gino's heard they've had a bust-up. My guess is that Plugge wanted Pickrang taken out so he tipped off Rocco that Pickrang was coming to Sydney, hoping we'd do his dirty work for him. You know Rocco – he always took things so personally. He would've decided to do Pickrang himself and Marty would've just gone along with it." He shrugged. "They must've bitten off more than they could chew. Obviously it was Pickrang who called the restaurant this morning; he's trying to work the same number as Plugge."

His father digested the summary solemnly. "So they're both responsible?"

"Well yes. If Plugge hadn't tipped off Rocco in the first place, I guess none of it would've happened."

"And this man Pickrang – do we have any idea where he is now?"

"It looks like he's gone back to Auckland. We've got someone out at the airport checking it now."

The head of the family rose. He put his palms on the desk and looked down on his son. "I want this taken care of by the time the boys are buried, Stefano," he said in a voice trembling with emotion. "I want you to supervise it personally."

Fucking wonderful, thought Steven. Your honour, could we adjourn for a few days? I've just got to jack up a couple of hits.

"I still recommend that we stay at arm's length," he said. "I just don't think it would be a good idea if our people are involved."

"You have someone in mind?"

"Remember that Maori gang we distribute through over there, the Blood Drinkers? Why don't we get them to do it?"

"Are they capable?"

"Well they're the scariest-looking people I've ever set eyes on which isn't a bad start," said Steven with some feeling. He'd personally negotiated the distribution deal with the Blood Drinkers' collective leadership, four scarcely human men-mountains who smelt like a third-world zoo in a heatwave. He shuddered at the memory. "They're animals. They'd scalp their grandmothers for a crate of beer and a Big Mac. The thing is, it would muddy the waters – the police'll see it as a turf battle."

"I'm leaving it to you, Stefano. Do it anyway you want but see to it – make sure it happens. I won't be able to look my sister in the eye until this is settled."

Steven nodded and started to leave.

"By the way," said his father, "what will the police do about Rocco and Martino?"

Steven shrugged. "They'll be a pain in the backside for a week or two. It gives them a good excuse to hassle us but in the end it'll be the same old story – just another wog vendetta."

Caspar Quedley dropped Louise Appleyard off at her house at 9.30pm that Sunday night. He declined her offer of coffee and a nightcap, pleading an early start the next morning. He suspected that she had more than coffee and cognac in mind and that, after the exertions of the afternoon and early evening, he would struggle to rise to the occasion if called upon to do so yet again. The widow, he thought, has taken to it like a stallion just out of quarantine.

By 10.15pm Quedley was in bed. After two late nights in a row and a physically demanding day, he was looking forward to nine hours' uninterrupted sleep. However when the luminous dial on his bedside alarm clock was showing 4.21am, Quedley sat bolt upright.

181

"I must be out of my fucking mind," he said out loud. "I actually believed the bitch when she said she'd throw it straight in the fire."

CHAPTER *19*

*C*aspar Quedley was at his desk by 7.45 the next morning, quite chipper despite his fitful night's sleep. As he set up the coffee machine he sang "Oooh-ooh Brown Sugar, how come ya dance so good? Oooh-ooh Brown Sugar, just like a black girl should", concluding his recital with a violent pelvic thrust. Quedley was cheerful because he saw light at the end of the tunnel. He'd tossed and turned for over an hour during the night, castigating himself for his childlike faith in Louise Appleyard. Eventually he succeeded in stirring his mind into a buzz of erratic activity which made slumber impossible. Finally however, there came a flash of inspiration among the random and unconnected images which cannoned around inside his head like dodgem cars. He'd got out of bed, gone into his study and written three words on a piece of adhesive notepaper which he'd stuck to his briefcase. Five minutes after getting back into bed, he was sound asleep.

The three words he'd written were "Dr Carl Plews". Dr Plews was an American, a graduate of Yale and the London School of Economics, who was often described in the media as a "world expert" in the new-fangled discipline of managing cultural change within large organisations. Quedley tended to doubt this; he reckoned that an American who really was a world expert would be back in the US of A where he could make a hell of a lot more money from transforming the completely fucking obvious into some sort of profound insight by dressing it up in a lot of new-age management-speak bullshit than he could in little old NZ. That wasn't to say that the doctor hadn't done pretty well for himself in New Zealand. He'd certainly earned some juicy consulting fees from advising government departments during their transitions into state-owned enterprises. There were three reasons for Quedley's conviction that Dr Plews would solve his problem: the first was the fact that Dr Plews' most recent client was New Zealand Post; the second related to the doctor's passion for gardening which was always mentioned in the profiles, usually just after the bit about how he was renowned for his volatile temper. That was the third.

Early one sultry evening the previous summer, Dr Plews, satisfied that his bow tie was symmetrical, had picked up the jacket of his tuxedo and called out to his wife Estelle that if they didn't get going within five minutes, they'd miss the start of the show. She'd hollered from her ensuite bathroom that she'd almost finished doing her make-up. Dr Plews smiled, a trifle smugly, and shrugged into his jacket. There was no need to leave for at least a quarter of an hour but his little pretence would ensure that Estelle was ready on time. Dr Plews liked things to go according to plan – his plan.

It occurred to Dr Plews that he had time to potter in the garden. He went downstairs and out through the drawing room French doors which opened onto the upper lawn. It was a beautiful evening; the light was starting to fade and assorted floral scents floated by on the soft sea breeze. Dr Plews closed his eyes and breathed in deeply. Halfway through his exhalation, he froze: a low, snuffling sound was coming from across the lawn. Although a squat bush obscured the source of the snuffles, Dr Plews knew instantly what they signified – there was a god-damn dog in his garden. He bounded across the lawn, swerved around the bush, and was confronted with a scene which caused the worm-like vein in his forehead to judder like a high pressure hose: the bed of delphiniums, which he'd

184

nursed through the squalls of spring and early summer from seed to glorious blossom, was in ruins, the blooms uprooted, scattered and trampled. The devastation couldn't have been more complete had a wild pig wallowed in the flowerbed. The culprit was in fact a young bulldog, scarcely more than a puppy, which stood there panting lightly and regarding Plews placidly through oyster eyes.

"Here boy," said Plews speaking in a strangulated croak.

The bulldog obligingly padded towards him. When it was within arm's length, Plews released a howl of rage, dropped to his knees, seized the dog by its collar, spun it onto its back, and began to throttle it. The dog took two long minutes to die. When it was over, Plews' lips were flecked with foam and his well-pressed trousers were smeared with dirt from the clods which the dog's excavations had left on the grass. Plews stood up; his chest heaved and he was sweating furiously. He mopped his face with a handkerchief and reviewed the situation: he knew the dog – it answered to the name "Rumpole" and belonged to his next-door neighbour, Mr Justice Smout, a High Court judge of flinty disposition. Only a few days before, Plews and the judge had discussed Rumpole over the picturesque if somewhat ramshackle lattice fence which separated their properties, after Estelle had placed her expensively shod right foot on one of the wee fellow's steaming fresh turds. The judge had been apologetic and promised to keep Rumpole on a tighter leash but his fondness for the ugly little brute was obvious. As Plews gulped in air in the gathering twilight, it occurred to him that convincing Justice Smout that his mutt had got its just desserts would be a tough assignment.

Plews reached a decision: he didn't want a vengeful and possibly litigious judge as his next-door neighbour, nor did he relish the prospect of becoming a hate figure for pet lovers and animal rights activists. He got a spade from the garden shed, carried the dead dog to the very bottom of the garden where the compost heap was located, and buried it. Having witnessed Rumpole's fate from an upstairs window, 17-year-old Kirsty Bolton decided that it didn't matter how well the Plews paid, there was no fucking way she was ever going to babysit for them again.

When Quedley heard the story of Rumpole's demise, he laughed so hard he fell off his chair which was not quite the reaction his informant, Kirsty Bolton's mother, had expected. He made no conscious effort to commit the incident to memory. He didn't have to: Quedley never forgot anything which cast someone else in a deplorable light.

At 8.15am Quedley rang Plews and effortlessly talked the doctor's secretary into putting him through.

"Dr Plews? Caspar Quedley here. We met in the PM's office last year."

"I remember it well Caspar. How're you doing?"

"Well I've got a little problem, I was hoping you might be able to help me out with it."

"Shoot."

"It's to do with the postal service . . ."

"Let me tell you Caspar, I know that outfit like the back of my hand. If a postie breaks wind, I get to hear of it. Tell me what the problem is and I'll put you onto the guy or gal who can set it to rights."

"Okay. Right now there's a piece of mail in the system which was posted in Sydney last week to a Mr Victor Appleyard in Takapuna. I want to get my hands on it."

"Excuse me?"

"I don't want that letter to be delivered; I want it intercepted and passed to me."

"This is a joke, right?" said Dr Plews in a tone which suggested he was going to get very cross if it wasn't.

"Carl, if I make a joke, you won't need to ask."

"Well buddy, you've come to the wrong guy," said Dr

Plews frostily. "I wouldn't even contemplate doing that for a friend and you sure don't qualify as one of them. Now if you don't mind, I got things to do."

"What, like strangle a dog?"

"What did you say?"

"Strangle a dog. That's what you did to Judge Smout's little pal, wasn't it – throttled the bugger with your bare mitts? All dressed up in your penguin suit too – Christ, it must've been a sight."

"I don't know what you're talking about and I'm terminating this conversation right . . ."

Quedley cut in, brisk and businesslike: "Carl, here's the deal: either you do this thing for me or I get on the phone to old Smout and tell him how you choked the living shit out of his precious puppy and planted him under your compost heap. It's your call – buddy."

Thirty seconds passed. Finally Dr Plews said: "Who'd you say the letter was addressed to?"

One hour before Caspar Quedley and Dr Carl Plews discussed tampering with Her Majesty's mail, a taxi pulled up outside a central city hotel. The taxi driver, a middle-aged Samoan, insisted on carrying his passenger's heavy suitcase into the hotel lobby; had he known that what appeared to be an attractive young blond woman was in fact a man, he would've left it to the bellboy.

Dean Delamore had left the Sparks residence in St Heliers without forewarning or explanation and while Reggie Sparks and his mother were still asleep. He registered under the name Lesley Gore and took the lift to the 14th floor, affecting not to notice the admiring appraisal of the 18-year-old bellboy. Once the bellboy had departed a dollar richer, Delamore undressed, removed the blond wig, and carefully hung his outfit, a smart lime-green suit, in the wardrobe. He then got into bed and slept for three hours to make up for the sleep he'd missed out

187

on due to the time difference between Australia and New Zealand and by getting up so early.

At 11am Dean Delamore clicked through the hotel lobby in high-heeled shoes which nicely complemented the green suit. He left his room key at reception and got into a taxi which he directed to the office building in Parnell housing Quedley Communications. He checked the directory in the foyer then took the lift to the fourth floor.

Delamore got out of the lift and looked around hesitantly. The receptionist behind the large desk smiled at him brightly.

"Can I help you madam?"

"I think I'm on the wrong floor," said Delamore. "This isn't Deco Design?"

"Next floor up. This is Quedley Communications."

"Oh I've heard of you. You do public relations, right?"

"We sure do."

"We could be in the market for some PR. Do you have a company brochure or anything like that?"

"Yes we do. Let me get one for you."

The receptionist went away and returned a minute later with a glossy brochure which Delamore put into his large black leather handbag. He thanked the receptionist, pressed the lift button, and got into the lift. The receptionist watched the lift panel lights and shook her head. What an airhead, she thought; I just told her Deco Design was the next floor up and what does she do? Goes down.

The letter-sized envelope postmarked Sydney, dated the previous Thursday and addressed to Mr Victor Appleyard, was delivered to Quedley's office shortly before five o'clock that afternoon. Quedley weighed it in his hand. That's odd, he thought; there can't be more than a single page in here. He tore open the envelope; it contained a note, in the same hand-writing as his recent letter from Julian Gage, which said:

Although this letter was sent to Victor Appleyard, I suspect that it's being read by Caspar Quedley.

If not, Victor, some explanation is required: not long ago, I wrote to Caspar to tell him that I'd written what I described as a little memoir of our school days. I was feeling particularly sorry for myself at the time and warned Caspar that unless he made contact with me before it was too late, the document would be sent to an interested party – your good self. In fact it was always my intention to tell the real story of what happened at Prince Albert in 1970; I have enough on my conscience without taking the truth to my grave as well. Thinking about it afterwards, I realised it was a mistake to forewarn Caspar; he is not the sort to sit back and do nothing. He would've set out to throw a spanner in the works and, given his talent for that sort of thing, he'd probably succeed.

I've therefore arranged for the material to be hand-delivered to you. If I've over-estimated Caspar's ingenuity, there's no harm done. If I haven't – well Caspar, for once you've been out-smarted.

Of course, whichever of you is reading this, the fact that it's being read at all means that I'm dead and gone. But not quite forgotten, eh Caspar?

Julian Gage

Quedley read the letter three times then laid it aside. He sighed and rubbed his eyes; he inspected his fingernails; he picked his nose absent-mindedly; finally he sat back in his chair and clasped his hands behind his head. After several minutes' reflection, Quedley reached the conclusion that something extremely shitty was about to happen. As usual, he was right.

Quedley was pouring his second bourbon when he got the message that there was a Mr Dean Delamore on line one.

He picked up the handset, pushed the button and said: "You've got it, haven't you?"

"Got what Caspar?"

"You know fucking well what I'm talking about," snarled Quedley. "The Julian Gage story – 'I was a Teenage Cocksucker'."

"Hmm, that's got a ring to it," said Delamore. "No wonder you're in PR. So Julian was right – you did get hold of the letter? How'd you manage it?"

"What the fuck does it matter? Why don't you get to the point? This whole thing's become balls-achingly tedious."

Delamore clicked his tongue and put on a posh accent. "Oh dear, one does dread being thought a bore. Okay; the point, Caspar, is that yes, I have got it and I'm taking offers for it."

"You're offering to sell it to me? I don't think that's quite what your sugar daddy had in mind."

"Appleyard's dead. As far as I'm concerned, that frees me from my obligation. Besides, you're a fine one to talk about respecting Julian's wishes – if you'd shown an ounce of common decency, we wouldn't be having this conversation."

Quedley grunted derisively. "I could've shown more compassion than Mother Teresa at a train crash and we'd still be having this conversation. Sorry to disappoint you, but I'm not interested. You see, I don't really think that what you're selling is worth buying. Why should I care? In the first place, it'd be my word against what – the lurid ramblings of a bitter and probably deranged man on his deathbed? Secondly, what are you going to do with it if I won't play ball? Give it to the newspapers? Give me a break – no newspaper here would print a word of it."

"That's not the impression I got from Reggie Sparks," said Delamore imperturbably. "And if you're so blasé about it, why did you send that animal Pickrang over to Sydney? Anyway, who said anything about the newspapers? Somehow I don't think your clients would be totally comfortable with some of the things you got up to as a lad. I've got one of your brochures in front of me as a matter of fact; goll-y, that's an impressive client list. Now, do you want to talk or should I go find myself a photocopier?"

"Is Sparks in on this?"

"Don't be silly."

"Oh well, no harm in talking I guess. Where are you staying?"

"Come now Caspar," said Delamore reprovingly. "That's unworthy of you – Julian made you out to be so clever. I went for a little wander today and Albert Park seemed a nice spot, especially at lunchtime with all those pretty young students around. Let's say tomorrow at 12.30."

"How will I know you?"

Delamore chuckled. "Don't you worry about that. I've got your brochure remember? God, what an ego trip – there must be at least a dozen photos of you in it. Not that you don't take a nice picture . . ."

Quedley told Delamore to get fucked and put the phone down with a clatter.

CHAPTER 20

*A*t 11am the following day, Tuesday, Dean Delamore walked through the lobby of his hotel and out onto the street. He was unshaven and wore jeans, sneakers, and a voluminous sweatshirt over a polo shirt; he didn't wear earrings or a blond wig or make-up. No-one gave him a second glance. He didn't leave his room key at the reception desk. As far as the hotel staff were concerned, the guest in room 1414 was a young blond woman and Delamore was anxious not to disturb that impression.

He had a cappuccino in a High Street cafe, bought a newspaper and a tuna, tomato and alfalfa sandwich, then strolled up through Albert Park towards the university. It was a mild spring day; clusters of dirty-grey cloud were blowing in from the west every half-hour with metronomic regularity and the smell of rain rose from the pavement when the sun broke through.

At 12.15pm Delamore sat down on a park bench opposite the university clock-tower and began to read his newspaper. There were plenty of people around, mainly students plus a few office types who'd come up from town to escape their colleagues, eat lunch, and enviously eye the students who canoodled and smoked cigarettes with an abandon suggesting they were unaware of the risks attached to both activities. At 12.25 Caspar Quedley walked up Princes Street and turned into the park. He stopped and looked around expectantly then shoved his hands in the pockets of his raincoat and pretended to take an interest in the large clock-face flowerbed. Delamore studied him from behind his sunglasses for a minute or two; having decided that the photos in the brochure didn't do Quedley justice, he turned his attention to the tuna sandwich.

At 12.45 Herman Pickrang got out of the red Mitsubishi which was illegally parked in a bikes-only zone on the other side of Princes Street and crossed the road. He walked towards Quedley, his gaze tracking slowly right to left through 180 degrees and back again. As he passed Quedley, he shook his head. Quedley shrugged. Delamore dabbed his mouth with a tissue, threw the tissue, sandwich wrapper and newspaper into a rubbish bin, got up and set off across the park. There were better ways to spend the afternoon than looking at microfiche in the city library but, he reminded himself, he was in Auckland on business, not on holiday.

Delamore got back to his hotel at 4pm. He thought about ringing Quedley but decided to soak in the bath first. Let him stew a bit longer, he thought. Delamore was enjoying the game of cat and mouse, all the more so because he was sure Quedley would hate being cast in the role of rodent. That was emphatically borne out when, shortly after five, Delamore finally made the call.

"What the fuck are you playing at?" the public relations man screeched down the phone. "I stuck around in Albert Park like a shag on a rock for half an hour . . ."

Delamore cut in: "Caspar, I've got to say you've been a big disappointment. All I used to hear from Julian – until he went off you – was Caspar this, Caspar that, Caspar's so smart, what an operator you were, Mr Cool. I mean, am I missing something here? I keep expecting class and style but, to be frank, all I see is clumsiness. I was in the park today, on time, ready to do a deal. If you'd just played it straight, you'd have Julian's stuff right now."

"What d'you mean, you were there? Where were you?"

"Well you'll just have to take my word for it. I saw you – you were in an ivory-coloured trenchcoat over a navy-blue suit. For what it's worth, I thought the coat was a shade . . . well, theatrical. I'm not sure that Humphrey Bogart look is really you."

Quedley's tone of shrill exasperation grew more pronounced: "If you were there, why the bloody hell didn't you show yourself?"

"Why the bloody hell do you think? I guessed you'd try something and I guessed right, didn't I? As I was saying, it was very clumsy Caspar. Jesus, you can spot that pet gorilla of yours a mile away."

"Okay," said Quedley sounding flat and tired. "You win. You're way ahead of me. Name a time and place and I'll be there – just me, no tricks, no frigging around."

"Uh-uh, not so fast, sugar," said Delamore in what he thought of as his southern belle voice. "I offered you first bite at the apple and you didn't take it. Now you've got to go to the back of the queue."

Delamore hung up in the middle of Quedley's protests and collapsed laughing on the bed, drumming his heels. When he stopped laughing, he went to his suitcase and retrieved the page he'd torn out of Reggie Sparks' notebook. On it was a list of names and phone numbers, one of which he dialled. The phone was answered on the second ring.

"Dermot Looms speaking."

"Hello, my name's Dean Delamore. I was a friend of Julian Gage's – a very close friend."

"Julian Gage – there's one out of the blue. I'd pretty well forgotten that name."

"You surprise me – I mean, considering what you've got in common."

"I think you've got the wrong end of the stick, my friend. You could cover all the stuff Gage and me have got in common without having to draw breath."

"Well Dermot – may I call you Dermot? – I'd have to disagree. Julian, you'll be sad to hear, passed away last week. Not long before he died, he sat down and wrote an account of his schooldays at Prince Albert College. When I read it, it struck me what a strong link there was between the two of you, a bond almost. I suppose you could say I've inherited that fragment of autobiography but it occurred to me that it might have some emotional value for you. It also occurred to me that you might be able to put a figure on that emotional value."

There was a very long silence which didn't surprise Delamore and which he made no effort to break. Eventually Looms said that yes, he supposed he might be able to do that.

"Good," said Delamore. "I felt sure you'd be interested. Well I guess the next step is for us to get together and toss a few numbers around."

Never again, thought Steven Perfumo. I don't give a fuck what happens or what the old man says, I'm never doing anything like that again – full stop.

He was sitting in the business-class cabin of an Air New Zealand Boeing 767. The aircraft was only an hour out of Auckland but Perfumo was already drunk. He took another noisy gulp of his Scotch and leaned back, closing his eyes. The scenes ran through his mind like frames from a favourite movie. He was living in a little country town or maybe somewhere up the coast – somewhere where the weather was good and everyone knew everyone else and you could go out at night and leave your place unlocked. He'd be in a little one-man legal practice, working nine to five then going home to the wife and kids, have a couple of beers, throw a few steaks on the barbecue in the backyard, maybe even wear a hat and an apron with one of those dumb sayings on it – 'Don't blame the cook, he's doing his best', some shit like that. Life would be simple and safe: no "family matters" to attend to, no looking over his shoulder, no hassles from the cops. Most important of all, there would be no 25-stone Maori sociopaths with yellow-rimmed, blood-streaked piggy eyes and obscene tattoos on their stupendous arms and dreadlocks down to their arses and filthy clothes stained with what looked like every type of fluid and waste matter the human body is capable of producing.

Perfumo had known from the outset that negotiating the terminations of Herman Pickrang and Barry Plugge with the Blood Drinkers would be a nerve-wracking and unpleasant experience. It had turned out to be far worse. As Gino, the acting head of the family's New Zealand operations, had explained on the way back to the airport, the Blood Drinkers Perfumo had met on his last visit were the gang's businessmen; the guys they'd just talked to were the shock troops.

What had been truly frightening about that hour in the Otara hovel was the knowledge that he was completely at the mercy of people to whom, quite clearly, the concept of mercy was as irrelevant as last month's balance of payments figures. Sure, Perfumo knew some cruel and vicious people; he was related to a few although their number had decreased by two at the weekend. But most of the bad things those people did, they did for a reason. They could be vicious when they had to be for business reasons. When they didn't have to be, they could and did behave more or less like human beings. But the Blood Drinkers – who could imagine what atavistic instincts they followed? Who knew what savage pagan gods they worshipped? How had he felt, an 11-stone Italian-Australian lawyer in a Giorgio Armani suit and little tassles on his beautifully polished loafers, being glowered at by a quartet of those cavemen? He'd felt like a bobby calf in the slaughterhouse pens, sniffing death in the wind; Holy Mother of God, he'd felt like dinner!

Christ alone knew what insane impulse had prompted it but he'd actually asked them where they'd got their name from. The leader, a pot-bellied colossus with a mangled ear and Maori markings on his chin, had chuckled, a sound like an underground bomb test.

"Our ancestor Te Kooti was a great warrior. He and his men killed some pakeha in a church one time and drank their blood, eh." He shifted on the burst and tattered couch, releasing a pocket of fetid air which made Perfumo's stomach lurch. "We don't do it, eh." He looked slyly at his companions. "Maybe if we ran out of piss." As the four Blood Drinkers bellowed with laughter and shunted one another like Sumo wrestlers, Perfumo made a snap decision to increase his opening offer by $10,000. He wasn't up to haggling.

Perfumo shuddered and signalled to the stewardess for a refill. At least his father would be happy; Pickrang and Plugge were dead men, utterly doomed. They had less chance of saving their skins than a cat in a Chinese takeaway.

Caspar Quedley had two couches in his office, one of them a massive affair which he'd installed following a painful experience involving a supple and adventurous secretary, some whipped cream, a bunch of grapes, and the corner of his desk. But that Tuesday evening he was simply grateful that the couch was long enough for him to stretch out full-length, collar unbuttoned and tie askew, as he sought to regain his composure and find a way out of the quicksand into which he was sinking.

How could they possibly have missed Delamore in the park? That moron Pickrang – he'd actually seen the little shit in the flesh; it defied belief that Pickrang wouldn't have recognised Delamore if he'd been there. He was there all right; he'd just been one step ahead of them. A disguise maybe?

Quedley groaned as it dawned on him how he'd been played for a fool. Pickrang had been adamant that Delamore was a transvestite; it seemed thoroughly unlikely but when his receptionist had said that yes, someone had been in to collect a brochure that day, a blond woman in a lime-green suit . . . well it all appeared to fit. Pickrang hadn't spotted him in Albert Park because he hadn't been in drag.

Back to square one. How do you track down someone when you don't know where they hang their hat or what they look like? You start with what you do know which amounts to two fifths of fuck all: he's a 20-something gay Australian man with a flair for cross-dressing. That's it.

Quedley had an idea; it was long shot but it was all he had. He went to his desk and rang a number he knew by heart. It was the number of his favourite restaurant, a brasserie in Ponsonby, whose owner was an identity on the local gay scene.

"Do me a favour Jerry – I'm trying to track down a character called Dean Delamore. He's gay, an Aussie, mid-to-late 20s, slim build, just come over from Sydney. He claims to be some kind of drag artist although I doubt he's wandering around the place in costume. He's probably staying in a hotel or motel; at a guess one of the better ones in the city – I'd say he's got a taste for the high life. Can you check around the traps and let me know if you hear anything?"

CHAPTER *21*

*I*t was a new-look Louise Appleyard who opened the door to Reggie Sparks. She was barefoot and wore large gold hoop earrings and a long, clinging floral dress with buttons all the way down the front; it looked like she'd started buttoning up at the waist and got sidetracked before she'd got too far in either direction. Her hair was tousled and unruly, the fringe cascaded down her face prompting frequent horsy head movements which Sparks found distracting. The lights were back on in her eyes and shining so brightly it was hard to believe they'd ever been dimmed. His phone call from Sydney had left Sparks apprehensive, sensing that unwelcome developments were in the wind; as he followed her inside, that vague uneasy feeling returned.

They were sitting at the kitchen bench.

"New look?"

She grinned happily. "Not really. I just felt it was time to loosen up a bit. What do you think?"

"I like it. It's sort of the gypsy look without hairy armpits."

Louise snorted with laughter. "Bloody hell Reggie, I'm not sure about that. Is that meant to be a compliment?"

The conversation moved along easily until Sparks brought up Julian Gage's posthumous dispatch. Then he discovered that Louise Appleyard had changed her mind along with her appearance.

199

"Hasn't arrived," she said, dropping her eyes.

"What? That's crazy. Delamore – Gage's boyfriend – posted it a week ago. You should've got it yesterday or the day before."

"Oh well, I guess it'll turn up," said Louise disinterestedly. Sparks tried to catch her eye but she examined the contents of her coffee mug. Neither spoke for a while. Finally she said slowly: "Look Reggie, I've been having second thoughts about this."

Sparks cupped his chin in his hand and stared at her unblinkingly.

"Oh yeah? What brought them on?"

Louise shrugged diffidently. "Oh I don't know. It's just that the more I think about it, the less likely it seems that one person's version of events that happened 20 years ago is going to prove a hell of a lot. Apart from anything else, who's to say he's telling the truth?"

"Who's to say he's not? The bloke was dying – why the hell should he lie?"

Another shrug. "Well, we don't know what his motivation was, do we? Maybe he was playing Vic along, pretending to know something about the girl's death. Maybe he had a grudge against someone and wanted to, you know, blacken their name."

Louise glanced up, caught Sparks' frown, raised her eyebrows defiantly as if to say "well, it's possible". She looked down again and continued: "Anyway, what I'm leading up to is that I can't guarantee that you'll get to see the letter. You're just going to have to trust my judgement, okay?"

Sparks sighed and turned his head, running his fingers through his hair. He found himself looking at a small blackboard on the wall next to the fridge. In the middle of the blackboard, surrounded by *aides-mémoire* – "pay phone bill", "new leotard" – boxed off, underlined and written in capital letters was the name "CASPAR" and a pair of phone numbers. One of the numbers had "home" in brackets after it.

Sparks spent 30 seconds considering the implications of this discovery and deciding they were all extremely negative. He picked up a packet of cigarettes that was lying on the bench.

"May I?"

"Help yourself."

He lit the cigarette and inhaled. It made him feel even more nauseous. What the hell, he thought. Let's get it over with. He cleared his throat and said, "Are you going out with Caspar Quedley?" He wanted it to come out casually, oh-by-the-way, but, to his ears, it sounded blunt and inquisitorial.

"What makes you think that?" she said, surprised.

Sparks took another drag on the cigarette and spoke through the smoke. "Just the thing on the blackboard there. Only thing missing is a heart with an arrow through it."

She smiled wanly. "Very droll. As a matter of fact, yes; we've been out a couple of times."

"And?"

"And what?" she said, her voice rising. "You want to put that in *New Nation* too?"

"I just meant how did it go," said Sparks stiffly. "None of my business obviously." He got up. "Thanks for the coffee – and the cigarette."

Louise Appleyard followed Sparks to the door thinking that she could have handled it worse – like she and Quedley could've been entwined on the front lawn when Sparks arrived. Sparks half-turned at the door, gave her an expressionless nod, and walked to his mother's car which was parked at the top of the drive, next to the letterbox. As he reached the car, a post-woman cycled up and slipped a bundle of letters in the box. Sparks looked around; Louise had gone back inside and closed the door. He retrieved the mail from the letterbox and shuffled through the envelopes; there was nothing from Sydney.

He walked back up the path to the house and knocked on the door. When Louise opened it, he handed her the mail.

"Is it there?" she asked. "Don't tell me you didn't look?"

"No it's not. If it's not a gross impertinence, can I ask you a personal question?"

Louise checked to see if there was a trace of irony behind Sparks' formality but found no evidence of it.

"Feel free."

"Did you tell Quedley that Gage's letter was coming here?"

She nodded.

"Could I use your phone?"

Sparks rang Jackson Pike and asked him if he thought Quedley had the clout to intercept other people's mail. Pike said he was buggered if he knew but he'd ask someone who would and call straight back. Sparks gave him Louise's number.

"Aren't we getting a tad paranoid?" she asked when he hung up.

"We'll see."

After that, they waited for Pike to call back in strained silence.

Pike called Garth Grimes and put the question. Grimes laughed. It wasn't his usual throaty wheeze; it was a full-blown cackle and it went on for a full minute. Then he said: "Jackson, you really shouldn't do that to an old man. I'm hanging up now; I have to go and lie down."

I guess that's a yes thought Pike and rang Sparks. Sparks listened to Pike, thanked him and hung up.

"Well?" said Louise.

Sparks gave her a long look which bordered on the unfriendly. "A guy who knows a lot more about your boyfriend than we do doesn't think I'm paranoid."

When Sparks had gone, Louise Appleyard went out onto the deck overlooking Lake Pupuke to reflect on the look Reggie Sparks had given her when he'd got off the phone. It took her the time it takes to smoke a cigarette to establish that the look bothered her. Working out why took a little longer.

As Reggie Sparks sat beside the pool at the Mon Desir Hotel drinking beer and thinking bitter thoughts about Dean Delamore, Louise Appleyard and Caspar Quedley, the latter was receiving good news.

"I think I might've found your lad," said his restaurateur friend. "The barman at the Rococo says an Australian calling himself Dean has been in the past couple of nights. He fits the description – right age, slim build and so forth. The barman and he got chatting and this Dean chap mentioned he was staying at the Regis. I didn't bother to ask if it was in the context of your place or mine; I didn't think it was germane."

The Regis, thought Quedley as he hung up. About time I got a break. They owe me for all the business I've put their way over the years. He rang the Regis' banqueting manager who was pleasingly servile and only too happy to check if there was a Dean Delamore staying in the hotel. There wasn't. Any name that was vaguely similar? Strike two. Quedley racked his brains; maybe Delamore registered as a woman? Why not? He was tricky enough and he could get away with it. Look how he fooled his receptionist.

Quedley asked the banqueting manager to run a check on the young, single women staying in the hotel. The one he was looking for would've been there for the past few days; she was slim, blond and she'd been seen around in a – what was it? – yeah, a lime-green suit.

The banqueting manager called back half an hour later to say that there were only three single woman guests; the one who fitted the bill most had checked in first thing Monday morning under the name Lesley Gore.

Lesley fucking Gore? thought Quedley. Wasn't she a pop singer? Christ, years ago. Did she do *C'mon baby, do the Locomotion*? No, that was Edie Gorme. *It's my party and I'll cry if I want to*? Something like that. Lesley Gore's got to be a little in-joke. Just like a faggot – too clever by half.

"All right," said Quedley. "Now we're getting somewhere. What's Ms Gore's room number?"

Delamore and Looms had arranged to meet in the Gateway to the North Tearooms in the foothills of the Brynderwyns, north of Wellsford, at 2.30pm. Delamore set off in a hired car just before midday. The concierge at the hotel had said it was about a 90-minute drive but he wanted to take his time and see some countryside.

The tearooms were a white-painted weatherboard box with a red corrugated iron roof and a glass frontage enabling customers to watch the lorries they'd overtaken with great difficulty 50km back down the road trundle past. Alongside was a scruffy little repair garage with a couple of petrol pumps. The tearooms were strategically located, just about the exact driving time from Auckland that it took the average family going north on holiday to start bickering. Just when the kids in the back seat would begin agitating for a comfort stop and an ice cream and Dad would be feeling like a break and a cup of tea before tackling the climb over the Brynderwyns, they'd spot the sign saying "Tearooms 200m ahead." Summer was the busy time; apart from the holidaymakers, the truck drivers and travelling salesmen would linger over a second scone and instant coffee to ogle the teenage girls in their shorts and tank tops.

There were only two cars in the parking area when Delamore pulled in five minutes late – a white station wagon with a car phone aerial and a Volvo. He parked and went in. A young man with frizzy red hair, densely freckled forearms and a row of cheap ballpoints in the breast pocket of his short-sleeved white shirt was debating the merits of ordinary milk versus the low-fat variety with the woman behind the counter. An older man, heavily tanned and mostly bald, was sitting by himself with his back to the wall at a table in the far corner. He observed Delamore over the rim of his cup. Farmer Giles I presume, thought Delamore.

He bought a Coke and walked over to the table in the corner.

"Mr Looms?"

"That's me. Sit yourself down."

Delamore pulled out a chair and sat down. Looms put his elbows on the table and hunched forward. His sleeves were rolled above the elbow and ropey veins ran down his forearms and wrists, branching off into tributaries which laced the backs of his thick, powerful hands. Looms' jaw jutted aggressively and his hard grey eyes stared out stonily from beneath bushy brows. This is a tough hombre, thought Delamore; not that you didn't know that already.

"So Gage wrote a little story, did he?"

Delamore nodded. "I'd describe it as a hair-raising tale – well, for those of us with hair."

"You're a funny little fellow aren't you?" said Looms without a twitch of reaction showing on his granite features. "How come you've got it?"

"Julian and I were friends."

"Bum chums?"

Delamore shrugged. "I've been gay-bashed three times so being called names doesn't bother me too much. But you go right ahead if it makes you feel better."

"I started losing my hair when I was 19; can't recall too many people taking the piss about it."

"Well there's a surprise," murmured Delamore. "Now that we've defined our respective areas of sensitivity, can we get on with it?" He looked around. "This is very cosy but it's not really my scene."

Looms raised his eyebrows as if amazed that anyone could find fault with the surroundings.

"Okay. You got it with you?"

Delamore tilted his head to one side. "Get real."

"Where is it?"

"In Auckland. In a safe place."

"It's not worth shit, you know?"

"I disagree," said Delamore confidently. "I can think of a number of people who'd be riveted by it – Mr and Mrs Ticehurst for instance. I checked them out; they're still around, still living in Auckland. He's a partner in one of those big accountancy practices – a man of substance as they say; the sort of man who could get the authorities to sit up and take notice. I think they'd find Julian's recollections convincing. Let's face it, deathbed confessions do have a certain credibility."

Looms frowned and rubbed his chin. "Maybe. So what's your angle?"

"This is my offer and it's non-negotiable: I get $100,000 Australian; you get Julian's rave from the grave and never hear from me again. You've got till the weekend to organise the money. I'll call you then and tell you where it's to be deposited. As soon as the bank confirms the transfer, I'll hand over the document."

"A hundred grand? You're off your fucking head."

Delamore smiled. "You can get help, split the cost. You're not the only one at risk so why should you bear the whole cost?"

Looms nodded dubiously. "Even if I could raise the money, what's to stop you making photo-copies and coming back for another bite?"

"Now that you mention it, nothing really. You're just going to have to trust me. The reality is, you're paying me to keep my mouth shut and go away. Which I'll do. Take it from me, I don't want to make a career out of this."

"Why not?" said Looms sourly. "You seem to have a talent for it."

Delamore stood up. "You're too kind. I'll be in touch."

Delamore hurried to the hired car and got in. As he put the key in the ignition, he felt something cold and metallic on the back of his neck. He looked around. A plump, moon-faced man with a ponytail and bushy white sideburns and wearing serious spectacles lay across the back seat. He cradled a single-barrelled shotgun pointed at Delamore.

Basil Batrouney smiled his other-worldly smile and said: "Just drive man – I'll tell you where."

CHAPTER 22

*T*here was nothing sophisticated about the way Dermot Looms interrogated Dean Delamore. Directed by Basil Batrouney, Delamore had driven his hire car to Looms' farm and into a lock-up garage. When Looms arrived a few minutes later, Delamore was herded at gunpoint to the woolshed which was 100m or so beyond the farmhouse, down a gentle slope. The woolshed was the size of a single-storey house. There were half-a-dozen holding pens, a massive wooden bench for wool sorting and a large space where the shearing was done. Even though Looms kept a clean shed, the devoutly urban Delamore found the smell – a blend of one part blood, several parts sweat and many parts sheep droppings and urine which had been stewing gently for three generations – almost overpowering. There was a rickety old highback wooden chair against the wall. Looms moved it to the centre of the shearing area and made Delamore sit on it. He pulled Delamore's arms behind him and around the back of the chair, tied his wrists together with twine then lashed his ankles to the chair's front legs.

Preparations complete, Looms stood in front of Delamore with his large, lumpy hands on his hips. Batrouney hovered in the background, humming to himself.

"Now then Sunshine," said Looms. "Where've you got this thing of Gage's hidden away?"

During the drive from The Gateway to the North

Tearooms to Looms' farm, Delamore had reached the conclusion that his best – if not only – chance of avoiding serious injury or worse was to refuse to divulge the whereabouts of Gage's letter. That in turn, he felt reasonably sure, would require him to withstand a considerable amount of pain.

As he'd told Looms, Delamore had on three occasions been a victim of the young men who, on Friday and Saturday nights, drive in from Sydney's working-class west to its trendy inner east – Oxford Street, Paddington, Darlinghurst – with the express purpose of beating up homosexual men. Delamore had taken his beatings fatalistically, assuming that there must be a genetic link between male heterosexuality, low IQ and the urge to consume huge quantities of cheap beer and gang up on gays. The third time it happened he'd tried to reason with them, pointing out that if it wasn't for all the queers, they'd have even less chance of getting girls. Perhaps it hadn't come out quite right because they just went ahead and gave him a kicking anyway.

While these experiences had left him less fearful of physical assault than the average person, he suspected that what he'd be subjected to in Looms' woolshed would be far worse: it wouldn't be drunken youths, half-mad with some sort of mob hysteria, flailing and hacking wildly and getting in one another's way; when it came to dishing out punishment, Looms, he felt pretty sure, would be both vigorous and methodical, a formidable combination. As long as that fat freak with the ponytail doesn't join in, thought Delamore. He's a psycho if I ever saw one.

So Delamore swallowed hard, licked his dry lips and said: "I'm afraid that's got to remain my little secret."

Looms tut-tutted and stepped forward to position himself within easy reach. He planted his feet.

"Sure about that?"

Delamore braced himself and gave a slight nod.

Looms swayed back, gathered himself, then drove his

right fist into the side of Delamore's face. The chair was flung over. Delamore lay on his side with his undamaged cheek on the floor. The stench of sheep droppings wafting up through the spaces between the floorboards was several times ranker than the general atmosphere. Batrouney was shadow-boxing, hopping from one foot to another, chirping: "Pow! Biff! Whacko! Take that Mr Bad Guy!"

Looms hauled the chair upright and let fly with a roundhouse left which caught Delamore just under the eye and knocked him sprawling again. As he propped up Delamore, he cocked an eyebrow.

"Well?"

Delamore could feel swelling coming up around his right eye. His upper lip on one side felt mashed and he could taste blood in his mouth. He shook his head.

"I can do this all afternoon if I have to," said Looms with a shrug. "You're not going to be a pretty sight."

Delamore closed his eyes for a few seconds. He opened them in time to see a big, brown, gnarled fist heading straight for the centre of his face. His nose was shattered and flattened in an explosion of blood and gristle and the chair pitched over backwards.

Delamore lay on his back with his bound legs in the air. He could hardly see and his entire face was ablaze with pain. He heard Batrouney's high-pitched scream: ". . . and the challenger hits the canvas for the third time. And here's the count: a-one, a-two, a-three, a-four . . ."

"Baz, you mad bugger, pipe down," said Looms amiably and walked over to Delamore. Then: "Hello, what've we got here?" Delamore, twisting his head to spit out blood, saw Looms stoop to pick up his hotel room key which had been jolted out of the back pocket of his jeans.

"Room 1414 at the Regis Hotel," said Looms. He hauled the chair upright again and peered into Delamore's face. "I'll bet that's where it is. Save it, Sunny Jim – I can see it in your eyes. Well the one that's still open anyway." He sighed and shook his head. "Christ, I told you – you could've saved yourself a few smacks in the scone by just giving me the bloody key in the first place."

Looms hitched himself up onto the bench. He flexed his right hand a couple of times. "I take my hat off to you, mister – I wouldn't have credited it in a blue moon. I thought one decent thump and you'd be howling the roof down." He looked at the key. "If this hadn't dropped out of your pocket, I probably would've been hammering the buggery out of you till teatime. Oh well, fat lot of good it did you. I'll shoot down to Auckland later on and find that fucking thing of Gage's. Then we'll have to decide what to do with you. What d'you reckon, Baz?"

"I do declare, hanging's too good for that varmint, marshal," said Batrouney in a hillbilly twang. "I say we do what the Injuns do – string him up by his nutbag and skin him alive with a red-hot knife."

At 9.10 that Wednesday evening Herman Pickrang, wearing his best suit and tie and carrying a briefcase, strode purposefully through the lobby of the Regis Hotel. The outfit and the briefcase, which he'd bought that afternoon, were intended to make him look like a businessman. In fact he looked exactly what he was: a thug in a five-year-old suit carrying a cheap plastic briefcase. Since the lobby was almost deserted, the thinness of his camouflage hardly mattered.

Pickrang took the lift to the 14th floor and found room 1414. The corridors were empty. He donned a pair of tight-fitting rubber gloves. As Quedley had promised, getting into the room wasn't difficult; the banqueting manager had been by a few minutes earlier to make sure of that.

Pickrang was not what could be termed a tidy burglar, one of those who pride themselves on leaving no trace of their visit apart from the absence of the stolen items. He violently stripped the bed, wrenched the mattress off the base, and scattered the contents of the drawers and wardrobes without finding anything.

The suitcase was locked. It had been a long time between knifings for Pickrang but impaling Rocco Perfumo had brought back to him just how satisfying knifework could be. On his return to Auckland, he'd procured a razor-sharp flick knife which he wore taped to his right calf as he'd seen Clint Eastwood do in a movie. He popped the blade and plunged it through the suitcase's canvas exterior. He ran the blade round the frame of the suitcase, cutting out the whole of one side. As he went to discard the material, he felt the envelope which had been sewn in between the canvas and the cloth lining.

Pickrang opened the envelope; it contained several typed pages. A quick scan satisfied him that it was what Quedley wanted. Pickrang replaced his knife, put the envelope in the briefcase, checked there was no one in the corridor, and left the scene.

He came out of the hotel, turned right and headed for his car which he'd left in a side street a couple of blocks away. As was usually the case at 9.30 on a Wednesday night, the city was near-empty and quiet.

Luther "Bad Louie" Potau awoke with a start when his mobile phone rang. He was sitting in the driver's seat of a 15-year-old Ford Falcon parked in the one-way inner-city side street directly opposite Pickrang's Mitsubishi. The caller was a fellow member of the Blood Drinkers who'd been stationed in the bus shelter across the road from the Regis Hotel waiting for Pickrang to come out; he was ringing to report that Pickrang was on his way.

Potau sat up and rubbed his eyes. He screwed the top back on the half-empty litre bottle of dark rum which was propped up between his massive fleshy thighs and slipped the bottle under the seat. For the third time that evening he broke open the sawn-off shotgun to check that it was loaded.

Just as he snapped it shut, he saw, in his rear view mirror, Pickrang round the corner. Potau laid the gun on the passenger's seat and wound down the window on that side. Pickrang walked a little way up the footpath on Potau's side of the road then crossed over to his car. He set down the briefcase and fumbled for his car keys. As he inserted the key, he heard a car door open behind him. He looked around. A huge Maori wearing a woolly cap and wraparound sunglasses got out of the beat-up Ford on the other side of the street and walked slowly around the front of the car. He leaned against the passenger door, folded his arms, and looked at Pickrang without speaking.

Pickrang picked him straightaway as a gang member, a species he despised despite the many things they had in common. After a few seconds' silence, he snapped: "What the fuck do you want, you big fat cunt?"

When Luther Potau reached in the open car window and brought out a sawn-off shotgun, Pickrang decided that a less confrontational approach might be in order. Because such an approach didn't come naturally, he was still trying to think of the appropriate words when Potau raised the shotgun and gave him both barrels. The blast hurled Pickrang onto the bonnet of his car. He rolled off the bonnet onto the road where he lay with his head in the gutter.

Potau, who didn't believe in looking gift horses in the mouth, walked across the road and picked up Pickrang's briefcase. He got into his car, threw the briefcase and the shotgun into the back seat, and drove off. As Potau turned out of the street, Pickrang lifted his head a few centimetres out of the gutter and coughed wetly. His chest hurt horribly. Perhaps, he thought, he should call for help. It went against his code of stoicism and self-reliance but, then again, he'd never found himself face down in a gutter with a chest full of buckshot before. When he tried to shout, he found he simply didn't have enough breath to make a sound. Before Herman Pickrang had

213

a chance to get to grips with the implications of his extreme shortage of breath, he died.

Cec Gilpin considered that he was extremely lucky to have a friend like Barry Plugge. Even though Plugge had made it – really made it – in life, he hadn't forgotten his boyhood mates. So when, at the age of 50, Gilpin had been made redundant by the city's parks and recreation department for which he'd worked for the whole of his adult life, Barry Plugge had put him on his payroll.

Plugge called him his "chauffeur and gofer". Gilpin didn't know and didn't care what a gofer was; he just did whatever Barry wanted. Sure, the pay was pretty ordinary – not much more than the dole if the truth be told – but the main thing was that he was occupied; he had something to do with himself, somewhere to go of a morning rather than moping around at home and having a blue with the missus. There was one other great benefit: he got to drive Plugge's cherry-red Jaguar Sovereign with the personalised number plate FLASH. Since he was a boy, Gilpin had regarded Jaguars as the ultimate in automotive excellence and style. If anyone had ever suggested that one day he'd be driving a Jag on a regular basis, he would've dismissed the notion out of hand. Yet here he was most days of the week, cruising the streets behind the wheel of this majestic machine.

Gilpin might've been less positive about both Plugge and the Jaguar if he'd been aware of the background to the Sultan of Sleaze's out-of-the-blue announcement a few months previously that Gilpin would henceforth chauffeur him around. It was to do with the threat from the Italians from Sydney. On the basis of the occasional television news reports from Sicily about prosecuting magistrates being blown to smithereens by car bombs, Plugge was of the view that the car bomb was once again the preferred assassination method of the Italian criminal fraternity. As any moviegoer knows, most car bombs were rigged up to go off when the car was started. Guarding against this eventuality meant going through the tiresome procedure of getting down on your hands and knees and inspecting underneath the car every time you wanted to go anywhere. The thought of a constantly cricked neck and soiled trousers didn't appeal to Plugge; furthermore, he was so ignorant of the workings of a car and things mechanical that he could conceivably have looked straight at a bomb without recognising it as such. A much better idea was to insure the hell out of the Jag and let someone else take the risks.

Thus it was that at 9.53 that Wednesday night, Cec Gilpin drove Barry Plugge's Jaguar out of the carpark, around the block, and double-parked it out in front of the Blue Angel strip club to await his employer. Knowing the wait could last anything up to half an hour, Gilpin turned on the car radio which he had tuned to a classic hits station. The first song to come on was Gene Pitney's *The Man Who Shot Liberty Valance*. Gilpin gave a grunt of delight and turned up the volume. In Cec Gilpin's pantheon of heroes, Gene Pitney ranked a close second to Barry Plugge. Sitting back in the soft leather and singing along to Gene with his eyes shut tight, Gilpin didn't see the battered Ford Falcon which came up Karangahape Road from the opposite direction, stopped a few metres away to allow a car to go by, then swerved across the middle line to pull up alongside the Jaguar.

Gilpin was doing his inadequate best to stay with Gene Pitney through the descending cadence of "He was the bravest of them all", when Luther "Bad Louie" Potau bellowed at him from less than three metres away: "Yo, white bread mother-fucker."

Gilpin swivelled his head towards the source of this unwelcome interruption. Potau poked his sawn-off shotgun through the car window, waited till Gilpin's expression changed from puzzled annoyance to eye-popping terror, and pulled the trigger. He gave him one barrel only but it was quite enough. As Bad L'ouie told himself as he roared down Karangahape Road towards the Symonds Street motorway ramp, he was only half the size of the other cunt, so why waste a second cartridge on him?

CHAPTER *23*

*D*ean Delamore's evening meal consisted of two slices of slightly stale bread, a lump of cheddar cheese, a glass of water and a handful of aspirins. He was then locked up for the night in the cellar under Looms' house. It was chilly and pitch-black and each creak and rustle caused him to wonder what other forms of life inhabited the cellar. After midnight the aspirins wore off and his wrecked nose set up a fiery throb which intensified as the night dragged on. The pain was enough to make sleep difficult; the combination of pain, the expectation of being scampered over or even gnawed by foraging rats, and dark thoughts of what the morning might bring which, try as he might, he couldn't block out of his mind, made it impossible.

At eight the next morning Looms let him out of the cellar to go to the bathroom. He examined his bruised, yellowing, misshapen face in the mirror. He decided it wasn't really the Rexette look. Suddenly he felt the delayed effect of all the pain and shock and fear which he'd gone through and he began to shake violently. When the shaking died down, he took a last look in the mirror. Remember, he told himself, big girls don't cry.

He came out of the bathroom. Looms, who'd been waiting outside the door, gripped him by the arm and pushed him down the corridor.

"I suppose you're wondering what's happening?" he

said. "Well I would in your shoes. I drove all the bloody way to Auckland and couldn't get within five blocks of the hotel. I don't know what the hell was going on but there were police everywhere, roadblocks, the works. So I'm going to have to do it all over again tonight. I should charge you petrol money." He stopped Delamore by the kitchen door and breathed in heavily. "Smell that? Bacon, eggs, tomatoes, fried bread and farm mushrooms – Baz's speciality. What did they used to say – 'the condemned man ate a hearty breakfast'?"

Having reviewed the events of Wednesday night, Detective Sergeant Tito Ihaka felt that, on the whole, it had been one of the better nights for the forces of law and order.

True, there was a shotgun killer on the rampage who didn't appear to draw the important distinction between legitimate targets and law-abiding taxpayers. But even then, Cec Gilpin hadn't died in vain: the shocking sight of his chauffeur's face plastered across the windscreen of his Jaguar had put a hurricane-strength wind up Barry Plugge. He'd drawn the obvious conclusion – that he, rather than his employee, had been the intended victim – and immediately sought sanctuary at the Central Police Station, the only place in Auckland where he felt safe. To ensure that the police didn't throw him back on the street, Plugge had demanded a tape recorder and started owning up. When Ihaka switched off the tape recorder four hours later, he estimated that Plugge would be eligible for parole sometime around the year 2015.

Plugge began by outlining the ingenious scam he'd cooked up with the jailed lawyer Trevor Lydiate. Then he'd explained the circumstances surrounding the demise of private investigator and candid photography specialist Wallace Guttle. No sooner had Plugge confirmed that Herman Pickrang had done for Guttle than the news came through that Pickrang

218

himself was past tense; he'd been the first of the unknown shooter's brace of victims.

Although Ihaka felt the shooter deserved society's heartfelt thanks for getting rid of Pickrang and couldn't suppress a twinge of admiration for his industry and no-nonsense approach, the pressure was on for a swift arrest. While Ihaka took a detached view of the previous night's events and, as always, was unable to get too worked up about what civilians did to one another – as far as he was concerned, the only sensible attitude for a policeman to adopt – the media were busy scaring the daylights out of the citizenry with its coverage of the double slaying. Ihaka didn't think the manhunt would be a long one. The way this merchant operates, he thought, he ain't exactly the Scarlet Pimpernel. The only question was how many people would be wiped out in the process of taking him out of circulation. Keep your wits about you, fat boy, Ihaka told himself; whatever happens, don't you be the first poor bastard through the door.

Detective Constable Johan Van Roon hovered nervously in front of Ihaka's desk, waiting for the sergeant to acknowledge his presence. Van Roon, who was 24, was a first-generation New Zealander, the son of Dutch immigrants whose fair northern European complexion he'd inherited. Ihaka had a sharp eye for others' distinguishing features or physical peculiarities and Van Roon's milky skin had immediately caught his attention. Van Roon, he'd announced to a crowded station room on the constable's first day at Central, was the whitest white man he'd ever seen.

Eventually Ihaka looked up.

"Well if it ain't the Milky Bar Kid. What's your problem?"

Van Roon tried to smile but didn't quite get there. "Sarge, there's something a bit odd about this Pickrang thing; it looks like he might've pulled a burglary at the Regis hotel just before he got hit."

"Oh yeah?" said Ihaka disinterestedly. "I'll bet it wasn't the only thing he pulled."

Van Roon soldiered on. "Pickrang copped it about 9.30. A bellboy saw him in the lobby just after nine and some time around then a guest's room got really turned over."

Ihaka sniffed noisily and looked at his watch. "Is this going to take long, constable?"

The constable, who'd heard that Ihaka's bark was worse than his bite but didn't believe it, swallowed hard. "Sure Sarge, I'm just about there. The guest whose room got done over is a Ms Lesley Gore from Sydney but immigration has no record of anyone of that name entering the country. There was an Aussie passport in the suitcase which the burglar took to with a knife – Pickrang had a knife on him by the way . . ."

"Hold it, what did he take to with a knife – the fucking suitcase or the fucking passport?"

The constable nodded hurriedly. "Sorry, sorry – the suitcase. He cut one whole side panel out of it. Anyway, that's a bit beside the point . . ."

"What is the point, son?" said Ihaka with quiet emphasis.

"The passport belongs to a 27-year-old man called Dean Delamore who flew in from Sydney on Sunday; the guest registered as Lesley Gore, and there were men's and women's clothes and toiletries in the room. The women who make the beds and that say they never saw any bloke's gear – it must've been kept in the suitcase – and they're certain there's only been one person in the room."

Ihaka said "Hmmm" and stood up. "How do they know that? They sniff the sheets or something?" He walked around and sat on the edge of the desk in front of the constable. "Have we tracked down the mystery guest?"

"No. There's no sign of him – or her. The staff at the front desk say they haven't seen Ms Gore for a couple of days. She always hangs out the "Do not disturb" sign when she's in the room. We showed Delamore's passport around and a couple of people seem to think Delamore and Gore are the same person but they wouldn't swear to it. Yesterday morning a guy the concierge identified as Delamore from the passport photo was asking about driving up north, somewhere round Wellsford."

"You check the car hire companies?"

"Yeah we did. Delamore picked up a Honda Civic from the Hertz place in town around midday yesterday. He used a New South Wales licence and said he'd have the car back by the weekend at the latest. I sent the number up to Wellsford and asked them to keep an eye out for it. We also faxed Sydney but haven't heard back yet."

"So Herman Pickrang burgled a man who's pretending to be a woman; then a few minutes later, a party or parties unknown spread his lungs over half of downtown. You seem to be right on top of things, son – what's your theory?"

"I haven't really got one, sarge. I just thought it was all a bit strange. If Delamore and Gore are one and the same – and it sure looks that way – you kind of think he must be up to something to go through all that carry-on. Oh by the way, we found this in the suitcase too."

He passed Ihaka a folded sheet of notepaper. Ihaka opened it. On it was a handwritten list of names, addresses and phone numbers; some had a line through them, some had ticks beside them, some question marks. It was the second time Ihaka had seen these particular names; the first time was on the long-dead Bronwen Ticehurst's dance card.

Ihaka stared at the list for a full minute.

"Son, you're absolutely right. This is definitely strange. You've got something else to tell me, haven't you?"

Van Roon racked his brains. "I think that's it, Sarge," he said uncertainly.

Ihaka looked at him wide-eyed, shaking his head. "Uh-uh. If Pickrang did the break-in, what'd he nick and where is it?"

"Nothing as far as we can tell. I mean, we didn't find anything on him or in his car. Oh shit, hang on – the bellboy said Pickrang was carrying a briefcase."

"But you didn't find a briefcase, right? So it's reasonable to assume that A, whatever he nicked from Delamore's room was in the briefcase and B, whoever pinged him took the briefcase."

Van Roon was so angry with himself for having overlooked the briefcase that he almost forgot to pass on his final piece of information. He had to go back and interrupt Ihaka's paperwork again.

"One other thing, Sarge," he said. "When Delamore filled in his immigration form, he didn't say he was going to stay at the Regis. He put down a private address somewhere in St Heliers – I've got it written down if you want it. It's the home of a Mrs Sparks – Mareena Sparks."

Mareena Sparks and Tito Ihaka greeted one another like old friends. After they'd finished assuring each other that they were in the pink, Mareena escorted the policeman to the downstairs den where her younger son lay on the couch watching TV. When she'd gone, Ihaka asked Reggie Sparks how his story was going.

"Shithouse," he said. "Next question."

"Yeah, it's good to be alive isn't it? I've got some news that might cheer you up – it's about your old sparring partner, Herman Pickrang."

Sparks rolled into a sitting position.

"Hang on – let me guess. Pickrang's body was found somewhere in the vicinity of Palm Beach, a little place on the coast just north of Sydney. He was shot by someone using a handgun, probably in the early hours of last Sunday morning. Am I right?"

Ihaka looked at Sparks as if he'd announced his intention to roller skate to the South Pole. "You quite finished? Pickrang's dead all right. His body was found in a side street in the centre of Auckland, a city situated on an isthmus separating the Waitemata and Manukau harbours. It happened around half past nine last night. And handgun, my black arse – he bought a full load from a double-barrelled sawn-off from as close as me to you. What's all this shit about some place north of Sydney?"

Sparks leaned forward staring at Ihaka. "What? He was killed here? Last night?" He slumped back on the sofa. "Last week I went over to Sydney, for *New Nation*. Pickrang was over there as well. I was at this place at Palm Beach when Pickrang turned up doing his 'I'm going to rip your ears off' routine. Then these two other guys showed up. Don't ask me who they were but they were dirty on Pickrang in a huge way – something to do with he'd shoved one of them in a pizza oven. Anyway, these guys had a gun, a pistol. They told us to get lost; it was pretty obvious what they had in mind."

"What was Pickrang doing over there?"

"I'm pretty sure he was sent by a guy called Caspar Quedley." Sparks told Ihaka about Julian Gage. He finished: ". . . but by the time he got over there, Gage was dead and his stuff was in the mail. Gage didn't know about Appleyard – that's why he sent it to him – but it hasn't arrived; I reckon Quedley's got his hands on it."

"How could he do that?"

"He's an operator, you know, he's got fingers in all sorts of pies, knows everyone who's anyone."

Ihaka nodded slowly. "Well if he's got the juice, I suppose he could. You know a guy called Dean Delamore?"

Sparks sat up again. "Yeah I do. He was a friend of Gage's; he posted Gage's stuff for him. Delamore was at Palm Beach when Pickrang turned up. He came over here with me on Sunday."

"Well that explains that. Where is he now?"

"No idea," said Sparks flatly. "He stayed here Sunday night then shot through without a word."

"Tell me something Sparks, how friendly are you and this character? The reason I ask is that I hear he likes dressing up in women's clothes. You don't have showers together and take turns picking up the soap, that sort of stuff?"

Sparks gave him a sour look. "Yeah, that's us all right."

"Hey, don't get me wrong; I've got nothing against it. Matter of fact, I wouldn't be surprised if the boy I sleep with is a bit that way."

Sparks' lips twitched. It was as close to a smile as he'd got in 24 hours.

"What about Delamore?"

"After Delamore left here, he checked in at the Regis Hotel – as a woman. Called himself Lesley Gore – that mean anything to you?" Sparks shook his head. "Looks like Pickrang's swansong was a B and E on Delamore's room. Typical Pickrang – tore the fucking place apart. Now what do you reckon he was after?"

"The stuff Gage wrote? Doesn't make sense. Delamore posted it in Sydney last week . . ." Sparks stopped in mid-sentence.

"You only got his word for it, right? I think your little mate's playing his own game." Ihaka passed Sparks the sheet of paper with the list of names on it. "We found this in his room."

"This is out of my fucking notebook, the little shit." Sparks put his head in his hands and thought hard. "If Delamore didn't send Gage's letter, Quedley couldn't have intercepted it. So Quedley finds out Delamore's staying at the Regis – how would he even know he's in town?"

"Delamore must've got in touch with him. Quedley must want this letter thing bad to send Pickrang over to Sydney. Why? Because it dumps shit on him?"

"I'm pretty sure it does."

"Well I'd say Delamore's trying to blackmail him."

Sparks thought about it. "I don't know about that. I can't see Delamore as a blackmailer."

"Grow up, mate. You've known him what – a few days? The way he pissed off out of here tells you he's up to something."

Sparks shrugged. "Okay, for the sake of argument, let's say you're right. But if Delamore had it and Pickrang stole it, where is it now?"

"We don't know for sure that he did. I mean, he left the place in a shambles but that doesn't prove he found anything. Pickrang was seen in the hotel with a briefcase which we haven't recovered, so the way it looks, if he did find it, whoever offed him has got it now."

Sparks rubbed his face wearily. "Jesus, this started out as just a story for a magazine."

"So it's a mess, so what's new? It's always this way for cops – nothing's ever simple. It's only you fucking journalists who make out it's ever any different, writing things up like they happened all nice and neat."

"Some journalist – I haven't written a fucking word yet. So where's Delamore now?"

Ihaka shook his head. "Christ knows. He's hired a car and looks like he took off up north. He was talking about going to Wellsford or somewhere."

Ihaka gave Sparks a quick rundown on the Plugge-Lydiate scam and its repercussions for Wallace Guttle then stood up. "Well I'll leave you to it Sparks. You're obviously a busy man, you got TV to watch, balls to scratch. Where do I find this Quedley joker? I'll think I'll go and talk to him about his ex-employee."

CHAPTER *24*

When Herman Pickrang didn't report in that Wednesday night, Caspar Quedley took it for granted that something had gone wrong. It stands to reason, he said to himself; everything else has. Bill Tench rang him in his office the next morning to report that, as he heard it from his police contacts, Pickrang had carried out his assignment in room 1414 of the Regis Hotel; shortly thereafter though, he'd found himself on the wrong end of a sawn-off shotgun. When Quedley wondered out loud who could've pulled the trigger, Tench spluttered with amusement and replied that the police didn't know where to start looking since a gathering of the enemies of Herman Pickrang would fill Eden Park. Afterwards Quedley reflected that if Pickrang hadn't found Gage's letter in room 1414, he was back to square one; if he had, then the likelihood was that at that very moment, Gage's account of life and death at Prince Albert College would be being studied, with some interest he imagined, at the Central Police Station.

Thus Quedley's spirits and shoulders sagged when he returned to his office after an early lunch to find Detective Sergeant Tito Ihaka waiting for him. He recovered himself quickly, pumped Ihaka's hand as if meeting him was the fulfilment of a long-held ambition, and ushered him into his office. Ihaka, however, proved difficult to charm.

"Didn't you used to play in the front row for University?" asked Quedley, examining him closely.

"Me? Shit no. You must be mixing me up with some other big coon."

"Yes, well, a lot of you folk are impressive physical specimens, that's for sure," said Quedley, undeterred by Ihaka's barely disguised truculence. "It's something to do with the bones, isn't it? Now Sergeant, what can I get you – coffee, tea, or something stronger?"

Ihaka shook his head. "I'm right."

"Of course you poor buggers can't drink on duty, can you? Well if you'll excuse me, I've just had a very grim lunch with one of those born-again wowsers who live on salad and mineral water. You know what alfalfa smells like?" said Quedley getting a beer out of the small fridge under the bar. "Get a whiff of it – you'll understand why they call it spunkweed." He poured the beer and raised the tall glass to Ihaka.

"Cheers. Now how can I help you?"

"Herman Pickrang's been working for you, right?"

Quedley's brow furrowed. "Herman who?"

"Pickrang. We have reason to believe you sent him to Sydney last weekend."

Quedley chuckled. "Reason to believe – isn't that what you lot say when you haven't got a shred of evidence? I'd love to know your reason Sergeant, because I've never even heard of the man."

"I suppose you don't know Dean Delamore either?"

Quedley rubbed his chin. "Delamore you say? Now that name does ring a bell. I can check with my secretary but I seem to remember getting a call from a Delamore the other day. I couldn't get rid of him; he was babbling away about Prince Albert College – I couldn't make head or tail of it. I think he was trying to screw a donation to the chapel restoration fund out of me. You never escape them, you know. You spend five miserable teenage years there and they pursue you relentlessly for the rest of your life."

Ihaka nodded. "Yeah I know what it's like. Tamaki

College is chasing me for money to re-lay the croquet lawns. What about Julian Gage – you know him?"

"Well I used to. He's dead. If it's not asking too much, would you mind telling me what this is all about?"

Ihaka stood up. "Seeing you never heard of Pickrang, you wouldn't be interested in the fact that he was shot dead last night."

Quedley drained his beer. "My, is that so?" he said blandly. "Just as well I didn't know him then – funerals make me depressed. Who did it?"

"We don't know yet but we'll find him. The thing is, the shooter took Pickrang's briefcase and we have reason to believe – there I go again – that there was something in the briefcase that a few people around town are fizzing at the bung to get their hands on. I thought you might be one of them. Wrong again, eh?"

Ihaka watched Quedley's expression turn thoughtful. He walked out of his office and got in the lift. On the way down he reflected that if the opportunity arose, he'd get enormous satisfaction from nailing Caspar Quedley to the wall – by his no doubt perfectly proportioned dick.

After leaving Quedley's office, Ihaka drove down through Parnell, up the hill past the university, and across town to Grey Lynn. He parked in Williamson Avenue and got out of his unmarked car. He was wearing jeans, running shoes and a zip-up bomber jacket. He put on a baseball cap and sunglasses and walked down a side street until he reached an old stone building. It was a church-cum-social club for one of the Polynesian communities; he had an idea it was the Tongans. There didn't seem to be anyone around. Ihaka followed the path down the side of the building to the rear where there was a low embankment. There was a two-metre-high wooden fence on top of the embankment which formed the boundary of the church property. Ihaka climbed up the embankment, swore, took a deep breath and hoisted himself up the fence. He squirmed over the fence and came down in a private and well-tended backyard. Ihaka walked up the lawn towards the house, a tidy old wooden villa. He tapped on the back door.

The man who opened the door was in his early thirties. He was tall and thin and had long, unkempt blond hair, an earring, and a little triangle of white fluff under his lower lip. He wore faded jeans, cowboy boots, and a tight black T-shirt bearing the legend "Kill 'em all and let God sort it out" in large white lettering. The man's name was Blair Corvine and he was an undercover policeman. By and large Ihaka was sceptical of the value of undercover police work; it took forever to get undercover men in place and then half the information they provided couldn't be used because it might blow their cover. A lot of them also turned into giant pains in the arse; he suspected it was all the dope they smoked. Corvine, on the other hand, had always been cut out for it; in fact Ihaka used to wonder how someone with such obvious criminal inclinations had ever got into the police force in the first place.

Corvine let Ihaka in. "Hey, it's big chief Ihaka," he said. "You and the bros dispossessed any hard-working honkies lately?"

"Well my man, the fight for justice is never-ending. I tell you what, they wear you down these pakehas, bleating about how their family's been there for 150 years and how they've levelled hills and cleared a thousand acres of bush and all this shit. You wouldn't believe the crap we have to put up with. Christ, we're not unreasonable people; we let you stay here – what more do you want?"

"I'd settle for not having that oily heap of shit with the tiki on TV every other night."

"I'm afraid you'll have to be more specific."

Corvine got two cans of beer out of the fridge and handed one to Ihaka. Ihaka, who hadn't enjoyed watching Quedley savour his beer, drank it in less than a minute.

Corvine took a careful sip of his beer. "Listen, I really enjoy it when you drop in," he said, "the way you trample on my flowers and hoover my piss and that, but is there a reason for it that's got anything to do with, like, our jobs?"

"Yeah I was going to ask you about that. I mean, what is it with you and all these flowers? Why don't you grow some fucking vegetables?"

"That's the Ihaka philosophy is it – if it you can't fuck it or eat it, it's a waste of time? I guess it's difficult for someone whose great-grandfather was a cannibal to grasp the concept of aesthetic pleasure."

"Watch yourself pal, I haven't had lunch. The reason I'm here, those Eyeties from Sydney who stirred up some shit in K Road a while ago . . ."

"The Perfumos."

"Yeah, they operate from a pizza joint, don't they?"

"Sure do – up the top of Queen Street there. They do a fucking good pizza as a matter of fact, lots of anchovies. I love anchovies. You like anchovies?"

"You're a sick man, Corvine. Didn't Herman Pickrang have a run-in with them?"

"The late, great Herman? Did he ever! They sent over these two brothers to run the show for them here; the pizzeria's the front. Apparently Herman barged into the joint and stuck one of them head first into the pizza oven. They reckoned you could hear the cunt scream in Henderson. I forget which one it was, Marty or Rocco. It was the dumb one; man, this fucker's so thick, you'd have to tell him what to do if his wang was on fire."

"That's pretty dumb. So where are they now?"

"The one who got cooked went back to Sydney; the other one's still around last I heard. What's up?"

"I just wondered if they had anything to do with Pickrang getting blown away. I mean, these guys are meant to be the Mafia, aren't they? You'd have thought they'd have been after Herman."

"Yeah you would, wouldn't you?" said Corvine. "The word was they decided to call a truce but maybe they were just biding their time. Why the hell are you chasing whoever did that scumsucker? Guy deserves a medal."

"Wheels within wheels, matey. You talk to the Sydney cops now and again, don't you? Why don't you give them a ring, see if they've heard anything about the Perfumos lately? Thing is, I heard Pickrang was over there last weekend and had a run-in with a couple of guys who sound like them."

"What, make a fucking international call on my phone?"

"Come on Blair, I've seen your expense claims. I bet you make a profit on it."

Corvine made the call. It took 10 minutes, half of which was obscene badinage, and was punctuated by frequent exclamations.

"Hey chief your source is red-hot," said Corvine when he put the phone down. "Martino and Rocco bit the big one last Saturday night: one of them got a third nostril, the other got a knife through the neck. The deal went down in a place called . . ."

"Let me guess – Palm Beach, a little place just north of Sydney?"

"You're on the ball chief, by Christ you are. So now we know who zapped Herman and why. Shit, I just thought of something."

"Must be a leap year."

"You know who moves most of the Perfumo's dope here? The Blood Drinkers. Those hits last night had Blood Drinkers written all over them – drive up with a sawn-off on your lap, boom, no fucking beg your pardons. 'What? We offed the wrong guy? Shit happens, we'll try again tomorrow.' That's them to a T. I'll bet what happened was the family put them on the case when Marty and Rocco got wasted, told 'em get Plugge while you're at it. Tell you what, I pissed myself when I heard how Barry scooted down to Central waving a white flag but fuck, if he's got those guys after him, it's the only way he's going to keep a head on his shoulders."

"The Blood Drinkers," said Ihaka. "That's just lovely."

Shortly after Ihaka got back to Central, he got a call from Reggie Sparks.

"How'd you get on with Quedley?"

"He's a cutie, isn't he? In a word, nowhere – he says he's never heard of Pickrang. He's lying of course. He didn't bat an eyelid when I told him Pickrang was dead and the turd's name hasn't even been released yet. He'd be happy that whoever did Pickrang's probably got Gage's letter; better than us having it and the chances are it'll be thrown away or lost or something. By the way, those guys who turned up at Palm Beach? It looks like they fucked up in the worst possible way." He told Sparks what had become of the brothers Perfumo. "So there you go," he finished. "I guess Pickrang found out what happens when you rumble with the big boys."

Sparks rang Louise Appleyard who said what a pleasant surprise it was to hear from him.

"Let's just say a surprise," said Sparks spurning the olive branch. "Going by what you said yesterday – that stuff about grudges and reputations being blackened – you and Quedley obviously talked about what Gage might've said in his letter?"

Louise decided to ignore the snub. "Caspar said he and Gage used to be quite close but they'd fallen out badly. Gage was all bitter and twisted and had threatened Caspar, more or less to destroy his reputation. He said the letter would just contain a lot of lies about him – he wasn't specific if that's what you mean."

"Did you believe him?"

There was a long pause. "Yes, but I suppose I didn't really think about it too hard."

"What does that mean?"

"It means I probably had other things on my mind at the time."

Sparks cleared his throat. "Look I want to ask Quedley a few straight questions; I'd like you to be there otherwise he'll just give me the run-around. How about it?"

"I think you might be overestimating my influence but all right. When?"

"Now, this afternoon."

They met an hour later in the reception area of Quedley Communications. Sparks, frostily polite, thanked her for obliging at such short notice. She was about to ask him how long she'd have to spend in Coventry when Quedley came out to greet them. He acted as if it was the most normal thing in the world for the two of them to turn up unannounced at his office in the middle of the afternoon. He seated them on the sofas arranged in a V formation in a corner of his office, Sparks on the two-seater, Louise on the larger. He perched on the arm of Louise's in what Sparks interpreted as a proprietorial statement. Louise, wearing snug-fitting dark green leggings and a loose white top, looked slightly anxious. Sparks, in no mood for small talk, got straight to the point.

"What happened at Prince Albert that you're so desperate to cover up?"

Quedley spread his hands and looked from Sparks to Louise with a bemused grin.

"And I thought this was a social visit. Jesus Christ, I don't mind you interrupting my work; I'm not even that bothered by the 'When did you stop beating your wife?' questions. But why drag Louise into it? What's your problem, Reggie? Are you all bent out of shape because of Louise and me so you want to make me look bad in front of her? Is that it?"

"Why stop there? Why don't you throw in my sister-in-law?"

"Your sister-in-law?" said Louise. "Where does she come into it?"

233

"A while ago Quedley tried to seduce her," said Sparks.

Quedley grinned ruefully. "Yes, that was rather unfortunate. When it comes to married women, I try to operate on the basis that what husbands don't know won't hurt them. How was I meant to know that Gavin was going to mount a room-to-room search?" He wagged a finger at Sparks. "But in the interests of accuracy Reggie, I must pull you up on your use of the word 'tried'. To say I tried to seduce dear old Heather implies that I failed. Now you and I both know that wasn't the case."

Sparks looked at Louise and said, "You can pick 'em." To Quedley: "She's here because I thought there was just the remotest chance that you'd be embarrassed to tell bare-faced lies in front of her."

"You're full of flattery today, aren't you? So are you here in your ace reporter role or what?"

"The chances are there won't be a story. The cops are involved now, shit, people have been murdered. It'll probably all be *sub judice* for months. Anyway, if you've got nothing to hide, what are you worried about?"

"So I have you to thank for the visit from Sergeant Plod do I? I wondered about that." Quedley heaved an exaggerated sigh and looked at the ceiling. "You're persistent, Sparks; you may be obtuse – you're certainly misguided – but you are persistent. Okay, if you really must know." He slipped down onto the sofa beside Louise. "This is strictly not for publication. As I was telling Louise, Julian was a bit of a slut at school. He used to tell me who he was playing doctors and doctors with and if I thought there was some mileage in it, I'd threaten to broadcast it far and wide unless they coughed up. It was hardly extortion on a grand scale – you know, it was hand over your pocket money or, I'll have that cake your mother brought today – but it's not the sort of thing you want written up in *New Nation*."

There was a long silence. Louise looked wonderingly at

Quedley who seemed to be examining his expensive-looking black brogues. Sparks' derisive snort broke the silence.

"Oh right, absolutely," he said, clicking his fingers. "You send a fucking psycho over to Australia because you don't want people to know that 20-odd years ago, you bullied a few spoilt kids out of some chocolate cake. You really think we're a couple of morons, don't you?"

"I can't conceive of any context in which I'd lump you together with Louise," said Quedley coldly. "I've answered your god-damn question; I can't help it if the answer doesn't suit your purposes but that's it."

"That's it huh?" said Sparks. "What about selling the exam papers?"

"Oh the history paper – I'd forgotten about that. I was quite proud of that little stunt; I broke into the master's common room to steal it and then sold copies. Fair cop, guv." He looked at Louise. "Well my sweet, now you know all my guilty secrets," he said, play-acting. "Am I beyond the pale? Does this mean you can never see me again?"

Louise looked uncertainly at Reggie, wondering if it was all over. He was sitting with his elbow on the arm of the sofa, his chin in the heel of his hand, and his eyes on Quedley. She recognised the expression; it was the same angry and disdainful look she'd got the day before.

"You know something?" said Sparks. "There's nobody dumber than a half-smart person who thinks he's really smart."

Quedley went and sat behind his desk. "I don't think that's original is it?" he said off-handedly. He pressed a button on his telephone and asked his secretary if there were any messages for him. Sparks stood in front of the desk and looked down at him.

"You don't know why Pickrang was killed, do you?"

Quedley looked up from his diary. "You still here? You've outstayed your welcome."

"When Pickrang was in Sydney, on your behalf, he killed

a couple of people – two brothers, Martino and Rocco Perfumo. The Perfumo family is involved in organised crime. Shit, why beat around the bush? They're Mafia. Now you know what those guys are like – you kill one of ours, we'll kill two of yours. Revenge is a way of life for them. If the Perfumos find out Pickrang was working for you, you'll be next in line for a shotgun facelift. And if you were going to ask 'how would they find out?' the answer is: because I'd tell them. And I'm pretty sure they'd believe me; I'd tell a good story because, you see, I was there."

Quedley sat back with his arms folded and looked steadily at Sparks who stared back. Then he picked up the phone and dialled.

"Ken? Caspar Quedley. You get *The Sydney Morning Herald* don't you? You got last Monday's handy? You mind having a quick look to see if there's anything about two brothers – someone and Rocco Perfumo – being murdered? Yep, I'll hang on." There was a short wait. "On the front page is it? What does it say?" Quedley listened for a couple of minutes, thanked his informant and hung up. He looked over at Sparks who was standing at the window with his back to him.

He coughed politely. "Sorry Reggie, what was the question?"

Sparks turned round. "Same as before: what would Gage have written that you didn't want people to read?"

Quedley walked over to the bar. "Anyone for a drink?" Louise and Sparks said no. He poured himself one from a heavy crystal decanter, added some ice, then went back to his desk. "The chaplain, a harmless old bachelor called Swindell, was infatuated with Julian," he said slowly looking at no one or nothing in particular. "He was also a masochist. He asked Julian to do things to him – I don't need to spell it out, do I? I blackmailed him. After a few weeks of it, he killed himself – drove his car into a brick wall."

"What about Bronwen Ticehurst?"

Quedley swallowed a mouthful of his drink and shook

his head. "Julian had nothing to do with Bronwen. He probably wouldn't even remember her. It's true, some people said it was my fault but how was I to know what a state she was in? I just told her the truth – that I didn't want to be tied to one girl. Christ, I never dreamt she'd go and kill herself."

"Have you heard from Dean Delamore?" asked Sparks.

Quedley nodded. "He offered to sell me the letter," he said dully. "Then he changed his mind, said he was going to talk to someone else."

"Who would that be?"

"I don't know. I wasn't sure if he was serious. I thought he was just going to make me squirm for a couple of days then come back to me."

Louise Appleyard went over and stood beside Quedley. "Caspar, why on earth did you do those things?"

He looked up at her. "My family . . . we weren't very well off. My father was a vicar and earned next to nothing. I only went to Prince Albert because clergymen's sons got a big discount. I saw how other families lived, the families of the boys I got friendly with. It was a different world, I mean money simply wasn't an issue for them. Say if little Simon wanted to go and stay with his friend in Fiji in the holidays? 'Well of course you can dear. Si-Si needs some spending money? Will $1,000 be enough? Let's make it $1,500 to be on the safe side.' When I wanted a new pair of shoes because I felt such a jerk wearing my black ones out of school, it was a major expenditure decision – my parents argued about it for a week. Then my mother died. All we'd ever really had was each other and that was taken away – we weren't even a family anymore. It just seemed like we had nothing and everyone else had too much."

Quedley sat with his head bowed. He reached out and took Louise's hand; she let him do it, neither withdrawing nor responding.

Sparks said, "Boo fucking hoo," and walked out of Quedley's office.

CHAPTER 25

*R*eggie Sparks sat behind the steering wheel of his mother's Peugeot, which was parked a little way up Parnell Rise from Quedley's office, pondering his next move. He'd made up his mind and was about to start the car when he heard his name being called. He looked up. Louise Appleyard was running up the footpath towards him. With her trim form, her dark hair bouncing on her shoulders and, as Sparks couldn't help noticing, her breasts bobbing perkily beneath the loose top, she looked as if she'd stepped straight from the pages of some glossy healthy living magazine. He wound down the car window.

She was panting slightly. "Are you in a mad rush?" she breathed.

He shrugged. "Not especially."

She walked around to the other side of the car and got into the passenger seat.

"That was a charming exit line," she said. "Didn't you feel even the slightest bit sorry for him?"

He looked at her incredulously. "Sorry for Quedley? You've got to be joking. As for the *Little House on the Prairie* routine, Jesus Christ." He shook his head. "How I managed to keep my lunch down, I'll never know."

"Didn't you believe him?"

"The stuff about his family? Yeah, I believed him – it's pretty much what I'd heard. But so what? Most kids feel hard done by at some stage. And what about the hypocrisy of getting his hooks into the chaplain? Presumably the poor bastard was no better off than Quedley's old man."

She raised her eyebrows non-committally. "What about the rest of it?"

"Hard to say. I still think he knows more about the girl's death than he's letting on. Once I'd hit him with the Perfumos though, I didn't have anything else to pressure him with."

"God yes, what was all that about? Did you really see those men get murdered?"

"Well, not exactly. I wouldn't be here if I had've."

"Tell the truth, Reggie: would you've really gone through with it?"

Sparks' mouth curved into a tight, coldly amused smile. Louise Appleyard was no longer in any doubt that Reggie Sparks possessed a mean streak. The only question was how big and for the second time that afternoon she found herself wondering if she'd underestimated the size of it.

"Shit yes," said Sparks. He held the smile for several seconds. "I still might."

She looked back at him, eyes narrowing. "I don't believe you."

Sparks looked away. "Relax Louise, I won't set the dogs on lover boy. You can scuttle back and tell him mission accomplished."

She laughed mirthlessly. "You know, you can be extremely bloody objectionable when you put your mind to it. As a matter of fact, I'm here because I wanted to let you know that that crack he made, implying that you were jealous – I didn't put the idea in his head."

Sparks gave a shrug of indifference. "You didn't need to. That's just the way his mind works."

"You're not a big fan, are you?"

"I actually quite like him in a funny sort of way," said Sparks mildly. "But the guy's an arsehole; it doesn't matter what you feel or I think, that's it." He twisted round in his seat to look at her. "You know how he gets away with it? He doesn't try to hide it; he lets people in on the secret – hey folks, look at me, I'm a walking, talking arsehole. People enjoy it because he's got a bit of style and because he says and does what they'd like to if they had the guts. Because he's upfront, they think it's an act; they think he's putting it on and deep down, he's not half as self-centred and contemptuous of the rest of us as he pretends. In fact, it's not a facade – he really is an arsehole."

Louise would've liked to have continued the conversation but Sparks brought it to a close by starting the car. She got out and held the door open.

"Where are you off to now?"

"I think I'll head up north," he said. "Who knows? I might find a damsel in distress."

What with having to go home and make sure it was okay with his mother to have her car for the evening and getting caught in the rush-hour Harbour Bridge traffic, Sparks didn't get to Looms' farm until just before 8pm. He followed the drive up to the house, parked right by the front door, and got out of the car. Loud rock music was coming from inside the house. Dermot Looms – rock 'n' roll animal, thought Sparks; I wouldn't have picked it. To the right of the house was a double garage. The roller door was raised and as he'd driven up, his headlights had illuminated a car parked inside. He went over for a closer look. The car was a Honda Civic sedan. It was unlocked and when he opened the driver's side door, the interior light came on. A plastic bag with a Hertz logo hung from one of the knobs on the dashboard. The paperwork showing the car had been rented by Dean Delamore was in the glovebox.

Sparks walked up the steps to the front door and knocked. There was no response. The music was incredibly loud. The bugger must be deaf, he thought. When three sets of knocks went unanswered, he began hammering. After 12 heavy thumps which shook the solid wooden door, it was opened by Basil Batrouney who blinked owlishly behind his thick lenses.

The corridor reverberated to Mick Jagger's lubricious screech: "Oh yeah, you're a strange stray cat/Oh yeah, don't you scratch my back/Oh yeah, you're a strange stray cat/I bet your momma don't know you scream like that/I bet your momma don't know you can sweat like that." Sparks found it vaguely disturbing that Batrouney should be listening to a song celebrating sex with minors.

"Could you turn the music down," Sparks bellowed, making a twisting gesture with his right hand.

Batrouney nodded once and ambled off down the corridor. Sparks followed him into the living room. The music was thundering out of a new-looking stereo system set on a sideboard against the far wall. Batrouney turned the volume right down and looked questioningly at Sparks.

"Who are you?" he said finally.

"Reggie Sparks," he said, his voice sounding strident in the hush. "I'm a journalist. I came to see you a while ago on Waiheke. You showed me your comic, what's it called – *Grub*?" he added in the hope the reference might trigger a reaction in the former rock star's burnt-out brain.

There was no indication in Batrouney's large moist eyes that a mental connection was in progress but something must have clicked.

"I remember you," he said, an accusatory note entering his voice. "You didn't like Jack Stack."

"Oh well you know, I guess it's an acquired taste," said Sparks weakly. "I'm sure if I read a few more . . ." Wait a minute, he told himself, you didn't come up here to exchange toilet talk with this anal retentive zombie. He changed the subject. "What brings you up here? I thought you were pretty much a homebody these days."

"Visiting Dermie. My friend."

Dermie and Baz? Talk about the odd couple. "Is Mr Looms about?"

Batrouney shook his head.

Sparks moved closer. "There's someone else here though, isn't there Basil? A man called Dean Delamore?"

Batrouney's large globular head vibrated violently. "No way Jose, no way."

"I know he's here, Baz. That's his car in the garage." He took Batrouney by the right arm, above the elbow. His fingers sank into soft, doughy flesh. "Where is he?"

Batrouney's head dropped and he tried to pull away. Sparks jerked him back and said in a hard voice, "Where the bloody hell is he? I want you to show me right now."

Sparks pushed Batrouney towards the doorway. Batrouney, his head still bowed, led him into the huge kitchen and took a key from a row of hooks by the back door. He went out the back door and down a few steps to a below-ground doorway. He unlocked the door and stood aside.

Sparks peered through the door into darkness. "In here?"

Batrouney nodded.

"Give us the keys."

Batrouney handed them over. Sparks took a couple of steps down into the cellar. Just then he remembered Batrouney saying at their previous meeting that he no longer listened to rock music. It occurred to Sparks that perhaps everything else the former rock star had told him was a lie but before he could advance this proposition, he was struck a fierce blow on the back of the head. He lost his footing, careered down the remaining few steps, and sprawled on the cold concrete floor. As he lay there stunned, jarred and disoriented, he felt the keys being ripped from his grasp and heard receding footsteps and the cellar door being slammed shut and locked, plunging the cellar into utter darkness.

Outside Basil Batrouney thoughtfully hefted the heavy

doubled-handed secateurs then dropped them back into the wheelbarrow parked by the cellar door. He said, "Good work, Batman," in a deep Hollywood voice and went back inside to listen to the other side of *Beggars Banquet*.

Sparks rolled onto his back and sat up. Blood trickled over his fingers as he gently prodded the welt which had already come up on the back of his head. As it dawned on him that he'd been out-smarted by someone whom he'd characterised, a few minutes earlier, as a zombie, Dean Delamore's hesitant voice came out of the darkness: "Is that you, Reggie?"

"No it's not," said Sparks with some bitterness. "It's Sir Lancelot."

Basil Batrouney felled Sparks with the secateurs at 8.25 that Thursday night. At 10pm police teams launched simultaneous raids on several premises in South Auckland believed to be occupied by leading members of the Blood Drinkers gang. Tito Ihaka led the team whose target was a flat in Otara, the last known address of Luther "Bad Louie" Potau. However, in keeping with his promise to himself, Ihaka was not the first man through the door; that distinction fell to an extremely gung-ho 26-year-old constable and member of the Armed Offenders Squad. Ihaka wondered if anyone had explained to the constable that his state-of-the-art rifle and flak jacket didn't guarantee complete protection against a sociopath with a sawn-off shotgun.

At the time of the raid Potau was sitting on a sofa watching television in the living room-cum-kitchen at the rear of the flat. He was surrounded by assorted debris including the packaging which had contained his supper – $35 worth of Kentucky Fried Chicken – and the leftover bones. A 19-year-old girl, whose name Potau was pretty sure was Christine but whom he called "woman" or "bitch" depending on his mood and who threw a better punch than any of his four previous de facto wives, sat on his lap. Christine had consumed four large bottles of beer and three stiff bourbon and cokes and was quite drunk. Potau, who liked to begin the day with a couple of bottles of stout but who never drank beer after sundown on principle, was just over halfway through his nightly intake of a litre of dark rum and therefore more or less sober, albeit not by any medical or legal definition.

When Ihaka banged on the door and bellowed "Police, open up", Potau went to shove Christine off his lap. However shifting 110kg of dead weight took some doing and by the time she'd been tipped onto the floor, the door had been breached and he could hear the raiders advancing down the corridor. Potau carefully set down the bottle of rum and picked up an empty beer bottle. He straightened up to find a rifle being pointed at him by a tall figure in a dark boiler suit who instructed him not to fucking well move. Ihaka entered the room just as Potau released an unearthly roar and commenced his charge. Having to negotiate his way over and around the recumbent Christine, two beer crates and the back seat from a 1966 Zodiac, which served as seating when he and Christine entertained, prevented Potau from building up much speed and saved his life. It gave Ihaka time to step around the constable and stop Potau in his tracks by clubbing him ferociously hard across the face with a baseball bat.

The subsequent search of Potau's flat proved productive: the sawn-off shotgun used on Pickrang and Gilpin was found under the bed; Pickrang's briefcase was amid the chest-high weeds in the backyard; and Julian Gage's memoir of Prince Albert College was on the kitchen table, splattered with grease and surrounded by unwashed dishes. Christine had made a shopping list on the back of one page and begun a letter to her mother in Gisborne on the back of another.

CHAPTER *26*

When Luther Potau woke up, he was taken to the Otara police station to be questioned about the murders of Herman Pickrang and Cec Gilpin. His sullen silence was standard Blood Drinkers' practise so it was some time before his interrogators realised that his speechlessness was not a matter of choice. He was ferried, under heavy guard, to Middlemore Hospital where X-rays of his spectacularly splintered facial bone structure swiftly became collector's items. At the Otara station Tito Ihaka re-read Julian Gage's letter before sending it into Central for Inspector Finbar McGrail's attention. Then he found himself a quiet corner and made three calls.

The first was to Reggie Sparks who, he learned from Mareena, had taken off up north somewhere and wasn't expected back till later. Her tone implied that it was already late. Under normal circumstances, Ihaka might've hesitated to ask her to go in search of the list of names and addresses which Dean Delamore had ripped out of her son's notebook but these were not normal circumstances. Because Mareena derived some comfort from Ihaka's interest in her wayward son, she did so. She found the list where her son had left it, in the downstairs TV room, and told Ihaka what he wanted to know, which was where Dermot Looms lived.

Ihaka thought long and hard before he made his next call. The obvious thing to do was to ring the Wellsford cops.

He imagined the conversation with whoever was on duty at the Wellsford station at that hour of the night: let's see, we've got a hanged girl at a private school ball in 1970, a dead witness and a blackmailing transvestite. And that's just for starters. What the fuck would they make of that in Wellsford? Christ, if someone rang him out of the blue at 11 o'clock at night with a story like that, he'd think the guy had been into the confiscated drugs. And assuming he convinced Wellsford to take it seriously, how about if they rousted a few guys out of bed and sent them out to Looms' place and the whole thing turned out to be a load of crap, a malicious fabrication? No two ways about it, he'd be the laughing stock of the entire police force.

So instead of ringing Wellsford, Ihaka's second call was to Blair Corvine, the undercover policeman.

"Mate, I need a gun."

There was a long silence. "Chief, last time I looked, we had more guns at Central than the fucking army so would you mind explaining why you're ringing me at this hour?"

"It's pretty complicated and I'm really stuck for time – let's just say it's a grey area."

"Now chief, think about this. Think about it very carefully. This sounds like it could be one of those fork-in-the-road-type decisions."

"Who wants promotion anyway? Just more fucking paperwork."

There was another silence. "It's your career buddy. What do you want?"

"A revolver will do."

"Oh just a revolver? I can't interest you in an Uzi machine pistol, you know 600 rounds a minute? What about a shoulder-launched missile, you let it go from the top of One Tree Hill and knock down the fucking Town Hall? Really get the job done."

"You're tempting me, you silver-tongued devil, but I'll settle for a revolver. Can you have it for me in an hour?"

They arranged to do the handover at midnight, by the Victoria Park pavilion.

Ihaka's third call was to Louise Appleyard. It was intended as a courtesy call, to let her know that they'd found Julian Gage's letter to her late husband. It turned out to be rather more than that.

"When can I read it?" was her first question.

"I don't know. We have to treat it like evidence so we can't go handing it round to the public."

"I'm not asking out of vague curiosity Sergeant," said Louise in clipped tones, "and I'm hardly just another member of the public."

"I'm well aware of that Mrs Appleyard. That's why I called in the first place."

"Well you've obviously read it; tell me what it says."

"Look I'm very sorry but I just don't have time. I'm a bit worried about your journalist friend Sparks."

"I saw Reggie this afternoon – he was okay. He said something about going up north."

"That's what worries me and that's where I'm off to now which is why . . ."

"What's up north Sergeant?"

Ihaka was wishing he'd never made the call. "A bloke called Dermot Looms."

"He was at the ball, wasn't he? Do you suspect him of something?"

"You could say that."

"I've got an excellent idea Sergeant. I'll go with you and you can brief me – isn't that what policemen say? – about the letter on the way."

Ihaka protested but Louise became very emphatic about how her late husband had started the whole thing and didn't that entitle her to some consideration? Ihaka thought of falling back on the excuse that it was police business but strictly speaking that wasn't the case. And while Ihaka could be an

247

accomplished liar when the need arose, he couldn't think of a single reason – apart from the obvious one of behaving like a responsible police officer – why he should deprive himself of the company of an attractive woman for the midnight drive.

It was 1.15am but the lights were still on in Looms' house when Ihaka pulled in behind Mrs Sparks' Peugeot which was still parked right by the front door.

"That's Reggie's car," said Louise.

Ihaka grunted and got the pistol out of the glovebox. In the deep, rural stillness, the music from the house was quite audible. It was Jimi Hendrix's *Hey Joe*, not that Ihaka recognised it, Hendrix having been a little before his time. "Listen to that," he said. "Sounds like they're having a party." He put the pistol back in the glovebox. "Guess I won't be needing it."

He told Louise, "You stay here – if I'm not back in 10 minutes, take off," and got out of the car. He walked up to the front door and knocked. No one came to the door. After he'd knocked again without response, Ihaka made his way around the side of the house.

The knocking startled Basil Batrouney. His friend Dermie had been due back half an hour before but, late or not, why should he knock when he had keys? Perhaps it was another of the nosey parkers with whom the Looms spread, despite its isolation, seemed to be infested. Batrouney decided to reconnoitre rather than answer the door. The upshot was that as Ihaka rounded the rear corner of the house and entered the rose garden, he trod heavily on the toes of an odd-looking specimen carrying a single-barrelled pump-action shotgun.

The former rock star received the bigger fright but not by much. Batrouney's perceptions of nosey parkers were largely based on Delamore and Sparks, neither of whom could be said to be physically intimidating. The third intruder had physical presence to burn as testified to by the appalling pain in his left

248

foot. For his part, Ihaka had had quite enough of lunatics with shotguns for one night. While this weirdo looked far less savage than Potau, Ihaka's instant impression was that he'd give Bad Louie a decent run for his money in the lunacy stakes.

They recoiled from the contact and eyed one another apprehensively for a few tense seconds.

"Whoa, take it easy amigo," said Ihaka holding up his hands in surrender. "I'm not looking for trouble. Sorry about the hour but I've got an urgent message for Dermot Looms. You him?"

Batrouney tightened his shaky grip on the shotgun and shook his head. Ihaka shifted his focus to a point over Batrouney's shoulder and flashed a bright grin. "You must be Dermot, right?"

The little charade was executed so smoothly that it would've taken in more alert individuals than Batrouney. Furthermore, being left alone to cope with the influx had made Batrouney fretful and therefore more susceptible to one of the older tricks in the book. His head whipped round as if on a spring. Ihaka shot out his right arm and wrenched the shotgun from his grasp. Batrouney looked back at Ihaka, appearing not to notice that he'd been disarmed.

"I can't see Dermie," he wailed. "Where is he?"

"My mistake," said Ihaka. "A trick of the moonlight." He leaned forward and tugged gently on Batrouney's woolly pullover. "Who are you?"

"Baz."

"Basil Batrouney?"

The former rock star nodded nervously.

"Well fuck me, the gang's all here," said Ihaka cheerfully. "Where's Sparks?"

"Who?"

Ihaka tightened his grip. "Reggie Sparks. His car's parked right outside the front door."

"I haven't seen him, I haven't seen anyone," jabbered

Batrouney. "I've just been grooving with Jimi and waiting for Dermie to come home."

Ihaka shifted his grip, gathering a handful of pullover from just below the neck. He jerked violently, hauling Batrouney up onto his toes. He put his face up to Batrouney's. "Do you want a fucking good hiding?" he asked in a tone of mild curiosity.

"Don't hurt me," moaned Batrouney, tears welling up in his eyes. "I'll show you."

He limped to the back door, took the key off the hook, led Ihaka down to the cellar door, and unlocked it. Ihaka stepped in front of him and pushed the door open. "Sparks," he called out. "It's Ihaka. You down there?"

"Look out," yelled Sparks from the darkness.

Ihaka whirled. Batrouney, teeth bared, stood on tiptoe with the secateurs raised above his head. As he began the downswing, Ihaka reversed the shotgun and jabbed the butt into his face, fracturing the former rock star's glasses as well as his nose. Batrouney shrieked piercingly and buried his face in his hands. Ihaka grabbed him by the pullover and held him at arm's length. "It's okay," he called into the cellar. "Come on out."

Sparks came out first followed by Delamore who had two perfect black eyes and whose badly bruised face glowed eerily in the half light coming from the kitchen window.

"Thanks for the warning," said Ihaka. "He get you that way, did he?"

Sparks nodded and gingerly rubbed the back of his head. "He sure did."

"Well if it's any consolation, I just gave him a fair poke right on the snotbox." He pushed Batrouney towards the door. "Okay pal, your turn in the dungeon."

Batrouney started to whimper and flap his arms but Ihaka shoved him roughly through the cellar door and locked it behind him.

Louise Appleyard was leaning back against the railing which fenced off the paddock to the right of Looms' house looking at the stars. She was getting cold and about to go back to the car when she saw headlights turn into the drive. The car came halfway up the drive but stopped when its headlights picked up the two cars parked in front of the house. The engine and lights were switched off and Louise heard a car door open and close. She moved deeper into the shadow of the garage.

Delamore, Ihaka and Sparks had just found a bottle of Scotch in a kitchen cupboard when Looms walked in the back door. He looked around slowly, took off his jacket and hung it over the back of a chair.

"Help yourself, why don't you?"

"Don't mind if I do," said Ihaka and took a hefty gulp. "You'd be Looms."

"And who might you be?"

"Ihaka's my name, Detective Sergeant out of Auckland Central."

Looms nodded impassively. "You're a ways from home, aren't you?" He walked over to the table, picked up the whisky bottle and took a swig. Ihaka casually dropped a hand on the stock of Batrouney's shotgun which lay on the table in front of him.

"Still, seeing you're here, Mr Detective Sergeant," said Looms, "I'd like to lay a complaint against Nancy Boy over there." He nodded at Delamore. "The cheeky little poof tried to blackmail me."

"Really?" said Ihaka. He studied Delamore who smiled shyly. "He looks as if he's got something to complain about himself." Ihaka turned back to Looms. "You know, there's one surefire way to take the wind out of his sails – just own up that you murdered Bronwen Ticehurst."

Looms frowned and was rubbing his chin as if he was seriously considering the suggestion when Lloyd Chennell slipped in the back door and pointed a .22 rifle at Ihaka.

"I don't think so," he said. "That would mean an awful lot of effort had been to no avail. Now if you'll put up your hands and step away from the table . . ."

They were in the living room, Delamore and Sparks sitting by the window on a large sofa with Ihaka in an armchair to their left. Looms and Chennell were on the other side of the room by the door, Chennell in an armchair with the rifle between his knees, its butt on the floor, and Looms on his feet, handling the shotgun like an extension of his arm.

Looms was speaking. "It's been a shit of a night, I don't mind telling you. First of all, I had to flag the Regis because there was a cop stationed outside the room, then Lloyd's flight was late . . ."

"Yoo hoo, anyone home?" Louise Appleyard's voice floated down the corridor from the back door. Sparks shot a horrified look at Ihaka who gave a short shake of his head, put his chin on his chest and massaged his forehead. Chennell, wide-eyed, turned to Looms who said "I don't fucking well believe this . . ." He held the shotgun down by his side and put his head round the door.

"Hi there," said Louise advancing down the corridor. "Pardon me for barging in but I seem to have mislaid my driver."

"He's probably in here," said Looms. "Half of Auckland is."

Louise entered the room. "Oh there you are," she said brightly, apparently oblivious to the charged atmosphere. "I got sick of sitting in the car so . . ." Her face fell as she noticed Chennell's rifle. "What's going on?"

Looms showed the shotgun. "Why don't you hop over there on that sofa?"

Louise sat next to Delamore, her hands clasped together between her knees but otherwise looking remarkably composed. Sparks did his best to give her an encouraging smile.

"Is that the lot?" said Looms wonderingly. "Or are there a few more wandering around out there?"

"You must be Dermot Looms," said Louise. "Is it true what Julian Gage wrote about you?"

Ihaka started to look up, then thought better of it. Looms looked puzzled. "How come you've seen that?" he asked.

"The sergeant showed it to me on the way up here," she said. Everyone exchanged glances. Louise looked at Ihaka. "Shouldn't I've said that?" she asked anxiously. Ihaka looked up, spluttered, and looked back at his shoes.

Looms guffawed. "Well bugger me. Here's me running all over the show looking for that bloody thing and we've got a door-to-door delivery." He stopped short. "Jesus, I completely forgot about Baz – where the hell is he?" He glared at Ihaka. "You didn't shove him in the cellar did you, you lousy bastard? The poor bugger'll be going frantic."

Looms swapped guns with Chennell. "I'm going to let Baz out and get Gage's letter," he said. "If they try anything Lloyd, let 'em have it." He left the room.

Chennell stood up and held the shotgun across his stomach, pointing away from his captives. When Louise heard the back door open and close, she reached under her loose white top and pulled Ihaka's revolver out of the waistband of her leggings. She pointed it at Chennell and told him to put his gun down.

Chennell stood stock still. Louise sat on the edge of the sofa holding the pistol at arm's length in both hands. Her eyes stayed on Chennells' face like a spotlight but she was struggling to hold the pistol steady.

"My dear," said Chennell huskily, "are you really prepared to kill me?"

The back door opened. The pistol wavered in Louise's grip. Chennell breathed deeply and shifted his hands on the shotgun.

"You do realise Louise," said Sparks conversationally, "that these fuckers killed Victor?"

Chennell saw something red flare at the back of Louise's eyes a split-second before she shot him through the fatty deposit above his right hip, the area sometimes referred to as a "love handle". He squealed, dropped the gun and clutched his wound.

Ihaka leapt across the room and snatched up the shotgun. He peered into the corridor. Batrouney was standing in the kitchen doorway fumbling with the rifle. There was no sign of Looms. Ihaka told Batrouney to drop the rifle. Batrouney squinted down the corridor, screamed "You locked me in the dark" and raised the rifle. At that moment Looms, having failed to find Gage's letter in either car and alarmed by the gunshot, opened the front door and received a bullet, meant for Ihaka, in the Adam's apple. He made an horrendous gurgling sound, fell over backwards, and proceeded to die noisily on the front porch. Ihaka hurriedly lined up on Batrouney's legs and fired. His intention was to disable Batrouney without killing him and in that he succeeded. His aim being high, he also put paid to the prospect of there ever being any little Batrouneys, not that the former rock star had shown any inclination towards reproductive activity for the better part of two decades.

CHAPTER 27

*T*en days later Reggie Sparks received a letter from Tito Ihaka. It said:

Kia ora Reggie boy,
Just to let you know where things are at, it looks like we're going to close the book on the whole thing. Batrouney hasn't said a word since the gunfight at the OK Corral – I know he wasn't too flash to start with but he's just a veggie now.

Chennell's a different kettle of shit: if we really bust a gut, we might be able to get him on some sort of conspiracy charge but those turkeys in the crown prosecutor's office aren't being much help – "in view of the most unusual circumstances of this case, we couldn't proceed against Mr Chennell with any real degree of confidence". You wouldn't believe the mealy-mouthed crap those characters come up with. Up at the farm, he didn't actually do that much apart from giving Calamity Jane a bit of target practice. There is a school of thought around here (ie me) which feels that the precise details of what happened up there should be allowed to fade into obscurity – if you get my drift. As you'd expect, anything to do with Bronwen Ticehurst just goes straight into the "too hard" file. We let Chennell know that, whatever happens, his school in

Sydney would hear all about it – his lawyer reckons he's already resigned – but we'll tell them anyway to bugger up his job prospects. Apart from that he'll probably walk.

Part of the reason we went easy on Chennell, as I guess you've heard from Louise, is that he explained what happened to her husband. After Gage told Appleyard the answer was on the dance card, he starting working his way through the names (and hired Guttle to check out Lydiate). He went and saw Batrouney on Waiheke and apparently coaxed part of the story out of him. When Batrouney realised what he'd done, he went frothing off to Looms. Looms set up a meeting with Appleyard somewhere here in town and pulled the same trick he pulled on Dolores Delamore – Baz in the back seat with a gun. About four in the morning they made Appleyard drive onto the Bridge with Looms in his car right behind, stopped at the top, and Looms just manhandled him over the edge. If they'd been really unlucky, they might've been spotted on the monitor but the cameras don't cover the whole Bridge the whole time and whoever was on duty was probably doing the crossword anyway. Fair go – some of the kids joining the force these days don't even move their lips when they read. He was a hard man, Looms. Good job Batrouney was such a fucking lousy shot.

Anyway, the insurance company has been advised so Louise gets her dough after all. While we're on that subject, a word of advice – strike while the iron's hot. It's obvious that you're keen on her but a woman like that won't be on her tod for long. I didn't realise she'd actually gone a few rounds with Quedley but I gather that's history. She told me you opened her eyes to what a complete cunt he was or words to that effect. That's not a bad start. Wasn't it Mahatma Gandhi who said that if you can open a woman's eyes, her legs will soon follow? Maybe it was Errol Flynn.

Well on that philosophical note, I'll sign off. Seeing there shouldn't be any legal complications, you can go full steam ahead on your story. Just go easy when you reach the bit about unregistered handguns popping up out of nowhere and retards getting shotgun vasectomies etc. Attached is a copy of Gage's letter which I thought might help. I don't ask much in return – just that your story should make it clear that my role in this little saga amounted to the niftiest piece of intuitive policework since the Crewe murder case. I'll also be very dark if you don't expose Quedley as a shiteating swine. You can quote me on that.

Hasta la vista

Chief Inspector Tito Ihaka (only a matter of time after the article comes out).

PS Burn this.

Sparks turned to Julian Gage's letter to Victor Appleyard.

Dear Victor,

First of all, let me repeat how very much I appreciated your gesture in the restaurant that night. I hope I'm wrong but I strongly suspect that very few men in your position would break off from a business dinner to speak to someone whose appearance rather encourages others to assume the worst. I also enjoyed and appreciated your subsequent visits and our chats. Many thanks too for the books. I know it's customary to tell giftgivers that they shouldn't have but I'll skip that fib and simply say I enjoyed them enormously, particularly the Jan Morris book about Venice which brought back some wonderful memories.

To say that your comments about poor Bronwen Ticehurst set me thinking would be a gross under-statement; I've thought of little else. I was deeply moved that you haven't forgotten Bronwen and are still troubled by her death (and deeply shamed by the invidious contrast with my own behaviour).

Once or twice I was on the verge of telling you the whole story but I just couldn't bring myself to do so. I suppose it's just a case that I've suppressed it for so long, I now find it terribly difficult to contemplate, let alone talk about. No doubt you found my coyness aggravating. I dare say my gesture of producing Bronwen's dance card with accompanying hints struck you as self-indulgently theatrical. I apologise. As I say, I have buried the knowledge of that episode so deep within me that it requires an immense, almost physical, effort to dredge it up again and these days my physical resources are limited. I might also say, in mitigation of my coyness, self-indulgence and theatricality, that it's not easy to break the habits of a lifetime.

Anyway so much for explanations and self-justification. Today has been rather a momentous day. I have finally come to terms with the fact of my imminent death. My doctor, bless him, still goes through convolutions to avoid stating the obvious and to find an aspect of my impressive range of ailments about which he can say something remotely encouraging. Like me however, he is fighting a losing battle, the futility of which becomes more pronounced by the day. His whole demeanour delivers an unmistakable message which he can't bring himself to put into words. In the wider scheme of things of course, this is making a drama out of the all-too-mundane; after all, I could hardly expect the laws of nature and medicine to be suspended on my behalf, could I? Nonetheless one lives in hope. Well I no longer do. I shall now concentrate on dying in peace.

The significance of my embracing fatalism is that it has concentrated the mind on the task of clearing out the emotional and spiritual baggage which I either won't need or don't want where I'm going. I have therefore resolved to tell you the full story of what happened at Prince Albert College in 1970. I shall write it down and have it sent to you when I've shuffled off this mortal coil. I know that's somewhat cowardly but it's the only way I can do it. It also has for me the immense attraction that I won't have to live with the knowledge of your contempt, for assuredly that is what you'll feel towards me when you've finished this letter. Your friendship and sympathy have meant a great deal to me and I am selfish enough to want to retain them for the short while I have left.

To begin at the beginning: I'm not sure how old I was when I began to suspect that I was gay but certainly by the time I started at Prince Albert in 1968. Of course, you were a day boy and I'm not sure how much naughtiness went on amongst the day boys. In most of the boarding house dormitories though, there was a constant hum of furtive activity, mostly what we called "mutuals" – tossing off the boy in the next bed after lights out providing he'd return the favour.

If I had to put a figure on it, I'd estimate that at least 50 per cent of boarders indulged in boy-boy sex. It had nothing at all to do with homosexuality in the sense of that being their sexual preference; it was simply a case of deprivation, through being in an all-male environment, on the one hand, and opportunity on the other. Sheer proximity is, after all, the most potent aphrodisiac. I can't say I ever came across anyone who refused to indulge because they had fierce moral objections; most of the non-participants either had extremely modest sexual appetites or were too timid or were so repulsive that no one with an ounce of self-respect would handle them wearing ski mitts.

As I say, there was no particular opprobrium attached to it in one's first and second year but once one reached the fifth form, it was a different matter. To continue from that point was considered to denote a preference; far healthier to satisfy one's urges in privacy with a *Playboy* and a wankie hankie. Those who kept at it were either too ugly or socially inept to get their fingers up during the holidays (excuse the coarseness but the disgusting schoolboy phraseology keeps popping into my head), or were blessed or cursed with excessive randiness or belonged to the tiny minority who just preferred boys and didn't give a hoot for the consequences in terms of being whispered about, sneered at or bullied. With all due modesty, I was the outstanding example of the latter. I have no doubt that I was the most sexually active Prince Albertian of my era; a respectable but nonetheless distant second would have been Caspar Quedley, which is where the tale really begins.

I became infatuated with Caspar in 1969, an easy enough date to remember. He was scarcely aware of my existence; with me being a second year and him a fourth year there were, under the rigid hierarchy of the boarding houses, limited opportunities for contact. Early the following year, however, we were both in the school play, Julius Caesar. Caspar was a thrilling Mark Antony while I had a non-speaking part as one of the friends, Romans, countrymen whose ears he borrowed. In the course of the rehearsals, I managed to inveigle my way into his acquaintance and, at the first opportunity, proclaimed my love and put myself at his disposal. Caspar wasn't in the least embarrassed or perturbed. He said he was flattered but didn't think it was quite his cup of Earl Grey; if he ever changed his mind or felt the inclination to experiment, he'd know where to come, as it were.

We became friends. We were both outsiders, in my case because of my hotly and widely rumoured filthy and unnatural tendencies; in Caspar's because he saw himself as underprivileged – it never ceased to amaze me how someone so well-endowed could feel so deprived – and this drew us together. Caspar didn't give a damn and had a perverse sense of humour so it amused him, being the official college stud, to ostentatiously keep company with the college queer. He also took an intense interest in what I got up to and insisted on being kept fully informed of my dalliances. I thought this was rather promising until I discovered that he was extracting money from some of my partners on threat of exposure. I was furious but Caspar could talk his way out of anything. He was also a very skilful flirt which kept alive the tantalising prospect of my yearnings being reciprocated, in my mind at least.

I was quite a holy boy, believe it or not. I was in the choir, by that stage a light tenor after a stint as the boy soprano – you might have heard me doing the *Once in Royal David's City* solo at the end-of-year carol service. I was also a sacristan which involved helping the chaplain, Padre Swindell, with various little chores around the chapel. The chaplain took a shine to me and was forever inviting me into his flat for a cup of tea and a chocolate biscuit. I thought nothing of this until one night he completely floored me by producing a cane and imploring me to thrash him. Not wanting to seem churlish, I obliged and the poor old thing just about put his back out trying to conceal his erection.

I'm sure you can guess the rest. I told Caspar who straightaway saw the commercial possibilities. The next time I took tea with the chaplain, I left the door off the lock and Caspar just happened to wander in while I was administering the medicine. He pretended to be shocked, horrified, revolted etc – he really was a superb actor – then told me to clear off so he could negotiate the price of his silence. Caspar told me afterwards that the chaplain was as worried about me as about his own position: he said something to the effect that "Julian is innocent in every sense of the word; he has no idea that he was providing me with gratification". That made it even worse when he drove his car into a brick wall a few weeks later.

Although it was presented as an accident, the rumours of suicide were soon rife. I worked myself up into a real state. Caspar eventually gave me a talking to: yes, Padre Swindell had killed himself, he said, but it had nothing to do with us. He claimed the chaplain had told him he had an incurable disease, hence the suicide. It was a lie, of course, as he admitted a few years later. He was worried that I'd break down and confess all and had made up the story to subdue my conscience.

After that you'd think we'd have shied away from these dangerous games but not a bit of it. The next to find his way into the honey trap was Lloyd Chennell, who taught history as you'd remember and was assistant house master in my house. However Lloyd was far from being the passive, guilt-ridden soul that Padre Swindell had been. I began picking up unmistakable signals from him and one night in his study, in the course of reviewing my academic performance, came the inevitable hand on the knee.

Although Lloyd was certainly no matinee idol, he was really my first sexual partner who was more experienced than I – he was about 26 then as I remember. A number of the boys I'd been with were older than me but I was always the knowing one, the one in control. Lloyd was quite adroit; he had the touch. Some do and some don't and, in my experience, it's almost impossible to tell in advance. Nor does having the touch seem to bear much, if any, relation to a person's general sexiness either in terms of their appearance or their ardour. Some of my most handsome and ardent lovers have been the most ham-fisted.

Of course I told Caspar and shortly thereafter he struck terms with Lloyd. It all seemed to be conducted in a very civilised manner. Lloyd certainly never took umbrage with me for telling Caspar although I suppose, in hindsight, he was rather addicted to me. Quite what Caspar got out of it I'm not sure – far more, in various ways, than he let on would be my guess. There was money of course and the famous episode with the exam paper which almost gave Lloyd a heart attack. He slipped Caspar the paper in advance solely for his own benefit, never dreaming that he'd make copies and sell them. Theirs was a curious relationship, not friendship exactly but certainly not the fear and loathing you'd expect under the circumstances. Perhaps Lloyd was bedazzled by Caspar too.

I'm sure you've found all this exceedingly distasteful and boring but I assure you it is relevant. So we come to the 1970 school ball. Needless to say I didn't go. The non-attendees had a free night but I stayed in. I forget why – it mustn't have suited my parents to have me home. Lloyd was one of the masters whose job it was to wander round at the ball and discourage tongue kissing and dry uprights (there I go again) on the dance floor. He suggested to me that if I felt left out, he could slip away from the ball at some point for a quickie. We arranged a rendezvous in the belltower, above the library, at 10.45pm.

I don't know if you ever saw the place but if you went up that spiral staircase from the library floor, you found yourself in this series of little rooms, a bit of a rabbit warren really, which were essentially used for storage. They contained the overflow from the library, books which had been weeded out, old furniture etc. We were in the third or fourth room along, playing with one another in the dark, when we heard approaching footsteps and the murmur of voices, one of which was unmistakably female.

We froze as they advanced through the rooms towards us. They stopped in the one next to ours. There were no doors – just a series of connecting rooms opening into one another – so we could hear every word. There were two boys and a girl and they'd come up for a smoke and a tipple. They debated whether or not to turn on the light; one of the boys, obviously the ring leader, said they wouldn't be able to see what they were doing otherwise and what did it matter anyway, there were no windows and who the hell was going to come up? So they switched on a light and began puffing and swigging and sniggering. Meanwhile Lloyd and I crouched in the dark just round the corner not even daring to put our trousers back on for fear of giving ourselves away. Lloyd, needless to say, was almost paralysed with fear.

After 10 minutes or so of eavesdropping, I'd worked out that the boys were Dermot Looms, a prime example of the large farm-bred louts whom Prince

Albert seemed to attract, and Basil Batrouney, a creepy youth known for his musical pretensions. It was apparent that something was amiss with the girl, whose name was Bronwen. Before long we learned that the agent of her unhappiness was none other than Caspar Quedley. From what we could gather, Bronwen had a major crush on Caspar but he'd just made it plain that it wasn't reciprocated. I couldn't help thinking, welcome to the club, sister.

After what seemed like forever but was probably less than half an hour, the booze – they had a bottle of brandy, Portuguese I think it was – was taking its toll. Bronwen started sniffling. Looms suggested that Caspar wasn't the only fish in the sea and why didn't she forget about him and have some fun. Nothing was said for a little while – I suspect she was sitting there a bit bamboozled by the brandy while Looms nibbled on her. Then the trouble started: Looms tried to force the pace and Batrouney wanted to join in. Whether they lured her up there with the aim of getting her drunk and taking turns or whether it was spur of the moment, I just don't know. Whatever, she was having none of it. She hissed at them to fuck off and leave her alone, that she wouldn't kiss Batrouney if he was the last boy on earth and that if Looms thought she'd take her panties off for him, he was even stupider than he looked. Looms called her a cockteaser; Batrouney accused her of being a stuck-up bitch. Their voices got louder as the violence of their language escalated. She said they could screw each other for all she cared but she was going; Looms roared back, like hell you are; she screamed at him to let her go. There was the sound of a struggle and a sharp slap; Looms called her a fucking slut, and then I heard this indescribable rasping choke. Without thinking about it, I ran in there pulling on my pants and screaming at them to stop it.

Then the four of us were staring at one another, thunderstruck, struggling to make sense of the evidence of our own eyes. The girl lay on the floor between us. At first, of course, none of us believed she was dead – we thought she'd fainted – and our concerns centred on having been caught in the act of considerably lesser crimes although Lloyd was staring professional ruin in the face. For a minute no one said anything. When I broke the silence by asking if the girl was all right, Looms knelt over her and tried to bring her round. Then he stood up and said quite calmly, "I'd say she's dead." She'd slapped him and he'd seized her by the throat and throttled her. It wouldn't have taken much; he was big and strong and Bronwen was quite delicate. Looms looked at Lloyd and said, "Sir, I think it would be for the best if we all forget what's happened here."

He was astonishingly cool. Batrouney was dazed – he was quite drunk and I don't think he really comprehended the situation; I was crying; Lloyd was in a state of shock, looking from Bronwen to Looms and saying "Of course, of course" over and over. Then he seemed to snap out of it. What was extraordinary then was how he and Looms suddenly seemed to be on the same wavelength. Crises create strange alliances, I suppose. It was only later that I came to realise that from Lloyd's point of view, Bronwen dying was a godsend. Her death necessitated the conspiracy of silence which also enveloped the lesser crimes and misdemeanours, of which his was by far the most serious.

He and Looms organised it between them. The hanging was Lloyd's idea. They used my tie; I was in the ordinary evening uniform, those pants that chafed like mad and a blazer with a standard school tie. The other two were in full black suits and couldn't go back into the ball without a tie, nor could Lloyd, so I had to provide the noose. There was a sturdy rail which must've been used for a curtain or drape to block off the doorway and they hung her from that. Lloyd looped the tie round her neck and stood on a chair to attach it to the rail while Looms held Bronwen off the ground. Then he let her go and she dangled there like a broken doll.

Lloyd told me to get back to the house and to go straight to bed, not to talk to anyone, and to see him the next morning. When I undressed, I found her dance card in my coat pocket. I didn't even remember picking it up. The next day Lloyd gave me a lecture about how it was a terrible accident, they hadn't meant to kill her, but what was done was done and nothing that happened now would bring her back. If the truth got out, all our lives would be ruined so it was better to forget about it, to pretend it never happened. He said I had to be really tough and tell absolutely no one even though there would be times when I'd want nothing more than to confide in someone to get it off my chest. It must've had some effect I suppose; until today, I've never told anyone. He also found me a new tie from somewhere.

I never went with Lloyd again. We did talk about Bronwen a few times; I remember asking him why it never came out that Bronwen had been drinking. He said they would've hushed it up for her parents' sake. For weeks afterwards I expected to be called down to the housemaster's study to find a policeman waiting for me but it never happened. Eventually it dawned on me that it suited everyone – except the Ticehurst family – to treat it as suicide. If the truth had come out, the scandal would've rocked Prince Albert to its foundations and there was far too much money and power and prestige tied up in the school itself and the old boy network – the old school tie syndrome – for that to be allowed to happen. Probably still is.

Perhaps you think that's cynical. Then consider this: if they knew that Bronwen had been drinking, it would've been a reasonable, if not irresistible, assumption that she wouldn't have done so on her own. Not many 16-year-old girls are solo drinkers and she'd hardly have headed off to the ball with a bottle of brandy in her handbag. That opens up all sorts of scenarios, so why didn't the police make an effort to find out who her drinking companions were?

Secondly, how was she supposed to have found her way up to the belltower? Some of the boys wouldn't have even known those rooms were up there. Thirdly, remember how we had to have a name label stitched onto every item of clothing including ties? Lloyd ripped the label off my tie; did the police think Bronwen had done it herself? And where had she got the tie from in the first place?

So there you are Victor. It hasn't salved my conscience but I feel better for knowing that I won't be taking this secret with me. Now that you know, what are you going to do with the knowledge? I'm sure you've heard the old curse – Chinese? – that may you get what you've always wanted? I find it hard to imagine that your peace of mind will be enhanced should you pursue the matter – if anything the reverse. On the other hand, I can vouch for the fact that to know and keep silent eats away at the soul like acid.

God bless you
Julian Gage

When he'd finished reading the letter, Sparks rang Tito Ihaka.

"Thanks for sending me Gage's letter."

"That's okay Reggie. Use it wisely."

"Was he right?"

"What about?"

"You know what I'm talking about – that the investigation was tanked because it suited everyone to call it suicide."

"How the fuck would I know? I was nine years old."

"Don't pretend you haven't looked at the file."

"Sparks, are you asking me as a journalist?"

"Yes."

"In that case, the answer to your question is no, Gage wasn't right. The investigation was properly conducted and thorough in every respect."

"Okay, just between the two of us."

Ihaka said, "Between the two of us, I'm surprised you have to ask," and put the phone down.

Two days later, a Wednesday, a foretaste of summer arrived unheralded in Auckland. A warm wind blew in from the north and the temperature nudged over 20 degrees for the first time in months. Reggie Sparks was driving Louise Appleyard to the airport to catch a plane to Brisbane. She was going to spend some time with her sister; an indefinite amount of time.

As they skimmed alongside the Manukau Harbour foreshore she asked, "Did you see Gage's letter in the end?"

"Yeah, Ihaka sent me a copy."

"What did you think?"

Sparks looked at Louise who looked back at him through big dark glasses. Her window was half open and the breeze whipped around her head, fluffing up her dark mane.

"I thought it was sad. Sad for Bronwen, sad for Gage, sad for Victor."

She nodded. "I've been meaning to ask," she said. "What

made you go up to Looms' farm? I mean, how did you know?"

"I didn't have to be Sherlock Holmes. Delamore knew the whole story because he'd had Gage's letter; I knew he'd gone north and when Quedley said Delamore had told him he was going to talk to someone else about the letter, the obvious conclusion was that he'd gone to see Looms."

"Where's he by the way?"

Sparks smiled. "Delamore? He went back to Sydney to get his face fixed up. He said if they could make him pretty again, he'd go back in the drag show. He's decided he's not quite devious enough to operate on the edge, plus it's too hard on his looks."

"Second question. How did you know Looms had co-murdered Victor?"

"Oh that was just an educated guess. It seemed to me all along that if Victor was murdered, whoever killed Bronwen must've done it. But I was just trying to give you a bit of motivation."

"Well you did. I needed some."

After a while he asked, "So why did you go up there?"

Louise gave him a brilliant, slightly mocking smile. "Reggie, don't tell me you haven't figured that out. You've been so clever about everything else."

He shook his head. "Sorry, you got me there."

"Because," she said, stretching out the word, "Tito thought you might be in danger."

Sparks nodded slowly. "Oh that's why? And here was I thinking you just wanted the chance to shoot someone."

He pulled up in front of the overseas terminal and carried her bags inside. She thanked him for the lift and told him not to wait around.

"Okay." He hovered awkwardly. "Well, have a nice trip."

"Thanks." She gave him a long look. It was part amusement and part fondness. He thought there might have been a part something else too but seeing she was going away and hadn't booked her return, he felt it was prudent to settle for amused and fond. "Reggie, I've been thinking that in a few weeks' time, when my sister and I are no longer on speaking terms, I might come home via New Caledonia. You speak French don't you?"

"Yeah pretty well. I used to think it was my only attribute but it's not a lot of use to me here."

"Oh it's definitely an attribute. I was wondering, perhaps you could come up and be my interpreter, you know, and introduce me to French culture and whatnot. Don't worry about the money – I'd take care of that, now that I'm rich." She tilted her head and raised her eyebrows questioningly.

"Sounds great," said Sparks hesitantly, wondering if he dared believe his ears. "But forget that stuff about paying for me – I'd feel like a kept man."

Louise nodded gravely. "Yes you're probably right. First of all I'd want to be sure you were worth keeping."

She gave him a sly smile from beneath lowered lashes that would throw his sleep patterns into disarray for several days, put one hand on his chest, and kissed him softly on the lips. "I'll be in touch."

Sparks drove home feeling slightly light-headed. He went straight to the desk he'd installed in the downstairs TV room. On the desk was a laptop computer which his brother Gavin had lent him and pages and pages of notes. Sparks studied his notes for a while, turned on the computer and stared at the illuminated screen.

Then he started to write: It was entirely appropriate that Wallace Guttle, the private investigator, should have spent the last hour of his life looking at pictures of other people having sex . . . .

ISBN 1-86958-068-0

Published in 1994 by Moa Beckett Publishers Limited,
P.O. Box 100-749, North Shore Mail Centre,
Auckland 1330, New Zealand.

Printed by Australian Print Group, Melbourne

The

Military Airfields
of Wales

The
Military Airfields
of Wales

Alan Phillips

bridge
books

Military Airfields of Wales
First published in Wales by
BRIDGE BOOKS
61 Park Avenue
Wrexham, LL12 7AW

A CIP entry for this book is available from the British Library

ISBN   1-84494-019-5

Printed and bound by
Cromwell Press Ltd
Trowbridge

Contents

Introduction and Acknowledgements

It was probably inevitable that certain parts of Wales would be chosen as the locations for airfields in times of emergency; the country is distant from continental Europe, making it a relatively safe area for both military bases and government establishments. This book is a study of the thirty-nine military bases that were constructed in the principality between 1914 and 1944 to put some facts and flesh onto the bare bones of a deserted control tower or former RAF canteen building. It is easy to forget those servicemen and servicewomen who worked, and in so many cases, died, in Wales either through enemy action, navigation error or simply a bad judgement call. This book, hopefully, does something to preserve their memory.

Before embarking on a study of the various military airfields it is perhaps worth looking briefly at some of the pioneers who brought aviation to the country.

In 1802 Francis Barret attempted to make the first balloon ascent from Welsh soil but, unfortunately, the balloon was destroyed. Ten years later, John Sadler flew over the Great Orme in a balloon whilst attempting to make the first attempt to cross the Irish Sea by air. The mantle was then taken up by Charles Green in Cardiff in 1847, but the first true Welsh-born pioneer was William Frost who, having read about the achievements of Yorkshireman Sir George Caley, made several attempts to fly a glider in 1895.

At the time that the Wright brothers were experimenting with their heavier-than-air powered flights at Kittyhawk, Captain A. E. Smith made several flights in Wales in 1901–03 and was followed by Charles Rolls of Monmouth who ended up, in July 1910, with the unfortunate claim to fame of being not only a partner in Rolls-Royce cars but also the first British man to be killed in an aeroplane accident. In 1910, former actor Robert Loraine made several attempts to fly to Ireland from north Wales, two years before Irishmen Denys Corbett-Wilson and Damien Allen attempted the crossing. The former successfully landed near Wexford on 27 April 1912, but the latter disappeared without trace having having last been seen after crossing the Welsh coast near Holyhead, *en route* for Dublin.

Numerous pioneers, including Gustav Hamel, Edwin Prosser, Henry Astley and Vivian Hewitt gave flying displays in Wales and John Herbert and Henry Howard were the first Welshmen to gain the Royal Aero Club Certificate. In 1913, the James brothers of Narberth in Pembrokeshire built their own aeroplane and were soon carrying passengers until their activities were interrupted by the outbreak of war in 1914. At the University College of North Wales, Bangor, Ellis Williams designed and built his own flying machine and carried out trial flights on Red Wharf Bay, Anglesey in 1913.

The major role played by Wales in the first air war (other than as a source for manpower for the infant Royal Flying Corps and Royal Naval Air Service) was as a base for anti-submarine patrols over the Irish Sea, Liverpool Bay, the Bristol Channel and the Western Approaches.

Perhaps the first post-war air enthusiast in Wales was Cardiff businessman Samuel Instone, who began a scheduled air service from Cardiff to London in 1919 (later extended to Paris). For most people, however, aeroplanes were a novelty, and pleasure flights were common from coastal areas such as Swansea Sands, Pendine Sands, Locks Common, Coity Fields, Red Wharf Bay and Rhyl Sands and, in the late 1920s, Sir Alan Cobham's flying circus introduced flying to many inland sites throughout the country. The events leading to the outbreak of the Second World War resulted in the earmarking of several sites in Wales for airfield development, a programme which proceeded rapidly once hostilities had begun. There were two main fighter stations (Valley and Fairwood Common) and a number of subsidiaries (e.g. Angle, Llanbedr, Pembrey and Wrexham). Most of the airfields and bases in Pembrokeshire played a significant role in the Battle of the Atlantic under the control of RAF Coastal Command. The bulk of the other airfields were involved in personnel training, especially gunners and bomb-aimers.

On the restoration of peace, most of the airfields were closed down, although some were converted to a civilian role (e.g. Aberporth, Fairwood, Rhoose and Withybush). Others were later re-opened for private flying (e.g. Llandwrog).

The RAF maintained four operational airfields throughout the 1950s viz Llanbedr, Sealand, St Athan and Valley while the Royal Navy took control of Brawdy. In 1974, Brawdy passed into RAF control. Today, the RAF has a presence only at Sealand, St Athan and Valley. Most of the other airfields have been redeveloped as industrial estates, have reverted to farmland or have been built upon.

My grateful thanks are extended to the following for their valuable assistance and information:
Airbus UK Ltd, Hawarden (Sue Cutts); Aircraft Museum (Wales), Cardiff Airport; RAF Air Historical branch; BAe Systems; Mr Norman Bird, RAF Sealand Museum; Caernarfon Air Park Museum, Caernarfon Airport; Cardiff International Airport; W/Cmdr A. P. Davies RAF (Retired); DERA, Aberporth (R. Unsworth) and Llanbedr; W/Cmdr Bill Doddsworth RAF (Retired);.Denzil

Edwards; Fleet Air Arm Museum, Yeovilton; S/Ldr Ivor Griffiths, RAF (Retied); Haverfordwest Aerodrome; Swansea Airport (Sarah Hopkins); Imperial War Museum, London; Mrs Wendy Mills; National Museum of Wales; Benjamin Owen; Pembrey Aerodrome; Pembrokeshire Aviation Group; various public libraries throughout Wales; National Archives, Kew; RAF Museum, Hendon; RAF Sealand; RAF Valley; Scolton Museum, Haverfordwest; *Western Mail*; *Western Telegraph*. I would also like to thank numerous individuals who contributed a wealth of information and photographs for this book and a special thanks to the ex-airmen and women and ground staff, without whose assistance the book would not have been possible.

Finally, my gratitude goes out to all those people who contributed photographs for the book, especially Air Heritage (Wales). All photographs are from the author's own collection or from Air Heritage unless otherwise stated.

Alan Phillips

1. Aberporth

Ceredigion

Aberporth airfield is located near the small village of Blaenannerch on the A487 Aberystwyth to Cardigan road, some four miles from the town of Cardigan. The main entrance to the base is just off the B4333 road that leads to the picturesque seaside village of Aberporth. Today, the main purpose of the airfield is to provide support for the Rocket Research Establishment that is situated on the headland south of Aberporth village. The airfield can be easily seen from both the A487 and the B4333 roads, as well as from other vantage points around its perimeter.

The airfield covers an area of approximately 118 acres and consists of one 3,003' x 75' tarmac runway (08/26) with linked taxiways to the two T2 hangars that were built in 1939. There are also two grass runways (04/22 and 15/33) which are still used by light aircraft and gliders.

The history of Aberporth (or RAF Blaenanerch as it was originally known) goes back to 1939 when land was acquired from local landowners to build an airfield. A large area was levelled to accommodate reasonably-sized grass landing strips with good approaches. Two T2 hangars were constructed, together with associated workshops. All the accommodation was of Maycrete or Nissen type huts, which were essential for such a bleak location.

The airfield was officially opened in December 1940 as part of RAF Army Co-operation Command to operate target facilities required by an Anti-aircraft Training Unit (AATU) stationed on the cliff top on the headland south of the base.

The first unit to occupy the base was Nº 1 AACU equipped with Wallace and Henley aeroplanes which were the main target-towing aircraft of the time. Although the first aircraft to use the new airfield was a Hawker Henley Mk III belonging to Nº 1 AACU (which was based at Carew Cheriton) on 3 August 1939. Throughout 1940 several aircraft from Carew visited the airfield, usually to the annoyance of the contractors that were still working on the airfield. RAF Blaenannerch was renamed RAF Aberporth later in the year.

On 11 April 1941, the Prime Minister, Mr Winston Churchill, visited RAF Aberporth, which drew a large crowd from all over the area.

The first flight to be transferred to Aberporth was 'L' Flight of Nº 1 AACU followed, on 1 July 1941, by 'Q' Flight. One flight of Queen Bee pilotless aircraft had already moved in during December 1941/January 1942 and were stored in

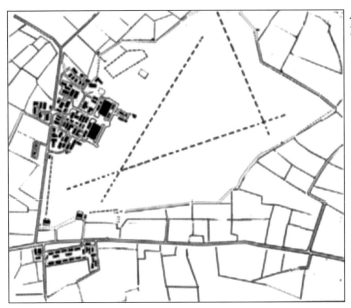

Aberporth airfield, 1944.

the two hangars. In a reshuffle on 1 October 1942 'B' Flight became N° 1607 Flight and 'Q' Fllight became N° 1609 Flight and the Queen Bee flight became N° 1621 Flight.

In November 1942 the aircraft inventory for N° 1608 Flight (which had arrived in July 1942) showed that it comprised six Henleys, two Wallaces, one Martinet, two Tiger Moths and two Hurricanes, but, within a year, it had been re-equipped, mostly with Martinets. The Flight was responsible for providing target-towing service for the gunnery ranges in the Cardigan Bay area for the three services. In July 1943 the unit provided air–air firing targets for Pembroke Dock-based Sunderlands and Catalina flying-boats.

The Flight was not without its accidents, some just resulting in damaged aircraft, but some were serious such as that of 25 May 1942 when a Henley crashed killing both crew members.

N° 1609 Flight's inventory was similar to that of its sister flight with Henleys and Tiger Moths but, until January/February 1943

A radio-controlled Queen Bee being put through its paces.

Hawker Hurricane 1c taxying on the grass strip at Aberporth. [RAE]

when they were transferred to RAF Bodorgan, Anglesey, it had also three Fairey Battles. The three AACU Flights were disbanded on 30 November 1943 to became part of N° 595 Squadron

In June 1942 a detachment of Avro Ansons of N° 6 AOS from RAF Staverton were transferred to Aberporth. They remained in west Wales until January 1943 when they returned to their former base.

To provide airfield defence a detachment of 185 NCOs and other ranks from N° 2758 Squadron RAF Regiment arrived on 9 September 1942.

From 1 December 1943 the main unit based at Aberporth was N° 595 Squadron which was split into three flights: 'A' Flight providing co-operation for the

Hawker Henley L3387 of N° 1609 Flight, forced landed in a field at Tregaron, 8 November 1943.

The Miles Martinet TT1 was the mainstay of N° 595 Squadron based at Aberporth.
[RAE]

gunnery camp at Aberporth; 'B' Flight providing co-operation with the light anti-aircraft practice camp at Aberaeron; 'C' Flight (with a detachment at RAF Carew Cheriton) providing target-towing services for the artillery school at Manorbier. The squadron was equipped with twelve Henleys, seventeen Martinets, two Tiger Moths and one Stinson Voyager, one Mustang I, one Oxford I, nine Hawker Hurricane IVC and five Spitfire VBs and XIIs.

The new squadron suffered its first fatal accident on 15 December when Henley (L3336) crashed near Kilgetty killing the crew of two. A Martinet crashed at Milford Haven killing the pilot New Zealander F/Sgt McMillan. On 4 July 1944 Polish pilot Sgt. Pilot Jurewicz crashed in his Hurricane (LB650) and was fatally injured. On 5 April 1945 a Spitfire, piloted by F/Lt Vickery, hit the roof of Blaemanerch church just after taking off from the airfield. The aircraft narrowly missed some houses crashing in a ball of fire in nearby fields.

The squadron was involved with all aspect of target-towing throughout west and south Wales, with its aircraft being detached to various airfields. The Martinets were also involved in leaflet dropping, window dropping (metallic strips designed to confuse radar) over the Bristol Channel and in the trials with towing the new winged glider targets. The Hurricanes often made mock attacks on various bombers from RAF Talbenny. One such attack resulted in a Halifax crashing into the Preseli mountain in poor visibility, killing all the crew.

On 17 August 1943 the squadron's detachment returned from Carew Cheriton, which caused parking problems at the airfield

On 29 November 1944 the squadron received the first of the seventeen American Vengeance aircraft to replace the Martinets, but these aircraft were neither popular nor ideally suited for the task and were replaced by Spitfires in July 1945.

On 26 April 1946 Nº 595 Squadron moved from Aberporth to RAF Fairwood Common. Its twelve Spitfires and six Martinets flying to their new base on the following day; eleven pilots then returned to Aberporth (in an Airspeed Oxford of Nº 691) to pick up the remaining Spitfires.

On many occasions the airfield had been used as an emergency landing airfield by varied types of aircraft but, as many a pilot discovered, its grass field was neither suitable nor large enough. On 31 March 1941 a Handley Page Harrow and a Bristol Blenheim made successful emergency landings. However, a Halifax (W1097) of Nº 405 Squadron was no so fortunate and crashed outside the perimeter fence. A Bristol Beaufort made a perfect landing on 25 September 1942, although a RAF Liberator made bumpy landing on 3 January 1943 when it ran out of fuel. Throughout 1943 it was mostly Whitleys and Wellington that used the airfield's grass strip. Most of the landings were successful, but there were also a number of crashes such as that on 3 September when Wellington III (HF634) crashed. In October, another Wellington from RAF Pershore hit the perimeter fence and crashed. On 17 February 1944, due to bad weather, three Dakotas transporting troops from the Middle East en-route to St Mawgan were diverted to Aberporth. On 22 February 1944 a USAAF Liberator on a flight from North Africa to RAF Valley made a successful emergency landing. Two Halifax IIIs of Nº 420 Squadron were diverted to the airfield on 29 February 1944 and one Halifax (LK643) of Nº 1644 HCU overshot and was damaged when it hit a hedge. Two more Halifaxes crashed in the vicinity of the airfield on 14 July 1944; one aircraft which crashed at Cardigan, was from Nº 158 Squadron, while the other crashed into Cardigan Bay. On 14 October 1944 a Vickers Warwick bomber crashed on approach to the airfield, killing two of the crew.

A number of fighters were also diverted to Aberporth including Hurricanes and Spitfires and a USAAF P-47 Thunderbolt. The most notable was on 24 October 1945 when eleven Spitfires of Nº 164 Squadron diverted due to bad weather and all landed safely.

The first jet aircraft to land at Aberporth was a Gloster Meteor fighter which, due to fuel shortage, made an emergency landing on 4 June 1945. This was the first time local people, as well as station personnel, had seen a jet aircraft so it generated some interest. It remained at Aberporth for three days awaiting more favourable weather conditions and a great number of onlookers gathered around the perimeter fence to see it take off.

On 15 May 1946 the RAF had no further need for the airfield and it was put on 'care and maintenance' as part of Coastal Command. Later the same year the airfield was handed over to the army to be used as a Polish Army Resettlement

Corps Depôt and remained such a camp until the last of the Polish forces departed in 1950.

The airfield return to its status as 'care and maintenance' basis until the Royal Aircraft Establishment took it over in 1951.

There had been continuous use of the airfield by the military between 1946 and 1951, mostly by Anson, Oxford and Hudson aircraft, which were used for light transport and VIP flights. Former German transport aircraft such as the JU52 and the JU352 made frequent appearances at the base.

Several types had been allocated to RAE duties including Havards, Spitfires, Seafires, Argus, Dominie, Vampire I and a Bristol Wayfarer, which was used for bulky transportation. A DH Devon and a Douglas Dakota became more or less permanent aircraft at the station, providing an air link between Aberporth and other RAE units in the UK.

However, over the years the aircraft types seen at Aberporth have completely changed; the post-war transport aeroplanes have been superseded by BN Islanders, Piper Navahos, Twin Commanches, Beech Barons, Andovers and helicopters which are becoming more common.

The airfield was used by a number of military aircraft, which were involved with various missile trials at the establishment across the bay. Aircraft that took part in these trials were Sea Vixens, Gnats, Hawks, Lynx and Gazelle helicopters, and in 1976 BAe Harrier, which caused as much interest as the first Meteor in 1945.

RAE Aberporth was part of DERA (Defence Evaluation & Research Agency) operating in support of the Missile and Rocket establishment that is situated south of the village of Aberporth.

Aberporth Airfield, showing the hangar and tower, 1990s.

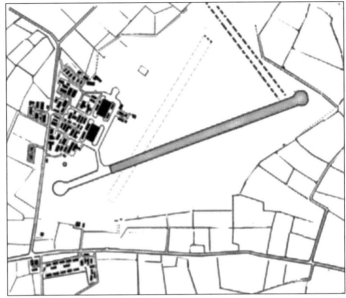

Aberporth airfield, 1970s.

The airfield is more or less the same now as it was in 1941, except that in 1956 a new hard surface runway with linked taxiways to the hangar aprons was built. Then, in 1968, a hangar apron was enlarged to provide additional parking space. This was again extended northwards in 1971 to form a helicopter pad. All other buildings are intact apart from two wartime blister-type hangars and one T-type hangar, which have been demolished.

The airfield is open daily for civilian flying between the hours of 0830 and 1700, but prior permission must be obtained. The airfield now consists of one asphalt-covered runway of 2,968 feet (08/26) and two grass strips. (04/22 and 15/33). Portable electric runway lighting is available, especially during the winter months.

In 2000, DERA announced a general reorganisation and restructure of its

One of the remaining Bellman hangars at Aberporth, 2000.

establishments. The airfield at Aberporth was regarded as surplus to requirement as it was not essential to the support of the Cardigan Bay missile range. The land was acquired by the Welsh Development Agency, which planned to develop the engineering, administration and domestic site as a business and industrial park while retaining the airfield for private and commercial flying. At the time of writing there is a limited amount of private flying, but Aberporth awaits a Commercial Operating Licence for general and commercial flying. The airfield has been renamed West Wales/Aberporth Airport.

2. Angle

Pembrokeshire

This wartime airfield lies just off the B4320 road, which connects the village of Angle and the castle town of Pembroke. One of the airfield perimeter tracks ran parallel with the public road. To the east lies the medieval equivalent to the airfield, the castle at Pembroke and, about ten miles away, the flying-boat station at Pembroke Dock. Today there is hardly any evidence left to remind us that Angle airfield ever existed and was one of the busiest of the Pembrokeshire airfields.

The runways, all the taxi-ways and the dispersal pens have been broken up and cleared. The main runways being utilised as the foundation for the road leading up to Pembroke power station. In the early 1990s the author was fortunate to see the last remaining buildings, the perimeter track and the firing butts before they too were broken up. Standing in the middle of the airfield where the main runways use to be, overlooking acres of ripen golden barley with sheep grazing on the cliff tops in the near distance, it is very difficult to imagine that some sixty years ago the roar of Merlin engines of the Spitfires and Hurricanes broke the still air.

So, within a short period of time, all traces of RAF Angle have disappeared; not a single monument survives to remind future generations of this once busy and important airfield. However, as the land has been returned to farming and the need for military airfields has declined, in a way there could not be a greater monument to those who did not return safely.

In its heyday, Angle had six fighter dispersal pens on the south-eastern side of the airfield, each with enough room for four Spitfires. There were a T2 hangar and four blister-type hangars, but by today there are no signs that they ever existed, even the concrete bases have been removed.

None of Pembrokeshire's airfields were very popular postings with RAF personnel. This is was because of their bleak location, especially those situated on the coast, and their remoteness. The wet, westerly winds that blew across the airfields, especially during the wintry months, did not help matters.

Angle was one of the airfields planned and built after the outbreak of the Second World War. It was completed during 1940 and was declared operational in May 1941. It was initially only used for training flights by various units based in the county. N° 32 was the first squadron to be actually based at Angle, equipped

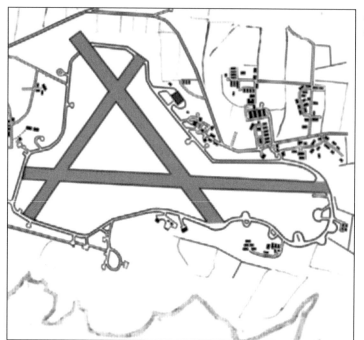

Angle airfield layout, 1943.

Angle airfield aerial photograph, 1946. [RAF Museum]

with Hawker Hurricane Is under the command of S/Ldr. T. Grier, DFC. It arrived from RAF Pembrey in early June and remained until transferred to RAF Manston, Kent in November 1941.

On 1 December 1941 Angle became a forward base in the Fairwood Common Sector under the control of N° 10 Group, Fighter Command whose responsiblity was to provided fighter cover for south Wales and the south-west of England, including the ports of the Severn estuary. From November 1941 to January 1942, N° 615 Squadron with its Hurricane Is & IIs became the airfield resident. The squadron came from RAF Manston under the command of S/Ldr. D. E. Gillam, DSO, DFC and Bar, AFC, who had seen distinguished service during the Battle of Britain. While at Angle N° 615 was primarily occupied with mounting convoy and shipping patrols over the Irish Sea. These patrols involved both sweeps seeking out enemy aircraft and escort duties for bombers and shipping. N° 615 Squadron left on 10 January 1942 for RAF Fairwood Common, on the Gower peninsula.

The first Spitfire unit to be based at Angle was N° 312 (Czech) squadron, which arrived, in early February 1942. This unit, after a non-operational period, was sent to Pembrokeshire to provide convoy patrols as well as an air defence of Milford Haven and its important installations.

While at Angle the squadron flew 231 operational hours and was involved in several skirmishes with enemy aircraft. One such encounter occurred on 16 February when some Spitfires went to the aid of a Coastal Command aircraft which was under attack. After the brief skirmish a Junkers JU88 was credited to the squadron. The Spitfires were fitted with bomb racks and took part in ground-attack exercises with the army. Although it was a Czech squadron, its commanding officer throughout their time at Angle was an RAF S/Ldr. H. Bird-Wilson, DFC.

In April 1942 N° 312 Squadron and its Spitfire Vbs left west Wales for RAF Fairwood Common and were replaced by the twin-engined Westland Whirlwinds of N° 263 Squadron under the command of S/Ldr. R. S. Woodward, DFC.

The Whirlwind was an attractive machine but never achieved its potential as a fighter aircraft. But, due to the sheer determination and bravery of its pilots, it did some very useful work in a bombing rôle. Armed with four Hispano cannons in the nose, the Whirlwind should have been an ideal platform for both air-to-air combat and ground attack, but it was constantly out manoeuvred by enemy aircraft and therefore suffered heavily. Throughout its brief service life it was also dogged by both engine and cannon problems. Although most of these had been ironed out by the time N° 263 Squadron arrived at Angle, it still caused considerable headaches for the ground crews. As if to compound matters, during

Westland Whirlwind F1, N° 263 Squadron, 1942. [RAF Museum]

Fitters maintaining the 20mm Hispano cannons of a
N° 263 Squadron Whirlwind, May 1942. [T. Rennie]

the squadron's move to Angle, a railway truck carrying the 20 mm cannon shells caught fire just outside Llanelli resulting in a spectacular explosion. Despite these problems the squadron provided convoy protection in the Irish Sea and took part in bombing raids on the continent, until being re-equipped in December 1943.

While N° 263 Squadron was based at Angle, a detachment of ten Whirlwinds was sent to RAF Portreath, in Cornwall, to take part in the first Ramrod operations over France. The first raid took place on 30 April 1942 when Whirlwinds, escorted by Spitfires of N° 310 Squadron, attacked enemy airfields at Lannion and Morlaix. Several enemy aircraft, mostly Heinkel He111s and Junkers Ju88s were destroyed or damaged, as well as several airfield installations. All RAF aircraft returned safely. Further raids were repeated on 5 June causing further destruction on enemy airfields.

The squadron's first casualty since moving to Angle was when two Whirlwinds were shot down by Me109s over France during a Rhubarb raid (a fighter sweep) on 23 July. Both pilots were killed.

In August 1942, N° 263 Squadron left Angle for RAF Colerne, and the sound of the Peregrine engines of the Whirlwind was replaced by the sound of the Merlin engines of N° 152 Squadron's Spitfires. The squadron's stay in Angle was short and, within weeks, it was re-posted to RAF Wittering where it was to be re-equipped with Spitfire Vbs.

From November 1942 to January 1943, N° 421 Squadron with its Spitfire Vbs, under the command of S/Ldr. F. E. Green, DFC, became the resident fighter unit at Angle, providing fighter cover for the area and for the Irish Sea convoys.

In January 1943, another change took place, this time N° 412 (Canadian) Squadron, equipped with Spitfires, moved in to RAF Angle under the command of S/Ldr. F. W. Kelly. Their stay was only temporary and they moved on to RAF Fairwood Common in February. All these short stays caused considerable problems for both the base and the squadrons themselves. On several occasions, by the time the various squadron ground crews had arrived at Angle, they found that squadron had already been posted on to another base, thereby causing some man-power shortages.

For the next few months there was a lull in squadron movements, which gave the airfield personnel a breather. The next visitor to Angle was a detachment of Whitley bombers and Horsa gliders which arrived in April 1943. The unit was involved in exercises with the 9th Parachute Battalion, which lasted for some weeks in preparation for airborne operations that were to follow.

Also in October 1943 the base was used by specially adapted Mosquitoes involved in trials with a new bomb designed by Barnes Wallis — code name 'Highball'. This bomb was developed for used against speciality targets such as railway tunnels, viaducts, fortified positions, certain types of buildings and, in particular, the German battleship *Tirpitz*. The bomb was spherical and would bounce on the ground/water towards the target in similar fashion to the famous dam busting bomb. Throughout the month De Havilland Mosquitoes armed with replica bombs made of wood and cast-iron made several sorties on various targets in the area. The most popular target was the Maenclochog railway tunnel, which closely resembled tunnels in Germany. Several attacks were made on the tunnel watched eagerly from across the valley by Barnes Wallis and other dignitaries. The trials were successful, as the tunnel was completely blocked and was out of action for some time. Several raids were made using the 'Highball' bomb. The most notable was against the Gestapo headquarters in Amsterdam.

By 1943, the importance of Angle as a Fighter Command station had declined and in July the airfield was temporarily taken over by the Royal Navy. Two Fleet

Air Arm squadrons arrived — a detachment of N° 759 Squadron, equipped with Proctors and Miles Masters and N° 794 Squadron, equipped with Hurricanes and Bristol Blenheim IVs. Both squadrons were responsible for training naval pilots and target-towing duties for Royal Navy ships.

On 5 September 1943 it was decided that the Fleet Air Arm should exchange its base at RAF Angle for RAF Dale, which was situated on the other side of Milford Haven. But it was not until November 1943 that the two target-towing squadrons actually moved to their new base.

The unit operated a variety of aircraft, including one Liberator V, one Halifax II, two Wellington Xs, one Warwick II, two Beaufighter Xs and Proctors for communication duties. The unit took part in various anti-submarine trials, but mostly was involved with tests to measure the audibility of aircraft from surfaced submarines. After the trials were completed the CCDU moved to its new base at RAF Thorney Island, but Angle remained under the control of Coastal Command. RAF Pembroke Dock controlled all flying on the south side of the Haven as there was a dispersed flying-boat flare path in Angle Bay. It was therefore essential that all night flying in the area was co-ordinated from one central control.

One notable event took place at Angle on 29 May 1943 when a Short Sunderland made the first ever dry landing. The aircraft in question was T9114E of N° 461 Squadron piloted by F/O Gordon Singleton operating out of Pembroke Dock. Having rescued a crew of another Sunderland (JM675) which had crashed due to enemy action, Singleton decided to pass them on to a French sloop but, while taking off in heavy seas, sustained considerable damage. A normal landing in the Haven was regarded as too dangerous and the only alternative was to land

Short Sunderland T9114, after emergency landing at Angle, 29 May 1943.

The station's firing butts, one of the few remaining structures in 1988.

on the grass area at Angle, the nearest airfield. With great skill Singleton landed the large flying boat without sustaining one casualty. Following an inspection by the salvage team from N° 78 Maintenance Unit at Pembroke Dock, it was decided that the aircraft was beyond economical repair as any attempts to try and move it to the nearest beach would have caused more damage. The aircraft was then dismantled and transported by road to the MU where it was used for spares and as a training airframe. Even that was no easy task, as a roadway had to be constructed through fields to reach the stranded Sunderland.

By the end of 1943 even Coastal Command had no use for the airfield, but it was kept under 'care and maintenance' and was used as an emergency airfield for the rest of the war. Angle airfield was officially closed on 1 January 1946, but several buildings had been dismantled earlier.

3. Bangor

Gwynedd

This First World War landing site was situated in a coastal area between Bangor and the village of Abergwyngregin on the edge of the Snowdonia mountain range. In 1915 the Admiralty was faced with the ever-growing problem of enemy submarine activities around the British coastline; several ships had been attacked and sunk by enemy submarines and pressure was being exerted on the Admiralty to keep the sea-lanes safe. Therefore an all-out effort was implemented to develop land bases for airships and land-based aircraft with priority being given to the former, which were thought to be more suitable for the task. As a consequence, it was not until 1918 that sites for anti-submarine land-based aircraft stations were identified and built.

Fifty acres of land, which consisted of most of Glan-y-môr Isaf Farm, were requisitioned in May 1918, and within a month two flights of N° 255 Squadron moved in (being part of the newly established Royal Air Force which, on 1 April, had been formed by merging the Royal Flying Corps and Royal Naval Air Service). Like all the coastal patrol squadrons this was under the control of N° 77 Wing, N° 14 Group (based at Haverfordwest).

Most of the airfield was very basic and easy to construct. At Glan-y-môr Isaf, hedges were removed to provide an enlarged area for landing and taking off and four Bessoneau hangars were constructed, usually on the grass. These hangars were the most common types at the time as they were constructed from just a wooden frame covered with canvas. All accommodation, officers and other ranks, were housed in variously sized tents. Stores, fuel and ammunition were stored in a site protected by sandbags and covered by tarpaulin in nearby woods away from the main site. Some farm buildings were confiscated for use as a wireless room and for briefing of crews.

As soon as most of the installations were in place another unit joined the base in August 1918. N° 244 Squadron equipped with eighteen DH6 fighter bombers, in three flights N°s 521 (A), 522 (B) and 530 (C). Two flights were based at Bangor and the third at Tallaght, Dublin. The Bangor flights were responsible for patrolling the area from Anglesey to Liverpool Bay, each patrol averaging $1^1/2$ hours.

On 7 September 1918 the squadron suffered its first fatal accident at the base, when a DH6 crashed just after take off. The pilot, Captain Tuck, and his observer,

DH6, which served with N° 244 Squadron, RNAS at Bangor, 1918.

Air Mechanic W. Shaw, were badly injured and taken to the C&A Hospital in Bangor where Shaw died from his injuries.

As there is no surviving airfield log it is very difficult to obtain much information about the base. It would appear that the squadron was involved in several coastal patrols and on a number of occasions went to the assistance of merchantmen in the area, but there are no records of any of the aircraft being involved with enemy submarines. However it does appear that one patrol went to the assistance of an airship from Llangefni which had mechanical problems and was in difficulty.

The squadron's greatest difficulty at Glan-y-môr Isaf Farm was serviceability. There was a shortage of trained mechanics and spare parts and, from a peak in October 1918 of seventeen serviceable aircraft, the numbers dropped in a few weeks to twelve and, at one stage, only two! Fortunately, by December the figure was up again to seventeen, but by now there were a shortage of pilots as some had left to join other squadrons.

The airfield itself caused a great many problems, especially during the winter months. As the result of heavy rain and strong winds, flooding made the base uncomfortable for its personnel who were accommodated in tents. Most of the time the airstrip was water-logged and unserviceable. On a number of occasions aircraft became bogged down in the mud. At one point the airfield was declared non-operational which caused a stir in the Admiralty. However, after the Armistice of 11 November, its importance declined and N° 244 Squadron was disbanded on 22 January 1919. Soon afterwards all the hangars and tented accommodation were taken down and the personnel, stores and equipment were removed by road to the railway station at Bangor. In May 1919 the land was released for farming and became Glan-y-môr Isaf Farm once more.

4. Beaumaris
Isle of Anglesey

During the German bombing of 1940, the flying-boat factories situated on the south coast of England became vulnerable to air attacks and various companies moved their factories to Cumbria and Scotland. Several sites were surveyed in Wales, where the best sites were already occupied by the RAF, namely the Dee estuary and Milford Haven. The Conwy estuary was surveyed but the area proposed for the factory, Conwy Morfa, was regarded as too wet and unstable. In 1937 this site had been put forward as a possible site for a proposed aerodrome, but had been rejected for the same reasons. The other site surveyed was the Menai Strait which, east of the Menai suspension bridge, had deep water which was an ideal alighting area and could provided a sheltered mooring. The high side of the Strait provided natural protection from preying enemy bombers.

The base was situated a mile from the town of Beaumaris, at Friar's House which became part of the complex. Here a small factory was built, consisting of two Bellman hangars, workshops, and a hard standing area connected to the sea by means of a concrete slipway. Beaumaris was not a military base, but it was available as a relief landing area for RAF flying boats.

Airfields attached to aircraft factories were given the highest priority for the construction of hangars and various faculties by the Ministry of Aircraft Production (MAP) and therefore, in August 1941, Saunders Roe had to dismantle one of their spare T2 hangars at Cowes, Isle of Wight and rebuild it at the new site at Beaumaris. Eventually, in December 1941, MAP built a T2 hangar and workshop sheds on the site. However over the years several modifications were carried out to the hangars.

During the early part of the Battle of the Atlantic, the RAF had an acute shortage of flying-boats for convoy escort duties. Most of the patrols were done by Avro Ansons and a few Sunderlands flying from bases in Pembrokeshire. The Sunderlands were an effective weapon against the U-boats, but the Anson lacked the range and weaponry for such a task. A new aircraft was required to supplement the four-engined Sunderland on patrol.

The American company, Consolidated Aviation was building the PPY5, a versatile twin-engined flying-boat for the US Navy, which could be based on both land and water. Arrangements were made to initially acquire seven of the type for evaluation by the RAF. After a series of trials and flight testing at Helensburgh, a

Two views of the modified SARO hangars at Beaumaris, 2001.

contract was placed under the lend-lease agreement to supply the RAF with the flying-boats which the RAF named the Catalina.

Saunders Roe was awarded a contract to modify the newly-arrived Consolidated Catalinas which needed to be fitted with various British components, including Browning machine-guns, British type bomb-racks, standard RAF radio equipment, ASV radars and Leigh lights, bringing them up to Coastal Command's specifications.

The first aircraft arrived at Beaumaris in April 1941, before the site received its first hangar and with the slipway incomplete. A further 11 Catalinas were delivered in 1941. The quantity increased to 63 in 1942, 70 in 1943 and a remarkable 114 aircraft in 1944. As the war in Europe came to an end and the threat to shipping ceased, delivery of the flying-boats was wound down. In 1945 only 38 Catalinas were converted with only a few being actually delivered to the squadrons; the rest remained moored in the Menai Strait until the war ended. However, the United States did not want them returned, but directed that they be

Consolidated Catalina IV on the slipway at Beaumaris.[BHC]

destroyed. Most of these surplus aircraft were scuttled in Lough Neagh, Northern Ireland with only a few hours flying on the clock.

After the work was completed the aircraft were flown by the Ferry Command pilots to their individual squadrons. In all, over 300 modified Catalinas passed through the Saunders Roe facilities at Beaumaris.

Like most flying-boat bases in the UK, Beaumaris suffered from a shortage of mooring facilities and it was decided that the aircraft should be ferried from America to Largs (on the Scottish coast) and then, as space became available, onwards to the Menai Strait. However some of the aircraft flew directly to Beaumaris and, in doing so, managed to avoid customs inspection and on several occasions, hauls of silk stockings, tobacco, spirits and chocolate were found on the aircraft.

The Consolidated Catalina was quite a formidable flying-boat. It was powered

Short Sunderland undergoing modifications at Beaumaris.

A prototype floatplane Supermarine Spitfire IX.

by two 1,200-hp Twin Wasp engines, which gave it a range of over 2,500 miles and a maximum speed of 195 mph. It was armed with up to six .303 Browning machine-guns and could carry a sizeable array of weapons (up to 12,000lbs of bombs). Coastal Command found the aircraft ideal for long range reconnaissance work, especially in the Far East.

Short Sunderlands were also visitors to the base, either because of weather diversions or because of the need for modifications; in 1944 several Sunderlands were sent by Short from Belfast for minor modification, before their onward flight to Pembroke Dock and Mount Batten.

The shelter of the Menai Strait was ideally suited for floatplane trials with various aircraft. Initially trials were conducted with Fairey Swordfish and Albacores fitted with floats, but these were superseded by Hurricanes as they became available and, in 1942, trials were carried out at Beaumaris by the Folland Aircraft Company with a Supermarine Spitfire fitted with floats, the first of which took place on 12 October using a Spitfire VB. Another two VBs were fitted with floats in 1943. However trials and evaluation moved to the Great Bitter Lakes in Egypt later in the year. On 18 June 18 1944 trials were begun with a Spitfire LFIXB (MJ892) fitted with modified floats, initially at Hamble and then at Beaumaris. None of the modified aircraft became operational, MJ892 was re-converted to a land plane, while the three based in Egypt were dismantled.

Other American flying-boats were evaluated by the RAF and Royal Navy at the MAEE (Marine Aircraft Experimental Establishment), Helensburgh and Saunders Roe, Beaumaris. Several Vought-Sikorsky Kingfisher reconnaissance seaplanes were tested and modified for the Royal Navy. On 29 April 1943 the large Consolidated Coronado flying-boat landed in the Straits from the States en-route to the MAEE where most of the trials took place. Another flying-boat that landed at Beaumaris before flying on to Helensburgh was the Martin Mariner, six of which were acquired by the RAF and equipped Nº 524 Squadron but, within a year, were withdrawn from service as they were classed as unsafe.

The Coronado did not fare any better. One was delivered to the civil airline BOAC for evaluation, but was rejected. After further modification at Beaumaris and at Nº 57 MU, six of the type were used by RAF Transport Command on the Scotland to Canada run. Saunders Roe at Beaumaris handled no further American flying boats.

Design work and various trials continued at Beaumaris during the post war period. As the Sunderland had provided such good service throughout the war years, several companies started designing a replacement. The Shetland flying-boat was planned as the Sunderland's replacement, and Beaumaris was involved in its initial development. However most of the Shetland work moved to Rochester in 1945.

Saunders Roe was looking forward to civilian flying-boat use which could carry fare-paying passengers non stop from Southampton to the United States. Their design team came up with the large Princess flying-boat for which a great deal of the design work and parts evaluation was done at Beaumaris, although the actual building was concentrated at Cowes. Sadly, the project was overtaken by long range land-based aircraft and eventually by jet powered airliners, and the flying-boat era came to an end.

In 1944, Auster conducted trials at Beaumaris with their Auster V (TJ207) float-plane, under the control of MAEE. The trials were discontinued but resumed at Beaumaris in 1955. Several were fitted with floats and were used throughout the world.

Martin Mariner beached at Beaumaris. [BHC]

Beaumaris, a Short Sunderland parked in front of the house 'Fryars'. [BHC]

After the war the future of the facility at Beaumaris was bleak. The site was put forward as a flying-boat base for the RAF, but was declined as they already had sufficient bases. Over the next few years Saunders Roe wound down all work at Beaumaris. In a move away from aircraft production the company concentrated on building motor torpedo boats and repair. It was also involved with light engineering and modifying vehicles for the military. This only lasted a short time and Saunders Roe moved all its manufacturing and testing to Cowes, where it became involved with the development of the hovercraft.

Today the site is used as an industrial estate, with all the old wartime buildings intact. The hangars and the slipway can still be seen and, with a bit of imagination, one could still visualize the Catalinas moored nearby.

5. Bodorgan

Isle of Anglesey

Bodorgan was a wartime grass airfield situated on the B4422, eight miles west of Menai Bridge, Anglesey. It was opened on 11 November 1940 as RAF Aberffraw and was initially involved with the launching of Queen Bee target drones, radio controlled versions of the famous De Havilland Tiger Moth trainer. These could be used either as conventional aircraft, using grass or concrete runways, or could be launched from a catapult. In its early days the system was very unreliable and thinly populated areas were chosen as bases. More Queen Bees crashed on their own than were destroyed by practice firing.

The site at Bodorgan was chosen because of its remoteness. Several fields were joined to make a grass landing area, dispersal areas were allocated in other fields adjoining the landing strip and the camp was tucked away in nearby woods. Originally one blister-hangar was built for engineers to work on the drones, but eventually two Bellman hangars were built which provided additional shelter for

the servicing crews. Wooden, Nissen and Maycrete huts were also built, which replaced the original tented accommodation. The airfield did not have a control tower as such but rather a watchtower situated in a 'bungalow' type building.

The first unit to be based at Aberffraw was 'Z' Flight of Nº 1 AACU providing target practice for the AA gunners at the Tŷ-Croes Range. The first pilotless flight took place on 2 December 1940 and the

Bodorgan airfield layout.

Queen Bee (P4804), after a faultless take off, remained aloft for nearly two and half hours, but crashed as it attempted to land. Two aircraft flew out to sea and were never seen again, while others went out of control and flew into the Snowdonia mountains.

A detachment of five Westland Lysander aircraft of N°13 Squadron from RAF Hooton Park arrived in March 1941 for night flying training during a full moon period. This was an exercise for the flying of agents into occupied France.

In April 1941 the base became known as N° 15 SLG under the control of N° 48 Maintenance Unit at Hawarden. The purpose of the SLG was to accommodate the overspill from Hawarden, which included repaired, surplus and factory production aircraft. Aircraft would be flown from the MU for storage at Bodorgan by Ferry Command pilots. The first aircraft to arrive were Westland Lysanders, Blackburn Bothas and Vickers Wellingtons. Surplus Hurricanes soon followed and, within a short period of time, further fields had to be requisitioned for storage. By the end of May there were 30 factory fresh Wellington bombers stored at the airfield.

Accidents were a common occurrence at the site, especially when RAF Collection Pilots picked up the Hurricane for delivery to their respective squadrons. These pilots were not accustomed to the small, uneven grass strip; several aircraft were severely damaged and were written off. The situation was so serious that N° 48 MU decided to use their own pilots for aircraft delivery, as they were more accustomed to the airfield.

However, because of shortage of propeller sets, once the aircraft had landed they were removed and taken back to Hawarden to be fitted on another aircraft. This procedure made the ferrying very laborious and they took twice as long. The original plan was for the squadrons to pick up the aircraft from Aberffraw, but after several accidents during take off it was decided to fly the aircraft back to Hawarden for collection.

Since the airfield opened there had been problem with the name. The English found Aberffraw a difficult name to pronounce resulting in delays to the postal service, mis-posting of staff and delays in obtaining spares. As a consequence, the name was changed to RAF Bodorgan on 15 May 1941.

In July 1941 a DH Dragon and a Lysander of N° 6 AACU were detached to Bodorgan for night flying training between the base and RAF Valley. This continued for a few months. Also in 1941 'J' Flight of N° 1 AACU with its Hawker Henleys, Tiger Moths and Miles Magisters joined 'Z' Flight at the airfield. On 1 October 1941 there was a general re-organisation of AACU, 'J' Flight became N° 1606 Flight and 'Z' Flight became N° 1620 Flight equipped with Queen Bees. N° 1606 Flight aircraft were eventually re-equipped with Martinets and Lysanders, which were used for target towing.

Bodorgan airfield, aerial photograph, 1943.

Nº 2 Maintenance Flight was also based at the airfield with the responsibility for the repair of Hawker Henleys based in the area. The unit was re-numbered on 1 December 1943 as Nº 3506 Servicing Unit.

The threat of enemy attack was real even in a remote spot like Bodorgan as *Luftwaffe* aircraft *en route* to bomb Liverpool often flew over Anglesey. With so many aircraft parked in the open it made a tempting target for enemy bombers. There would be at least thirty aircraft, mostly Wellingtons, parked in the fields between the airfield and Bodorgan Hall to the east. Fortunately it was never attacked, whether enemy bombers failed to see the base or perhaps thought it was too obvious and that the aircraft were dummies. Airfield protection was the responsibility of RAF Valley, but in October 1941 an airfield defence flight was formed by Nº 48 MU. Training began with Westland Lysanders, which included an invasion exercise with two Ansons making dummy attacks on the airfield and nearby towns. The airfield defence flight was meant to be equipped with four Hurricanes, but never materialised

Westland Lysander which served with N° 13 Squadron at Bodorgan, 1941.

As with most Welsh grass fields there was the problem of flooding, which meant that the airfield had often to be closed during the winter months.

On 10 January 1943 two Fairey Battles (R7378 and P6727) joined N° 1606 Flight from RAF Aberporth. However the type was not suited for target towing and was not very popular with the pilots so the two aircraft spent most of the time in storage.

RAF Bodorgan was not without its accidents, thankfully most were minor, resulting in only superficial damage to the aircraft. However on 8 June 1942 a Lysander (V9604), piloted by a Polish airman P/O Kalarus, based at the airfield, was in collision with a Spitfire of N° 350 Squadron based at RAF Valley. Tragically both pilots were killed.

By December 1944 the threat of enemy activity in the area had declined and

Bodorgan airfield, 1990s.

Bodorgan camp, looking towards Holyhead Mountain, 1990s.

the dispersal of aircraft such a distance from MUs was no longer necessary and N° 48 MU decided to consolidate its activities nearer to the main base. RAF Hooton Park was taken over for storage and the SLG at RAF Bodorgan was not required. All storage aircraft were removed by 30 December and the airfield lost its status as an SLG.

In early 1944 a detachment of N° 577 Army Co-operation Squadron, equipped with Martinets and Lysanders, arrived at the airfield and was joined in November by more Martinets of N° 650 Squadron. These remained at Bodorgan providing training and target towing until September 1945. After the squadron left there was a general run down of the airfield and on 30 December 1945 RAF Bodorgan was officially closed. The land was returned to its original owners, while the two Bellman and blister hangars were demolished. By today there is not much evidence left of the wartime airfield. Part of the technical site and domestic accommodation area is used by light industry, while the hangar foundations and apron is either a car park or used for storage.

6. Brawdy
Pembrokeshire

Brawdy airfield is situated just off the A478 Haverfordwest to St David's road, the nearest village being Pen-y-Cwm. During its existence it has been in the control of all three services. The airfield was opened as a RAF base, was then taken over by the Royal Navy's Fleet Air Arm, reverted back to RAF ownership and finally became an Army camp.

The airfield became operational on 2 February 2 1944 as a satellite to RAF St David's which is about seven miles away. On 1 November 1945 the station headquarters and its squadrons were officially transferred from St David's to Brawdy, leaving the former to become the satellite airfield.

The runways at Brawdy were constructed so that all three crossed each other to take advantage of the prevailing winds which was completely different to the standard war time triangular pattern previously used at St David's, which suffered severely from the wind blowing in various directions. As a consequence, aircraft were able to take off fully loaded. Previously Halifaxes used for anti-submarine patrols would 'bomb up' at St David's, but only take on a light fuel load. They would then land at Brawdy to 'top up' their tanks and then proceed on patrol, a routine which was unsatisfactory in wartime conditions.

The first squadron to be based at Brawdy was N° 517, equipped with their four-engined Handley Page Halifax Mk III and Mk V bombers, which had been modified for meteorological duties. This aircraft was ideally suited for the task as it could carry various equipment and a sizeable fuel load, giving it up to ten hours duration in the air. The squadron arrived at St David's on 2 February 1944, but soon transferred to Brawdy. It remained at the new base until September 1945, when it moved to RAF Weston Zoyland. The squadron was disbanded at RAF Chivenor in June 1946.

The meteorological unit was responsible for gathering weather information over the Atlantic Ocean and the Bay of Biscay, which proved invaluable for the military high command during operational planning. It was such units that provided regular, precise forecasts for the D-Day landings. Despite its function (or perhaps because of it) the squadron was not immune to the problems brought about by bad weather (and occasional mechanical problems) and on several occasions aircraft were diverted as far as Gibraltar or to bases in North Africa.

N° 517 Squadron was regarded as a front-line operational squadron and on a

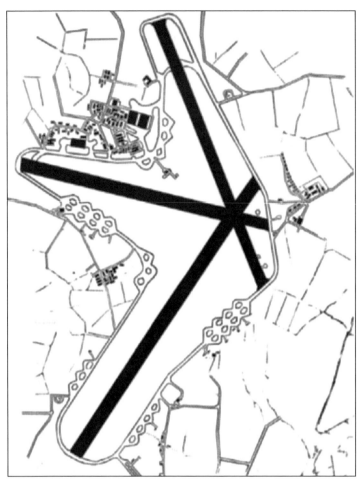

Layout of Brawdy airfield, 1945.

number of occasions was involved in skirmishes with enemy aircraft, especially the *Luftwaffe's* Focke-Wulf Condor long-range reconnaissance air-craft. One such encounter took place in June 1944, when a Halifax piloted by F/O Aveling, a Canadian serving in the RAF, was on a weather-gathering mission in connection with the D-Day operations. Well into the mission the aircraft developed mechanical and engine failure some 800 miles from Pem-brokeshire. After deciding there was no hope of returning to Brawdy or any other airfield, Aveling ditched the Halifax in the Atlantic and the crew were able to climb into their dinghies and were all eventually picked up by an American ship and taken to the United States. However other crews were not so fortunate, like the crew of Halifax LK962, which crashed into the Atlantic in November 1944 with no survivors.

Handley Page Halifax BIII, Mk III & IV operated with
N° 517 Squadron at Brwady in 1944. [Air Heritage]

The base only once drew the attention of enemy aircraft when a large force of Junkers Ju88s were intercepted and shot down over St Bride's Bay by fighters from RAF Angle and RAF Fairwood. A returning Halifax was caught up in the firefight and was presumably been shot down, as only a single main wheel was ever found. Another Halifax managed to dodge the combat area and was able to reach the airfield in safety.

During the early part of 1945 other units became lodgers at Brawdy. One such unit was a detachment from N° 8 OTU (Operational Training Unit) from Haverfordwest with its photo-reconnaissance Spitfires and Mosquitoes. Another visitor during 1945 was a detachment of 33 target-towing Spitfire VBs and XIIs of N° 595 Squadron from RAF Aberporth. They arrived on 27 February and remained until June when N° 8 OTU left Pembrokeshire for their new base at RAF Mount Farm. The detachment was involved in trials with target gliders, providing practice for the coastal AA batteries. These target gliders were built by the International Model Aircraft Company, which was famous for the scale model plastic kits sold under the brand name 'Frog'. The gliders TG Mk I had a 16-foot wingspan and were fitted with a skid undercarriage and at the time were an improvement on the standard tow. It was a strange irony that during Brawdy's early days the airfield was ear-marked as a base for pilotless aircraft, but was shelved.

After September 1945 there were virtually no flying at the base and by the end of the year the airfield was put on care and maintenance but, due to its prominent position, the Admiralty immediately took a keen interest. On January 1 1946, RAF Brawdy airfield was officially handed over to Admiralty control and became HMS *Goldcrest II* as the relief landing ground for Dale, which was HMS *Goldcrest I*.

While under Admiralty control, an RAF Radio Meteorological Flight, equipped with six Airspeed Oxfords, was based at Brawdy from January to July 1946.

The first naval squadron to be based at the new station was N° 748 equipped with Grumman Hellcats IINF, North American Harvards and Fairey Fireflies, with a small detachment at Dale. The squadron's main responsibility was the training of navy fighter pilots in the art of night fighting. It remained at Brawdy until 30 September 1946.

N° 759 Squadron, equipped with Martin Martinets TTI, became resident from March 1946 and provided Royal Navy ships with target-towing facilities for gunnery practice off the Pembrokeshire coast.

The next squadron to be based at the airfield was N° 811 with its De Havilland Sea Mosquito T33s (the only naval Mosquito squadron) which arrived in December 1946 and remained until April 1947 when it moved to Eglinston.

As Dale was the main Fleet Air Arm base in the county, Brawdy was regarded as surplus to requirements and was put on care and maintenance from August 1947 to July 1952. However the Admiralty had drawn up further plans for the airfield and in 1951 a major modernisation programme took place bringing the base up to peacetime standards. For the next five years the base looked more like a construction site rather than an aerodrome.

The main runway was lengthened by 500 feet and resurfaced; new taxiways were built while the original ones resurfaced; a new up-to-date airfield lighting system was installed; the control tower was modernised with new radar and communication systems; new concrete aprons were constructed as well as three inter-connecting hangars and a brand new technical support facility. All the wartime Nissen huts were replaced by brick buildings, which included a new mess hall and accommodation block. Although the rebuilding was not completed until 1956, the airfield was re-commissioned as active on 1 September 1952 providing a shore base for Fleet Air Arm aircraft while their carriers were in dock, front line replacements for naval squadrons and additional training facilities and support. The only resident units at the base were communication aircraft, search and rescue and various training units. All other squadrons were on a short period detachment.

To accommodate the new breed of jet aircraft (such as the Sea Vixen and the Scimitar) that were entering service with the Fleet Air Arm it was decided to lengthen the runway by another 1500 feet and between 1961 and 1963 the airfield was occupied once more with construction workers. Hangars were modernised, further accommodation was built for the ratings (as well for the WRNS that were about to be posted to base). After the extensive modernisation, flying activity was resumed on 1 August 1963 and for the next ten years the airfield was involved with the training of Fleet Air Arm crews and also became the base of a Royal

A squadron of Hawker Sea Hawks about to take off. This was the most common type to be based at Brawdy during the 1950s. [D. Edwards]

Navy Aircraft Support Unit which was responsible for overhauling, storing and modifying all the Fleet Air Arm's aircraft. Its storage system was unique, as the aircraft were moth balled and stored in a humidity free environment.

The search and rescue unit with its Whirlwind helicopters remained at Brawdy during this period.

By the late 1960s, the Royal Navy's carrier force was down to three fleet carriers, HMS *Hermes*, HMS *Eagle* and HMS *Ark Royal*. With the scrapping of the last aircraft carrier the *Ark Royal* scheduled for the late 1970s, the Royal Navy's presence at Brawdy was coming to an end.

N° 759 Squadron was decommissioned on 24 December 1969, followed by N° 738 Squadron and by 8 May 1970 all the Hunter squadrons and their personnel had left the base. The only unit to remain was N° 849 with its Gannet aircraft but

Sea Hawk F2 of N° 898 Squadron FAA on a wet apron at Brawdy.

it too departed for Lossiemouth on 19 December 1970. The last ever naval training flight from Brawdy was carried out by N° 849 Squadron's Gannet aircraft on 1 December.

Admiralty control of the airfield came to an end in January 1971 by which date all naval property had been removed and distributed to various destinations. It is worth noting that from January 1950 to its closure the civilian firm of Airwork Ltd. was contracted out by the Admiralty to undertake conversion-training courses on heavy twin-engined aircraft for naval crews. Originally the unit was equipped with DH Sea Mosquitoes and Sea Hornets, but later was re-equipped with Meteor T7s. The unit moved to St David's airfield in September 1951, where they operated a jet conversion course. However they returned to Brawdy in October 1958 when space became available and remained there until the base closed.

From 1971 to 1974 the base came under the control of the Department of Environment and there was great concern over the closure as the airfield contributed to the finance of the county, particularly in terms of employment. After a defence review, the government decided that the RAF would use the airfield, but at the time its rôle had not been decided upon — eventually it was decided to use the base for operational conversion training.

The RAF again took control of the airfield in January 1974, after a modest modernisation programme. The first unit to use the base was 'D' Flight of N° 22 Squadron equipped with Westland Whirlwind search and rescue helicopters. It was not until 4 September 1974 that N° 229 OCU equipped with Hawker Hunter T8s moved in to their new base. This unit was eventually re-named N° 1 Tactical Weapons Unit (N° 1 TWU) with its sister unit N° 2 TWU based at RAF Chivenor. These units were responsible for training RAF operational pilots in the skills of air combat, air-to-ground attack and tactical low flying, which became a regular occurrence over the Pembrokeshire countryside. Brawdy's TWU had three squadrons, N°s 63, 79 and later 234, all equipped with Hawker Hunters.

In 1978 the British Aerospace Hawk T1 replaced the TWU Hunters, although some Hunters remained on the squadron's charge until 1984. The Hunter was a firm favourite with many of its pilots, but the Hawk proved to be a superb replacement and a very capable aircraft.

N°s 63 and 79 Squadrons dealt solely with weapon training for pilots who had graduated from the Flying School at RAF Valley. After completing the course at the TWU the pilots would be posted to an Operational Conversion Unit flying Buccaneers, Harriers, Phantoms and Tornadoes. N° 79 Squadron only provided refresher-training courses.

After 1978 all the weapons training was flown in the BAe Hawk T1A . Most of the Hunters were returned to the manufacture to be resold or put in storage at

In 1974 the RAF regained control of Brawdy. A Hawker Hunter FGA9
of Nᵒ 79 Squadron, Nᵒ 229 OCU.

Nᵒ 32 MU St Athan, although few remained at Brawdy as station flights.

About 72 Hawks from Nᵒˢ 1 and 2 TWU were armed with two 30mm Aden cannons and Sidewinder air-to-air guided missiles and, in a war situation, could be used as secondary defence aircraft and distributed to various airfields throughout the UK. Brawdy was also used as a forward operating base for RAF Phantom aircraft and on many occasions detachments of Phantoms were regular seen at the airfield.

Another resident at the base was the United States Navy Oceanographic

Hunter GA 11 (XF297) of No 738 Squadron embedded in a
hangar after a mishap during landing. [J. James]

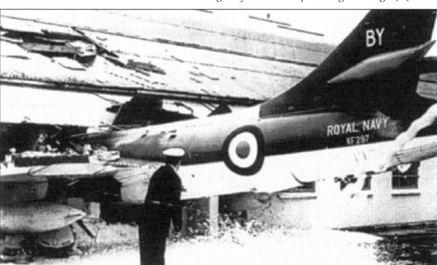

BAe Hawk XX191 flying over the Welsh coast. The Hawk replaced the Hunter for weapon training.[via RAF Brawdy]

Research Unit operated by USNAVFAC. This secretive unit was situated away from the airfield's operational side and its existence was often denied.

In January 1992 the Ministry of Defence announced another review and decided to cease all flying training at Brawdy. The last training flights taking place by 10 Hawks on 28 August 1992. Both No[os] 79 and 234 Squadrons were disbanded and the Hawks were either distributed between the other squadrons or put in storage. However, 'B' Flight of N[o] 202 Search and Rescue squadron, with its Westland Sea King HAR3s (which had replace N[o] 22 Squadron in 1979) remained, maintained by Support Unit personnel. The search and rescue service,

The Westland Sea King HAR3 of No 202 Squadron over the Pembrokeshire countryside. [via RAF Brawdy]

(Naval and RAF) which Brawdy had provided since the mid 1950s eventually came to and end in 1998.

It is worth noting that 'B' Flight of N° 202 Squadron had an impressive record e.g. in 1991 it responded to 162 call outs, both military and civilian. In all, 214 people were airlifted to safety, which was just an average number rescued during the flight's stay at Brawdy.

Brawdy airfield is perhaps one of the best airfields in the UK and, over the years, various type of both military and civilian aircraft have used its runways. During the 1987 General Election, campaign BAe 748s and BAe 1-11s of the various political parties used the airfield during the visits of politicians to the county. During one of its annual air displays in June 1987, a RAF Lockheed Tristar landed on its runway, but the heaviest aircraft to land anywhere in Pembrokeshire was an USAF Lockheed C141 Galaxy transport aircraft which landed in 1991 to remove US Navy oceanographic research equipment.

Brawdy has been renowned for its air displays, which had been started in the mid-1950s by the Fleet Air Arm and continued by the RAF until its closure. The displays gave the people of the county an opportunity to see what was going on at the base and a chance to marvel at the professionalism of the pilots who flew from the airfield.

During Brawdy's naval control period, local schools were encouraged to visit the airfield and be the Navy's guests for a day, a service which was highly appreciated by both the school children and the education authorities — a wonderful public relations exercise as well as perhaps a source of future recruits.

The airfield has had close ties with Pembrokeshire and over the years thousands of servicemen and women, who have served at the base, have settled in the county adding to the richness of the community. The base was so much a part of the county that in 1984 a new station badge was awarded, depicting a red sea-dragon supporting with one claw the feathers of the Prince of Wales. In the other claw is the sword of Strike Command. The station motto was '*Amddiffynfa y Gorllwein*' which means 'Stronghold of the West'.

At the time of writing the airfield has been taken over by the army as a base, keeping the military presence in the county. The hangars are used for storage of army vehicles and

The crest of RAF Brawdy. [via RAF Brawdy]

equipment, but the runways are kept in operational readiness and are occasionally used by army and RAF helicopters.

Summary of Naval squadrons and aircraft based at Brawdy

The first squadron to be reformed at Brawdy was N° 849 on 7 July 1952, equipped with Douglas Skyraiders AEW I. It remained there throughout the Fleet Air Arm's stay at the base until its closure in December 1971.

It was followed by the front line N° 804 Squadron, equipped with Hawker Sea Furies FB 2, from 20 November 1952 to 16 January 1953 when it was deployed aboard HMS *Indomitable*.

From 1953 to 1958, which were the glorious years of the Fleet Air Arm, various naval squadrons visited Brawdy. The following is the list of squadrons and their equipment and dates when they were based at Brawdy.

N° 727 Training Squadron; 4 January 1956–16 December 1960 (disbanded). Aircraft included Sea Balliol, Sea Prince and Sea Vampires.

N° 736 Squadron; 25 June–2 July 1960. Equipped with the Fleet Air Arm only supersonic fighter the Supermarine Scimitar FI.

N° 738 Squadron visited Brawdy on a regular basis. The first visit was in November 1954 followed by others in 1956, 1957, 1958, and 1959. The squadron was equipped with various marks of the Armstrong Whitworth Sea Hawks naval fighter-bombers. In the early 1960s the squadron was disbanded and reformed as a training unit at Lossiemouth. However, in 1964, N° 738, equipped with Hawker Hunter T8s and GAIIs, was transferred to Brawdy were it remained until 1970. The squadron was responsible for training naval pilots for a 12-week period which included tactical formation flying, simulated air-to-air gunnery, air-to-ground firing (with both cannon and missiles).It also it trained pilots in air-to-air combat as well as low-level flying (a rôle similar to that of the RAF's N° 1 TWU).

N° 751 Squadron; a detachment was based at Brawdy between 13 and 15 May 1957. It was equipped with North American Avenger AS4s, but had been re-equipped with D.H. Sea Venoms by the time of its next visit between 11 and 19 September 1957.

N° 759 Squadron; from 1 August 1963–24 December 1967, equipped with Hawker Hunter T8s, and T8Cs. This eventually became the last Fleet Air Arm squadron to be permanently resident at Brawdy.

N° 800 Squadron visited the base on a regular basis from November 1954 while the various aircraft carriers they served on were in dock. The squadron operated various marks of Hawker Sea Hawks.

N° 801 Squadron; 1957–60, equipped with Sea Hawk F1s, F2s and FGA6s.

N° 802 Squadron; from 12 May–16 June 1953, equipped with Hawker Sea Fury

DH Sea Venom of A Flight N° 831 Squadron, RN, Brawdy, 1964.

FBIIIs which was deployed aboard H.M.S. *Theseus.*

N° 804 Squadron; from August to September 1959, equipped with Sea Hawk FGA6s.

N° 806 Squadron; the first Naval squadron to be equipped with jet aircraft, the Hawker Sea Hawk F1, was based at Brawdy from 2 March 1953 – 5 February 1954.

N° 807 Squadron; the first naval jet squadron to be based at Brawdy, equipped with Sea Hawks. Further visits took place in May 1954 and between 19 February and 3 March 1955. The squadron's last visit to west Wales was in July 1955.

N° 813 Squadron; X Flight, 18 March– 5 April 1957 and again from 20 May– 5 August 1957, equipped with the turbo-powered Westland Wyvern S4 which was deployed on the aircraft carrier H.M.S. *Eagle.*

N° 824 Squadron; 7 June–1 July 1955, equipped with Fairey Gannet AS1s.

N° 831, A and B Flight; 16–19 November 1964, equipped with Sea Venoms and Sea Princes.

N° 849 Squadron; this was more or less a permanent resident from 1959 to 1970. At the beginning it was equipped with Douglas Skyraider AD4s and later with various marks of Fairey Gannets.

Headquarters, A, B, C, and D Flights N° 849 Sqaudron. This unit was based at Brawdy from December 1964 to May 1965 and at various other times, right up to the base's closure in 1970. The unit was equipped with Gannet AEW3s, AS4s, COD4s and T5s. When not at Brawdy the flights were deployed on Royal Navy carriers.

'A' Flight was deployed on HMS *Victorious.*

'B' Flight on HMS *Centaur.*

'C' Flight on HMS *Ark Royal.*

'D' Flight on HMS *Eagle.*

N° 891 Squadron; from 2–4 March 1956, equipped with D.H. Sea Venom FAW21s.

N° 892 Squadron; equipped with D.H. Sea Vixen FAW2s was based at Brawdy for a naval exercise from 21 August –9 September 1956.

N° 893 Squadron; 6–24 October 1959, equipped with Sea Venoms FAW21s.

N° 895 Squadron; 23 April–25 June 1956, equipped with Sea Hawk FGA4s and 6s.

N° 898 Squadron; the second naval squadron to be re-equipped with pure jet aircraft — Sea Hawks — it was stationed at Brawdy during August 1963.

N° 1831 Squadron; 28 July–10 August 1956, equipped with Sea Balliol trainers, Sea Vampires and Supermarine Attackers.

During the naval presence at Brawdy there was also a resident station helicopter rescue service. The unit was originally equipped with Westland Dragonflys then with Westland Whirlwind HRs and eventually the turbine-powered Whirlwind HAS7s.

In 1958, following the decision to decommission the aircraft carriers, there was a general run down of naval fixed-wing aircraft and the threat of closure hung over Brawdy once more. But, after a revision of the plans, the airfield was reprieved but its status as a support base for front line forces was gone and it became involved in advance training. The first training squadron to move in was N° 738 equipped with its Hunter T8s and GA11s.

7. Carew Cheriton

Pembrokeshire

The remains of this airfield can be found just off the A477 Pembroke Dock to St. Clears road, wedged between the villages of Carew Cheriton and Sageston on the B4318 road, only six miles from Tenby and five miles from Pembroke.

Today there is hardly anything remaining of this proud war time airfield except for few short lengths of the main runway and the perimeter track which still can be found in amongst the overgrown hedges and the fields. A number of wartime buildings are in reasonable condition (including a rare turret training building) and are used by local farmers. Most of the domestic site was demolished during the widening of the A477 road. On the airfield side, with access from the public road, there is the very unusual control tower, which has been renovated by its owner the businessman Mr Gevan Davies, who at the time of writing was intending to use it as a museum, which will be a small memorial to all those who were stationed at Carew Cheriton. Part of the parking area, workshops and foundations of where the hangar stood are today occupied by a caravan site. During the summer months a Sunday market occupies the area.

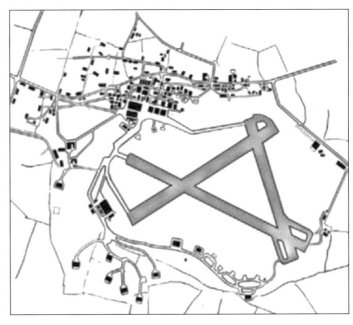

Layout of Carew Cheriton airfield, 1945.

Aerial view of the Bessoneaux hangars at Carew Cheriton, 1943.
[National Assembly for Wales]

Carew Cheriton is regarded as the oldest aerodrome in Pembrokeshire. Its origins go back to the First World War when it was used as a Royal Naval Air Service airship base, known as RNAS Milton, which occupied land close to the village of the same name. This base was run down and eventually demolished in the 1920s.

During the early 1930s defence in the United Kingdom was not given the same priority as it was in some European countries. However it was decided to build a number of new airfields for the Royal Air Force. Airfields in areas around London and the south coast were allocated to Fighter Command, East Anglia and Yorkshire for Bomber Command, Wales, the south west and Scotland to Coastal and Training Command.

It was decided to build a new airfield at Carew in support of the flying-boat base at Pembroke Dock. Its purpose was to provide initial training on twin-engined aircraft prior to pilots being transferred to flying-boats, and also provide land based aircraft for patrol work.

With the sounds of war echoing through Europe, the airfield was modernized and brought up to the standard required for operational use. New concrete and asphalt runways were planned and eventually built replacing the grass strip, additional parking pens were built and new hangars and associate workshops were constructed. Due to its close proximity to Pembroke Dock it was decided from the beginning the airfield should be under control of Coastal Command, as a land base support for the flying-boats based on the Haven.

Prior to the arrival of Coastal Command aircraft, the resident aircraft at the airfield were a mixture of training and communication aircraft like Tiger and Hornet Moths belonging to the Coastal Patrol Flight. A coastal patrol flight was formed at Carew equipped with civilian Leopard Moths, Hornet Moths and Tiger Moths and it remained at the airfield until disbanded on 27 May 1940. The impressed aircraft were allocated to various AACCU and Flying Training Schools

The majority of Welsh airfields suffered from poor drainage, which caused severe problems throughout their existence. During the extremely wet March of 1940, parts of the airfield became water-logged. An urgent requisition was made to local timber yards for wooden duckboards, which could be used to construct temporary taxiways.

In June 1937, the first Command aircraft had arrived at the airfield — a detachment of Avro Anson Is of N° 217 Squadron then based at RAF Tangmere. It was replaced in August 1939 by another detachment, again from N° 217 Squadron but, by now, based at RAF Warmwell. It remained at Carew until October 1939. The squadron badge was a demi-shark erased with a motto 'Woe to the unwary'. For most of the time spent at Pembrokeshire, its aircraft carried the squadron markings 'MW' on their fuselages. While at Carew the squadron took part in coastal and shipping patrols just like their predecessors from RNAS Milton during the First World War. The Anson was never really a threat to the U-boats, as they were very lightly armed, but, nevertheless, were the only aircraft available and were a reassuring sight to the convoys and other shipping.

The airfield's first wartime casualty was a visiting Vickers Wellington (L4232) of N° 99 Squadron which hit a taxing Henley whilst landing. Both aircraft were

DH Tiger Moths and Leopard Moths of the Coastal Patrol Flight, 1940.

damaged but there were no casualties amongst either crew. The Wellington however, was beyond economical repair and was dismantled for spares. For some reason the airfield official records erroneously recorded that the Wellington crashed during take off, due to strong crosswinds.

In November 1939 a detachment from N° 75 Squadron, equipped with Wellington Is, arrived at Carew from their home base in East Anglia, but before the end of the year returned to their home base.

Throughout the winter months, N° 217 Squadron kept detachment of aircraft and personnel at Carew. However on 8 July 1940 the squadron completely moved from the airfield to its base at St. Eval, in Cornwall, and was replaced by a flight of Ansons from N° 48 Squadron, which was based at Thorney Island.

In May 1940, members of the Royal Netherlands Naval Air Service, in a collection of 26 land- and water-based aircraft, escaped from Holland when German forces invaded that country. The Fokker T-V111W seaplanes remained at Pembroke Dock while the rest were attached to Carew Cheriton. After familiarisation and training on Anson Is, the Dutch Naval personnel began to receive their own aircraft and on 1 June 1940. N° 321 Squadron was born and, by 28 July, were ready to take part in patrols over the Irish Sea. These patrols continued until January 1941 when the squadron was disbanded. N° 321 Squadron's personnel provided crews for N° 320 (Dutch) Squadron, which by then had been re-equipped with Lockheed Hudson aircraft at Leuchars in Scotland.

Between 14 and 18 June 1940 the airfield became the base for Fairey Swordfish of N° 818 Squadron, Fleet Air Arm, which were attached to Coastal Command to assist with anti-submarine and patrol duties.

RAF Carew was the only 'land-plane' airfield in Pembrokeshire to be bombed by the enemy during the Second World War and drew the wrath of the German

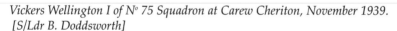

Vickers Wellington I of N° 75 Squadron at Carew Cheriton, November 1939.
[S/Ldr B. Doddsworth]

Avro Anson I of N° 48 Squadron on patrol.

Avro Anson I of N° 10 Radio School, Carew Cheriton. [D. Edwards]

bombers a total of five times; the first raid was in July 1940 and the last was on 15 April 1941. Very little damage was done by any of the raids and each time the airfield was fully operational within a matter of hours.

Milford Haven and Pembroke Dock had been targets for German bombers since the beginning of the war. During a raid on Milford Haven on 19 July 1940 a lone Heinkel He111 dropped eleven bombs on Carew, causing slight damage to the perimeter track and the runway, but there were no casualties. According to German archives the airfield was not the intended target that night, the Heinkel crew appear to have failed to locate Milford, their designated target.

During the raid, a Stranraer flying-boat from Pembroke Dock was sent up to try and intercept the intruders, luckily for the crew no contact was made as the elderly aeroplane would not have stood much of a chance against a He111.

The next raid on the airfield was on 1 October 1940, when a Junkers Ju88 approached the airfield from the direction of Carmarthen Bay, dropping its ordnance across the airfield. This time Carew was not so lucky; a Bellman hangar was destroyed, two-parked Avro Ansons were completely burned out and a Hawker Henley was seriously damaged. It also resulted in the airfield's first wartime fatality when one airman was killed and four others seriously injured. The Junkers returned safely to its base in France.

The next raid was on 10 October, when two Anson's returning from patrol, were followed by a German bomber which dropped a stick of bombs across the airfield. Damage was minimal and there were no casualties. Two visiting Hurricanes were scrambled but no contact was made. There was then a lull in the bombing raids until April 1941.

The most serious raid was actually the last one on 15 April when six Heinkel He111s attacked the airfield, dropping a mixture of high explosive bombs and incendiary devices across the airfield, where they hoped to cause the most damage. Seven Blenheims (of N° 236 Squadron), a Hurricane and an Anson were damaged but all were repairable. There were, however, a number of casualties including twelve airmen who were killed when a bomb hit and destroyed the sick bay. Damage to installations and runways were minimal, civilian workers and RAF personnel made repairs in record time and the airfield was fully operational within twelve hours.

As the result of these nuisance raids a decoy site was built a short distance away, which was bombed by a lone German bomber in October in what was to prove the last raid on the county by the enemy. Angle, Dale, Talbenny and St. David's were more directly involved with combating the U-boat menace and it is strange, therfore, that Carew was regarded as a more serious target by the *Luftwaffe*. The only conclusion which can be drawn was its close location to the First World War airship base at Milton, which the Germans had clearly marked on their maps. Unlike the other airfields in Pembrokeshire, RAF Carew was built in the 1930s, prior to the outbreak of war, and was therefore known to the Germans.

The airfield at Carew Cheriton was used mostly for training, although at the beginning of the war was used as a base for convoy patrol by N° 15 Group Coastal Command, providing in-shore coastal protection to shipping. During its existence the airfield became the base to a variety of aircraft.

On 22 October 1941, N° 22 Squadron detached three Bristol Beaufighters from RAF Bircham Newton to provide long-range escorts for seven Bristol Blenheims which had already arrived from Aldergrove, Northern Ireland. These aircraft were to take part in convoy escort duties over the Irish Sea. Several skirmishes took place between Carew's aircraft and Fokker F200 Condors and Junkers Ju88s, but none was reported as having being shot down.

Bristol Blenheim of N°234 Squadron just returned from a sortie.

Convoy escort duties were Coastal Command's main occupation in Pembrokeshire, but, in 1941, two specially equipped Beaufighters of N° 22 Squadron were detached to Carew to keep an eye on the elements of the French fleet that were bottled-up in French ports, especially Brest. N° 236 Squadron, with eleven Bristol Blenheim IVs and seven Bristol Beaufighter Ics arrived at RAF Carew in March 1941 and remained at the base until February 1942. This squadron was also involved in reconnaissance flights over Brest, using St. Eval as its forward base, and both members of one of its crews, Sergeants Mooney and Phillips, were awarded the DFM. The squadron was also responsible for providing escort duties for BOAC Douglas DC3 flights from Lisbon to the United Kingdom.

Due to the attention the airfield received from German bombers in the early part of 1941, a detachment of Hawker Hurricane Is from N°s 32 and 238 Squadrons from RAF Pembrey were sent to Carew. The fighters remained at the airfield between April and June 1941 and were not once called on to defend the base, except the occasional false alarm scramble. They were, however, called upon to provide escorts for maritime patrol aircraft.

A CCDU (Coastal Command Development Unit) spent a year at Carew between November 1940 and December 1941. It came from Ballykelly in Northern Ireland and was responsible for the service trials of new airborne signalling equipment using a variety of aircraft including Lockheed Hudson Is, Bristol Beauforts and Armstrong Whitworth Whitleys. The unit was scheduled to receive a number of flying-boats in early 1941, but did these did not materialise and Short Sunderlands from nearby Pembroke Dock were utilised in the trials.

Nissen huts photographed at Carew in 1945.

The unit carried out tests of new A.S.V. radar, various types of bombs and depth charges (on both submarines and surface vessels) by both day and night, the latter attacks being carried out with the aid of parachute flares and the newly developed Leigh light (a search light fitted under an aircraft wing and controlled from the cockpit). Other trials conducted by the unit included the installation of beam approach in the Haven for flying-boats. Another little-known trial undertaken at the airfield was the fitting of a tail parachute to a Hudson; the idea being to use the aircraft as a dive-bomber but, after a few hazardous engagements, the idea was dropped.

On 6 January 1942, the airfield was a host to VIPs, namely HRH Prince Peter of Greece and the Polish General Sikorski, both who had escaped from their overrun countries. They had been flown to Pembroke Dock, then travelled by road to Carew where they boarded a DH Flamingo of N° 24 Squadron which flew them on the last leg of their journey to Hendon.

Carew aerial photograph, taken from the Sunderland flying boat, 1944.

Mess hall at Carew before demolition.

Throughout the early wartime life of the airfield a Coastal Command communication flight was based at Carew. Its equipment varied a great deal over the years, but one of its aircraft was the Westland Lysander, which became a common sight in the area. The control of the airfield was handed over to RAF Training Command on 24 July 1942 by which time all Coastal Command activities had ceased.

The first new resident to move in was 'B' Flight, N° 1 A.A.C.U. which was tasked with target towing for the Army School of Anti-Aircraft Defence at Manorbier and the N° 4 Armament Practice Camps. In December 1942, N° 4 Radio Direction Finding School (equipped with ten Airspeed Oxford, twin-engined trainers) of N° 1447 Flight from RAF Hooton Park moved in. This flight was re-designated the following year as 'A' Flight, N° 10 Radio School. In January the school received its second flight, equipped with surplus Ansons from N° 5 O.T.U. at RAF Turnberry. During the Allied advance through Europe in 1944–5, five of the school's Ansons were loaned to H.Q. T.T.C. Communication Flight for use in France and Belgium and, when the aircraft returned to Carew, they boldly displayed the invasion stripes on their wings and fuselages.

As a number of Carew's dispersal areas were not connected with paved sections, a Sommerfield trackway and standing area was laid in 1943 by N° 5017

The unusual control tower at Carew.

Aerial photograph of Carew taken by N° 541 Squadron, 15 April 1946.
[National Assembly for Wales]

Westland Lysander of RAF Coastal Command flight based at Carew.

Airfield Construction Squadron who also re-sited three of the airfield's blister hangars.

In December 1943 N° 4 APC moved to RAF Talbenny and was replaced by 'C' Flight of N° 595 Squadron equipped with Miles Martinets from RAF Aberporth. The flight continued to provide target-towing for both the army at Manorbier and the United States Navy off the south Pembrokeshire coast.

On 31 January 1943 the airfield, which had not previously handled a four-engined aeroplane, was the scene of a forced landing by a USAAF B-24 Liberator which had run short of fuel.

Throughout 1944 the airfield was gradually run down, even by Training Command, and, with the exception of an occasional visiting aircraft, witnessed very little flying activity. Only the Radio School, which had provided the RAF with hundreds of wireless operators for all Commands, remained. The school was eventually disbanded on 13 November 1945, when its aircraft were flown to holding depôts to await disposal. Within ten days the R.A.F. station was officially closed.

When the RAF left in 1945, flying at the airfield ended until June 1976 when Westland Wessex helicopters of N° 846 Squadron, Fleet Air Arm, were based at Carew for three weeks while taking part in an exercise at the nearby Castle Martin Tank Range.

It is worth noting that in 1949 the airfield of Carew was put forward by Tenby Council as a regional airport for the county of Pembrokeshire, but lost out to Withybush which was felt to be better preserved and more centrally situated.

8. Chepstow

Monmouthshire

This airfield, situated on the Chepstow racecourse, became operational on 13 May 1941 as N° 7 SLG under the control of N° 19 MU St. Athan. It was a common practice during both World Wars to use horseracing courses as landing strips, as they provided instant and cheap aerodromes, with hardly any necessary construction required. During the First World War several were used by the Home Defence Units, but by 1939/40 they were more suited for aircraft storage and as emergency landing strips. Although the racecourse at Chepstow was not used in 1914/18 it was earmarked for such use in 1941. The area is situated between the A466 road and the River Wye and two miles from the town of Chepstow. Today there is no evidence that a SLG existed, as no permanent building or aprons were ever built. Some of the original racecourse buildings were used by the station personnel.

Also it was common practice to use the local Home Guard to protect the SLG, as there was a serious shortage of regular army personnel.

As early as 1941 N° 19 MU at St. Athan was experiencing problems with a shortage of storage space as well as the constant threat of attack posed by enemy aircraft. The first aircraft to be stored at Chepstow were some 15 Spitfires and few Hurricanes. Over the next few months several types passed through Chepstow, mostly flown in from St. Athan, usually stored in the open and flown back to the MU when required.

On 21 February 1942 the racecourse SLG was handed over to N° 38 MU Llandow which was also experiencing a lack of storage space.

Unique shields made of wire wool and netting was built to protect and camouflage parked aircraft, but during the summer of 1942 these were replaced by bays built into clearings in the surrounding woodland which considerably increased the storage capacity of the base. It was quite normal to see at least 30–40 aircraft in storage — in May/June 1943 the base had 34 aircraft on its charge, mostly Spitfire and Mustang fighters, with a few Boston and Albemarle bomber.

For the next twelve months the SLG at Chepstow continued to store aircraft for Llandow but, as the war progressed and the threat of enemy attacks diminished, the importance of the airfield diminished and, by December N° 38 MU declared the base closed. It was eventually return to its owners on 31 March 1945 and within months horse-racing was resumed.

The strip did witness a number of emergency landings such as the one on 6 June 1942 when a Spitfire of N° 53 OTU developed an engine fire. The pilot made a crash landing, seriously damaging the aircraft, but fortunately escaped unhurt.

9. Dale
Pembrokeshire

The Dale airfield is located a quarter of mile from the delightful, picturesque seaside village of the same name. It is situated just off the B4327 some 12 miles from Haverfordwest. To the north of the airfield is the little village of Marloes and to the south the scenic St. Anne's Head with its outstanding views and lighthouse.

Both the airfields of Angle and Dale stood in prominent positions on either side of the entrance to the Haven and were in an ideally suited location to protect the important bases at Pembroke Dock and Milford Haven. Dale consisted of three runways in the revised wartime configuration, two of which had approaches over the cliff top that is known locally as Hooper's Point. During the winter months the weather could be very cruel, especially with the cold westerly winds blowing across the bleak cliff tops. However, the scene could completely change in the summer when the wild and beautiful rugged coastline was transformed into a naturalists paradise. As one airman who was brought up in the city remarked, he didn't know such beauty existed until he was posted to RAF Dale.

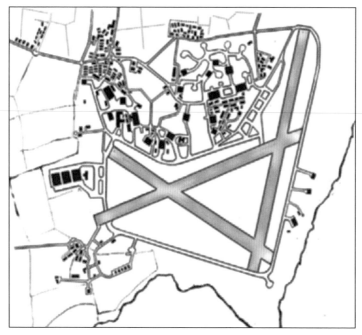

Dale airfield layout, 1945.

Aerial view of Dale airfield, 1990s.

But even during the summer months bad weather was not unknown. On 12 August 1942, when high winds were blowing in from the sea, driving waves hard against the rocky coastline and heavy rain was lashing down on the runways, all coastal shipping was anchored in the shelter of the Haven. The runway into the wind was unserviceable, so patrolling aircraft had to use the North–South runway. Vickers Wellington HX384 of N° 304 (Polish) Squadron, taking off on an anti-submarine patrol, failed to get airborne in the crosswind and disappeared over the cliff edge. After hectic efforts to get to the stricken plane to save the crew, both men and machine disappeared under the rough seas. As with most of the coastal airfields, sea birds were also a great problem. On a number of occasions, birds caused incidents, mostly minor, but there were a few serious ones, resulting in fatalities.

Dispersal points, hangars, workshops and accommodation blocks were to the north-west of the runways with the main entrance toward Marloes. At the time of writing the airfield is in remarkable condition when compared with the other Pembrokeshire wartime airfields. The main runways are more or less still intact and have not been ploughed up — unlike those at RAF Angle, its neighbouring airfield across the Haven. The perimeter track and some of its dispersal pads are still visible but are breaking up and overgrown with weeds and will no doubt eventually be reclaimed by nature. Local farmers and local firms use the watch tower and a hangar, as well as several buildings on the domestic site.

Vickers Wellington 1c N° 304 (Polish) Squadron 1942/3. [RAF Museum]

Dale airfield became operational on 1 June 1942 as a satellite base to RAF Talbenny under the control of N° 19 Group, RAF Coastal Command, tasked with flying anti-U-boat patrols over the Bay of Biscay and protecting convoys in the Western Approaches. The command flew mostly flying-boats from bases like Pembroke Dock but, because of the threat to the convoys, the life line of Britain, several land-based squadrons were transferred to convoy duties and they required modern airfields.

The first squadron to be based at Dale was N° 304 equipped with Vickers Wellington bombers. This Polish squadron had just completed a year of bomber operations over Germany prior to its transfer to Coastal Command. It arrived at Dale on 15 June 1942 from RAF Tiree and was to support another Wellington squadron, N° 311 (Czech) at RAF Talbenny, which had arrived in the county at the beginning of June. Up to then Coastal Command land based aircraft had consisted of a collection of obsolescent light aircraft for submarine spotting. (Ansons, Swordfish, Austers, Tiger Moths, Lysanders, etc). The Vickers Wellington bomber was powered by two 1500 hp Hercules engines, which gave it the top speed of 255 mph, an operational range of over 2,000miles and an ability to carry a 2,000 lbs bomb load, the Wellington was a formidable weapon against the U-boat menace and paved the way for later types such as the Warwick and the Halifax to enter service with Coastal Command in 1943/44.

The squadron's first operation was on 10 July, when seven aircraft were airborne on an anti submarine reconnaissance patrol. Wellington 'T' for Tommy spotted a surfaced U-boat, which it attacked dropping four depth charges on the target, but sinking was un-confirmed. On 27 July 1942 aircraft from N° 304 Squadron were again in action, this time a Wellington attacked an Arado Ar196 floatplane during a patrol. Unfortunately, due to low fuel, they had to break off the attack, whilst the enemy aircraft was seen leaving the vicinity with smoke trailing from its engine. In August, N° 304 Squadron, together with its sister squadron from RAF Talbenny, took part in the high-level bombing of a tanker in La Pallice and in anti-shipping raids in the Gironde Estuary.

The Wellington was a very robust design, and on a number of occasions was able to limp back to base, where other aircraft would have crashed. One such example happened on 16 September, when 'E' for Ella took off from Dale on a routine daylight patrol in the Bay of Biscay. The lone Wellington was attacked by six Junkers Ju88s, was credited with shooting down two of them, but was badly holed with several six-inch holes in its starboard fuel tank, the oil tank badly ruptured with oil pouring everywhere and the starboard engine so shot up, that it had to be shut down. To make the situation intolerable the fuselage was full of acrid black smoke. The aircraft did not have sufficient fuel to reach Dale and had to try and land at RAF Portreath in Cornwall. With enough fuel to make just one attempt the pilot, F/O Targowski, made a faultless landing and for his gallant exploit was awarded the DFC. However tragedy struck on 16 October, when F/O Targowski and his crew failed to return from another Bay of Biscay patrol.

After spending another winter at Dale, N° 304 Squadron left in March 1943 for Docking in Norfolk. A Coastal Command Development Unit from Tain replaced the unit in April and was joined for few weeks by N° 303 FTU from Talbenny while that airfield's lighting system was upgraded.

During this period there was a lull in flying activity at Dale which lasted until 1 September 1943 when the Royal Navy exchanged its base at Angle with RAF Dale. For some time the RAF considered Angle a better located airfield for their purpose, especially in support of the flying-boat base at Pembroke Dock. So Dale airfield became HMS *Goldcrest*.

The Admiralty made several changes to the airfield, a new concrete apron was added, a standard RN pattern four-storey control tower was built (which was not finally completed until 1945). Several BCF concrete huts replaced the wooden ones and two naval Mainhill hangars were built to supplement the airfield's T2s and blister hangars. The Main or Mainhill hangars were modified naval versions of the extended blister hangars. The hangars were 72' x 60', with a sliding-door only at one end and were designed to accommodate folded-wing aircraft.

The first naval unit to occupy the airfield was N° 764 Naval squadron which arrived on 10 September. This was an air target-towing unit equipped with Defiants, Fulmars, Masters and Martinets. However their stay was short lived as on 22 November they left for Henstridge.

The Fleet Air Arm was short of large airfields with good length runways especially for their twin-engined aircraft. So, on 31 March 1944, N° 762 Squadron moved in with its twin-engined aircraft, Blenheim IVs, Beaufighters, Beaufort T11s and later Mosquitoes. The unit was responsible for training Fleet Air Arm

Seafire of Nº 790 Squadron, Fleet Air Arm parked in front of the Mainhill hangar.

crews on twin-engined aircraft. This training continued more or less non-stop until the squadron moved to Ford on 20 June 1945.

Between February 1944 and August 1945 Dale was one of the Fleet Air Arm's busiest shore bases. As well as being involved in training, several first-line operational squadrons passed through the airfield including Nᵒˢ 809 and 897 Squadrons with their Supermarine Seafire L11cs, Nº 1770 Squadron Fairey Firefly Mk VIIs and Nº 748 Squadron with its American Corsairs.

30 August 1945 saw the arrival of Nº 790 Squadron with its Fireflies, a training and conversion unit, which remained at Dale until 13 December 1947, when it moved to the new base at Culdrose. However by then the unit had became 'B' Flight Nº 790 Squadron RN.

From 15 January 1946 Dale became the home of the FAA Night-Fighting School with Nº 748 Squadron as its core. The squadron was equipped with a night-fighter version of the Grumman Hellcat 11 and a few Mosquitoes. The unit was involved with training Fleet Air Arm pilots in night-fighting as it was intended to base detachments on various carriers. As the war was over there was a general run-down in all the three services and Nº 748 Squadron was disbanded at Dale on 10 September 1946.

Another squadron that became a resident at Dale was Nº 861 (Royal Netherlands Navy) Squadron, which was formed at Dale on 16 September 1946, equipped with four Fairey Fireflies. After completing the squadron's training under the Fleet Air Arm, the aircraft were sold to the Dutch to become one of the units embarked on their newly acquired aircraft carrier the *Karel Doorman* Nº 861 Squadron was disbanded.

When the training school left Dale the airfield's closure was imminent. Various departments and sections at the airfield closed and staffing was reduced. The only flying was by visiting aircraft from other shore bases, although during

Fleet Air Arm control tower, Dale, 1945.

the summer months the airfield was occasionally used by aircraft from carriers that were in dock. By the end of the year, most of the sailors had left and all sections closed down, except for a small administrative staff that remained until the base was officially closed on 13 December 1947.

Surprisingly there are various RAF and Admiralty buildings still standing including Maycrete, Nissen and BCF huts, although the three-storey Admiralty control tower has been demolished. Situated just off the perimeter track, overlooking the sea, is the station Battle Headquarters. At the time of writing the naval Mainhill hangar still remains (see photograph).

Remains of a RN Mainhill type hangar in 1988.

Dale domestic site as it was in 1988.

10. Fairwood Common

Swansea

Fairwood Common is situated on the Gower peninsula, just off the A4118 Swansea to Port Eynon road and some 5 miles from Swansea. From its planning stage Fairwood Common was be a fighter station which took just over twelve months to construct, using large quantities of industrial spoil to level the site, which was once a bog. The airfield followed the usual Air Ministry pattern of three runways: runway 23/05 northeast–southeast, which was 4,800 feet in length; runway 29/11 west–east which was 4,100 feet; 33/15 northwest–southeast which was also 4,100 feet in length. The airfield has a unique system of taxiways, interconnecting the three runways, dispersal points and the hangars. Three Bellman hangars and eight blister hangars were built during the war years. Two bay extensions to the blisters were built in February 1945. On the western and southern sides of the airfield there were six single-engine pens (each accommodating two single-engined fighters) and nine twin-engined pens. The airfield had also twenty-nine fighter hard-standings around the perimeter track.

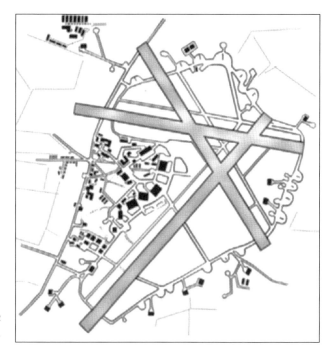

Fairwood Common ground plan, 1944.

71

Pilots of N° 303 (Polish) Squadron pose in front of a Spitfire.
[Swansea Airport]

The domestic sites, which were numerous, accommodated the continual in- and out-flow of squadrons. They were situated in the fields to the north and east of the airfield, and comprised of twelve large sleeping sites, sick quarters, concert halls, NAAFI and other miscellaneous buildings; all were of wooden construction. The Officers Mess was at the requisitioned Fairwood Lodge.

The airfield was opened on 15 July 1941 within N° 10 Group Fighter Command and became the most important fighter base in south Wales. The first aircraft to be stationed here were the Hurricane Is of N° 79 Squadron which were transferred from nearby Pembrey on 14 June 1941. One of the squadron's most famous pilots was Roland Beaumont, DFC, who was a flight commander at the time. Bristol Beaufighter IIs of N° 600 Squadron replaced the Hurricane squadron and they were in turn replaced by Spitfires of N° 317 Squadron from RAF Colerne. Although the squadron's stay was short, it made a name for itself by shooting down a Ju88 some ten miles south of the base on 14 July 1941. The airfield became a full sector station on 25 October 1941.

During the *Baedecker* raid by the *Luftwaffe* on Bath on the night of 26/27 April 1942, N° 125 Squadron Beaufighters, Defiants and Hurricanes from Fairwood and RAF Charmy Down flew several patrols over the city. During one of the ensuing two skirmishes they claimed one enemy aircraft probably destroyed and one damaged. On another occasion a N° 125 Beaufighter shot down a Ju88 off the Pembrokeshire coast.

Fighter squadrons were rotated through Fairwood at a very fast pace because of the two armament practice camps based at the airfield, which were involved in

Women of the ATS attached to the Ops Room at
Fairwood Common, 1943/4 [Ann Jones]

air-to-air and air-to-ground firing. In most cases the courses would last from ten days to two weeks. However, during their stay, the squadrons would also be involved in various convoy patrols around the Welsh coast as well as in the air defence of important installations and cities. The station was often used as a rest base for some of the front-line squadrons. Towards the end of the war Fairwood was often used for squadron conversion and re-equipping.

The two armament practice camps based at Fairwood Common were primarily used by fighter-bomber units of N° 83 and 84 Groups and of the 2nd Tactical Air Force. N° 11 APC was formed at Fairwood on 1 October 1943 and N° 18 APC in August 1944. The main target range was Broughton Burrows near Llangennith, which was used by Spitfires and Typhoons for cannon- and rocket-firing practice. The other range was near Margam, where floating targets were used. A stretch of railway line at Rosebush in the Preseli Hills was also used for a short period in 1944 to train pilots in ground attacks on railway lines using 500lb bombs and damage assessment; for some time the RAF had been bombing railway lines in occupied France, but reconnaissance photos showed that the lines

The Duke of
Gloucester meeting
members of N° 307
(Polish) Squadron,
4 June 1943. [PRO]

were back in operation within two days. To assess the findings it was decided to carry out trials on the Rosebush section of railway. Typhoons, armed with two 500 lb HE bombs, bombed the line causing considerable damage but, within 48 hours the damage was repaired and the line was again operational. As a result of this, a change of tactics was adopted and it was decided to concentrate future attacks on bridges, tunnels and rolling stock.

Like most active airfields, Fairwood Common drew the attention of enemy bombers. The worst raid was on 16 February 1943 when eleven enemy bombers dropped bombs on the airfield. The accommodation section was badly hit and three WAAFs were killed. However, a Beaufighter of N° 125 Squadron managed to shoot down two Dornier Do217s.

Fairwood night fighters were responsible for the protection of south-west England and patrols around the Exeter area became a standard pattern. During one patrol, on 27 March 1944, two Beaufighters of N° 307 Squadron were diverted onto a group of enemy aircraft. One Ju88 was shot down near Wells and the rest limped home with cannon shell holes in their fuselages. By the summer of 1944 the threat of enemy bombers had diminished and, with the departure of N° 68 Squadron with its Beaufighter VIs in June, the station's status as an active operational airfield ceased and it became a training station for Fighter Command, remaining under the control of N° 10 Group.

On 1 October 1 1943 N° 11 APC was formed at Fairwood, with the responsibility for training crews in ground attack. A section of disused railway line was requisitioned and driverless trains provided targets for rocket and cannon fire. In all, twenty-nine squadrons passed through the unit before it closed on 1 July 1945. N° 18 APC was formed at Fairwood in August 1944 and remained at the airfield until 1 July 1945.

Also based at the airfield was a detachment of Lysanders, which provided ASR (Air Sea Rescue) coverage for the area. 'C' Flight, a detachment from N° 595 Squadron, equipped with five Martinets, had been stationed at Fairwood since September 1944 on target towing duties. The flight left on 14 November 1945.

Fairwood was used as a diversionary airfield by Bomber Command, Transport Command and the USAAF. On 29 March 1944 a B24D Liberator of the 405 (Heavy) Bombardment Group, based in Italy, was diverted to Fairwood because of bad weather. It seems it was on a secret mission to pick up radar equipment from RAF St Mawgan when it was diverted. As the aircraft approached Fairwood it ran out of fuel resulting in a total loss of power on all engines. Four of the crew baled out and landed safely, while the pilot and the crew chief stayed with the aircraft. The pilot tried to land the aircraft but failed and made a crash landing near Kittle Lane in which both were badly injured. The pilot later recovered from his injuries but unfortunately the crew chief did not.

On Easter Sunday, 9 April 1944, a Halifax Mk III of Nº 1658 Heavy Conversion Flight 'R' for Roger, based at RAF Pocklington, Yorkshire, crashed while making an emergency landing. Unfortunately the aircraft demolished a WAAF hut where some airwomen were sleeping at the time. One WAAF was killed while several others were slightly injured.

In August 1944, a Wellington with an engine fire attempted to make an emergency landing but crashed after hitting some trees.

From April 1946 the airfield became the permanent home for Nº 595 Squadron, which was responsible for providing target facilities for all the services. The unit was equipped with Miles Martinet Is, Airspeed Oxford Is & IIs, and Spitfire Mk IXs and LF16s. As there was a shortage of pilots, it took the unit two days to move all the aircraft, and 'on loan' pilots were ferried back to Aberporth in Nº 691 Squadron Oxfords. Nº 595 Squadron remained at Fairwood until October 1946 when it left for Pembrey where it was renumbered as Nº 5 Squadron. On 12 March 1946, one of Nº 595 Squadron's Spitfires, piloted by F/O Abbott (based at Aberporth) was diverted to Fairwood, as his home airfield was water-logged. For the next few weeks he operated out of Fairwood, but, on 21 March, while flying in cloud, the aircraft crashed for no apparent reason and he was killed.

Nº 691 Squadron made a brief appearance at the airfield in 1946 arriving in July from RAF Weston Zoyland and departing for RAF Chivenor in October. The unit was equipped with Oxford Is, Vultee Vengeance IVs, Martinet Is and Spitfire LF16s. Although it was officially a training squadron, its aircraft were used for light transport and special flights.

In all, sixty-five different squadrons passed through RAF Fairwood Common, some visiting more than once.

Nº 19 Squadron, a detachment was based at Fairwood during October 1942 equipped with Spitfire VBs and VCs.

Nº 33 Squadron, for few weeks in August 1944: equipped with Spitfire LF IXs.

Nº 41 Squadron with Spitfire XII, 16 May–26 May 1944.

Nº 65 Squadron with Mustang IVs from 13 August to 6 September 1945.

Nº 66 Squadron from 20 February–16 March 1945 equipped with Spitfire XVIs.

Nº 68 Squadron, March 1944 to June 1944 equipped with Bristol Beaufighter VIFs under the command of W/C D. Haley Bell, DFC. Squadron left for RAF Castle Combe in June.

Nº 74 Squadron, from 7 January–15 February 1946 equipped with Gloster Meteor F3s. This was the first jet squadron to visit Fairwood.

Nº 79 Squadron arrived from Pembrey in June 1941 equipped with Hawker Hurricane Is & IIs. This unit participated in the daylight raid on Brest on 24 July

Handley Page Halifax III after crash-landing at Fairwood Common, 9 April 1944.

1941 with N° 504 Squadron's Hurricane. It left Fairwood in December 1941 for RAF Baignton and eventually on to India.

N° 91 Squadron, two weeks in July 1945 equipped with Spitfire Mk XXIs.

N° 118 Squadron, August/September 1945 with Mustang IIIs under the command of S/Ldr. A. Drew, DFC.

N° 124 Squadron, detachment equipped with Spitfire VIIs from March to July 1943. The squadron returned to the base in February/March 1946 with Meteor F3s.

N° 125 Squadron, September 1941–January 1942: equipped with Defiant Is, left for RAF Colerne but a detachment returned to Fairwood in May 1942. By the end of May the whole squadron had arrived and was re-equipped with Bristol Beaufighter IIFs. The squadron moved to Exeter in April 1943.

N° 127 Squadron February/March 1945 with Spitfire LF IXs and XVIs. (C/O F. W. Lister, DFC).

N° 131 Squadron for one week in February 1944 with Spitfire IXs.

N° 132 Squadron for one week in March 1944 equipped with Spitfire VIs.

N° 164 Squadron, with a detachment at Peterhead from January to February 1943 equipped with Spitfire VBs left for RAF Middle Wallop. The squadron was again stationed at Fairwood Common from November 1945 to January 1946, this time with Spitfire IXs.

N° 165 Squadron for one week March 1944. with Spitfire IXbs.

N° 183 Squadron with Spitfire IXs and Tempest IIs from 8 October–15 November 1945.

N° 193 Squadron with Typhoon Ibs from 18 September–6 October 1944.

N° 197 Squadron again with Typhoon Ibs from 28 November–12 December 1944.

N° 198 Squadron equipped with Typhoon Ibs from 6–21 November 1944.

N° 222 Squadron with Hawker Tempest Vs from 4 June–25 June 1945.

Spitfire XII of N° 41 Squadron, 1944. [Swansea Airport]

N° 245 Squadron equipped with Gloster Meteor F3s from 18 February–20 February 1946.

N° 247 Squadron from 7 January–16 February 1946 with Tempest IIs.

N° 257 Squadron August 1944, while being re-equipped with Typhoon Ibs, prior to a return posting to France (St Croix).

N° 263 Squadron equipped with Westland Whirlwinds FIs February/March 1942 under the command of R. S. Woodward, DFC. The squadron left for RAF Angle on the Pembrokeshire coast. A detachment returned to Fairwood in September 1942 and remained until January 1943.

The squadron was re-equipped with Typhoon Ibs and returned for a few weeks in January 1944 and again in January/February 1945.

N° 264 Squadron arrived from RAF Predannack in July 1943 and left for RAF Colbey Grange on 12 November 1943 equipped with Mosquito night fighters.

N° 266 Squadron equipped with Hawker Typhoon Ibs from April to June 1945.

N° 268 Squadron equipped with Mustang IIs, from 13 January to 9 February 1945.

N° 276 Squadron. A detachment was based here from January 1942 to 4 April 1944. This was an air-sea rescue unit equipped with Walrus, Spitfire IIas, Defiant Is, Ansons and Sea Otters.

N° 285 Squadron, again a detachment equipped with Martinets, Beaufighters and Hurricane Is.

N° 286 Squadron, a detachment was based at Fairwood for various periods from April 1942 to 1944, with Hurricane IIs.

N° 302 (Polish) Squadron, with Spitfire Vcs, arrived from RAF Northolt in December 1943 and returned to RAF Northolt within a couple of weeks. However the squadron returned to Fairwood with their LFIXe series in August/September 1944 prior the squadron return to Lille in France.

N° 306 (Polish) Squadron arrived from RAF Coltishall in October 1945 with

Westland Whirlwind of N° 263 Squadron, winter 1942. [MAP]

Mustang IIIs and remained for a month.

N° 307 (Polish) Squadron, equipped with Mosquito Mk IIs, April to August 1943, left for RAF Predannack.

N° 308 Squadron from April to June 1945 with Spitfire XVIs.

N° 312 (Czech) Squadron, January 1942 while on transit from RAF Ayr to RAF Angle in Pembrokeshire. The squadron was equipped with Spitfire IIbs, but when they returned to Fairwood between April and May 1942 was re-equipped with Mk Vbs.

N° 315 (Polish) Squadron, November/December 1945, with Mustang IIIs.

N° 317 (Polish) Squadron with Hurricane Is from RAF Colerne on June 1941 left six weeks later for RAF Exeter.

N° 322 (Dutch) Squadron, equipped with Spitfire LF IXb under the command of C. M. Van Eendenberg. The squadron only remained for three weeks in October 1944.

N° 329 Squadron with Spitfire IXs from 16 July–10 August 1945.

N° 331 (Norwegian) Squadron made two brief visit to the base with its Spitfire IXs: 19 September–6 October 1944, and 14 March–2 April 1945.

N° 332 (Norwegian) Squadron (AH) 11–31 December 1944 with Spitfire IXs (C/O Major J. Tyedte).

N° 345 (French) Squadron, for one week in October 1944 and again in March/April 1945 while being re-equipped with Spitfire HF IXs. The unit came from and returned to Schijndel.

N° 401 Squadron, April 1944 equipped with Spitfire IXs from RAF Biggin Hill left for RAF Tangmere.

N° 402 (Canadian) Squadron May 1942 equipped with Spitfire Vbs was involved in convoy duties.

N° 403 (Canadian) Squadron September to October 1944 with Spitfire IXbs under the command of E. P. Wood.

N° 411 (Canadian) Squadron with Spitfire IXs from 17–22 April 1943.

N° 412 Squadron. The first time the squadron was stationed at Fairwood was during February/March 1943 with Spitfire Vbs; the unit arrived from RAF Angle and left for RAF Hurn. The squadron returned during April 1943 and again in March/April 1944.

N° 421 (Canadian) Squadron was based at Fairwood for most of 1942. The squadron was equipped with Spitfire Vbs.

> May–June 1942 C/O was F. W. Kelly.

> July–October 1942 C/O was F. C. Wills.

> October–November 1942 C/O was F. E. Green, DFC.

The squadron left for RAF Angle in Pembrokeshire.

N° 456 (Australian) Squadron arrived from RAF Colerne on 14 November 1943 and left for RAF Ford on 20 February 1944, equipped with Mosquito IIs.

N° 485 (New Zealand) Squadron equipped with Spitfire IXs from 2–26 November 1944.

N° 504 Squadron, 21 July–12 August 1941 with Hurricane IIs under the command of S/Ldr P. T. Parsons. The squadron's Hurricanes took part in the daylight raids on Brest on 24 July. The squadron left for RAF Chilbolton.

N° 536 Squadron (Turbinlite Unit) arrived early October 1942 equipped with Havoc Is & IIs. These aircraft were fitted with a searchlight in the nose for night-fighting. A detachment was based at RAF Exeter. The squadron was eventually disbanded at Fairwood on 25 January 1943.

N° 577 Squadron. This was an anti-aircraft co-operation unit which operated

Hawker Typhoon IB of No 266 Squadron, 1945.

throughout Wales at the north-west of England providing target-towing facilities for aircraft and ground gunners. It was equipped with Hurricanes, Oxfords, Beaufighters, Vengeances and Spitfires.

N° 595 Squadron. This was another anti-aircraft co-operation unit formed at RAF Aberporth and remained in Wales for most of the time. Its function was similar to that of N° 577 Squadron. The complete unit was based at Fairwood from 27 April–October 1946 operating only Spitfire XVIs.

N° 600 Squadron equipped with Beaufighter VIs for about ten days in June 1941.

N° 609 (West Riding) Squadron equipped with Typhoon Ibs, 6–20 February 1944, and again from 4–23 June 1945. This was originally a Royal Auxiliary Air Force squadron, which was formed at Yeadon Aerodrome, Leeds in 1936.

N° 610 (City of Chester) Squadron, Royal Auxiliary Air Force, December 1943–January 1944 equipped with Spitfire Vbs.

N° 616 Squadron, April–May 1944 with Spitfire VIIs under the command of S/Ldr L. W. Watts, DFC.

N° 691 Squadron with Harvard IIbs from July–October 1946.

By the end of 1946 all RAF squadrons had left Fairwood Common and over the next twelve months the airfield was put on care and maintenance and for three years there were hardly any aircraft movements at all until Cambrian Airways made an offer to re-activate the airfield for civilian passenger flights. But it was not until 1956 that the land was de-requisitioned by the Air Ministry and the aerodrome was handed over to Swansea Corporation who re-opened it as

Swansea Airport 1990s.

Swansea Airport on 1 June 1956. In 1951, Cambrian Airways had been awarded a five-year agreement to operate a Haverfordwest–Swansea–Cardiff service but, as Fairwood had not been de-requisitioned, only the Haverfordwest to Cardiff sector was operated. Cambrian's first flight from Swansea did not take place until 1 June 1957, when DH Heron G-AORT inaugurated the Swansea–Jersey scheduled service. Initially, the service was three times weekly but, due to a promising load factor, was increased to a four times weekly service. Over the next few years further flights took place to Dublin and Ostend. In 1968 the airline withdrew the last of its Dakotas, which led to the pruning of flights from small airports, and all flights from Fairwood ended in 1968.

Another airline that took an interest in the airport was Morton Air Services, which in April 1959 introduced a Brawdy–Croydon scheduled service with a stop at Swansea. Their first service via Swansea was inaugurated on 2 June 1959 by Heron G-AOGO. Subsequently stops at the airport were only made when traffic demanded. Gatwick replaced Croydon as the London destination aerodrome in October 1959 and the last Croydon flight from Swansea was on Tuesday 29 September by Dove G-ANAN, piloted by Captain Jeffrey. The London (Gatwick) services were increased to daily flights by 1967. British United Airways took over the entire airline scheduled routes from Fairwood, but, by 1968, had dropped Swansea from all their operations.

Trans European Airways Ltd, was founded at Fairwood Common in May 1959 to provide passenger and freight services with two DH Dragon Rapides but, by the end of the year, they moved their operations to Coventry Airport.

Other airlines that used the airport were the Midland based Derby Airways and Dan Air, which took over the Channel Islands services. Air Anglia was awarded licences to operate a service between Aberdeen, the Isle of Man and Swansea in 1964, but the service never materialised.

Severn Airways was another regional airline to include Fairwood in its schedule, when on 5 May 1975 inaugurated the Bristol–Swansea–Cork service. However, on 12 May, Dove G-APZU with six passengers over-ran the runway while landing in wet conditions and failed to stop before crashing through the boundary fence. By the end of the year the airline had ceased trading and Swansea was again without a scheduled passenger service.

In August 1960, Swansea Airways tried to start a Fairwood-based air charter operation using a Percival Prentice and a Dragon Rapide. Unfortunately the company ceased trading in early 1961.

Due to the introduction of heavier aircraft, especially turbo-prop and jet powered airliners, the airport put forward plans for redevelopment in the early 1970s, but, by then, it had been decided that Rhoose was to be the main south Wales international airport. A modest investment was put into the aerodrome:

The modified control tower at Swansea Airport.

one runway was resurfaced and extended to 6,000ft, but the shorter runways were reduced from 4,100ft to 3,200ft because their over-runs crossed the A4118 road. A terminal building was also built which could handle up to 100 passengers.

Swansea Airport has the same problems facing other small regional aerodromes in Wales: the lack of interest and support by airlines, the local population, the business fraternity and some local authorities.

Today most of the aircraft movements at Swansea Airport are by private aircraft, which makes it fairly busy at weekends but does not generate a fraction of the aircraft movements that the airfield has been used to. There is a successful flying school based at the airport, that attracts enthusiasts from all over south Wales.

In 2002 Air Wales, obtained a licence to operate Swansea Airport on behalf of local council. The airline began a twice weekly service to Cork from Swansea, other scheduled services were planed but never materialised. By today, all services from Swansea have been discontinued. Until early 2000, the De Havilland Aviation flying museum was based at the airport with four DH Vampires, Venom and a Sea Vixen, but sadly the museum moved to Bournemouth in May 2000.

Gradually, this unique wartime airfield is disappearing, although the original control tower is still in use but has changed its appearance over the years. Only one of the Bellman hangars remains and has been renovated. The station armoury, the tractor and trailer shed and several other minor buildings have also survived. The fighter pens and most of the taxiways along the western side are overgrown and are being reclaimed by nature. Runway 15/33 is no longer in use.

11. Fishguard Harbour

Pembrokeshire

Fishguard harbour became a Royal Naval Air Service seaplane base as the result of the mounting enemy submarine attacks on Allied shipping in the Irish Sea during 1917. Over the years, attacks on coastal shipping had trebled; enemy U-boats were using the rugged coastline of southern Ireland as shelter and, by the time a warship reached the scene, the U-boat had disappeared, either into the open Atlantic or to the safety of the Irish coast. The only solution was to set up seaplane bases at strategic positions along the coast. Fishguard Harbour, with its sheltered bay, was an ideal location for such a base.

The Royal Naval Air Service stationed only six seaplanes at the base, consisting of three Fairey Hamble Babies and three Short 184 seaplanes. All belonged to N[os] 426 and 427 Coastal Patrol Flights of N[o] 245 Squadron. The serial numbers of the aircraft are not certain as the seaplanes tended to be inter-changed with other coastal patrol flights. The Commanding Officer of the base was Major F. Denhamm Till.

The base consisted of one small hangar, constructed with a wooden frame covered with canvas, which was used mostly for aircraft maintenance rather than storage, as the seaplanes were usually moored in the bay. All accommodation was

Aerial photograph of Fishguard Bay showing clearly the breakwater, the port of Goodwick and the site of the RNAS station outside the outer breakwater.
[K. Williams]

*Short 184 seaplane of Nº 427 Coastal Patrol Flight of Nº 245 Squadron,
based at Fishguard in 1918.*

also under canvas, except the Officers Mess which was located in the Bay Hotel
and a nearby requisitioned cottage.

According to records the seaplanes based at Fishguard made several
sightings, but there are no records of any submarines being either damaged or
sunk. However their presence was a deterrent as on a few occasions surfaced
submarines made a hasty retreat when a seaplane appeared on the horizon. One
such sighting occurred in November 1917 when two aircraft from Fishguard went
to the aid of a trawler which was being attacked by a surfaced U-boat. By the time
the aircraft got to the scene the submarine had gone and the trawler was limping
back to port. But, on their return to Fishguard, one of the aircraft spotted what
looked like a periscope trail in the sea. The Short 184 made a low pass and
dropped two 25 lb bombs, at least one of which exploded but they could not
confirm a kill.

None of the seaplanes based at Fishguard were shot down or damaged by
enemy fire, although accidents were common and several mishaps occurred
during take off and landing. The only fatal casualty occurred when, on 22 April
1917, a Sopwith Baby (N10330, piloted by Lt Eldon Bush, failed to stop when
landing and crashed into a cliff, the pilot dying of his injuries few days later in
hospital.

The base was dismantled and its personnel and equipment transferred to
other bases on 10 May 1919, leaving no evidence whatsoever that a seaplane base
had ever existed. However, according to local residents, a few concrete moorings
did survive for some time and were used by local fishermen to moor their boats.
They too disappeared with redevelopment and the strengthening of the sea
defences. At the time of writing only the concrete slipway remains.

12. Haroldston

Pembrokeshire

Situated some five miles west of Haverfordwest, Pembrokeshire and two and a half miles from the Broad Haven road, a short distant from the hamlet of Haroldston this is one of the lesser-known airfields of Wales. It should be described as an airstrip, or a relief landing ground, rather than an airfield as it consisted of two fields with the hedges removed. It was opened as a relief landing area for the new airfield at RAF Withybush towards the end of February 1942, months before its parent airfield was officially opened. A local cottage (Tongs Cottage) at the edge of the field near the public road was requisitioned and was later used by the two or three airmen that were on permanent duty at the location. Their duty included placing markers out on the field for incoming aircraft as well as guard duty, which included a duty in a makeshift gun post.

There is no official record of any aircraft making an emergency landing at the site. Although local inhabitants recalled of a small biplane, probably a Tiger Moth or a Queen Bee making an emergency landing the summer of 1942. Also, one of Carew's Ansons, returning from a patrol in August 1942, circled the field twice, but decided it was safer to proceed to RAF Talbenny. All emergency landings were done at nearby Talbenny, which had tarmac runways and full emergency services.

Haroldston closed in 1943, as there were by then sufficient other airfields in Pembrokeshire to cope with any emergency. Tong Cottage was returned to its rightful owners a year later.

13. Haverfordwest (Withybush)

Pembrokeshire

This aerodrome is situated at Withybush, about two miles north of the county town of Haverfordwest, on the A40 trunk road to Fishguard. It is only a short distance from the new hospital, which was built on the site of the old war-time Withybush Hospital.

The history of Withybush airfield goes back to early 1940, when the site was chosen for the development of a full airfield. Within weeks of the decision being made, people were given twenty-four hours to move out of their homes and shortly afterwards the heavy plant machinery of the airfield construction units moved in. It soon became apparent that the area chosen was not an easy site to build an airfield on as problem after problem occurred, mostly with the weather and the contour of the land, which delayed the official opening until 10 November 1942; even then the airfield was far from complete but, as the heavy plant and most of the labour force had been transferred to the construction of the new airfields at St Davids and Brawdy, the task of completing the airfield and buildings was handed over to a number of local firms.

When four Whitley bombers of N° 3 Operational Training Unit (the first unit to be officially based at RAF Withybush) complete with ground crew, arrived from RAF Cranwell on 30 November, the whole airfield was covered in mud and water, most of the accommodation section had not been completed and those buildings nearing completion were lacking a roof. Construction work on the hangars had not been started and only the control tower and runways had been completed. The Whitleys were refuelled by civilian tankers that were on the base

Armstrong Whitworth Whitley of N° 3 OTU at Withybush. [B. Owen]

Ground plan of Haverfordwest (Withybush) airfield.

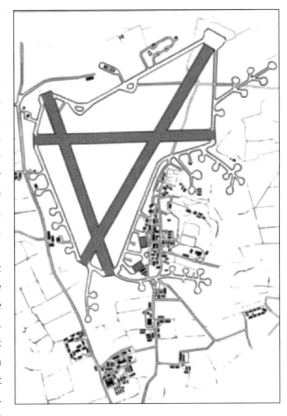

and returned to Cranwell the same day. Later, the unit's Whitleys, Wellingtons and Ansons arrived and set up a reconnaissance training programme. From 5 October 1943–1 November 1944 the unit's Polish flight, equipped with Wellington bombers, operated out of Withybush.

Another problem that became apparent at the time was the overloading of the town's only power station, resulting in a blackout not only at the airfield but also in the town of Haverfordwest and the surrounding area. This was only remedied a year later when an oil-powered generator was installed at the airfield.

Eventually N° 3 OTU's ageing Whitleys were replaced by more Wellington bombers. However, due to limited space at Withybush, 'O' Flight was detached to the satellite airfield at RAF Templeton, while the Ansons were despatched in December to join N° 12 Radio School at RAF St Athan. N° 3 OTU was disbanded on 4 January 1943.

In May 1944 General Reconnaissance Aircraft Preparation Pool was formed at the airfield, but moved to RAF St David's on 1 October 1944, where it remained until the unit was disbanded January 1946. The unit operated Wellington XIVs, Liberator GR Vs, GR VIs and Halifax GRIIs.

On 4 January 1944, N° 7 OTU, equipped with Wellingtons, arrived from RAF Limevady, Northern Ireland. This unit's main responsibility was general reconnaissance and A.S.V. training. On 16 May 1944 the unit was renamed N° 4 Refresher Flying Unit, but it too was disbanded in September. During its short stay at Withybush the unit was involved in training crews, mostly for Coastal Command, as well as ferrying aircraft to various Coastal Command units throughout the UK.

Armstrong Whitworth Whitley of Nº 3 OTU waiting for the completion of the final maintenance checks prior to a training flight. [Air Heritage]

In January 1945 the airfield vibrated to the sound of the Merlin engines of the photo-reconnaissance Mosquitoes and Spitfires of Nº 8 OTU from RAF Dyce near Aberdeen. The unit was involved in training photo-reconnaissance pilots for the RAF, in both high- and low-level flying. Areas around the Preseli Mountains were often use for low-level training, much to the annoyance of local farmers. The unit's secondary role was to carry out an aerial survey of the British Isles, which continued until April 1945 when it was taken over by a specialised survey unit. Nº 8 OTU consisted of five flights, of which four was based at Withybush ('B', 'C', 'D' and 'F'), while 'A' flight was stationed at RAF Templeton airfield.

In early 1945, Withybush had an acute parking problem as it had twice as many aircraft as it had been originally intended to accommodate. Plans were put forward to re-open the Rudbaxton grass strip but, on 27 February, it was decided to move thirty Mosquitoes and Spitfires to the newly completed satellite airfield at RAF Brawdy. Their stay there was short lived, however, as on 21 June all of Nº 8 OTU moved to RAF Mount Farm airfield, near Benson, which was to be the main RAF photographic reconnaissance base.

While on a reconnaissance exercise over Snowdonia on 20 February 1945, a Mosquito (NT221) of Nº 8 OTU made a forced landing on the beach at Harlech due to an engine fire. Initially the landing went well, but the aircraft was unable to stop and hit a sand dune and caught fire. Unfortunately the pilot died from his injuries in RAF Llandwrog sick bay.

The last operational RAF unit to leave Withybush was the Aircrew Holding Unit, which left for Thorney Island on 22 November 1945. Within a matter of months, most of the RAF personnel had left the base and a care and maintenance staff remained over the winter months, but in January 1946 the airfield was officially closed. Throughout the year contractors removed all equipment from the base, but it was decided that all buildings would remain intact. Surprisingly the airfield remained in reasonable condition during the ensuing six years of neglect.

Pembrokeshire County Council took over the responsibility for the airfield from the Air Ministry in 1952, with a view of developing the site into a civil airport for the county and west Wales. A need for an airport had been drawn up in 1949, when Haverfordwest Council but forward Withybush as a contender, while Tenby Council, with the backing of other local councillors, put forward Carew Cheriton as their choice. Both councils put their proposals to the Ministry of Transport. After some lengthy considerations, Withybush was selected as it already had most of the structures in place, the runways were in better condition and it was nearer to rail and road links. It took another three years before the airport was ready for any form of private or commercial flying.

As soon as it was officially opened, several proving flights took place by a number of companies using varied types of aircraft including Dragon Rapides, Dakotas, Proctors and Doves. After the initial interest, only Cambrian Airways began any sort of scheduled service having been awarded a twice-daily service to Cardiff (Pengam Moor), with connecting flights to London, the Channel Islands, Liverpool and Weston-super-Mare. The first flight took place on 24 May 1952, operated by the airline's Dragon Rapide G-AJCL. It departed Haverfordwest at 10.45am and arrived at Pengam Moor at 11.30am, but the return flight only took a mere 30 minutes. A stop-over at Swansea was added to the schedule later in the year.

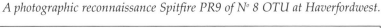

A photographic reconnaissance Spitfire PR9 of N° 8 OTU at Haverfordwest.

Aerial photograph of Withybush airfield, taken by Nº 541 Squadron, April 1946.
[National Assembly for Wales]

Haverfordwest control tower with a T2 hangar in the background.

On this inaugural flight the passengers included the mayors of Haverfordwest and Tenby, as well as other local dignitaries and newspaper reporters, the latter giving the flight a fair coverage in their newspapers. The cost of a single fare to Cardiff was £3 12s. 0d. a substantial sum in 1952 but it did not deter local people from taking advantage of the service. Cambrian used the larger Doves and Dakotas on some flights, especially at the weekends or when there was a rugby international taking place in Cardiff. During the summer months a few charter flights were flown from the airport to Ireland. In the beginning, load factors were quite encouraging but the novelty soon wore off and within two years the airline withdrew the service and severed all links with Haverfordwest.

With no apparent airline interest in using the airport, the council support evaporated. All the enthusiasm of 1949 had completely gone, resulting in the aerodrome falling into disrepair, with the buildings and most of the surviving wartime facilities becoming overgrown. Even the runways began to break up with weeds taking over. Some councillors were talking of selling the land off for housing or developing it as an industrial estate.

When Morton Air service expressed an interest in establishing a service from Pembrokeshire to London (Croydon) in 1958 they found the aerodrome to be unusable and chose Brawdy instead.

However things looked better in the 1960s as Channel Airways was given permission by the ATLB to operate a air car-ferry service between Haverfordwest and Cork in Southern Ireland. Throughout the year the airline made extensive preparation at the aerodrome, building special concrete ramps for the cars to board the Bristol B170, car parks, a reception centre in a converted Maycrete hut, a waiting room and administration offices. Even the council allocated some money for resurfacing one of the runways and providing other facilities for the airport. One weekend the airline flew in a Bristol Freighter to the aerodrome to access the work already done. But, to everyone's surprise and disgust, the airline dropped the project and dismantled all the work that had been done and Haverfordwest airfield fell into another period of disrepair and neglect, becoming

Refuelling a Spitfire at Withybush, mid 1945. [B. Owen]

a favourite venue for learner drivers and illegal car racing.

In the early 1970s the county council saw the potential of redeveloping the aerodrome as an airport for west Wales. After the initial clearing up and all-round tidying session, various people and companies began looking at the airfield with a view to possible development. The engineering section just off the A40 road was either sold or rented out to local businesses and other facilities were sold off generating extra cash for redevelopment. In 1974 Air Swift (Wales) a subsidiary of the Blackbushe air taxi service operated a twin-engined Piper Seneca between Haverfordwest, Swansea and Cardiff, mainly in connection with the exploration of oil and gas off the Welsh coast. This continued well into the following year when the exploration came to an end.

Interest in private flying continued to grow and more people began to base their light aircraft at the aerodrome and the West Wales Gliding Club was formed and became a regular user of the airfield. Various air taxis continually used the airfield.

Welsh Airways, a local air taxi, had ambitious plans of starting a regular scheduled service between Haverfordwest, Cardiff and London and even converted a club house as a small terminal with its check-ins and departure lounge. Sadly due to insufficient financial backing the plan was dropped.

Throughout the 1970s and 1980s there was on-going redevelopment at the airfield, bringing it up to modern standards. In recent years the airfield has had a number of additions, including an additional hangar and a new control tower.

During the 2004 'Aviation in the UK' review it was decided that Wales was in need of a flexible air service connecting north to south as well as east to west, feeding on to the main hub at Cardiff Wales International Airport. Haverfordwest was an obvious choice for one of the satelite airfields and further redevelopments are planned for the near future, including the building of a passenger terminal adjacent to the apron.

Due to the investment in the airfield since 1989, Haverfordwest has attracted the International Air Rally that has provided the airfield with world-wide recognition. Today it attracts two 'Fly-ins' (usually in May and August), the BPPA Regional Competition in June and October and the BPPA Rally following the June competition. The first such event took place on 9 August 1989 and attracted competitors from eighteen different countries. Altogether sixty different aircraft were parked around the airfield, the largest number since its heyday in 1945. Since then the number of competitors and aircraft has continued to grow.

One of the competitors in the 2001 London to Sydney Centenary Air Race was Mr Maurice Kirk from Barry, Glamorgan ,who had his 1943 Piper J35C-65 Cub based at the aerodrome. He took off in this aircraft (G-KIRK) from Biggin Hill on 11 March 2001 on the epic 14,000 miles adventure. Half-way through the race he was disqualified as he had diverted too far from the planned itinerary, but he nevertheless succeeded in flying his D-Day veteran Cub to Sidney.

Other events at the aerodrome have not been welcome, like the light aircraft accident on 19 May 2001 when the pilot decided to return to the airfield after experiencing mechanical problems. He failed to reach runway 04 and crashed on the grass area between the A40 road and the runway, badly injuring both himself and his passenger.

Today, only two of the wartime runways have been resurfaced and are in use; 04/22 is 1221 x 45 metres and 09/27 is 1040 x 45 metres. The third runway is used as a taxiway between the two thresholds of the useable runways. Two new hangars have been built to accommodate the ever-growing private flying from

A good view of the remaining T2 hangar at Withybush.

the aerodrome. In 1999/2000, as a part of a modest modernisation programme, the old Welsh Airways terminal was demolished to make room for a new hangar, and a new terminal building was built accommodating a café and a small waiting area. A new entrance has been constructed just off the A40 trunk road as all the southerly part of the airfield which included the old main entrance, the 'T2' hangar and the old control tower has been taken over by private interests. The other T2 was sold to Rhoose Airport in the late fifties for £100,000.

At the present time, only runway 04/22 has a permanent inset runway lighting system as well as PAPIS. The aerodrome has a non-directional beacon for navigation and a green identification beacon; all are in the process of being updated. Next to the newly built hangar there is a fuel point for both Jet 1 and 100LL aviation fuel and oils. The most recent addition to the aerodrome is a new café, 'The Propeller' which is popular with both aviators and the local population.

The aerodrome has a licence to handle every type of light executive public transport, single- and twin-engined aircraft used by most air taxi companies and public transport aircraft up to twelve metres in length. However, over the next few years, the County Council (owner) is hoping to continue its development and upgrading programme. Future plans include another hangar, a control tower with a small terminal, improvements to the airfield's communication and navigation facilities and improvements to its fire services.

The airfield was opened for private flying on an unlicensed basis in June 1973. The County Council, in consultation with the CAA, decided to convert the old wartime airfield to civilian use as they foresaw a time when the county would benefit from having its own airport.

Haverfordwest (or Withybush as it is known locally) is the only Pembrokeshire wartime airfield with the majority of the original architecture

Fragment of the casing of a Highball bouncing bomb that was aimed at Maenclochog tunnel on 7 October 1943, now on display at Withybush aerodrome.

The refurbished Second World War control tower at Withybush.

more or less intact. One of the standard T2 hangars is still used by a local firm. The RAF control tower is still standing, although slightly altered with a sloping roof. A new control tower became operational in 2004. Around the airfield there are various types and sizes of Nissen huts and good examples of Maycrete huts. Even one old guard room is still standing, although badly overgrown. The remaining blister hangar and technical site were demolished during the construction of the A40 Haverfordwest by-pass.

The airfield had seventeen dispersal points; some of which are still visible in the overgrown grass areas, and the wartime refuelling section can be seen at the northern end of the airfield. These are likely to disappear unless some steps are taken to preserve them.

With continued support from the local authorities, local aviators and general interest from some airlines there is a bright future for the airfield.

14. Hawarden

Flintshire

To emphasize the importance of Hawarden/Broughton as a wartime airfield and an aircraft factory the history needs to be split into two parts, the first briefly covering the story of the aircraft factory and the second, the RAF station. It is doubtful if the airfield would have been built if it were not for the aircraft factory and a need for an adjoining airfield.

The Broughton Factory

In 1935, Parliament issued a proposal for building a number of 'shadow aircraft factories' in the event of a war so as to provide mass production of certain aircraft types and aero engines that were already in service, or at least in the production stage. This would enable the main factories to develop new aircraft or improve existing types. These shadow factories were to be located close to centres of population from which a labour force would be drawn, had to have good road and rail access and, where possible, be sited close to an airfield or a location where an airfield could be built. After the outbreak of the war all responsibilities

Hawarden airfield ground plan.

The famous Vickers flight shed at Hawarden, 1944. [BAe Systems]

for these factories were taken over by the Ministry of Aircraft Production (MAP).

Broughton in north Wales was chosen because it was a flat site and, as well as accommodating a factory, had sufficient space available to develop an airfield. It was also close to towns such as Chester and Wrexham from where the necessary workforce could be recruited. The factory was originally to be part of the Vickers Armstrong Group, but soon became a government owned factory (under the guise of MAP) but managed by Vickers.

Work on the factory and the airfield began in November 1937 and by February 1939 the massive factory of some 141,000,000 square feet, larger than any other aircraft factory in Europe, had been completed. From the outset the factory was geared for the production of the Vickers Wellington bomber.

The first contract for 750 Wellingtons was placed in May 1939. Initially parts was transported from Weybridge in Surrey to be assembled at the new factory, until the new production facility got started. While the factory was being built, all assembly was done in the Bellman hangar that was built on the edge of the airfield.

The first Broughton assembled Wellington was L7770 which made its maiden flight on 2 August 1939 but, due to flooding at the newly constructed airfield, the aircraft was flown to Weybridge for flight testing. Production of various marks of the Wellington continued until 1945 and, at its peak, the factory built 130 aircraft a month. By the time production ended a total of 5,540 Wellingtons had been built at Broughton.

The Wellington was a remarkable aircraft and was highly regarded by the crews that flew in it. As a result of its construction technique and the sturdy design of Barnes Wallis, the aircraft could withstand tremendous punishment from enemy fire and on several occasions, although shot to pieces, brought its

The Vickers Wellington production line at Broughton. [Vickers]

wounded crews back to their home bases. Most of the variants were powered by two types of Bristol Hercules engines producing some 1,500 hp each. Some later variants (and particularly the Vickers Warwick) were powered by two Pratt and Whitney R2800 engines. The aircraft dimensions were: length 64ft7ins, span 86ft 2ins, weight 29,000lbs. It had a maximum speed of 255 mph. Armament included six .303in Browning machine-guns (increased to eight in the Wellington II) and a 4,500 lbs bomb load. It was in a Broughton built Wellington that Sgt. James Ward won the Victoria Cross when, on a night raid over Germany on 7 July 1941, Wellington L7818 was attacked by an enemy night-fighter, setting the wing on fire. Sgt. Ward climbed out onto the wing and succeeded in putting the fire out with an engine cover as a result of which both the aircraft and crew managed to return to base safely.

Another Wellington that was of special interest to the workers of Broughton was R1333 which was subscribed to by the employees who raised a sum of £15,000 for the aircraft, which was named *Broughton Wellington*. Unfortunately the bomber never saw any action as it was destroyed in a raid on the airfield on 14 November 1940.

On 27 August 1942 the King and Queen visited the factory and were amazed by the great skill, determination and enthusiasm of the local work force.

By 1943 new, larger four-engined bombers were being built for the RAF. As the Broughton factory had some spare capacity 500 Lancaster aircraft were ordered from Vickers-Armstrong on 15 April 1943. The first was delivered in June 1944,

The famous 'Broughton Wellington', 1940. [BAe Systems]

but only 235 had been delivered when production ceased in September 1945. Another Avro design, the Lincoln bomber, was also built at the Broughton factory.

By the end of 1945 all the Ministry of Supply contracts had been completed and uncertainly hung over the factory. As there was a housing shortage the factory was contracted to build pre-fabricated houses (pre-fabs), a contract which continued until 1948 by when nearly 28,000 units had been completed. In 1948 the factory was taken over by the de Havilland Aircraft Company who had a substantial order book for their aircraft from the RAF and foreign air forces. As their base at Hatfield had insufficient space, some of the designs were re-located

King George VI and Queen Elizabeth visiting the Broughton factory, 1942. [Vickers]

Crew from Nº 3 Ferry Pilots Pool posing in front of a newly completed Wellington at Hawarden. [Air Heritage]

to Broughton.

Thr de Havilland company took control of Broughton on 1 July 1948 and commenced the production of three different aircraft: the twin-engined Mosquito, the twin-engined Hornet and the Vampire jet fighter. The first Mosquito flew in October, while the first Hornet did not fly until 1949. The delivery of Vampires to Sweden and Switzerland from the Broughton complex commenced in November 1949. In 1950 an additional production line was built for the Chipmunk trainer and the twin-engined light transport aircraft the Dove. The Venom fighter-bomber was the next aircraft to be built at the factory. In all eight types were built at Broughton in just four years.

In the early fifties alterations were made to the production facilities in order to extend the scope of the factory's work. In 1952 work began on the Comet Mk 2, unfortunately, due to a number of accidents, the aircraft was grounded and production was suspended in 1954. However, work commenced a year later on a modified version of the Comet for the RAF. In 1958 work started on the Comet 4 which continued unitil production ceased in 1966.

In the early 1960s Broughton saw the production of the DHC Beaver aircraft for the British Army and the naval fighter the Sea Vixen, which continued until 1966. In 1961, the jet replacement to the Dove, the DH125 was revealed to the public and went into production at Broughton a year later.

In 1963, as part of a massive reorganisation of the British aircraft industry, the company was renamed Hawker Siddeley (de Havilland Division). Production of the popular 125 continued at Broughton as well as the fuselage of the Nimrod aircraft (a development of the Comet).

In 1971, Hawker Siddeley began producing wings for the Airbus A300B. New advanced machine tools, skin milling machines and manufacturing jigs were installed and the first completed wing set was despatched from Broughton to Toulouse in November 1971. Since then, the factory has produced wing sets for all the Airbus family of passenger aircraft. Today, all wings are transported directly from Hawarden to Toulouse or Bremen, in a specially built aircraft the Beluga (an adapted A300-600T).

On 29 April 1977 the merger of the British Aircraft Corporation, Hawker Siddeley Aviation, Hawker Siddeley Dynamics and Scottish Aviation, resulted in the formation of British Aerospace. Another merger took place, with Marconi Electronics, on 30 November 1999 creating the present company — BAE Systems. With the continually growing Airbus order book, the future prospect of Broughton continuing as an aircraft factory seems to be quite healthy.

Hawarden Airfield

With the building of the aircraft factory the airfield gradually took shape, albeit without the same urgency as the factory itself.

Hawarden airfield is situated just off the A55 North Wales Expressway, some three miles west of Chester. It was built on requisitioned land adjoining the Vickers Armstrong factory, part of which had been used by RAF Sealand as their relief landing ground. A single short concrete runway was laid for testing the Wellington bombers, but the other runways were not built until the spring of 1941 (by Gerrard Construction of Manchester). From the beginning the airfield was intended to have three concrete runways, but it was only when the airfield became water-logged and production aircraft were unable to be tested, that a sense of urgency was put in force. Several types of hangars were built for the use of the aircraft factory and the RAF units that were to be eventually based at the airfield.

The first RAF unit to arrive at Hawarden was N° 48 MU on 6 March 1940. The unit was responsible for the preparation of Wellington bombers for operational use prior to their delivery to their respective squadrons. The MU dealt with other types such as Lysanders, Herefords and the Bothas, as well as providing storage facilities for a variety of service aircraft (Magisters, Henleys, Hurricanes and even some Rocs).

Throughout the war years the airfield was the home for several Operational Training Units (OTUs) responsible for the training of fighter and fighter-reconnaissance pilots.

The first of these was N° 7 OTU, arriving on 15 June 1940 with twenty-five Spitfires, fourteen Hurricanes and thirteen Masters, under the command of W/Cdr J. R. Halling-Pott, DSO, a distinguished fighter pilot. However N° 10

Spitfire of N° 57 OTU at Hawarden, with Czech pilot J. Striver.

Group declared that the unit should standardise with only Spitfires, and by August the unit had fifty-eight Spitfires (plus seventeen Masters and six Fairey Battles which were used for target-towing duties). During 1940 and the period of the Battle of Britain, training was rather a haphazard affair. Due to the pressing shortage of trained pilots, recruits left OTUs after completing as little as ten or twelve hours on Spitfires or Hurricanes. Some even had their first experience of the type they were to fly in combat when they reached their operational squadrons which contributed to the very high loss of lives during this period. The course at Hawarden normally lasted two weeks and was mostly involved with familiarising the pilot with the Spitfire, but with only a few hours of actual flying.

The airfield did not escape the wrath of German bombers and several raids took place. Fortunately the factory escaped most of the bombing, although the MU suffered several hits. Two of the hangars (a 'K' and 'J' type) received direct hits, destroying three Magisters and Wellington R1333 the *Broughton Wellington*, a further twenty-four aircraft were damaged.

As the result of enemy air raids, a battle flight was formed with three Spitfires that were always armed and kept in the state of readiness. The flight's first encounter with enemy aircraft took place on 14 August 1940 and resulted in the shooting down of a He111, which just had bombed RAF Sealand. The next combat was on 7 September when Sgt. L. S. Pilkington, DFM, a veteran of N° 73 Squadron, who was on exercise in the area, received reports of a Ju88 heading towards him on a homeward run after bombing Liverpool. An air battle took place resulting in the enemy aircraft crashing into the hills of Merionethshire. The next successful venue for the Hawarden battle flight was off the Anglesey coast, when a Do215 was shot down on 18 September 1940.

On 28 December 1940 N° 7 OTU was renumbered N° 57 OTU.

Hawarden suffered from an acute shortage of storage space. The factory was producing over a hundred aircraft each week which could not be quickly despatched to the squadrons. The MU was overflowing with various aircraft that were awaiting delivery and by 1941 all the aircraft dispersal areas in neighbouring fields were full. The situation was eased when the Satellite Landing Grounds (SLGs) at Aberffraw (Bodorgan) and Tatton Park became available.

Aircraft ferrying between Hawarden and the SLGs or the respective squadrons was done by the Air Transport Auxiliary, a civilian organisation. N° 3 Ferry Pilot Pool (FPP) was established at Hawarden where it served until being disbanded in November 1945 after delivering thousands of aircraft. 'B' Flight of N° 4 FPP was also attached to Hawarden from October 1940 until 31 January 1941.

Another ferrying unit was N° 3 Delivery Flight, which was responsible for delivering fighters to N°ˢ 9 and 12 Groups. The unit was at the airfield from 7 April 1941 until 10 January 1942.

Even with the SLGs, Vickers had great problems with congestion on the airfield, and the Air Ministry decided to move N° 57 OTU to RAF Eshott in November 1942. It was replaced at Hawarden on 11 November by N° 41 OTU equipped with North American Mustangs tasked with the training of pilots in army co-operation. The unit remained at Hawarden until it was disbanded on 1 June 1943.

Another satellite airfield at RAF Poulton (between Chester and Wrexham) became operational in March 1943 and provided some much wanted relief for Hawarden's congested aircraft parks.

Hawarden attracted several visitors to the airfield, some unexpected like the thirteen Halifaxes of N°ˢ 420 and 425 Squadrons which landed there on 9 June 1944 while returning from a raid on marshalling yards in northern France.

USAAF aircraft became a common sight at the airfield, mostly Liberators returning from raids over southern Europe, or US in-bound flights which had missed landing at RAF Valley. On 13 January 1944 two Douglas C-54 Skymasters of RAF Transport Command flew to Hawarden directly from the Azores with a secret load. US General George Patton, in his Dominie aircraft, was another distinguished visitor to the base.

Hawarden was a distance away from the airfields that were directly involved in the D-Day operations, but it was used on 16 July 1944 when over a thousand US troops were transported in fifty-nine Douglas C-47s to the forward airfields in Normandy. Another smaller operation took place on 7 August, when 420 troops were transported from Hawarden in twenty-one C-47s.

The next visiting units to be based at Hawarden were two Royal Navy Fleet Air Arm squadrons, N°ˢ 808 and 885, equipped with Seafires, during September and October 1944. The squadrons were attached to N° 41 OTU for tactical reconnaissance training.

Aerial photograph of Hawarden taken on 17 January 1947, with large numbers of aircraft parked all over the airfield awaiting disposal. [National Assembly for Wales]

In 1945 there was a general reorganisation of all training units and the OTU fighter reconnaissance wing was transferred to Chilbolton, retaining the designation N° 41 OTU. while the day-fighter wing at RAF Poulton returned to Hawarden to become N° 58 OTU on 12 March. However the unit was short lived as it closed on 20 July 1945.

In August 1945, control of the airfield was handed over to N° 41 Group Maintenance Command and all storage aircraft in various locations were returned to Hawarden so that the SLGs could be de-requisitioned. By the end of

*The original Vickers factory dominates the upper part of this
photograph of the BAe factory at Broughton.*

June there were a total of 1,091 aircraft in stock including those at RAF Hooton
Park, but the figure dramatically increased during July, reaching a peak of 1,177
aircraft in September. The airfield had reached saturation point, as every grass
verge available was used for aircraft storage. Most of the aircraft were due to be
broken up but the MU was heavily involved with various modifications and the
supply of new aircraft to the RAF.

In April 1946, a detachment from N° 577 Squadron with its Spitfire XVIs,
Oxford IIs and Vengeance aircraft moved in. The unit provided target-towing
facilities for army co-operation training in the area and remained at Hawarden
until it was disbanded on 15 June.

Over the next few years Hawarden's MU was mostly involved in the disposal
of surplus aircraft including Wellingtons (some of which had been built at the
Broughton factory), Ansons, Martinets, Masters, Halifaxes as well as Hotspur and
Horsa gliders.

When most of the disposal work had been completed, N° 48 MU was
disbanded on 1 July 1957, followed by N° 173 Squadron (which had been formed
from N° 4(H) FU in 1952) on 1 September 1957. The only military unit to remain
was N° 631 Gliding School with its Sedbergh and Cadet gliders until it too moved
to RAF Sealand in May 1963.

On 31 March 1959 the RAF station closed and N° 47 MU was disbanded and
the airfield was handed over to de Havilland who opened it to private users and

Hawarden control tower as it is today.

were keen to encourage civilian airlines to use the airfield as a local airport for Chester.

The first company to take a keen interest in establishing a passenger service from 'Hawarden Airport' as it became to be known, was the Liverpool based Starways Ltd. which began a Liverpool–Hawarden–London Heathrow scheduled service on 2 April 1962. At first the service was flown by Dakotas before being upgraded to the larger Douglas Skymasters and eventually the turbo-prop Vickers Viscount. Starways made its last Skymaster (G-ARIY) flight from Hawarden on 23 December 1962 piloted by Captain Goodman. Starways assets and routes were taken over by British Eagle in November 1963, but continued to operate the service using Viscounts until December 1966.

Several companies have been interested in establishing an air link from Hawarden. In 1977 Air Wales began scheduled services from the airport. The twice-daily flights to Cardiff were inaugurated on 6 December 1977 using a Piper Navajo Chieftain (G-BWAL). At first, load factors were very encouraging and the airline introduced an Embreaer Bandeirante on the route, enabling Air Wales to extend the service to the continent. The service continued until the airline ceased operation on 6 April 1979 when it was taken over by the British and Commonwealth Shipping Company and was integrated into Air UK on 1 June 1980.

In recent years, further interest has been shown by various operators wishing to use Hawarden as a local airport but, although private flying has increased from the airfield, nothing significant has materialised. The airfield remains more or less as it did during the war. The factory today makes wings for the European Airbus and a new west factory was built for the manufacture of high tech wings for future generations of Airbus airliners. The new facility will safeguard the future and importance of Broughton. Most of the wings are transported by air to the final assembly plants in Bremen and Toulouse, using the Beluga transport aircraft (A300-600T). However, the sheer size of the wings for the new A380 mean that they will have to be transported by barge to Mostyn docks and then by ship to Toulouse.

The old MU site has been taken over by light industry and hangars adjacent to the railway line are occupied by the Raytheon company which has taken over the production of the 125 business jet under the evocative name 'Hawker'.

15. Hell's Mouth

Gwynedd

The airfield known as Hell's Mouth (or Porth Neigwl as it is known locally), was built to support the bombing range in the nearby Hell's Mouth bay after which the airfield took its name. The site was originally prepared as far back in 1937 as a range for N° 5 Armament Training Camp at RAF Penrhos, some ten miles away. The base, with its grass strip, was inland as the foreshore was used as part of the gunnery range. The nearest village was Llanengan, with Abersoch some two miles away, on the A499 road.

In its early days Hell's Mouth consisted of a grass strip, tented accommodation and a few Nissen type huts which were used as workshops. However, in the early 1940s four Bellman hangars were constructed, together with an adjoining concrete apron which led to a short perimeter track. Some Nissen and various wooden huts were also built for accommodation and administration.

The gunnery range consisted of target floats moored in the bay and moving targets mounted on a specially built narrow-gauge railway line on the foreshore, operated by a pulley system at each end of the track.

The range and the airfield were at the mercy of the weather and on numerous

Hell's Mouth, an aerial photograph taken by No 540 Squadron, July 1946. The four Bellman hangars are clearly visible. [National Assembly for Wales]

A mobile power-operated turret training rig at Hell's Mouth.
[T. Rennie]

occasions all bombing practice had to be curtailed because of sea mist and bad weather. Eventually, because of these problems, the airfield was forced to close. However, due to shortage of landing spaces in the area, the base was reopened as a Relief Landing Ground (RLG) for RAF Penrhos under Flying Training Command. Due to the shortage of space at Penrhos several Ansons of N° 9 (O) AFU became residents at Hell's Mouth. Other aircraft that used the airfield were usually diversions from other nearby airfields such as Llanbedr, Towyn, Bodorgan and even Valley. It was also used by aircraft which were lost such as the two Westland Whirlwinds of N° 263 Squadron, based at Fairwood Common, on patrol over the Irish Sea on 22 May 1942 which had been vectored onto an enemy aircraft, but had to break off the chase as their fuel was low. They were unable to contact their base and decided to make for the Pembrokeshire coast, but got lost. Eventually, after a long search they found the small strip at Hell's Mouth. Both landed safely with only a very small quantity of fuel left, insufficient even for taxing. Other aircraft were not so fortunate such as the Wellington (X3541) which crashed on 3 August 1944 whilst attempting a forced landing or the USAAF P-38 Lightning based at RAF Atcham in Shropshire,which got lost and was unable to get its bearings around Snowdon. It landed at Hell's Mouth without incident but was unable to take off again for few days because of bad weather.

By 1944 the airfield's importance had diminished, even the bombing range activities had been wound down as other more suitable ranges had been established elsewhere. For the remainder of the war, Hell's Mouth remained a RLG for RAF Penrhos, but was eventually closed in July 1945, although the buildings were not demolished until 1946/47.

Today there are virtually no signs that an airfield ever existed here. All buildings have been removed and even the perimeter track has been lifted (except for a section which has been used as part of a minor road). There are still some air-raid shelters dotted around the site. Like most of the wartime bases in Wales, Hell's Mouth is now just a name, as all the evidence has gone, removed or reclaimed by nature.

A Westland Whirlwind F1 twin-engined fighter of No 263 Squadron, after making an unscheduled landing at Hell's Mouth on 22 May 1942. The tip of the starboard wing appears to have been damaged.

16. Lawrenny Ferry
Pembokeshire

This small marine base was situated about four miles from Pembroke, just a short distance from the village of Lawrenny. It was always over shadowed by the larger flying-boat base at Pembroke Dock, and therefore very few people knew of its existence. At the beginning of the war the Royal Navy had been looking for a suitable base to train its seaplane crews. This part of the upper Haven, not far from where the Western and Eastern Cleddau rivers joined, was the ideal sheltered area for such activity.

Local cottages were taken over for accommodation and administration and a blister type hangar was built next to a concrete parking area, which led to a slipway. Several Nissen type huts were also built as accommodation. Other buildings in nearby Lawrenny village were also used on a number of occasions. The base was commissioned on 1 February 1942 as a Royal Naval Air Station for advance seaplane training, although it had been regarded as operational from May 1941.

The main squadron to use the base was Nº 764 Seaplane Training Squadron, Royal Naval Air Service, equipped with mostly Supermarine Walruses. Towards the end of 1942, the squadron was supplemented with American-built Sikorsky Kingfishers, three-seater single-engined aeroplanes which proved difficult to fly

Chance Vought Kingfisher floatplane of Nº 764 Squadron, Royal Navy, which was based at Lawrenny Ferry before moving to Pembroke Dock.

Supermarine Walrus seaplane.

and operate from such a confined place as Lawrenny. In early 1943 a few Sea Otter spotter planes joined the squadron.

N° 764 Squadron personnel arrived at Lawrenny on 4 October 1941 followed by their equipment during November and December. The squadron was disbanded on 24 October 1943. During its existence it trained hundreds of crews for spotter plane duties on battleships and cruisers.

Towards the end of 1943 the Lawrenny base reverted to care and maintenance and, by the summer of 1944, the need for such a base diminished and the base was officially closed. Today very little remains of the base other than the slipway, which is used by local pleasure boats.

17. Llanbedr
Gwynedd

The airfield of Llanbedr is situated on the coastal strip west of the A466 Harlech–Barmouth road and the Porthmadog–Machynlleth railway line. It is approximately ninety miles from the RAE Aberporth and forty-five miles from the Aberporth range head. It is surrounded by many world famous places and landmarks and an area steeped in ancient Welsh history and folklore. Until recently the airfield was primarily a target aircraft base providing piloted and pilotless target facilities for Aberporth and the RAF Missile Practice Camp at Valley. Its secondary role was providing refuel facilities and emergency assistance to RAF and other NATO forces aircraft.

The airfield was constructed during 1940 on low-lying land between the mountain and the sea at the northern end of Cardigan Bay. The main runway is aligned so that approach and landing are mostly over the sea, avoiding the high mountain ranges inland. It was officially opened as a RAF camp on 15 June 1941 under the control of RAF Valley.

The first aircraft to use the airfield was a Wellington bomber which, on 28 June, got lost after a bombing raid on Germany. The next aircraft to land on the

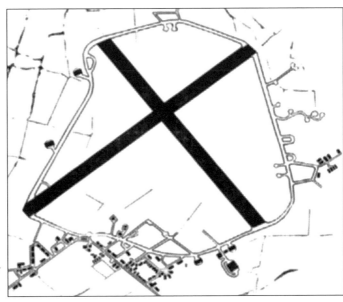

Layout plan of Llanbedr.

Spitfire Vb of Nº 602 (Canadian) Squadron at Llanbedr.

new airfield was a Defiant, piloted by Christopher Deanesley, on 1 July. Several RAF units had designs on the airfield but control was handed over to Nº 9 Group.

The first unit to occupy the base was the Elementary Flying Training School operated by the civilian company Airworks Ltd., equipped with de Havilland Tiger Moths, most of which were requisitioned civilian aircraft. On 24 August 1941 a detachment of Nº 6 AONS from Staverton arrived with six Avro Ansons, remaining at the base until October 1941.

The first front line operational squadron to arrive at Llanbedr was Nº 74 Squadron with its Spitfire IIs on 4 October 1941, commanded by S/Ldr R. G. H. Matthews, DFC. The squadron was involved in convoy patrols over the Irish Sea and the occasional scramble. On 26 November a pair of Spitfires encountered three Junkers Ju88 and one enemy aircraft was shot down, but, unfortunately, P/O Williams was shot down and killed. The squadron left Llanbedr for Long Kesh in Northern Ireland in January 1942.

The next squadron to arrive at Llanbedr was Nº 131 from RAF Atcham, equipped with Spitfire IIbs & Vbs in February 1942, and left for RAF Valley on 10 March 1942. Due to problems with soft sand blowing in off the sand dunes at Valley the squadron returned to Llanbedr in April 1942 before finally leaving for Merston in May.

In May 1942 Spitfires of Nº 232 Squadron were based at Llanbedr for three months. While at the airfield the squadron was detached to Merston to take part in the ill-fated Dieppe raid. The squadron left in August for Turnhouse airfield to take part in the protection of the city of Edinburgh and the Firth of Forth.

In 1943 the airfield became a temporary home for two Polish squadrons, Nᵒˢ 302 and 306 between March 1943 and March 1944; a Czech squadron, Nº 312, for two weeks in December 1943, and a Free French, Nº 340, in May 1944. For three weeks in March 1944 Nº 485 New Zealand Squadron commanded by S/Ldr J. B. Niven became the resident defence squadron. All were equipped with Supermarine Spitfires.

From March to April 1944 N° 129 Squadron with its Spitfire IXs arrived from RAF Heston, commanded by S/Ldr C. How, DFM, Order of Lenin (one of the few foreigners to win such decoration).

Spitfire squadrons were usually sent to Llanbedr for a rest period, but they were still shared in the responsibility for air defence of the north-west and provided patrols over the Irish Sea. The author has only included some of the squadrons that were based at Llanbedr. Numerous squadrons just stayed for a brief period ranging from few hours to a few days, which caused great strain on the ground crew at the base.

It was not only the RAF that used the airfield and on a number of occasions USAAF Thunderbolts, P-51 Mustangs and P-38 Lightnings shared the facilities.

The USAAF 2025th Gunnery Flight, equipped with British-built Lysanders, was based at the airfield from March 1943 working in support of visiting US fighters. During the summer months of 1942 eight P-38 Lightnings of the USAAF 48th Fighter Squadron were based at RAF Llanbedr for air-to-air firing practice. It was joined by the 49th squadron from Atcham. While at the airfield, the units were put under the command of N° 9 Group and took part in air defence and patrol duties.

By the summer of 1944 enemy activities over the north-west and the Irish Sea had diminished and therefore Llanbedr was no longer required as fighter base. It had always played an important part as a gunnery training base. N° 12 Gunnery School was located at the airfield between 1942 and 1944. The Armament Practice Camp provided static targets on the beach, floating targets in the bay and air targets (usually towed over Cardigan Bay by Martinets). The practice range was located at Tal-y-Bont beach.

Like most airfields, Llanbedr was not free of accidents. On 15 October 1941 a

A line up of the personnel of N° 41 Squadron. [RAF Museum]

Wellington (N2866) of N° 18 OTU from Bramcote suffered engine failure and attempted to make an emergency landing at Llanbedr. The aircraft was forced to make a crash-landing in the foothills east of the airfield but, because of the great skill and courage of the pilot, Sergeant D. K. M. Mendleson, made a perfect belly landing in a field. On 27 March 1943 a Lysander on a target towing flight sustained engine failure. Unfortunately only one of the crew managed to bail out safely.

Perhaps one of the saddest days in Llanbedr records was on 22 October 1942 when three Spitfires belonging to N° 41 Squadron went missing. Two aircraft were believed to have collided and crashed near Dolgoch waterfalls, north of Machynlleth. The wreckage of the other aircraft was not found, and is believed to have crashed into the sea. Then in August, while the squadron was detached to Tangmere to take part in the Dieppe Raid, six pilots including the CO were reported missing.

One interesting experiment that took place at Llanbedr in March/April 1944 was the fitting of 250lbs and 500lbs bombs to Spitfire Vbs of N° 602 (City of Glasgow) Squadron, which was on detachment from RAF Detling in Kent. The idea was to adapt the Spitfire as a dive-bomber for attacking the ski-shaped launch platforms for the V-1 flying bomb. The trials were successful and the Spitfires were used for the task. Unfortunately according to station records a N° 602 pilot was killed when his aircraft crashed during a dive-bombing practice run at Dyffryn.

The last RAF unit to be based at Llanbedr was N° 631 Squadron from Llandwrog, equipped with Henleys, Spitfires, Hurricanes, Vengeances and Martinets. The unit was responsible for providing simulated targets and target-towing for the APC. The squadron was disbanded in February 1951 and re-numbered N° 20 Squadron on 7 February and re-equipped with Beaufighter *Fairey Firefly U9 drones. [DERA]*

View of the airfield after its closure. Note the T2 and Bellman hangar.

TT10s, Spitfire IXs and Vampire F1s. Then, on 16 October 1951 the unit was disbanded once more and its tasks were taken over by N° 5 CAAU equipped with Mosquito TT20s and Meteor TT8s.

The RAF Mountain Rescue unit from Llandwrog moved to Llanbedr in 1945 and remained at the base until 1949.

RAE period from 1951 to Present Day
In the early fifties the airfield remained in RAF control and was used extensively by the army for training troops for the Korean War. During the period of transition and refurbishing N° 5 CAAU personnel attended a short familiarisation course on Mosquitoes and Meteors at Valley, which also provided target drones for RAE Aberporth. Short Bros and Harland was awarded the contract to operate the unit, initially under the RAE element supervision. Eventually in 1956 all RAF involvement was phased out and the base became wholly operated by civilians.

In 1952 a new aircraft was introduced to CAAU inventory the Fairey Firefly, which had been under development at RAE Farnborough for some time. The Firefly could be used either as an ordinary aircraft towing various target drones or pilotless. However the Firefly was not aneasy aircraft to fly because of the high propeller torque from the Rolls Royce Griffon engine. The first successful shoot ing down of a Firefly by a missile fired from Aberporth was in 1954 (a Bristol Bloodhound). The last Firefly flight took place in June 1960.

The next target drone to be introduced was the Gloster Meteor U15 in January 1957. Initially flight tests with a Meteor drone began in 1954, with the first take off and landing under automatic control taking place on January 17 1955. Meteors were converted by Flight Refuelling at Tarrant Rushton. The U 15 as pilotless target drones and the Meteor TT2O for target towing.

The Meteors were used extensively during the development of the early air to air Fireflash missiles.

All pilotless Firefly and Meteor drones were accompanied always by a shepherd plane to take manual control if required. These were usually Fireflies Mk 9 or Meteor TT2O.

Gloster Meteor U15 which replaced the piston types at RAF Llanbedr.

In mid fifties the Australian Government Aircraft Factory began developing a cheap pilotless target aircraft to British specifications. As the result the Jindivik target drone was born(Jindivik-Aborigine name 'the hunted one').

The first Jindivik Mk102 arrived at Llanbedr in May 1960 and since thousands have been built in Australia and in the UK, and have provided valuable service. It is worth noting that Llanbedr celebrated its 7,000th Jindviks sortie in 1999.

The Jindivik performance surpassed that of the Meteor in speed and in altitude, and was more suited to testing the newer breed of guided missiles that were entering service.

Over the years different variants have entered service and were based at Llanbedr. They were manufactured in Australia and final assembled by Fairey Avation at Ringway.

The original Viper engine being designed as a throwaway unit which had an endurance of some forty minutes.

The Jindivik takes off from a three wheeled trolley that remains on the

Llanbedr's aircraft flying over Harlech Castle. [DERA]

Line up of aircraft used by RAE i 1970: Canberra, Hunter and Jindiviks. [DERA]

runway, whilst the landing is on a centrally mounted skid. Development of the drone has continued over the years, most of which is done at Llanbedr, but with the introduction of heat seeking missiles like the Firestreak and later the Red Top, the Jindiviks became vulnerable, so the drones were adapted to tow targets for the missiles. Others were involved in trials with various radars and fitted with wide-angle cameras.

In recent years DERA Llanbedr has provided support and target drones for the missile test range, whether they were ground-to-air missiles fired from the Aberporth range or air-to-air missiles fired by aircraft usually based at Valley.

RAF Tornado F3, Harrier GR 3, and Naval Harrier FA 2 have been involved with live firings of various marks of the Sidewinder and Sparrow A-A missiles. Also, in the late nineties and early 2000, numerous test firings of the new ASRAAM missile (replacement for the Sidewinder) have taken place over the Cardigan Bay range.

Target drone Jindivik flying over Cardigan Bay. [DERA]

Commemoration of the 2,000th Jindivik sortie, 12 June 1969. [DERA]

Over the years CAAU inventory of aircraft has changed. Canberra twin-engined aircraft and theHawker Hunter has replaced the post war types. In the nineties several ex Royal Navy de Havilland Sea Vixen were adapted by Farnborough as supersonic drones and operated out of Llanbedr. However, they were replaced by the Stiletto supersonic target drone. The remaining Sea Vixen was acquired by the De Havilland museum based then at Swansea Airport. At the time of writing the museum has moved to Hurn and the Sea Vixen is regularly seen at air displays and other events (initially in the Llanbedr colour scheme).

The Stiletto target is an air launched expendable drone developed and built by the Beech Aircraft Corporation of America as the AGM 37A US Navy target. Performance of the drone is incredible. It has a maximum speed of Mach 3.0 and a ceiling of 70,000 feet. Propulsion is by a liquid fuel rocket engine. A Canberra carries the Stiletto under its wing and, after launch, the control of the drone is taken over by DERA Aberporth.

At the time of writing aircraft based at Llanbedr were as follows, Canberra 82(TT), Meteor U16, BAe Hawk T1, Jindiviks Mk 4 and the Stiletto target drone. The Meteor and the Canberra are coming to the end of their fatigue life and are being withdrawn from service. The Hawk was indented as their replacement, but due to an acute shortage of the type in RAF service, a number of ex-*Luftwaffe* Alpha Jet trainers were acquired for use at Llanbedr and RAE Bedford. In recent years the range has been used by various military helicopters for missile testing and machine-gun firings. The most unusual test took place in 2001 when an A-150 airship was based at Llanbedr conducting trials of a Remote Minefield Detection System.

With a new century DERA (formerly RAE) changed its name to QinetiQ in July 2001, which was felt represented the company better in the new millennium. For a number of years due to its location the future of Llanbedr is promising as it is situated in an ideal position providing target facilities for the missile establishment at Aberporth and the missile Practice Camp at Valley. The airfield approaches are unique as they are over the sea and therefore avoiding any built up areas. Over the years there have only been minimal changes to the airfield. The runways have been resurfaced a number of times, new hangars and workshops have been built and in early sixties a new control tower was built to accommodate the equipment required to operate the pilotless drones. Also with the introduction of the jet equipment an arrester barrier was installed across the main runway. The airfield is also used as an emergency diversion airfield for RAF Valley, as on average about a dozen emergency diversions by Hawks and other aircraft from Valley are made at Llanbedr.

However, by 2000, the writing was on the wall for Llanbedr airfield and the target facilities provided by the airfield. As in early 2002 MOD announced that the base was to close in 2004. Reason given that because of the range, altitude and complexity of modern missiles, Cardigan Bay was not regarded as a safe place anymore, as a number of civilian flights over flew the area.

Throughout 2004 flying activities was gradually run down. The final sortie was flown by Jindivik Mk4A Series 800. serial no. ZJ495 on October 28 2004. The Jindivik and its towed target were pitched against an AMRAAM armed Tornado F3 of N° 11 Squadron. The missile hit the towed target as planned and the Jindvik returned safely to Llanbedr with its chase plane an Alpha Jet. After refuelling Llanbedr two Alphajets were flown to their new base at Boscombe Down. The Jindiviks were transported by road for storage to 16 MU RAF Stafford on 18 and 19January 2005 to await disposal. All future target operations will be done by the smaller, more modern Italian produced Meteor Mirach targets. These will be ramp-launched and operated from Aberporth. At the time of writing QinetiQ and MOD are looking for a buyer for the airfield, hoping to use it for private flying and perhaps some schedule services.

Llanbedr's wartime control tower as it is today (2005).

18. Llandow
Vale of Glamorgan

The history of RAF Llandow dates back to the early 1930s, when the Air Ministry was investigating possible sites for future airfield development. Work began on clearing a site near the village of Llandow, which had reasonable access to both rail and road. Originally it had only a few basic wooden buildings with a grass strip.

The first unit to be based at the new airfield was N° 614 Squadron equipped with Hawker Hinds, Hectors and one Avro Tutor. The squadron had been formed at Pengam Moor on 1 June 1937 as part of N° 22 Group and had an equal proportion of reserve and regular officers, under the command of S/Ldr R. Cadman.

The squadron was responsible for army co-operation and several of the unit's aircraft were involved in exercises in both the Brecon Beacons and on Salisbury Plain. Pre-war, the squadron's aircraft were often seen at Llandow because of commercial traffic at Pengam Moor, an arrangement that survived until the squadron moved to RAF Odiham in October 1939.

Llandow layout plan.

Hawker Hector of N° 614 Squadron RAuxAF.

N° 614 Squadron RAAF personnel with their Hector and Hind aircraft. [H. Lewis]

For the next few months there was some redevelopment and building at Llandow. Workshops, additional accommodation quarters, concrete aprons and an 'L'- type hangar were constructed before the airfield reopened on 1 April 1940 as an Aircraft Storage Unit under the control N° 38 MU.

The first aircraft, three Lysanders, arrived by road on 4 April followed by three Tiger Moths, a Fairey Battle and two Fox Moths. Later aircraft, which flew directly from the manufacturers, included several Blenheims, which flew in from

A mixture of Spitfires, Hurricanes, Austers and Ansons stored in field adjacent to the airfield at Llandow, 1941. [Central Library]

Woodford. During August a number of Spitfires and Whitley bombers arrived for storage.

Work on the runways began in early June, but it was not until late autumn that they were completed and ready for use.

With the sharp increase in parked aircraft, eleven Super Robin hangars were built during the winter months, followed in the early part of 1941 by an additional six 'L'-type hangars. Throughout the rest of 1941 and most of 1942, two 'K'-type, one 'J'-type, two T2s, one A1 and twelve blister type hangars were built on several different sites around the airfield. All were connected to the main runways and aprons by miles of concrete taxiways.

The locations of most of the airfields built in the 1930s were marked on various maps and, consequently, they became targets for the *Luftwaffe's* bombers. On 6 August 1940 a Ju88 dropped at least four bombs on the station main site, causing slight damage to the 'L'-type hangar (which was repaired within two weeks.

In 1943 N° 38 MU became responsible for the twin-engined Albemarles and the American Boston light bombers that were beginning to arrive from the States. Later, Mustang Is began to arrive as well as Avro Lancaster bombers from Woodford, Broughton and Yeadon. As the war progressed the number of aircraft in storage rose considerably and by May 1945 there were 500 machines parked on the airfield, rising by November to 856. This number of aircraft had not been anticipated when the airfield was planned and the shortage of storage space became such a problem that adjoining fields and car parks were used. After the cessation of hostilities in 1945 the airfield remained as a storage base for some time, mainly for aircraft awaiting disposal.

Spitfire V of N° 53 OTU at Llandow. [H. Lewis]

Llandow was also the base for N° 53 OTU equipped with Spitfires and Masters, which moved in from Heston on 1 July 1941, the unit being responsible for training pilots on single-seat fighters. W/Cmdr F. W. 'Taffy' Higginson, OBE, DFC, DFM, recalled the Great War ace, W/Cmdr Ira Jones, DSO, MC, DFC and Bar, MM, as OC N° 53 OTU at Llandow. The OC Flying had given clear instructions that Jones, who was determined to become involved in combat, was not to be allowed anywhere near a Spitfire as he was certain to damage it. One evening, a fire broke out in one of the perimeter buildings which was quickly brought under control. In the distance, the 'fire fighters' heard the sound of a Merlin bursting into life and saw a Spitfire suddenly lurch forward and immediately tip up on to its nose. Rushing to the rescue of the pilot, they found Ira Jones hanging by his harness in the cockpit. As soon as the potential rescuers arrived, Jones called out (he always had a stammer when over-excited), 'This b-b-b-bloody p-p-p-plane is broken! F-f-f-fetch me another!'

Llandow was not an ideal airfield to

W/Cmdr James Ira Thomas Jones, DSO, MC, DFC and Bar, MM, Cross of St George. Highest scoring Welsh fighter pilot of the Great War with 40 confirmed victories. He commanded N°ˢ 53 and 57 OTU at Hawarden and Llandow. [W. Alister Williams via Ira Jones]

Aerial view of Llandow taken on 8 March 1944, with various aircraft parked in every available space. [National Assembly for Wales]

Avro Lancaster of N° 149 Squadron awaits disposal at Llandow. [H. Lewis]

land at or take off from, as the runways had a rise in the middle which gave the pilot a very misleading impression that the runway was shorter than it actually was. On several occasions pilots aborted their landing thinking that they did not have enough runway left.

The only aerial action to be carried out by any pilots based at Llandow was when an OTU pupil pilot got lost and decided to attack an enemy motor vessel off the Cherbourg peninsula. He was in turn attacked by two Fw190s but luckily managed to escape into clouds and eventually reach home. The OTU left Llandow on 9 May 1943 for Kirton-in-Lindsey.

On 1 July 1943, N° 3 Aircraft Preparation Unit was formed at Llandow to prepare aircraft for ferrying abroad. Types of aircraft handled by the unit were Beaufighters, Wellingtons, Warwicks and Venturas. The unit moved to RAF Dunkswell on 12 August 1945.

N° 614 (County of Glamorgan) Squadron was originally formed at RAF Pengam Moor in 1937 and was re-formed at RAF Llandow as an Auxiliary fighter squadron on 26 August 1947 equipped with the Spitfire LF 16e, which was in turn replaced by Spitfire F22s in July 1948. The squadron was equipped with DH Vampire F-3s from July 1950 to July 1952, Vampire FB-5s July 1952 to July 1957 and finally Vampire FR-9s for a brief period in 1957. The squadron was finally disbanded in March 1957 when all Auxiliary units were abolished.   To demonstrate its close links with Wales the squadron adopted red and green as the colours of its insignia and remained at Llandow for most of the time except for the occasional detachment and various exercises.

Another unit that became a resident at the airfield was 'A' Flight of N° 633 Squadron, equipped with Auster AOP6s from July 1949 to March 1957.

Before all civil flying was transferred to Rhoose in 1954, Pengam Moor had been the municipal airport for Cardiff, but due to its location and limited space

The Llandow control tower as it was in 1998.

for redevelopment it was unable to handle aircraft larger than a Dakota. Consequently, most of the charters that used a larger passenger aircraft operated from Llandow.

Unfortunately, the airfield will be remembered for the tragic air disaster of 12 March 1950 when an Avro Tudor (G-AKBY) passenger aircraft, belonging to Fairflight, was returning with rugby supporters from Belfast. It crashed at Sigginston on its approach to the airfield. Out of the eighty-three passengers aboard only three people survived what was, at the time, the worst air disaster ever. Soon after, all passengers charter flights were suspended before being transferred to Rhoose.

Throughout its existence Llandow airfield remained a storage satellite for nearby RAF St Athan. Reserve aircraft would be brought out of storage on an annual basis, prepared for flight at either St Athan or Llandow, with most of the flight trials being carried out at the latter. After testing, the aircraft would be once again prepared and returned to storage. The bulk of the aircraft stored at the airfield at this time were Meteors, Venoms, Gnats and Hunters. The 1,650 yards runway was not suited for the heavier type of jet aircraft that were beginning to enter service with the RAF, so all future trials were conducted at RAF St Athan.

Today, Llandow's main runways form part of the public road network that crosses the airfield. The B4270 follows part of a perimeter track, while at the southern end of the field there is a go-kart racing circuit, which occupies part of the main runway and the perimeter track. Most of the wartime hangars still exist, along with the control tower which has been transformed into offices. The main site now forms part of the Llandow Industrial Estate, whilst other sites are surrounded by high fences and are still used for storage. Some accounts of the airfield state that a 'perimeter track' led all the way to RAF St Athan and was used to move aircraft between the two bases. Travelling along present roadways between the two bases, it is very hard to imagine that such arrangement ever existed.

19. Llandwrog

Gwynedd

Today, Llandwrog is the home of Caernarfon Airport, which also operates the Caernarfon Airworld Museum, and is owned by Mr Roy Steptoe. The Museum specialises in the history of the airfields in the Gwynedd area. There are at least fifteen aircraft in store as well as a number of interesting exhibits. The airport is the home of an annual air show, usually held in July, which has grown in popularity over the years.

The RAF station at Llandwrog was officially opened on 11 July 1941 and is situated four miles from Caernarfon, just off the A499 Caernarfon to Pwllheli road, on a minor road close to the beach development of Dinas Dinlle.

The airfield was built as a training base in 1940, on the site of a former tank training ground, the west coast of Wales being regarded as an ideal area for training new air crews, relatively safe from the threat of enemy aircraft. The airfield had three concrete and tarmac runways in a triangular layout. Runway lengths were as follows; 03/21 was 3,100ft x 150ft. 32/14 was 2,990ft x 150ft and 09/27 was 3,000ft x 150ft. There were eight hangars built all together, although

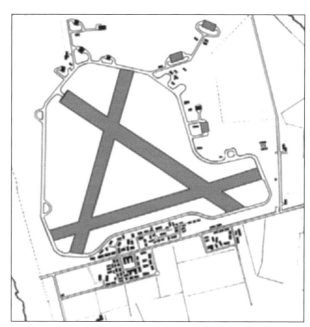

Layout of Llandwrog, 1944.

Airspeed Oxford N6250 of N° 11 FTS, Llandwrog.

some were added later. The airfield had two 'T' types, one Bellman and five Over Blister hangars. The technical site, together with the administration section, the sick bay and the control tower, were situated on the south side of the runways. The accommodation section was a mile away, on Blythe and Chatham farmland, over an inlet of Foryd Bay and accessed by a small wooded bridge. Approach to the airfield from the landside was rather hazardous, with mountain ranges rising to over 3,000 feet only four miles from the edge of the runways, while the other ends were extremely close to the beach and the sea. Around the sea perimeter of the airfield a dyke was erected which caused problems for aircraft taking off — on 8 September 1943 an Anson (EF978) hit the dyke when taking-off and crashed into the sea, killing one of the crew.

The first unit to use the airfield was N° 11 FTS which arrived on a training exercise in June/July 1941, with its Tutor, Audax, Gauntlet, Battle and Anson aircraft. The airfield was officially opened as a base for N° 9 Air Gunnery School which was formed at Llandwrog on 7 July 1941, equipped with Armstrong-Whitworth Whitley bombers, Avro Ansons, Bolton Paul Defiants and Westland Lysanders. The latter would tow target drones over Caernarfon Bay for firing practice by gunners aboard the Whitleys, Defiants and Ansons.

Like most units, N° 9 AGS was not exempt from accidents. On 16 July 1943, a Whitley (T4153) crashed while being delivered to the unit by a ferry pilot. Then, on 10 October, two Whitleys (K7252 and K9041) collided when one aircraft attempted to land on top of the other, which was taking off. Seventeen airmen died in this tragic accidents.

Llandwrog airfield was attacked on 23 January 1942 by a solitary Junkers Ju88 believed to be returning from a raid. The enemy aircraft made a low-level machine-gun attack across the airfield. Luckily the only casualty was one Whitley slightly damaged, but it was repaired and flying the following day.

Armstrong Whitworth Whitley, a large number of which were converted for use as twin-engined trainers.

On 28 May 1942 three Whitley IVs (N1345, N1428 and T4155) of N° 9 AGS were flown to RAF Driffield to join in the first 1,000-bomber raid over Germany, but unfortunately Whitley N1345 was shot down.

On 13 June 1942 N° 9 AGS was disbanded and most of the aircraft were passed on to various holding units and MUs, but a few Ansons and Lysanders remained at Llandwrog. With the importance of the base diminishing it was decided that the airfield would become a Satellite Landing Ground of N° 9 (O) AFU at RAF Penrhos. However, on 11 February 1943, the station headquarters was moved from Penrhos to Llandwrog as the satellite proved to be a much better airfield. Penrhos had only a grass strip, which was often water-logged whereas Llandwrog had three concrete and tarmac runways. By the end of 1942, station personnel at the Caernarfon base exceeded the parent station by nearly one thousand airmen.

Navigation and gunnery training continued, although not on the original scale. By the autumn of 1943 the urgency attached to training in safe areas, away the threat of enemy bombing had diminished and the importance of Llandwrog, like so many other training bases in Wales, also declined. Gradually the base strength was reduced until the AFU eventually closed on 14 June 1945. By then all flying had more or less ceased. For a few months the buildings were used to accommodate N° 2 ACHU while the RAF was reorganising.

Other units from other training establishments visited the airfield. On 13 June 1943, a flight of Oxford twin-engined trainers of N° 11 FTS from RAF Shawbury used the airfield and its facilities for night-flying exercises. N° 595 Squadron Martinets were also often seen at the airfield.

Because of the airfield's close proximity to the beach, it had quite extensive defences. Several pillboxes were constructed around the perimeter — even the control tower and other buildings had reinforced concrete pillboxes attached to them. Personnel from the RAF Regiment manned all these defences, which were based at Llandwrog from 1941. Several of the pillboxes and other defences can still be seen today.

There were ASR launches based at neighbouring Belan, a Napoleonic fort on the tip of the peninsula, which often worked in conjunction with aircraft from Llandwrog.

RAF Llandwrog was put on care and maintenance on 29 July 1945 but at the time there were no foreseeable future military use although there was a rejected proposal to use the airfield in support of the Royal Artillery establishment at Ty Croes. At the end of the war a large amount of chemical weapons was discovered stockpiled by the Nazi regime in Germany. It was decided to bring some of these to the UK for safe disposal and several disused airfields were considered for the task. Llandwrog was finally chosen because of its remote location and it became N° 277 Maintenance Unit (Explosive Disposal Unit) on 29 July 1946. Over the next few months the site was made ready for handling the dangerous munitions.

'Operation Dismal' as it was known, began in October 1946. Over 71,000 250kg bombs were landed at Newport Docks in south Wales before being transported by train to N° 31 Maintenance Unit at Glyn Rhonwy, Llanberis. They were then transferred by road to N° 277 MU at Llandwrog. Over the next few months, 21 Bellman hangars were built on the airfield's three runways for storage and by 1947 there were 14,000 tons of Tabun nerve gas stored there. In 1954 it was decide to dispose of the gas by sealing it in cargo containers in ship holds and sinking the ships in the Atlantic.

The disposal operation, code-named 'Sandcastle' began in January 1955, with the first consignment leaving Llandwrog the following June. The deadly cargo

Llandwrog's wartime control tower in the early 1980s. It has since been renovated and adapted for modern use.

Llandwrog airfield, 1990s. (Caernarfon Air Park]

was loaded on to landing ships at Belan Fort on its way to Cairnryan, near Stranraer, to be loaded on to the cargo ships that were to be sunk in the Atlantic. The site was made safe with demolition or removal of all the buildings associated with the chemical weapons and eventually closed on 21 October 1956. All the hangars, even the ones built during the war, were demolished and, when more or less completely cleared, the site was was put up for sale.

There were no serious buyers and over the next twenty years the airfield was more or less forgotten and went into decay. However, in 1975, with an increase in pleasure flying, Llandwrog was opened for civil use. The airfield was tidied, some of the buildings were repaired and runway 08/26 (09/27 — wartime heading) was resurfaced. The airfield had been used extensively by light aircraft, helicopters and military aircraft during the investiture ceremony of the Prince of Wales at Caernarfon Castle in 1969. As a result, Keen Air Service of Liverpool took over the running of the airfield and renamed it Caernarfon Airport. The company was involved in pleasure flights during the summer months and *ad hoc* charters all year round. During the 1980s several more wartime buildings were demolished, but the control tower was saved and refurbished.

In mid 1990, Air Caernarfon, a subsidiary of Air Atlantique, was formed to run the airfield, the museum and the company's historical flight (equipped with several vintage aircraft, often seen at the airfield). Throughout the summer months Air Caernarfon's DH 86 Rapide, Avro Anson and Piper Cherokee Warrior provided pleasure flights. Following the take-over of Air Caernarfon by Roy Steptoe in 2002, the historical flight moved to Coventry.

Today, the main operator of the airfield is QDM Aviation, providing flying training and trial lessons on both fixed wing aircraft and helicopters. The company also provides a variety of pleasure flights over north Wales and Snowdonia.

Mountain Rescue Service

The Snowdonia range was notorious for aircraft crashes. During a five-month period in 1942 there were ten major accidents in the area with the death toll of least forty air crew but only eight of the casualties were recovered. So serious was the situation that some local airfields banned training flights near the mountain range. However aircraft still flew over or near Snowdonia and further crashes occurred.

At first the Air Ministry seemed not to be interested in the formation of a rescue service, which would be trained to recover crews from the scenes of crashes, so it was left to local individuals to come up with some ideas. On 17 October 1942 a Boston light bomber of N° 419 Squadron crashed on Carnedd Dafydd. Fortunately a young airman and his girlfriend came across the wreck while walking on the mountain. Amongst the wreckage were three bodies one of which was found to be still alive. The newly formed mountain rescue unit at Llandwrog was informed and before long they were on the scene and Sgt Mervyn Sims was rescued suffering from exposure and multiple injuries, from which he later recovered.

So RAF Mountain Rescue Service was born at Llandwrog thanks to people like

F/L George Graham, the Medical Officer at the station. In January 1943 he was awarded the MBE for his services to mountain rescue. Flt Lt Graham's (or 'Doc' Graham as he became known) exploits were so numerous that they cannot be included in this book. Tragically, he died in 1980 but his name will live on among today's mountain rescue teams, especially those who still risk their lives saving others in Snowdonia.

George Graham (centre) and members of the Llandwrog Mountain Rescue Team, 1943.

20. Llangefni

Isle of Anglesey

The First World War U-boat campaign began on 4 February 1915, when the German High Command announced that any shipping in the vicinity of Britain and Ireland were legitimate targets. Up until then it was only warships that had been targeted by enemy submarines and surface warships. As Liverpool was one of the main ports in the British Isles it drew considerable interest from the enemy and within weeks of the announcement, three ships were sunk off Liverpool and a further two off the north Wales coast. Several ships in the Irish Sea reported sighting submarine periscopes and even surfaced vessels.

The most formidable deterrents against submarines were warships armed with depth charges, but the response time was not ideal. From the time a submarine was sighted, to the time when a warship would reach the scene, could be several hours by which time a ship may have been sunk and the submarine on its way home. The only solution to the menace was aircraft but in 1915 there were no machines available that had sufficient endurance, capability or reliability and airships were utilised to filled the gap.

For some years the Admiralty had been using various dirigibles for fleet patrols, operated from ships and shore bases, and found they had remarkable

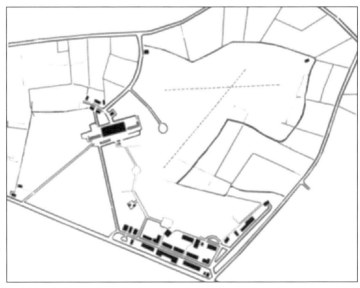

Ground plan of Llangefni.

SSZ50, which clocked up a remarkable 770 hours whilst at Llangefni. [Real Photos]

endurance, provided the weather was fine. After numerous experiments and modifications at Farnborough several airships were armed and adapted for sea patrols and eventually the Sea Scout type went into limited production. The Admiralty then decided to build a number of airship stations around the British Isles, two of which were intended to protect the Irish Sea — one at Luce Bay and the other in Anglesey.

Several sites in Anglesey were considered before the Admiralty eventually acquired over 200 plus acres of farm land three miles from the town of Llangefni. The site was located between the A5 and B5109 roads, which had reasonable clearance all around for operations. The nearest village to the base was Heneglwys, which was the name given to the RNAS station. However, over a period of four years, it also was called RNAS Bodfordd and RNAS Gwalchmai before eventually settling on RNAS Llangefni, changes which not only confused the enemy but everyone concerned.

Over the summer months of 1915 the base took shape as hedges were flattened and an airship shed (120ft x 318ft, with windshields on both ends), workshops, gas production units and wooden accommodation huts were constructed. A Bessonneau hangar was later added to accommodate the DH4 and DH6 aircraft that used the base. The main administration and accommodation section was built near the junction of the A5 and B5109 roads, with the main entrance on the crossroads. All the buildings were of wooden and corrugated iron construction with some tented accommodation for the personnel.

RNAS Llangefni was commissioned on 26 September 1915 as part of N° 14 Group, which was responsible for the protection of the British coastline. The first airship arrive at the base on 26 September when SS18, crewed by FSL Urquat and Kilburn, flew in from Kingsnorth. Within weeks the rest of the airships — SS22, SS24, SS25 and SS33 had arrived completing the initial establishment. The first

A somewhat indistinct aerial photograph of Llangefni, 1918. [Air Heritage]

station commanding officer was Major George Scott (who eventually became Deputy Director of Airship Development, but tragically lost his life ion the R101 crash in France in 1930). The first escort duty by the station's airships was in October when an SS (Sea Scout) escorted a Liverpool bound convoy, and the Dublin to Holyhead ferry. Llangefni patrol sector covered an area from Bardsey Island to Dublin and up as far as the Isle of Man and Morecambe Bay — a considerable area for only four airships!

The station had its mishaps for on 9 November 1915 SS18, on detachment to the base, struck a cow while landing in an adjoining field. It then hit a control car becoming uncontrollable and flying out to sea. Eventually its pilot managed to gain control of the gas valve and was able to let the dirigible down onto the sea. The pilot was rescued but, unfortunately, the engineer was drowned.

For most of 1916 the airships were involved with escort duties and long patrols. During this lull the station was involved in experiments with hydrophones, whereby an underwater microphone was lowered into the sea from the airship. This could detect the sound of a submerged vessel. Although the system was never used operationally during the First World War it has proved invaluable since. These experiments continued well into 1918. During the following year enemy submarine activity in the area increased considerably and in February 1917, six coastal vessels were sunk near Bardsey Island, causing some concern at the Admiralty. In June the SS series of airships were replaced by the Mark II, known as SSP airships. These types had an increased gas volume (over 70,000 cubic ft.) and a crew of three. Only six of the type were built, three of (SSP1, 5 and 6) which replaced the older type at Llangefni.

RNAS officers posing for the camera outide the mess at Llangefni. [PRO]

As a refuelling point during the long patrols, an airship mooring station was built near Dublin allowing not only an opportunity for the airship to be refuelled and rearmed, but allowing the crew a short respite during their long patrols.

In November 1917 six DH4 aircraft were despatched from Castle Bromwich in the Midlands to join the airships at Llangefni. However, things did not go according to plan and due to bad weather only two aircraft reached north-west Wales, one landing on Traeth Lavan near the village of Abergwyngregin, while the other crashed within sight of the base at Llangefni. Luckily the pilot emerged with only few scratches, but the observer was badly injured. The other four aircraft, completely lost, decided to return to their base in the Midlands.

On 6 June 1918 Nos 521 ('A' Flight) and 522 ('B' Flight) Coastal Patrol Flights were formed at Llangefni, equipped with eight Airco DH6s. The flights, which were part of N° 255 Squadron RNAS, remained at Llangefni until 15 August when the unit left for the new base at Aber (Bangor) where it was renumbered to N° 244 Squadron. While at Anglesey the squadron was involved in coastal patrols in conjunction with the airships.

During December 1917 enemy submarines sank nine vessels of various tonnages off the coast of Anglesey. As the result, the number of patrols were increased considerably.

A new airship appeared in 1918, the SS Zero type which was a big improvement on its predecessors. Most of the development for the SSZ was made at RNAS Pembroke (Milton). It was powered by a 75-hp Rolls Royce Hawk engine that gave it between 16 and 40 hours endurance depending on the speed. The airship bomb load was increased to 320lbs, either 3 x 100lbs or one 230lb bomb. Llangefni's SSPs were replaced by six Zero types — Z31, Z33, Z34, Z35, Z50, Z51 with Z72 and Z73 at the Malahide mooring in Dublin. The base's first SSZ patrol took place on 18 April 1918, carried out by Z35, but, after some seven hours over Liverpool Bay the airship suffered engine failure. The crew had no choice other than to make an emergency landing. Fortunately the airship came

RNAS Airco DH4 which was based at Llangefni for some time in 1918.

down near a fishing boat which eventually towed it to safety so it could be beached at Llandudno.

With the formation of the Royal Air Force on 1 April 1918, all land-based air operations were handed over to the new force, and RNAS Llangefni became the responsibility of the RAF. Initially there were no changes whatsoever, the base was still run by naval personnel and the aircraft and airships retained their original markings.

Llangefni's airships made several contacts with enemy U-boats, especially in the final year of the war. On 18 May 1918, SSZ50 located an enemy submarine near the Skerries, dropped a 100lb bomb (with no effect), climbed a further 100 feet and dropped a 230lb bomb, which exploded on hitting the water. Royal Navy destroyers joined in the attack with depth charges but were unable to confirm a kill.

Another attack was made by SSZ 51, south-west of Bardsey. The airship crew spotted a periscope wake in the sea, dropped a 230lb bomb but again with no effect. SSZ35, which was in the area, joined in the attack dropping another 230lb bomb, again without success. Four RN destroyers of the Irish Sea Patrol Fleet joined in with depth charge attacks and eventually oil and debris was seen floating nearby, so it was confirmed as a kill. After the war German officials confirmed that UB119 left a German port on 27 April but never returned.

Further attacks followed such as that on 27 May when SSZ 34 dropped a 230lb bomb on a suspicious target, with no confirmation. SSZ51 also dropped bombs on some bubbles appearing in the water but again had no confirmation of a kill. Although there is no record of any airship sinking a submarine, their presence on

Officers' Mess at RNAS Llangefni.

escort duties and patrolling was more of a deterrent than actual threat.

With the war coming to an end and land-based aircraft becoming more advanced and bigger, it was felt in some quarters that the airship era was coming to an end. In an effort to counter this there was an all-out effort to prove that the dirigible was still an effective weapon. On 29 June 1918, SSZ35 broke the airship endurance record by flying north from Anglesey, across Scotland, down towards the Isle of Man, then eastward towards Blackpool, Liverpool, returning via the north Wales coast to Holyhead, across Caernarfon Bay down Cardigan Bay and the west coast of Wales before finally returning to Llangefni twenty-four hours later.

On 21 October 1918 all U-boats were recalled to their bases, ending a gruelling submarine campaign around the coast of Wales.

When the Armistice came on 11 November, there were great celebrations at the Llangefni base, part of which entailed a flight by an airship under the Menai suspension bridge. After the war the base remained opened for a while and a few airships were occasionally seen there before the Admiralty finally relinquished the site in 1920 when it was transferred to the Government Disposal Board. On 20 November 1920. Anglesey County Council bought the site converting several of the buildings into a small local hospital. Other buildings were used for storage, but the airship sheds and associated building were demolished and sold. Today there is no evidence whatsoever that the First World War base ever existed as the present day Mona airfield was built on the same site.

21. Manorbier
Pembrokeshire

Manorbier cannot be classed as an airfield in the true sense, but rather an established army camp, with a grass field belonging an Army anti-aircraft training school. The camp and its grass strip was situated a mile east of the town of Manorbier, just off the B4585 road, and five miles from Tenby and some eight miles from Pembroke Dock. It dated back to the mid-1930s, when 'B' Flight of N° 1 Anti Aircraft Co-operation Unit was formed in July 1937. The unit experimented with an early form of radio-controlled target aircraft which was very crude and unreliable, but over the years the system was perfected and the Pilotless Aircraft Unit was formed which became available for the training of all local anti-aircraft army gunners.

At first most of the accommodation and workshops were of the canvas type, but as years progressed these were replaced by more permanent brick buildings. A Bellman hangar, which was built to house and modify the drones based at the camp, is still there today. Although the army camp covered a large area, the actual grass strip was just a small part of the whole complex. It consisted of one grass strip heading out to sea towards Old Castle Head. This was lengthened in 1940.

DH Queen Bee, used as a manned and remote target drone by N° 1 AACU at Manorbier.

Aerial view of Manorbier Camp, [National Assembly for Wales]

From the outset the area was troubled by flooding, especially during the autumn and winter months, caused by very poor drainage and a slight dip in the landscape. The strip therefore became unserviceable for long periods and training had to be curtailed. A novel solution to the problem was the construction of hydraulic catapults, similar to the ones install in the Royal Navy's light cruisers, on the cliff tops so that training would not be disturbed.

The standard pilotless target aircraft used the time were Queen Bees, the radio-controlled drone version of the famous primary trainer the De Havilland

Tiger Moth. Over 420 Tiger Moths were converted to Queen Bee drones, most being fitted with the conventional undercarriage but those used for catapult launching were fitted with floats. These were quite remarkable aircraft for their time. During their early development in the mid 1930s the craft required a pilot for take off and landing, but could be flown by remote control once in flight. However, these early drones were only used to tow a drogue. Later Queen Bees were fitted with a trailing aerial wire which, when it touched either the sea or land, automatically landed the craft. It was during the war that a fully remote-controlled system was developed.

The coastline around the Manorbier area was very rugged and was composed of high cliffs with no suitable beaches for the drone's recovery. It was therefore decided to use the beaches at Tenby some five miles away an area often used as a relief flying-boat mooring area.

The normal procedure was for the drones to take off from Manorbier, climb to around 5,000 feet, fly to their designated target area (which was usually just off the coast) then return to land at Tenby. Once recovered by a team based in the town the drone would be returned by road to Manorbier. Operations did not always go according to plan and on several occasions the take off went disastrously wrong—probably because of a faulty radio control—and the drone went out of control and crashed into the sea. On one occasion the Queen Bee lost all control and decided to fly out to sea and was later picked up floating on the crest of the wave 100 miles away. Another drone was hit several times by anti-aircraft shells but still managed to return and land at Tenby. As the war progressed these teething problems were eventually solved and the pilotless drones became more reliable, but for most of the time the gunners had to be contented with targets towed by manned aircraft.

Like most bases built during the early 1930s, Manorbier was known to the German authorities, but surprisingly the *Luftwaffe* usually gave the place a wide berth, probably because the camp was an anti-aircraft gunnery school. However on 17 January 1941 a low-flying raider approached the base and was fired at by various low-calibre guns. Several people claimed that the aircraft was damaged as a plume of smoke was seen coming from one of the engines, but there is no record of it crashing. As well as being protected by anti-aircraft guns of various calibres Manorbier also had a remarkable device, a Hamilton-Picket retractable pillbox, which could be fitted with a variety of different calibre guns or cannons. Situated on the cliff top, this could be lowered or raised hydraulically when required.

The Pilotless Aircraft Unit remained at Manorbier throughout the war years and provided a steady stream of well trained anti-aircraft gunners for the army. However by 1946 its importance had declined and the unit was gradually run

*DH Queen Bee drone ready for a catapult launch on the
cliff top at Manorbier.*

down and eventually closed. Since then the airstrip was used by various Army
Air Corps aircraft including DHC Beavers and Otters, Auster AOP aircraft and
other liaison and communication aircraft. More recently the main visitors have
been Army Westland Scout helicopters.

Today with the introduction of helicopters the need for the airstrip has
disappeared, and it has therefore been returned to nature. There are only small
tell-tale signs that the strip ever existed—concrete bases for the catapults and the
rusty base for the retractable pill box. At the camp itself there is ample evidence
of its existence in the buildings and the Bellman hangar. Several new buildings
have been constructed, including a new hangar, several helicopter pads,
administration building and engineering blocks, with a replica of a Thunderbird
air-air missile on its launching base.

22. Milton

Pembrokeshire

This First World War base became known as RAF Carew Cheriton during the Second World War. It occupied more or less the same area as the latter airfield did. The German submarine campaign had started on 4 February 1915, and pressure was put on the Admiralty to combat this threat that was becoming a problem around the coast. An all out effort was made to develop airship and land plane bases as well as seaplane bases around the British coastline. As a consequence, the Admiralty bought 228 acres of land near the village of Sageston, just off the main road between Pembroke and Carmarthen, with the intention of building an airship base. A similar acquisition had occurred in north Wales with some land near Llangefni.

The base at Milton did not take shape until early February 1916, when two 40yds x 106yds. hangars were built of corrugated iron, together with large windshields, which could house the largest airships then operated by the Royal Naval Air Service. Two lots of hydrogen storage tanks were constructed adjacent to the hangars. Wooden huts and canvas workshops were also built, supplemented by tented accommodation for the personnel. Several hedges and trees were removed to make a clear area for the airships to operate. The base steadily grew during the year, so it became necessary to acquire more of the adjoining land to accommodate additional tent space.

Milton, or RNAS Pembroke, became the main base for the SS Zero airships of the Coastal Patrol Flights. Photograph shows SSZ36 landing at Milton.

BE2 Scout airship being manhandled at RNAS Pembroke.
[Imperial War Museum]

A satellite base was built at Killeaugh, Co. Cork, Ireland, for the purpose of providing moorings and refuelling facilities for airships in the area. Milton's patrol area covered St George's Channel and all of Cardigan Bay, reaching as far as Llŷn Peninsular and Dublin in the north and Cork and Lundy Island to the south.

During the early months of 1916 the base became predominantly a stopping point for airships attached to various warships patrolling the Irish Sea. This arrangement was quite useful to Milton personnel as it gave them considerable experience in handling the craft. A number of both RFC and RNAS land based aircraft made use of the clear and fairly level land at the base, which made the authorities realise the potential of Milton. However it was not until September 1916 that Milton officially became a base for the Submarine Scout BE airship.

The drawback with the early flying machines was their range and loiter time, which was insufficient for patrol work. Several attempts were made to extend the range, by adding extra fuel tanks and by using a balloon or an airship type system to keep a crew aloft for longer periods. The SS BE 20 combination was one of the more serious attempts to deal with this problem during the early years of the war and it paved the way for further development in later years.The craft was a BE 20 aircraft hung underneath a 143ft. airship powered by a 70–75hp. air-cooled Renault engine. Several design improvements were made to the S.S. B.E.20 at Milton which were eventually built into later production models e.g. a special extended fuselage to house three crew members. This was a great improvement to the earlier examples as the engine could be restarted from within the fuselage. Being a 'pusher' type of craft the engine could be cranked from the inside. Previously, restarting the Renault engine mid-flight was a hazardous task, as a brave crewman had to climb out of his cockpit and balance on one of the skids

A Submarine Scout Zero 16 airship (SZ28) landing at Milton after a patrol over the Irish Sea. [Real Photos]

while trying to spin the propeller. Originally these airships were armed with a single .303 Lewis machine-gun and two 100lb bombs. Later, after modifications at Milton, they were able to carry two 250lb bombs or four 150lb delayed action bombs as well as an additional Lewis machine gun.

In 1917 the base became to be known as RNAS Pembroke, but most people still referred to it as Milton Airship base.

By 1917 the German U-boats were creating havoc amongst Allied shipping around the British coast especially in the Western approaches. N° 14 Group was given the task of patrolling the Atlantic sea approaches and flights of airships were attached to Llangefni, Pembroke and Mullion (Cornwall), and as Pembroke and Mullion were nearest to the main concentration of enemy submarine activities it was their craft that saw most of the action.

Initially three coastal type airships were allocated to Milton, C13, C5A and C6 but, due to their limited endurance, they were found to be unsatisfactory. The newer 'Zero' type was then entering service and RNAS Pembroke, because of its strategic position, was one of the first bases to be equipped with the new machine. Two flights, A & B, each comprising eight SSZ patrol craft, attached to N° 255 Squadron

A rather indistinct enlargement of the fuselage of the SZ28 airship (above) showing the crew arrangement and engine position. [Real Photos]

147

Coastal Patrol airship becoming airborne at Milton. [B. Owen]

RNAS were established at Pembroke and by the end of 1918 this had increased to fourteen SSZ airships.

The SSZ was a development of the BE type, powered by a 75hp Rolls-Royce Hawk engine. Most of the development had been done by Milton in the previous year. It was a non-rigid airship with a total volume of 70,000 cubic feet, a beam of 30ft and an overall height 44ft 6ins. The carriage (fuselage) was over 18ft long. Its fuel capacity was 102 gallons, which gave it an endurance of 16 hours at 50mph, or 40 hours at 20mph. It had a crew of three in a modified BE 20 fuselage.

From May 1917 Milton's airships were involved in numerous convoy duties and submarine patrols —some lasting up to ten hours. Several U-boats were sighted and attacked but none were sunk, although it was believed that some were damaged causing them to break off their patrols. On the afternoon of 17 December SSZ 16 attacked a surfaced submarine with a .303 Lewis machine-gun. Fortunately the submarine did not return fire but rather dived for safety. Another incident happened on 12 January 1918 when two airships from Milton spotted a U-boat laying in wait for one of the coastal convoys. Both craft attacked and dropped their bombs on the target but the submarine had been able to dive and the convoy sailed on in safety. According to German records, at this time one of their submarines had its rudder damaged in an incident with airships and had to return to base. The airship patrols proved to be more of a deterrent than an actual efficient weapon system, as no convoy was attacked by a U-boat while under an airship escort.

The SSZs did not escape without casualties. On 13 September 1917, SS42A broke away from its mooring in a strong wind. After a desperate attempt by its crew to get it under control it crashed north of Bull Point killing its three crewmen. Another accident happened in early November, when an SSZ (believed to be SS46) accidentally deflated when about to take off. No one was hurt and the airship was only slightly damaged.

From early in 1917, RNAS Pembroke, because of its location and it's fairly level ground with a clear area for operations, had been ear-marked as a station for land based aircraft. These aircraft were to operate in conjunction with the airships in patrolling the Irish Sea. On 29 April 1917 the first Sopwith $1^1/2$ Strutter aircraft arrived at Milton (the aircraft got their name from an unusual arrangement of short and long pairs of centre section struts). These were naval bombers fitted with the RNAS Equal Distance Bomb Sight which was regarded as the most sophisticated and most modern of all bomb-aiming equipment. The aircraft were powered by a single 110hp. Clerget engine which gave a maximum speed of 108mph and were armed with one Vickers machine-gun, a Lewis machine-gun and four 25lb bombs.

In August 1918 a new type began to arrive at Milton in the shape of the new Airco DH6. These bombers were much slower than the Sopwiths but had a longer range and were more adaptable to patrol work. The DH6 was powered by a 90hp RAF 1A engine which gave it a speed of 70mph and over three hours endurance. It was armed a .303 Lewis gun and a bomb load of 120lb. The DH6 Flight, N° 255 Squadron RNAS, was formed at Milton on 16 August 1918 and was disbanded on 14 January 1919. The flight's emblem was a panther's face painted on the fuselage. N° 255 Squadron was formed by amalgamating N°ˢ 519 ('A' Flight) and 520 ('B' Flight) of the Coastal Patrol Flights. To accommodate the fixed-wing element, several additional wooden buildings were constructed, including a Bessonaeux hangar, which survived until 1940.

Both Fishguard and Milton came under the command of N° 14 Group; initially its headquarters was at RNAS Pembroke —but in July 1917 it was moved to Haverfordwest where it was felt it would be more central for operations around

Sopwith $1^1/2$ Strutter scout of N° 519 SDF, N° 255 RNAS squadron at Milton.
[Air Heritage]

Submarine Scout Zero airship on convoy patrol over the Bristol Channel, 1918.

the Pembrokeshire coast. Also under its command was a sub-station at Wexford in Ireland, which were occasionally used by Milton's airships and by the N°9 Kite Balloon base at Milford.

Today there is nothing left of the original First World War base. The two corrugated airship hangars were dismantled in the late 1920s when the area was re-developed for the RAF airfield. (See Carew Cheriton)

23. Mona (Heneglwys)

Isle of Anglesey

Mona airfield is situated on the site of the old First World War airship station of Llangefni. From its planning stage it was decided that the airfield would not be called Llangefni so as not to confuse it with the former airship station. Initially, it was called RAF Heneglwys, taking the name of a nearby village, but, due to the difficulty of the English in pronouncing Heneglwys, it was decided to rename the airfield RAF Mona, which was the Roman name for the island of Anglesey. The airfield can be found just off the A5, tucked between the Menai Bridge to Holyhead road and the B5109 road, near the villages of Heneglwys and Bodffordd.

The basic construction of the base was completed by mid 1942 but the site was not accepted by the RAF until December, when the hangars had been completed. Three T1 hangars were built on the site of the old airship mooring area. Over the next few years no fewer than 17 blister type hangars were built around the perimeter track.

Mona was opened on 1 December 1942 under RAF Training Command as part

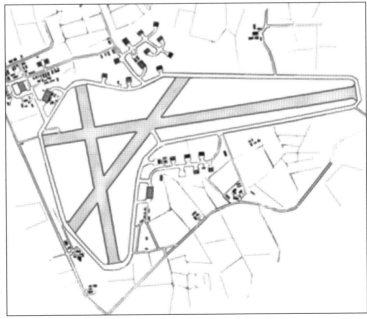

Ground plan of Mona airfield, 1944.

of N° 25 Armament Group. The first commanding officer was G/Cpt G. Bourne. The first unit to arrive was N° 3 Air Gunnery School, moving from Castle Kennedy in Scotland with 48 Blackburn Bothas, 8 Miles Martinets and 6 Fairey Battles, all used as target tugs. The unit was re-equipped with Avro Ansons in May 1943, but returned to Castle Kennedy on 1 November of that year. During February and March 1943, a flight of Masters from N° 5(P) AFU (Advance Flying Unit) from Tern Hill was based at Mona, training some Turkish Air Force officers. N° 3 AGS was replaced by N° 8 (Observers) AFU which was formed at Mona on 15 November, equipped with Avro Ansons, newly delivered from the manufacture. The purpose of the unit was to train navigators, bomb aimers, wireless operators and air gunners and it remained at Mona until it was disbanded.

One of the unit's Ansons was involved in an accident on 12 July 1944 — MG804 was approaching Llandudno when the ailerons broke off, making the aircraft uncontrollable. Despite tremendous efforts by the pilot, the aircraft crashed near Marl Farm, killing all the crew.

During 1943, concrete runways were laid at Mona enabling the airfield to handle all types of aircraft and curing the drainage problems that dogged most of the Welsh airfields. As a consequence of this, in January 1944, the airfield became a temporary home for a detachment of Martinets from RAF Bodorgan whose airfield was unserviceable because of floods.

Mona regualrly received unannounced visitors, especially aircraft of the USAAF; on 14 March 1944 a B-24 Liberator inbound from Marrakesh in North Africa landed having mistaken the airfield for RAF Valley. In April, three Douglas C-47s on flights from the United States made unscheduled landings, followed by a C-54 Skymaster of Air Transport Command on 11 April.

On 19 May 1945 all flying training ceased at RAF Mona and N° 8 (Observers) AFU was disbanded on 14 June 1945. With the war nearly over, the need for aircrew training was no longer a priority and along with most other training airfields in Wales, Mona was run down and eventually closed on 6 May 1946. The airfield remained on Care and Maintenance until 26 July 1951 when it was reopened as a relief landing ground for RAF Valley which was then the home of N° 202 Advanced Flying School (AFS), operating Vampire jet trainers (later replaced by the Folland Gnat T1 of N° 4 FTS).

Due to the introduction of jet equipment the airfield was partially modernised, the main runway was resurfaced and lengthened to 6,000 feet, new, up-to-date electronics were fitted into a modified control tower and new runway lighting and approach lights were installed. The other two runways were withdrawn from use. Today N° 4 FTS operates BAe Hawk trainers, the standard RAF trainer which are regularly seen over north Wales. Mona is still used as a

Aerial view of Mona airfield, 1944. The A5 road from Menai Bridge to Holyhead runs on the south side of the airfield. In latter years, vehicles travelling along here were stopped by traffic lights whenever an aircraft was landing or taking off on the main runway. [National Assembly for Wales]

Starting an Avro Anson of Nº 8 AFU at Mona, 1944.

relief landing ground and the Hawks are often seen at the airfield.

As the airfield is only used by RAF Valley during weekdays, it is open to civil use at weekends and most evenings. Since 1974 the airfield has been the home for the Mona Flying Club which operates a variety of light aircraft.

Mona airfield looks very much the same today as it did in the 1940s. Although all of the blister hangars have disappeared, the wartime control tower (slightly modified) remains, as well as a number of wartime buildings. Of the T1 hangars, only one remains.

Unlike some other Welsh airfields, RAF Mona never had a distinguished record. However, it did make the news in 2001, sadly not in the world of aviation, but in the foot and mouth epidemic as a location for burying carcases.

24. Pembrey

Carmarthenshire

Work on the airfield at Pembrey began before the declaration of war in 1939. The site chosen was land known as Towyn Burrows, which was situated between the railway line and the sea, two miles from Burry Port. Access to the airfield was just off the A484 road on some minor, unclassified roads. Originally the airfield had only a grass landing strip, which had a tendancy to become water-logged and unserviceable. Three concrete and tarmac runways were built during the summer of 1940, enabling the airfield to be operational around the clock and in all weather. An assortment of wooden, Maycrete, Nissen and brick buildings were built to form the domestic site, many of which survive today. Unusually for 1940, two different sizes of 'VR' type hangars, with side openings, were also built.

Due to heavy enemy activity over the south Wales coast, and especially the location of some of the UK's major steel and coal production areas, it was decided from the offset that RAF Pembrey would be a fighter station providing air defence for industrial south Wales, the docks of Cardiff, Swansea and Llanelli, as well as the coast around south and west Wales. At the time, the airfields at Fairwood and Angle were only in the planning stage and were not opened until 1941.

The first squadron to be based at Pembrey was Nº 92 in June 1940 flying in from RAF Hornchurch equipped with Supermarine Spitfire Mk IIs, under the command of S/Ldr P. J. Sanders, having been withdrawn for a rest period from the early stages of what was to become the Battle of Britain. Whilst at Pembrey the squadron provided convoy patrols around the south Wales coast and beyond. The squadron's first action occurred on 4 July when the unit's Spitfire shot down a Ju88 over Wiltshire. Patrols continued throughout the summer months but there were no more enemy actions. Nº 92 Squadron returned to RAF Biggin Hill on 9 September which was the height of the air battle.

In response to the *Luftwaffe's* increasing night attacks on south Wales during the early part of 1941, detachments from Nᵒˢ 256 and 307 Squadrons, equipped with Defiant IIs, were based at the airfield. Nº 256 Squadron eventually departed for RAF Colerne in February 1941 and Nº 307 moved to nearby RAF Fairwood Common in April 1943. The latter squadron was re-equipped with Beaufighter iFs in August 1941 whilst based at Pembrey. No successful engagements were recorded by the squadron and the detachment left south Wales in August 1943. The next unit to arrive at Pembrey was Nº 79 Squadron with Hawker Hurricane

Oblique view of Pembrey airfield as it is today. Note the hangar foundations. [Pembrey Country Park]

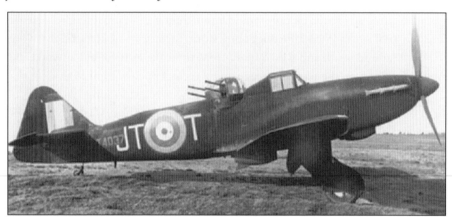

Boulton Paul defiant I of N° 256 Squadron, based at Pembrey for night fighter defence in early 1941.

Ilbs in September, and it remained at the airfield until 14 June 1941 when it left for the newly constructed airfield at Fairwood Common on the Gower Peninsula. Whilst at Pembrey the squadron saw some action such as in early November, when a section of nine Hurricanes engaged a formation of eleven He111s off St David's Head, Pembrokeshire, claiming one destroyed and another as a probable. Another kill was recorded on 20 November 1940 when a Ju88 was shot down by an aircraft patrolling near Pembroke Dock seaplane base. On 12 April 1941, N° 79

Side opened 'F' type hangar at Pembrey. [Pembrey Country Park]

Squadron was joined at Pembrey by N° 32 Squadron (also equipped with Hurricanes) and both continued with convoy patrols until they left in June 1941. Also in April N° 238 Squadron, flying Hurricane Is and Ils, was stationed at Pembrey with a detachment at RAF Carew Cheriton. On 14 February 1941, N° 316 (Polish, City of Warsaw) Squadron had been formed at Pembrey, equipped with Hurricane Ils. A few days later, on 1 April, after becoming operational, the squadron had its first skirmish with the enemy, when a burning ship was spotted off Linney Point still being attacked by two Ju88s. In the air battle that followed the enemy aircraft withdrew but one was claimed as 'probably destroyed'. The squadron first confirmed kill was on 10 April 1941, when a He111 was shot down just off St Anne's Head off the coast of Pembrokeshire. Another enemy Ju88 was attacked over Porthcawl, but after a short chase was eventually downed near Ilfracombe. By the time the squadron left for RAF Colerne on June 16 1941 it had

Hawker Hurricane Ic of N° 32 Squadron at Pembrey. [W/Cmdr A. P. Davies]

Spitfire of N° 92 Squadron, Pembrey.

earned a respected reputation. From February to April 1941, N° 118 (Dutch) Squadron with Spitfire Is, under the command of S/Ldr F. J. Howell, DFC, arrived in Pembrey for a brief rest period.

The next fighter unit to be based at the airfield was a detachment of four Curtiss Tomahawks from N° 26 Squadron who were at Pembrey for two weeks in June whilst on exercise with the army at the School of Artillery at Sennybridge.

By the middle of 1941, RAF Fairwood and its satellite airfield at RAF Angle had taken over the air defence of the south Wales sector. Pembrey was re-allocated to RAF Flying Training Command on 15 June 1941 as N° 1 Air Gunnery School, equipped with Blenheim 1s & IIs and a few Lysanders. The first gunnery course began on 21 June. In May 1942 the Blenheims were flown in secrecy to RAF Upwood to be used as second line aircraft in the first 1,000-bomber raid on Cologne. The Blenheims, however, were not needed and returned to Pembrey within a few weeks. By the autumn, the Blenheims were replaced by Avro Ansons straight off the production line.

Due to its location next to the Towyn Burrows and the sea, the airfield was regularly used for test trials of new aircraft and weapons. In December 1941, the Royal Navy, using a Fairey Albacore, tested a new anti-submarine bomb designed to explode in twenty feet of water. In the autumn of 1942 a Whitley bomber was based at the airfield carrying out night firing trials using illuminated towed targets. In April 1944, trials of the new Vickers Warwick bomber (a development of the Wellington) were conducted at Pembrey by the Air Ministry. A year later, it was intended to conduct flying trials of the proposed new Windsor bomber.

Pembrey was chosen because of its ideal location away from prying eyes and the side opening doors of the VR hangars which could accommodate the large wing span of the new bomber.

Pembrey airfield played host to a number of visiting aircraft, the most notable being a Focke-Wulf FW190 on the evening of 23 June 1942, when the pilot *Oberleutnant* Faber, having become completely disorientated, mistook north for south and the Bristol Channel for the English Channel, and landed at Pembrey thinking it was an airfield in France. Faber had been in a skirmish with Spitfires from Exeter during which he had shot down a British aircraft before breaking off the engagement as he was running short of fuel and ammunition. When he realised his mistake he tried to destroy the FW190 but was overpowered and captured before he could do any damage. The valuable prize was then flown to the Royal Aircraft Establishment at Farnborough where its capabilities were evaluated, resulting in development of the Spitfire IX.

Other stray visitors were a Halifax (DT551) on 9 December 1942, which landed on three engines after a patrol over the Bay of Biscay. On 18 January 1943 a USAAF B-24 Liberator running short of fuel was diverted to Pembrey. On 19 May 1943, the GOC of the USAAF IXth Air Force, Brigadier General Hoyt Vandenberg arrived from Marrakesh in a Boeing B-17 Fortress *en route* to Bovington. During April 1944 several B-24s *en route* to RAF Valley made unscheduled stops at Pembrey either because of low fuel or having lost their way. The airfield was also used by C-47s evacuating wounded service men from the Normandy battlefront in 1944.

The N° 1 AGS Ansons were replaced by Vickers Wellingtons during the latter part of 1944, the first six aircraft arriving during September. Simulated fighter attacks were made by Miles Martinets, augmented by Spitfires in 1944 to make training more realistic. A total of 114 courses passed through the AGS since it was formed, with courses lasting approximately seven and a half weeks. Training continued until the unit was disbanded on June 14 1945.

The airfield's accommodation was taken over by N° 3 ACHU (Aircraft Holding Unit) in July, which remained on the site for most of the year. At this time, flying was at a minimum and comprised mostly visiting aircraft from RAF Fairwood. On 22 October 1946, N° 595 Squadron, equipped with Martinets and Spitfires, was transferred from Fairwood and the airfield's control was return to RAF Fighter Command.

In 1949, N° 595 Squadron was re-equipped with some Vampire jet trainers and, on 11 February, was re-numbered to N° 5 Squadron. The unit stayed at Pembrey (with a detachment at RAF Valley) until the airfield closed for flying in July 1956, although an RAF element remained on site for few more years. Another unit resident at Pembrey from March 1950 to July 1955 was N° 233 OCU equipped

Avro Anson of Nº 1 AGS, Pembrey. [B. Owen]

with the Hawker Tempest TT5, the last unit to operate this aircraft in the UK.

During the early 1950s several squadrons made brief visits to the airfield, usually during various exercises, and in the 1960s an air to ground firing-range was opened on the edge of the airfield, utilised used by Nº 1 Tactical Weapons Unit (TWU) from RAF Brawdy and Nº 2 TWU RAF Chivenor. Since the closure of Brawdy, the range has been used by detachments based at RAF St Athan and Hawks from RAF Valley. Today only one of the airfield's runways is in use; the other two and most of the taxiways are breaking up and overgrown.

Since 1998 the airfield has become a popular venue for private flying and had a boost in 2000 when a new airline, Air Wales (Awyr Cymru), reported plans to commence a scheduled service linking Haverfordwest, Pembrey, Cardiff and Stansted, commencing on 20 March. The airline also planned to establish its

Avro Anson of the station flight, Pembrey, 1957.

A squadron of Venoms of N° 125 Squadron, temporarily based at Pembrey during the 1950s. [MAP]

headquarters at Pembrey with the building of a hangar and offices. Shortly afterwards the airline declared that the smaller Welsh airports were unsuitable and postponed their plans. The service was eventually started using only Cardiff-Wales Airport.

Today, there are still remnants of the Second World War buildings surviving: two remainingVR hangars (used for agricultural purposes), the control tower and an astrodome that was once used to train air gunners. Most of the perimeter track is breaking up, although one end is used by the Motor Sport Centre as a racing circuit. The area between the airfield and the sea is dominated by the Pembrey Country Park and Forest.

Pembrey based Hawk of N° 234 Squadron, over the firing range.

25. Pembroke Dock

Pembrokeshire

The flying boat base at Pembroke Dock was officially opened on 1 January 1930 although, in the beginning, there was not great deal to be seen that would associate it with a seaplane base — only a few wooden huts, a hurriedly built blister type hangar (which was demolished when the modified 'B' types were built), a wooden jetty and a wooden slipway. A form of floating dock was later added to berth the flying-boats. Maintenance was mostly done in the open until the large hangars were built in 1935. The Blister type hangar was found too small to accommodate the flying boats of the day and was therefore used as an engine maintenance facility.

During the 1930s the base was gradually modified and the facilities extended: a new concrete slipway was constructed in 1936 to replace the wooden one built a few years earlier; new brick quarters were built for the station's personnel, together with permanent workshops to cope with any problems that might arise. Eventually the base also had two modified 'B' type hangars that could accommodate the largest type of flying-boats then in service with the Royal Air Force. A 'T2' hangar was built for storage and to accommodate the smaller flying-boats. An elegant Georgian style Officers Mess was built which became a landmark for miles around. By the outbreak of the Second World War, Pembroke Dock flying-boat base was one of the premier flying-boat stations in the United Kingdom. Other RAF and Royal Navy flying-boat bases in the U.K. during the

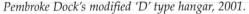
Pembroke Dock's modified 'D' type hangar, 2001.

Three Singapore flying boats of N° 203 Squadron on patrol. [RAF Museum]

war were Castle Archdale (Co. Fermanagh), Mount Batten, Oban, Sullom Voe (Shetlands) and Woodhaven (Fife). All bases became famous in their own right during the war and contributed a great deal to flying-boat operations, and controlling the U-boat menace.

A variety of flying boats and seaplanes used the base, either for training or on operational duties, including search and rescue. In 1934, Seal seaplanes of N° 821 Royal Naval Squadron made a brief visit while on a training flight, but the first squadrons to be permanently based at Penbroke Dock were N°ˢ 210 and 230 Squadrons RAF.

On 1 March 1931, N° 210 Squadron was re-formed as a flying-boat squadron at Felixstowe and moved to Pembroke Dock in May. The squadron was equipped with the Short Southampton II, but was also involved in the developing trials of other types. Eventually, due to the squadron's close connection with Wales, it adopted a dragon as its badge and a Welsh motto '*Yn y nwyfre yn edfan*'. The squadron returned to Pembrokeshire in October 1935 and was re-equipped with Rangoon I flying-boats. In September 1935 it left Pembroke Dock but returned again (with Singapore III aircraft) in 1936 to be re-equipped with the new Short Sunderland I.

In July 1940, N° 210 Squadron moved to Oban, but, when it returned in October 1942, it had been re-equipped with the Consolidated Catalina I. On 30 May 1943, Catalina JX264 was badly damaged by cannon fire from a surfaced U-boat. With one crewman dead, the flying-boat limped back to the safety of the Haven, but, after an emergency landing, the badly holed fuselage sank just after the crew had managed to get clear. The squadron was disbanded at Hamworthy

Short Singapore III of N° 240 Squadron taking off from the Haven.

Junction in December 1943, but was re-formed by renumbering as N° 190 Squadron at Sullom Voe. A detachment of the squadron's Catalinas was stationed at Pembroke Dock from January 1944 to June 1945.

While N° 230 Squadron was re-formed at Pembroke Dock on 1 December 1934 it did not get its equipment (Short Singapore IIIs) until April 1935. In September 1935 the squadron moved to Aboukir and Alexandria in Egypt, but returned to Pembroke Dock the following September where the squadron was re-equipped with Short Sunderland Is. Their stay in Wales was a short one and the squadron was posted to the Far East and Africa where it remained throughout the war. It did return to Pembroke Dock in February 1949.

Another RAF unit that made Pembroke Dock its home base was N° 228 Squadron, which re-formed there on 15 December 1936, with an interim selection of aircraft, including one Supermarine Scapa (K7306), a Saro London (K5258) and two Short Singapore IIIs (K4579, K6913). However it was not until the following April that the squadron received eight Supermarine Stranraer Is. In September 1938 the Squadron moved to Invergordon for a month, but returned to Pembroke Dock prior to their move to Kalafrana in May where it was re-equipped with Short Sunderland Is. A week after war broke out the whole squadron returned to Pembroke Dock, where they remained until June 1940. N° 228 Squadron did not return to its Welsh base until 4 May 1943 when the Sunderlands were flown direct from Lough Erne to the Haven and the ground crew and other personnel were flown in Horsa gliders, towed to Talbenny by Albemarle bombers, escorted by the Sunderlands. The squadron remained at Pembroke Dock until it was disbanded on 4 June 1945.

The Short Sunderland was RAF Coastal Command's main long-range flying-boat during the Second World War. The prototype first flew from Short's factory at Rochester, Kent on 6 October 1937 and entered service on 28 May 1938 and provided maritime patrols, anti-submarine patrols, convoy escorts, search and rescue and transport duties until the early 1950s.

The Sunderland was developed from the famous Short 'C' class flying-boat, which had opened up air routes to the Middle East, the Far East, West Africa and Australia with Imperial Airways in the early 1930s. This mighty flying-boat was powered by four Pegasus XXII engines, but later models were powered by the even more powerful Pratt & Whitney Twin Wasp radial engines. The Sunderland was found ideal for patrol operations, having sufficient room for the crew and a useful range and endurance. The Mk. I's range (fully laden) was 1,780 miles, but with the Pratt and Whitney engines, this was increased to well over 2,200 miles carrying an useful ordnance load of 2,000lbs. As the war progressed, enemy aircraft began to treat the Sunderland with a great deal of respect, as from the Mk III onwards they were armed with up to 14 x .303 machine-guns and 2 x .50 machine-guns. The aircraft soon became known to German pilots as 'The Flying Porcupine'. The Sunderland served with a total of twenty RAF Coastal Command squadrons in every theatre of operations. But it was during the Battle of the Atlantic that the flying boat became a star.

In total, ten Sunderland squadrons were stationed at Pembroke Dock, some on a permanent basis while others were on detachment, re-equipping or on exercise. The squadrons were Nᵒˢ 10, 95, 201, 210, 228, 230, 422, 461, and Nᵒ 4 OTU (re-numbered Nᵒ 235 OCU in July 1947). At least seven different Sunderland squadrons were stationed here together at one time which caused some parking problems in the Haven.

The following paragraphs deal with some of the exploits and bravery of crew from various squadrons while based at Pembroke Dock.

Nᵒ 201 Squadron arrived at Pembroke Dock in March 1944 and was immediately involved with sweeps of the English Channel protect-ing the invasion fleets. The squadron's Sunder-lands made two notable U-boat attacks in June. One encounter by F/Lt Baveystock resulted in

Supermarine Walrus at Pembroke Dock's Empire Day, 1939. [S. Broomfield]

Short Sunderland flying boats moored on the Haven.

Short Sunderland of Nº 10 Squadron RAAF, taking off from the Haven. [S. Broomfield]

Sunderland MR5 of Nº 235 OTU at her moorings.

the sinking of U-995 on 7 June, but the another caused the loss of S/Ldr Ruth and his crew. The squadron was again in action on 11 July when F/Lt I. F. B. 'Wally' Walters attacked and sank U-1222 in the English Channel. On 18 August F/Lt Baveystock scored his third kill, sinking U-107.

Nº 228 Squadron returned to Pembroke Dock at the outbreak of war, and was involved from the beginning with anti-submarine patrols and convoy duties in the Atlantic. On 9 September 1939, Sunderland L2167 attacked a U-boat which had just sunk a merchantman, the S.S. *Vancouver City*. The Sunderland then circled the lifeboats until the occupants were rescued by another ship. The following day, the Sunderland N6135 sank during a landing accident. It was eventually beached but was too badly damaged to be repaired and was broken up for spares. On 11 September the squadron was in action again, when the S.S. *Kensington Court* was attacked by U-boats. Various patrolling Sunderlands picked up a distress signal, three of the aircraft being from Nº 228 Squadron. Sunderland N9025 piloted by F/Lt Thurston N. W. Smith (who had been with the squadron since June 1938) was the first to arrive on the scene, by which time the U-boat had departed leaving the survivors clinging to anything that would float. Smith landed his aircraft near the stricken ship and rescued twenty of the survivors. By now, the aircraft was dangerously overloaded, but with great skill he managed to take off. Another Sunderland from Mount Batten, which rescued the remainder of the ship's crew, later joined the rescue mission. Both aircraft returned to their respective bases and both pilots received the DFC for their exploits. On 21 October 1939, a Sunderland commanded by F/Lt Brooks made an unsuccessful attack on a U-boat attack. A total of thirty-five sorties, mostly convoy escorts, were made during the month. In December 1939 the C.O. made an attack on a submarine, and F/Lt Brooks was in action again in January.

When the squadron returned to Wales in May 1943 it was again involved in patrolling the Western Approaches and the Bay of Biscay. The squadron sortie rate went up and before long the casualty rate also increased. Two Sunderlands and their crew were reported missing, but F/Lt French attacked and destroyed a U-boat. Losses continued to mount during June and July, but the squadron had its successes as at least two submarines were sunk. Three more successful attacks followed in August, including the destruction of U-383 (sunk by F/Lt S. White of Nº 228 Squadron) and U-106 which was shared by F/O R. D. Hanbury (of Nº 228 Squadron) and F/Lt I. A. F. Clarke (of Nº 461 Squadron). On 7 Novemebr F/O A. J. L. Bonnett damaged U-123. By December 1943 Nº 228 Squadron was flying sixty-four anti-submarine sorties a month from Pembroke Dock.

During January 1944 the squadron lost three crews through enemy action and aircraft failure. The squadron made very few contacts until June, when a number of squadrons were involved in sealing the western end of the English Channel ready for the invasion. On 7 JUNE 1944 F/Lt C. G. D. Lancaster sank U-970 followed by U-333 damaged by F/Lt M. E. Slaughter on 11 Jue. Several more successful attacks were made on U-boats during later in the year.

Nᵒ 461 Squadron, Royal Australian Air Force, was another of Pembroke Dock's busy Sunderland units. On 2 May 1943 F/Lt E. C. Smith sank U-332 and on 2 June 1943, during a patrol in the Bay of Biscay, two Junkers Ju88s and two Focke-Wulf Fw190s, and later, a further eight Ju88s, attacked F/Lt Colin Walker's aircraft (EJ134). After a continuous pounding by cannon and machine-gun shells, the Sunderland was so badly damaged that most of its instruments were not functioning, the port outer engine was out of action and the hydraulic system to the gun turrets was damaged. Only the manually operated guns could by used. The rear gunner was wounded, one of the waist gunners was dead, but, in spite of their dilemma, three, possibly four, of the attacking Ju88s were shot down. Due to the condition of his aircraft and crew, Walker decided to break off the engagement and head for safety. There was no chance of reaching Pembroke Dock, as it was nearly 300 miles. The only solution was to make for the nearest British coastline and he managed to land the damaged flying-boat 300 yards off Pra Sands near Marazion, Cornwall then running her aground in shallow water before she could sink. For his gallantry and airmanship Walker was awarded the DSO while his second pilot, F/O W. J. Dowling, received a DFC, two were awarded DFM and a fourth a Mention in Despatches.

A month later on 30 July 1943, Nᵒ 461 Sunderlands were again in action. This time they were joined by a Liberator and a Halifax and a US Navy Liberator in an

Sunderland on the slipway at Pembroke Dock.

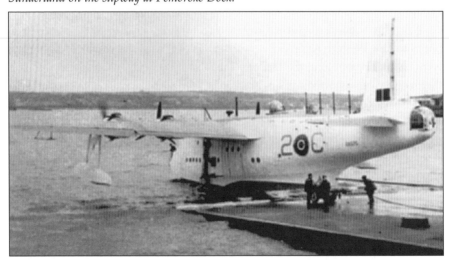

attack on three surfaced U-boats. The aircraft were kept at bay by the heavy flak put up by the submarines until the Halifax managed to score a direct hit, resulting in the sinking of one of the submarines. Meanwhile, a N° 461 Squadron Sunderland, piloted by F/Lt Dudley Marrows, dived through the barrage of flak from 37mm and 20mm cannons put up by the remaining U-boats, dropped its depth charges on, ironically, U-461, which cut the submarine in half. Despite of the other U-boat continuing to put up constant anti aircraft fire, Morrows returned and dropped a life dinghy for the U-461's survivors. On his homeward return to Pembroke Dock Morrows spotted a lone U-boat on the surface which he attacked with machine-gun fire and depth charges, but without any success. By this time his aircraft, badly damaged by the relentless flak put up by the submarines, was running low on fuel and he nursed her back to friendly shores and, as there was no chance of returning to base, made an emergency landing near St Mary's in the Isles of Scilly.

Two weeks later Morrows was again in action, this time he was patrolling just off the Spanish coast when he was attacked by six Ju88s. After a fierce fight, the enemy broke off, but the Sunderland was badly damaged. Having great difficulty keeping the Sunderland airborne, Morrows had no choice but to ditch. A Royal Navy destroyer picked all the crew up safely the following day. On 2 August 1943, F/O R. D. Hanbury sank U-106.

Like all the squadrons based at Pembroke Dock, N° 461 Squadron had its casualties. On 13 August W/Cdr Halliday, the squadron's commanding officer, was killed attempting to land in a heavy swell to rescue the crew of a ditched Wellington which had been involved in a clash with a Fokker Wulf F200. Only one of the Sunderland's crew survived.

One of the squadron's Sunderlands made history by being the first flying-boat to make a dry landing. On 29 May 1943, Sunderland T9114, piloted by an Australian, Gordon Singleton, made the landing at RAF Angle. During a take off in heavy weather the aircraft sustained extensive damage to the fuselage and a landing on water was regarded as being too dangerous. As Angle was the nearest airfield, the pilot headed there and with great skill landed the large flying-boat without any casualties. After a close inspection by salvage team from N° 78 MU, the Sunderland was deemed to be beyond repair, was dismantled and transported by road to the maintenance unit at Pembroke Dock.

N° 95 Squadron, which was formed at Pembroke Dock in January 1941, equipped with Short Sunderland Is, but after a brief crew familiarisation, the squadron was posted to Freetown in South Africa.

Another unit, N° 119 Squadron, was formed at Pembroke Dock and equipped with the Sunderland I. It moved to Lough Erne in April 1942 where it was re-equipped with Catalinas. It returned to Pembroke Dock in August 1942 to be

A flight of Sunderlands on patrol.

equipped with the new Sunderland III, but, due to a shortage of trained crews, was disbanded at the base on 17 April 1943. Most of its crew and aircraft were transferred N° 461 Squadron and N° 4 OTU. During its short time at Pembroke Dock the unit completed several sorties in the Channel and the Bay of Biscay.

N° 240 Squadron was based at the base between May and July 1940. It was equipped with Supermarine Stranraer flying-boats under the command of W/Cdr A. W. Bates. Ironically one of the squadron's Stranraers was scrambled when the airfield at RAF Carew was bombed on 17 July.

There were two Canadian Sunderland units based at Pembroke Dock, N°s 422 and 423 Squadrons. The former was based in the Haven between November 1944 and July 1945 and was involved in a flurry of anti-submarine activity in the Channel and the Bay of Biscay between 5 and 8 March 1945. Its Sunderlands made several depth-charge attacks on enemy U-boats, but after that, the squadron began to run down. On 2 July 1945 the squadron left Pembroke Dock to reform as a Liberator bomber squadron, part of the Tiger Force, a very long-range bomber group intended for operations against Japan. The re-formation, however, never took place and the squadron was disbanded on 3 September 1945.

N° 423 Squadron, RCAF, was heavily involved with the U-boats' last exploits in the English Channel. The squadron's Sunderlands were credited with the last U-boat fight of the war which took place on 4 May 1945.

A US Navy squadron, VP63, equipped with Catalinas, made a brief appearance in 1943. The unit made several patrols and anti-submarine sweeps in the Bay of Biscay and the Western Approaches before being posted to Port Leyautey in North Africa in December 1943.

N° 4 OTU was another Sunderland squadron formed and based at Pembroke Dock. The unit was formed in March 1941 and remained at the base until it disbanded in April 1951. However, in July 1947, the unit was re-named N° 235 OCU. During its time at Pembroke Dock it operated various type of flying-boats: Stranraers, London IIs, Lerwick Is, Catalina Is and Short Sunderland Is, IIs and Vs.

Another resident at the base was N° 78 MU which was involved in all major Sunderland servicing and repairs. The MU was also involved with all modifications and updating of aircraft. Due to its importance and heavy workload, a 'T2' hangar was built at Pembroke Dock in November 1943, which remained standing until a few years ago.

RAF Pembroke Dock had two daylight alighting areas, one opposite Milford Haven and the other to the east of the RAF station. The night alighting area was opposite Angle Bay, which was also used for beaching should the need arise. This night landing area consisted of flare path buoys. However, on a number of occasions, the Coastal Artillery searchlight unit at the blockhouse at St Anne's Head was switched on to assist incoming flying boats that were in serious trouble attempting to land.

It was not surprising that a base as important as Pembroke Dock attracted the attention of *Luftwaffe* bombers. There were a number of raids on the ports, the fuel storage tanks and other military installations in the Haven area and, because of the base's close proximity, several bombs landed on the RAF station. The first of these was on 19 August 1940, when three enemy bombers slipped through the air defences and bombed Llanreath oil storage tanks, which burned for some days after and could be clearly seen as far as the Preseli hills. Another raid was in May 1941, when enemy bombers dropped bombs and mines on the local town and

Sunderland GR5 on the slipway in front of a 'B' type hangar. [RAF Museum]

army bases. None of the moored flying boats were damaged but one land-mine hit the base, causing some damage and killing an airman. The town, however, received a number of hits causing severe damage and a number of casualties. By the end of 1941 more fighter squadrons had arrived in the county thereby deterring any further raids.

In 1945 most of Pembroke Dock Sunderland squadrons were disbanded and the Australian and Canadian personnel returned home to their own countries. Only N°ˢ 201 and 230 Squadrons, together with N° 4 OTU (later to be renamed as N° 235 OCU) remained at the base operating the Sunderland GR5, equipped with latest Pratt and Whitney engines.

In the post war period, the Pembroke Dock aircraft were used for maritime patrols and long-range air sea rescue. N° 230 Squadron aircraft was involved in the Berlin Airlift and in August 1952, a detachment from Pembroke Dock was providing transport and support to the British North Greenland Expedition. A month later, the squadron's aircraft was providing support to islands in the Ionian Sea which had been affected by earthquakes.

But the flying-boat era was coming to an end. Coastal Command was re-equipping with a maritime version of the Lancaster and, later, the Avro Lincoln bomber. On the drawing board was a specially designed long-range maritime aircraft, the Avro Shacklelton. The last Sunderland was officially withdrawn from RAF service in February 1957 and N° 208 Squadron was disbanded at Pembroke Dock. In future, all RAF Coastal Command aircraft were to be land based and Pembroke Dock was placed on Care and Maintenance on 31 March 1957. In 1959,

Sunderland ML824 made a brief return to Pembroke Dock in 1968. It is now at the RAF Museum, Hendon.

*An unusual sight at Pembroke Dock in early 1944, a
Fokker TVIIIw of N° 320 Squadron.*

the base was officially closed and the site returned to the Admiralty, which sold
the land for redevelopment.

Since its official closure the base has attracted a great deal of interest. In 1961,
a Sunderland (ML824) was acquired by the Short Sunderland Trust who intended
making a small part of the Pembroke Dock base into a museum. This particular
aircraft had served with N°ˢ 201 and 330 (Norwegian) Squadrons and had flown
sorties from the base during the war before being purchased by the French Navy
for service with Flottille 27F in the Pacific. The aircraft was acquired by Mr Peter
Thomas of Skyfame Museum and was presented to the Trust by the French
Government on 25 March. The aircraft was on view to the public at Pembroke
Dock until it was given to the RAF Museum at Hendon where it still can be seen
in its wartime colours and is a permanent memorial to all the crews that flew in
them.

More recently, another visitor to the Haven was a PBY5a Catalina (G-BLSC),
painted in the colours of JV928 of N° 210 Squadron, which landed in the Haven on
4 September 1987.

26. Pengam Moor
Cardiff

The RAF station at Pengam Moor was originally Cardiff Municipal Airport. It was situated near the coast, about two miles from the centre of Cardiff. Today the area has been redeveloped with housing and light industry; a factory and car park now stands where the main runway used to be.

The aerodrome was opened in September 1931 and was known as Splott, after the nearby suburb of the city. The site was flat, semi marshland, between a housing estate and the sea, known as Pengam Moor. To combat flooding problems during the spring high tides, a sea wall was built the whole length of the area that was to be used by the aerodrome. Initially there were only a few wooden huts with an extremely uneven grass strip. The name Splott was dropped in early 1936 and the aerodrome was renamed Pengam Moor.

Layout of Pengam Moor in 1945.

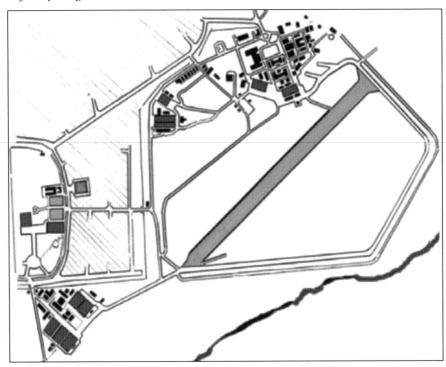

Oblique view of Pengam Moor, 1944. [National Assembly for Wales]

The first scheduled service from the airport was inaugurated on 11 April 1933 by Great Western Railway Air Service, using a Westland Wessex (G-AAGW) on the Cardiff–Haldon–Plymouth route, piloted by Captain Gordon Olley. The Wessex was on hire from Imperial Airways as the Great Western Railway Air Service did not have a suitable aircraft to carry the dignitaries on the inaugural flight. Later flights were flown by the airline's own DH Dragon aircraft. The return fare to Plymouth was £6, a small fortune to people in the early 1930s. However, by the end of the year, a total of 714 passengers had been carried on the route, but by the following year the service was dropped.

In 1934 the Railway Air Service was formed and GWR Air Service, like other railway owned airlines was absorbed into the new company which was to be standardized on one type of aircraft, the DH84 Dragon. However these machines were replaced by the larger DH86 Dragon Rapides in 1938.

Another airline that operated from the aerodrome in the 1930s was Western Airways which, in September 1933, inaugurated a Cardiff – Weston Super Mare scheduled service, which was extended to Bournemouth a year later. Surprisingly, this service continued operating until the outbreak of the Second World War. The company was the first to introduce services to the continent when, on 17 May 1935, the Cardiff–Le Touquet–Paris service was inaugurated by the company's DH84 Dragon.

Although Railway Air Services ceased operating flights from Pengam Moor in

The Great Western Railway Westland Wessex G-AAGW that made the inaugural service from the airfield in 1933. [Cardiff Central Library]

the latter part of 1938, an off shoot — Great Western and Southern Air Service — operated some services from the aerodrome. The company was the first airline to operate a night air service between Cardiff and Weston in October 1938.

In 1939 ATLA (Air Transport Licensing Authorities) came into being and was soon re-organising the airline industry in the UK. As a result, Western Airways was given the monopoly on routes from Cardiff, except for summer flights to the south-west coast resorts already being flown by GW & S Air Services. By this time the aerodrome had acquired several new buildings including a wooden terminal hall and hangars.

On 3 September 1939 the Air Navigation (Restriction in Time of War) Act became law, which prohibited civil flying in certain areas of the UK. Although Pengam Moor was not directly affected, civil flying, especially schedule services, fell drastically.

It is worth noting that Nº 614 Squadron (City of Glamorgan) Auxiliary Air Force was formed at Pengam Moor on 1 June 1937 with S/Ldr Cadman as CO and F/O M. G. F. Pedley as his Adjutant. Initially, the squadron was equipped with two Avro Tutors, these were joined by Hawker Hinds and Hectors during 1938. Although the squadron's offices were at Pengam, most of the training flights were flown from RAF Llandow, because of the upsurge in commercial flying at Pengam Moor. This arrangement continued until the squadron was posted to RAF Odiham on 2 October 1939.

On the outbreak of the Second World War, like most civilian aerodromes, Pengam Moor was requisitioned by the Air Ministry and was renamed RAF Cardiff. Almost immediately, aircraft from various airlines and private individuals were flown to Pengam to provide a pool for the newly formed National Air Communication Unit. However the organisation was short lived and was disbanded in May 1940. The aircraft were then flown to other units and destinations.

In November 1940 N° 8 AACU arrived at Pengam from RAF Weston Zoyland, equipped with a varied collection of aircraft, mostly requisitioned civilian types, and a few early Blenheims and Lysanders. The unit was responsible for providing support and co-operation for the 9th Anti-Aircraft Division in the south Wales area. In early 1941 the unit was re-equipped with DH Dominie (the military version of the DH Rapide) with the underside of the wings painted in an illuminating paint to help train searchlight units to work out the height and bearings of an aircraft. Some machines were fitted with lights to illuminate their undersides. Eventually Airspeed Oxfords and Miles Martinets replaced the Dominies and the unit was disbanded at Pengam in December 1943, its aircraft and crews becoming the nuclei of six separate squadrons situated in various parts of the UK.

The only other flying unit based at the airfield was a detachment of N° 587 Squadron equipped with Martinets which was there for two weeks in September 1944, while in the process of being transferred to Weston Zoyland.

On the outbreak of the war the RAF had a shortage of MU facilities, especially in packing and the storage of aircraft. As a consequence, in February 1940, N° 43 MU was opened at the airfield, which was responsible for the packing and despatch of aircraft for overseas service. The MU took over an area near the entrance of the aerodrome, where some allotments were levelled off. Sites were prepared for timber storage that would be used for the packing cases and the old

Flight of three Hawker Hectors of N° 614 Squadron over Glamorgan.

1930s hangars were refurbished and several hard standing aprons were built. The first aircraft to be packed by the unit were seven Vickers Vildebeests, which arrived by road, en-route for the Far East. A week later three Tiger Moths were flown direct to the unit from Brize Norton. In the first month of operation, sixty-three aircraft were delivered to the MU, packed and despatched. Most arrived by road as the landing strip was in poor condition for most of the time.

On 13 March 1941 the unit was renumbered to N° 52 MU and the next batch to pass through were 78 Hawker Hinds en-route for South Africa. On 4 May 1943, 21 Miles Magister trainers, plus two Supermarine Walrus amphibious aircraft and a Percival Vega Gull, were shipped to Egypt via Cardiff docks. To keep up with a large influx of aircraft, the N° 2 Ferry Pilots Pool, based at Whitchurch, stationed a detachment at the airfield. N° 52 MU was also responsible for handling and packing all Fleet Air Arm aircraft, two Fairey Sea Fox en-route to Malta being the first naval machines to pass through the unit.

Cardiff and especially the dockland area were a prime target for enemy bombers and due to the proximity of the airfield, great effort took place in trying to camouflage the site by painting the aprons, roads and buildings in various shades of green, brown and grey. Also the city's barrage balloon defence was increased, which covered Pengam airfield.

During an air raid on the city and docks on 27 February 1941 several stray bombs fell on the airfield causing minimal damage, except for one of the old hangars, which was replaced in May by a brand new Bellman.

Throughout 1941 the main type to be prepared and packed by the MU were Hawker Hurricane Is, Ics and IIs, mostly destined for the RAF in the Middle East. In October three Hurricane IIAs were packed for transit to Archangel in Russia, via Liverpool docks. In July 1942 a total of 173 Hurricanes of all marks were prepared, packed and despatched. Other types that were also beginning to pass through the MU at this time were North American Harvards and Supermarine Spitfires. By the end of 1943 the MU dealt with an average of 153 aircraft per month.

Accidents were, thankfully, fairly rare at the base, most flying ones occurring during approach and landing. In early 1941 a Harvard severed a balloon cable and, although damaged, landed safely and had to be returned for repair. In February 1941, a Dominie belonging to N° 8 AACU crashed on approach to the airfield. The crew members were rescued by a local man who was awarded a British Empire Medal for his brave effort. Other accidents mostly involved aircraft being dropped or damaged during preparation at the MU.

Leading up to D-Day, Pengam Moor was used for the storage of aviation fuel in jerry cans, which was kept secret from the civilians working on the base, and especially from the public, as the aerodrome was situated close to heavily populated areas. During April 1944 the jerry cans were removed by the USAAF transportation section, to another location on the south coast of England.

As well as packing and despatching aircraft the airfield was used for storage. During August 1944 there were a grand total of 898 aircraft being stored or in the process of being despatched. In November 1944, the MU was in the middle of another flurry, when a USAAF C-47 made numerous shuttle flights between Pengam Moor and the forward airfield in Northern France, carrying spares and other supplies that were being stored at the airfield.

In November 1944, a squadron of crated Piper Cubs were unpacked, assembled and tested by the company staff. They were temporary based at the MU, before being flown direct into battle.

In early 1945, the MU activities had dwindled and most of the deliveries were of Supermarine Seafires for the Fleet Air Arm. As the war drew to its conclusion in Europe, the RAF took over all deliveries from the Air Transport Auxiliary in July 1945 and the MU closed on 31 October.

In 1948, the RAF based N° 3 Reserve Flying School, with Avro Ansons and DH Tiger Moths, at Pengam Moor, where it remained until disbanded in the early 1950s.

During the war years there had been a number of alterations to the airfield, like the new Bellman hangar that was built in 1941 to replace the bomb damaged one. Also, in 1941, a Sommerfeld trackway was laid to keep the strip operational throughout the winter months. Eventually, in 1942, a new 2,800 feet concrete strip was laid which enabled the airfield to remain open all year round and for all types aircraft to be flown in for despatch.

As soon as the restriction order on private flying was lifted on 31 December 1945, civilian flights were re-started at most aerodromes. Cambrian Air Service made the first post-war charter flight from Pengam Moor to Filton, Bristol, on 1 January 1946.The aircraft used was a Taylorcraft Auster carrying a load of aircraft spares from the MU, piloted by Captain Eric Symmons. Soon more flights by Cambrian followed and in May 1948, in partnership with Western Airways, Cambrian was granted a BEA Associate Agreement to operate all the pre-war services between Cardiff and Weston-Super-Mare. Cambrian used its DH Dragon Rapides, while Western used their newly required ex-RAF Avro Ansons on the route. Further services soon followed to other destinations including the Channel Islands.

By 1948 the Cardiff–Weston scheduled service had increased to six flights per day in both directions, with additional flights at the weekends. The following year Cambrian took over all Western flights from Cardiff and became the sole operator at Pengam. During 1950/51 the airline added more Channel Island flights, Liverpool (which was to play an important part in the airline's future

*Cambrian Air Services DH Dragon Rapide G-AKUB (named 'Glamorgan')
at Pengam, 1948.*

expansion programme) Haverfordwest and Swansea to its route network from
Pengam, as well as continuing the Weston route.

After the war the Douglas C-47 Dakota became the mainstay of most airlines,
large and small. Over 10,000 were built for the Allied forces in Europe and the Far
East, to be used as transport carriers, for cargo and glider tugs. When the war
ended, a large number were converted for civilian use. Cambrian, like other
airlines, was in the market for the twenty-seater aircraft, but Pengam Moor, with
its cramped position and no suitable spare land for expansion, a short runway
and the lack of night flying facilities, severely restricted the aerodrome becoming
a major airport for the area.

In 1949, Rhoose airfield, situated twelve miles south-west of the city, was
handed back for civil use, and on 1 April 1954 all civil flying was transferred to
the new airfield and Pengam Moor aerodrome closed.

Heath Park

This is one of the least known airstrips in the Cardiff area. It was situated in the
Heath Park suburb of the city and was known as Camp Heath. The camp became
the base for a field artillery unit of the United States Army in the spring of 1944,
in the build up for the D-Day landings. A landing ground was cleared, adjacent
to the camp, for use by the unit's observation aircraft. The first aircraft to use the
strip were Piper L4 Cubs, which remained at the camp until the unit moved to
France in July 1944. However, in November 1944, the US 7th Infantry Division
with its L4 spotter aircraft arrived at the camp, but within a month the unit was
moved to southern England, *en route* to France.

Today there are still some remnants of the camp remaining, like the camp
guard room, the drill hall and various Nissen huts scattered in the vicinity. The

landing strip has been returned to public use as a park and football pitches.

Llanishen

Llanishen was another of Cardiff's lesser-known airstrips. The landing area was situated on a fairly level area between Tŷ Glas Road, Coed Cae woodlands and Crystal Woods, with the railway line to the south. The strip was allocated to the Air Training Corps in 1941. A blister hangar was constructed to store the gliders and other equipment.

In 1943, the ATC and their gliders were moved to Pengam Moor, as the airstrip was required by the US Army Air Observation Units with their Piper L4 spotter aircraft. To accommodate the influx of personnel, tented accommodation was erected near the Tŷ Glas Road, while the hangars were situated on the north-eastern corner of the camp. According to some sources there were at least 20 observation aircraft based at the camp. Prior to the D-Day landings on 6 June 1944, the unit and its aircraft moved to a new base on the south coast of England.

During June/July 1944, like so many other landing grounds in the Cardiff and the south-western area, the landing ground was used by light aircraft of the US Evacuation Units transporting casualties from the Normandy beach head.

By today, all the land used has been returned to public use.

27. Penrhos

Gwynedd

RAF Penrhos was situated three miles west of Pwllheli on the Llŷn Peninsula, just off the A499 Abersoch road. During the early 1930s, when there was no perceived emergency that warranted the creation of new military establishments, any that were planned met with a great deal of opposition from local inhabitants.

In early 1936, the Air Ministry acquired land on the Llŷn Peninsula with the intention of developing the area and vicinity as a gunnery range. Altogether, seven farms were purchased at Porth Neigwl (or Hell's Mouth), with the intention of developing a gunnery range and small support airfield. Another farm of some 250 acres was acquired west of the town of Pwllheli, to be used as a landing strip and a base.

The airfield was built on a low plateau, the south-west boundary of which is

Ground plan of Penrhos, 1943.

Aerial view of Penrhos, 1943. The main Pwllheli–Llanbedrog road can be seen from bottom right to centre left. [National Assembly for Wales]

some ten feet above the surrounding fields. Most of the huts were of wooden construction, but some concrete ones were added later. Initially there was a Bessonneau hangar but this was replaced by two Bellman hangars in 1939. A further ten blister hangars were later built at the airfield.

There were considerable local objections to the building of the airfield, but the building stage promised at least 200 local jobs. Jobs were more important at the time of hardship in the thirties. Most of the hostility came from the Welsh Nationalists who, on 8 September 1936, while the base was being built, managed to break in and set fire to a constructor's hut, workshops and a stack of timber. As the buildings were of wooden construction, considerable damaged was done. The arsonists gave themselves up and were sentenced to nine months imprisonment. So, RAF Penrhos had some unwanted publicity even before it became operational. Ironically, today the only memorial at the old RAF Penrhos is a plaque commemorating this arson attack. Several books have been written on the subject of this incident and the ensuing legal case and the author is not including it in great detail in this publication.

The airfield with its grass strip was opened on 1 February 1937, under the command of W/Cdr T. V. Lister, as N° 5 Armament Training Camp, equipped with five Westland Wallace aircraft. A marine section was also formed at Pwllheli harbour, with five small patrol boats to act as tows for the floating targets and to provide an air-sea rescue service. The first course began on 3 April with 34 aircraft of N° 10 FTS based at Tern Hill arriving at the airfield together. Leading the group was Acting P/O 'Pat' Pattle, in a formation of five Gloster Gauntlets. Pattle would

Hawker Audax of N° 5 FTS at Penrhos in the late 1930s.

Mishaps were common at Penrhos. A Hawker Fury of Nº 6 FTS with undercarriage failure on 21 April 1937. [C. F. Chandler]

would become the RAF's the top-scoring fighter pilot before his untimely death in an air action in Greece. The ground crews at Penrhos had great difficulty coping with such a large quantity of aircraft at one time and some aircraft, very low on fuel, had to do emergency landings in nearby fields. All the aircraft were recovered the following day. Courses lasted one month and involved all aspect of bombing and gunnery training.

In 1938/39 various aircraft of Nᵒˢ 4, 13, and 600 Squadrons stopped at Penrhos for refuelling on round the Britain long distant endurance flights. As a public relations exercise, an Empire Air Day was held on 28 May 1938, which attracted well over 11,000 spectators, who were able to glimpse at close hand the aircraft then operated by the RAF.

Handley Page Harrow (K962) of Nº 7 AGS at Penrhos.

Hurricanes of Nº 312 Squadron parked on a snowbound RAF Penrhos. [Z. Hurt]

On 9 September 1939 RAF Penrhos became known as Nº 9 Air Observers School, but on 1 November was renamed Nº 9 Bombing and Gunnery School equipped with Handley-Page Harrow bombers and Fairey Battle light bombers.

From March to April 1940, Nº 12 FTS, with its Tutor, Hart, Oxford and Battle aircraft, used the airfield on training exercises.

During the period known as the 'Phoney War' the school was on a war footing. During a routine training exercise, the crew of a Harrow spotted a submarine conning tower two miles south of St Tudwal's Island. Details were sent to Coastal Command who despatched an aircraft to investigate, but by the time it reached the scene there was no trace. Another incident involved an Irish steamer that was acting suspiciously. As the result of these sightings a Fairey Battle was kept at readiness at Penrhos, fully armed with bombs.

On 9 July 1940, the peace at Penrhos was shattered when a single enemy bomber dropped a stick of bombs across the airfield. Three blocks of the officer quarters, a hangar and two Hawker Henleys of Nº 1 AACU was destroyed. Unfortunately two airmen were also killed in the attack. Four more attacks followed until the autumn, causing some damaged, but thankfully there were no further casualties.

Following these attacks a detachment of Spitfires of Nº 611 Squadron from Tern Hill arrived at Penrhos. They were replaced during the winter months by Hurricane Is of Nº 312 Czech Squadron from Speke. The detachment eventually left to join the rest of the squadron that had been posted to RAF Valley in April 1941.

On 21 January 1942 N° 9 Gunnery School was transferred to the newly built airfield at RAF Llandwrog, which was better suited to night flying training and a new unit, N° 9 (O) AFU, was formed at Penrhos on 28 February equipped with De Havilland Dominies and Avro Ansons. In 1942, the RAF had not yet standardised its flying training policy, and N° 9 AGS at Llandwrog was disbanded and the base became a satellite for Penrhos which then concentrated on the air gunnery course, rather than the observers. The first course began on 30 August 1942, training 41 air gunners for Bomber Command. The last course was completed on 25 November 1944.

An AML Bombing Teacher and Turret Training System was introduced at Penrhos in 1942. It was rather unusual as it was fitted inside a blister hangar with a screen attached to one end wall. A film of various aircraft flying and manoeuvring was shown while students sat inside an electrically operated Boulton Paul turret. The guns were removed and replaced by a light projector, which projected a light beam on to the target on the screen.

RAF Penrhos, like every other airfield, had its fair share of accidents. In October 1937 an Audax aircraft (K5161) of N° 5 FTS, on a training exercise, nosed over during a landing on the damp airstrip. During another exercise in November 1937 two Avro Ansons belonging to N° 224 Squadron collided while taxiing, resulting in one Anson being written-off and the other badly damaged. Fortunately none of the crew were seriously hurt. Another incident happened in the spring of 1944 when a Halifax made a forced landing crashing into and damaging an Anson before going over the edge of the airfield. On 6 November 1944, a US Navy Catalina made an emergency landing due to engine failure, failed to stop, and struck a hangar.

The headquarters was moved from RAF Penrhos to RAF Llandwrog because the latter had three concrete runways, and Penrhos was reverted to a satellite station. Then on 16 June 1945, N° 9 (O)AFU was disbanded.

A number of camouflage schemes were employed on various Welsh airfields, some of which were very effective while others were not

Armourers work on a Hurricane of N° 312 Squadron.

so. Serious efforts were made to camoufalge Penrhos, a number of hedges were painted on the airfield to depict fields but, when the airfield was photographed from the air an Anson was seen parked on top of a 'hedge'! The airfield was handed over to Nº 21 ACHU in July 1945, which occupied the vacant accommodation block until the station closed in 31 March 1946.

Part of the main domestic site became a home for Polish ex-servicemen and has remained so until today. The area once occupied by the Bellman hangar and the engineering section is a caravan and camping site.

There are a few concrete buildings still standing around the perimeter area. Most of the perimeter track remains, but the old grass airfield now has a new 1,200 ft tarmac runway, built to cope with the growing interest in weekend private flying.

28. Rhoose

Vale of Glamorgan

Rhoose, which officially became the main civil airport for Cardiff on April 1st 1953, is situated some twelve miles south-west of the city of Cardiff, and three miles from Barry, on the B4265 road, but today it can be reached via the A4232 and the A4050, with the A4226 leading to the airport. Today's airport, however, bears no resemblance at all to the wartime airfield.

The Air Ministry requisitioned land near the little village of Rhoose in 1940 and the airfield was built in 1941/42 as a satellite to nearby RAF Llandow which, by 1942, had an acute storage problem. Rhoose runways formed an unusual cross-shape, with the perimeter track forming a square around the airfield. This layout was one of several experimented with by the Air Ministry. Four enlarged over-blister hangars were built to accommodate up to four Mosquito sized aircraft. Other hangars were planned but were not built.

Ground plan of Rhoose, 1945.

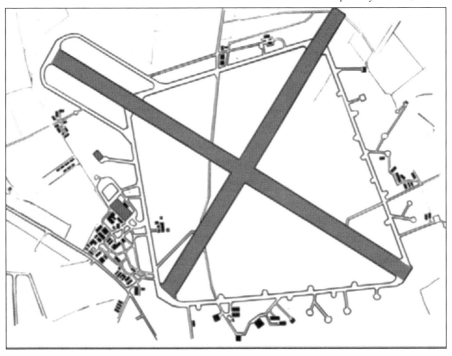

The first aircraft to use the airfield was a Spitfire (K9933) of N° 53 OTU on 8 October 1941, when it made a crash-landing on the ploughed ground after engine failure. The pilot emerged from the aircraft uninjured, and the aircraft was transported to RAF St Athan for repair.

The two runways were completed in early 1942, and the station was officially taken over by N° 53 OTU on 7 April. The first aircraft to move in were the unit's Spitfire and Masters, although work had not been complete and certain parts of the airfield were still building sites. During this period of construction several accidents occurred — overshooting the runways, taxiing off the taxiway, aircraft undercarriage becoming stuck in the mud and colliding with plant machinery. Accidents were a common occurrence with the ageing Spitfires, most of which had already clocked up a very high number of flying hours with their previous units. At least ninety Spitfires were involved in various accidents, some of which were fatal. However, these machines, veterans of the Battle of Britain, trained thousands of Commonwealth pilots for the RAF. While at Rhoose several Mosquitoes were added to the unit's inventory.

The most common cause of these accidents involving OTU aircraft were air collisions, especially during formation flying, take-off and landing incidents, stalling and pilots loosing control during a spin. There were also numerous technical failures. Typical examples of such accidents are as follows: 7 July 1941, two Spitfires (X4024 and X4607) collided during a training exercise. Unfortunately, X4024 crashed on a dwelling in Merthyr, killing the occupants and the pilot (Sgt L. Goldberry). Both Spitfires had taken part in the Battle of Britain with N° 92 Squadron. On 9 July 1941, an ex N° 64 Squadron Spitfire crashed and was totally destroyed. On the same day, Spitfire P9383 crashed killing the pilot, Sgt F. G. T. McGaby. The following day Spitfire X4982 spun out of control while practising dog-fighting manoeuvres and crashed at Macross. On 6 August 1941, N° 53 OTU suffered another acccident when Spitfire X4381 crashed into a hill at Ton Pentre, killing the pilot, F/Lt Goodman. These are just a few samples of accidents that occurred in two months with N° 53 OTU.

The OTU left the Rhoose on 7 May 1943 for RAF Kirton-in-Lindsey, which left the airfield unused until 8 February 1944, when N° 7 Air Gunnery School from RAF Stormy Down used it as a satellite while their base was being improved. The unit's full strength of twenty-three Ansons, twenty Martinets, accompanied by the pilots and ground crew moved over to Rhoose. Within two weeks the first course was ready to commence. Like all training units, N° 7 AGS was not without its accidents. On 8 May 1944, eight of its crew were killed in an air collision when three Ansons and a Martinet collided during an exercise over the sea just off Porth Cawl Point. The work at Stormy Down took longer than first anticipated, but the AGS eventually moved back on 2 August 1944.

A formation of Avro Ansons from N° 7 AGS at Rhoose.

The layout at Rhoose was far from ideal and caused a lot of congestion in the marshalling areas and, as a consequence, two airmen were positioned at each aircraft's wing tips to prevent taxiing accidents. Like a number of airfields built in 1942/43 period Rhoose was built without a definite role and by mid 1944 was no longer required and was put on care and maintenance. However, by the end of the year, it was decided to us the airfield for storage and from 1 November 1944 Rhoose was transferred to N° 40 Group Maintenance Command. As hangar space was limited most of the aircraft were stored in the open, covered with tarpaulins. It remained an aircraft storage unit until the end of the war.

In 1946, for a brief period, Rhoose became a sub site for N° 214 MU at Newport and was used as a bomb storage depôt, the blister hangars being used to store various bombs. This was kept secret from the local population for fear of causing alarm and complaints. But when the MU closed in 1948, the Rhoose site was not needed and the station was closed. Rhoose was one of hundreds of satellite airfields built for no apparent reason, as throughout its brief military history the authorities were undecided on its role. The airfield was finally handed over for civil use in 1949.

For the next few years Rhoose lay dormant, except for the occasional civil aircraft that was diverted there from Pengam Moor. At one point, the land was marked out for an industrial estate, but by 1950 it was being regularly used by civilian passenger charterflights that were unable to use the Pengam airfield. As a consequence, in 1952, a decision was made to develop Rhoose as a civilian airport, initially to handle larger aircraft that were unable to use the small strip at Pengam Moor. After some redevelopment, on 1 April 1954, all civilian flying

Servicing one of Nº 53 OTU's Spitfires at Rhoose, early 1943.

was transferred to Rhoose which came under the control of the Ministry of Civil Aviation. A new terminal building and new hangars (civilian Bellman type) were built on the village side, providing airlines with office and hangar space. Cambrian Airways, which had been operating out of Pengam Moor since 1946, moved its headquarters and maintenance base to the new airport. Soon, new services and more airlines began operating scheduled services from Rhoose to the south of France, Belfast and Cork and licences for other destinations were applied for. By the end of the year, Cambrian alone carried 25,000 passengers from the airport.

In the early 1960s, holiday charters to the Mediterranean began to be flown from Rhoose. Glamorgan County Council took over the control of the airport in April 1965 and, before long, put forward their plans for future redevelopment and the airport was re-named Glamorgan (Rhoose) Airport.

Spitfire MV-P of Nº 53 OTU at Rhoose 1943.

Miles Master I of Nº 53 OTU at Rhoose. [Air Heritage]

More airlines began to use the airport and passenger and freight traffic grew continuously so that, by 1970, to meet the growing demand, £5 million had to be invested in a new terminal, control tower (with modern equipment) and radar. In addition to this, runway 12/30 was increased in length to 7,000 feet and resurfaced. These improvements enabled the airport to operate the new jet-powered aircraft that were entering service with various airlines. The new terminal building was opened by the Duke of Edinburgh in 1972 and the airport was re-named Cardiff Wales Airport.

In 1974, Cambrian Airways began operating as part of BEA, but, in 1976, the Welsh name disappeared after 40 years of operation.

Several airlines tried unsuccessfully to introduce scheduled services between Cardiff and the rest of Wales; companies like Air Wales and Welsh Airways. The most successful to date is Air Wales, founded in 1999 by a Swansea porperty financier, Mr Roy Thomas. The airline operated scheduled services from Cardiff International to various destinations in the UK and abroad, using a fleet of ATR 42-300s. Sadly, in April 2006 the airline announced it was ceasing all scheduled flights from cardiff and concentrating on charter and freight services. Other airlines have expressed an interest in taking over some of the routes. Another airline that has boosted operations at Cardiff is bmi Baby, the low-cost arm of bmi (British Midland International).

Various holiday charter airlines have been formed and based at Cardiff — Diamond Airways, Inter-European Airways (a subsidiary of the Cardiff-based Aspro Travel Group) and, perhaps the most nationalistic of all, Airways International Cymru. Over the years, Cardiff Wales Airport has attracted British, Continental and American airlines. Some have ceased operating, such as Dan Air

Aerial view of Cardiff International in the 1980s. [National Assembly for Wales]

Cambrian Airways BAC One-Eleven parked by the terminal building at Cardiff.

which connected Cardiff to Amsterdam, Belfast, Cork and the Channel Islands; the Leeds based Capital Airlines, which operated the Cardiff – Leeds/Bradford, Glasgow and Jersey links; Air UK, which took over the original Air Wales network in 1979, operated from the airport for a while; Netherlines took over the Amsterdam schedule. Today, other airlines, including Metropolitan, Air Europe, Aer Lingus, British Regional Airways, KLM, Ryan Air and Manx Airways as well as a number of holiday charter companies, operate scheduled services from the airport. Like most airports in the UK, the appearance of Concorde always made a great impression with all spectators and grabbed the local headlines. The first Concorde to visit Cardiff was an Air France aircraft in the summer of 1986.

Further development took place in the 1980s when a £1 million extension to the main runway brought it up to 7,725 feet which enabled the airport to take the heaviest aircraft and operate a trans-Atlantic service. In 2000, Cardiff International (as it is now known) handled 1.5 million passengers for the first time and was placed among the UK's top five fastest-growing airports. At the time of writing further expansion is planned, to bring it up to the standards required of a major British airport. In recent years British Airways has established a large engineering complex at the airport, capable of handling Boeing 747s. A flying club also operates from the airport and, on the north-east side, just off the airport approach road, is the Welsh Aircraft Museum. It was opened in 1976 and over the years has acquired an interesting collection of aircraft, mostly types that were once based in Wales and associated with the country, the prize exhibit being a Vickers Viscount in the colours of Cambrian Airways.

Aerial view of the terminal building and apron in the 1980s. [Cardiff Airport]

Concorde at Cardiff International Airport. [Cardiff Airport]

29. Rudbaxton
Pembrokeshire

This little known airfield has probably the shortest history of all Pembrokeshire's wartime airfields. There were over fifty satellite landing grounds in the UK, ranging from large park land on private estates to race courses and farm land. Buildings on these SLGs were kept to the minimum and usually comprised of existing houses and out-buildings which were requisitioned. Blister and Robin hangars were built for maintenance, together with concrete aprons and hard areas. Sometime a paved perimeter track was constructed to the grass landing strip with dispersal areas. Defence of the SLGs was usually the responsibility of the local Home Guard unit.

The SLG at Rudbuxton was situated half-a-mile north-east of RAF Withybush and came into being in April 1941 as N° 4 SLG for the aircraft storage unit of N° 38 MU at RAF Llandow. At the time, N° 38 MU was responsible for the storage of Tiger Moths, Lysanders, Blenheims, Whitleys and Spitfires. As parking space was limited at Llandow, and the threat of air raids was ever present, it was decided to construct a SLG in a safe area, away from the MU. Some land near Rudbaxton was chosen, having been designated some months before as a potential airfield site. The site consisted of fairly level ground with clear approaches. Entrance was along a long, narrow, concrete road leading from the B4329. The SLG had a grass runway, which was sufficient to operate a lightly-loaded Whitley, but was often unusable in wet weather. The camp consisted of two Nissen huts and tented accommodation. A blister hangar was constructed and a Robin hangar was planned, but most of the aircraft were stored in the open or under tarpaulins.

Within two years the station was closed, partly due to its location — by 1942 the new airfield at RAF Withybush had became operational and as the approach to the new airfield's main runway was directly over Rudbaxton it was regarded as too dangerous for safe operation and the threat of enemy bombing raids on the Severn estuary had decreased considerably thereby reducing the need to disperse aircraft to SLGs.

In September 1942 N° 38 MU handed over the station to the Ministry of Aircraft Production. On 1 July 1943 the SLG was officially closed, the hangar and the Nissen huts were dismantled and re-erected at the new airfield at Withybush. Eventually the land was returned its owner. Only sporadic use had ever been made of the SLG, mostly used for storage, although some test flights were conducted from the airfield. According to records, there were only ever about thirty aircraft stored here at any one time.

Today there is hardly any sign left that the SLG existed. The remnants of the narrow concrete roadway leading up to the camp still exist and is now part of a farm lane. The concrete base of the blister hangar was broken up in 1943.

Another SLG was planned for the county at Picton Park adjacent to Picton Castle, west of Haverfordwest, but the site was not required.

30. St Athan
Vale of Glamorgan

RAF St Athan is one of the largest stations used by the Royal Air Force today and is one of only two left in Wales. Today, as in the past, St Athan is a Maintenance Unit supplying and supporting the RAF in its worldwide role.

St Athan is situated alongside the B4265 road, seven miles west of Barry. Even when it was built it was an exceptionally large airfield by any standards. Construction work began in January 1937, taking eighteen months to complete with the official opening by the commanding officer, G/Cpt E. Brownsdon-Rice, taking place on 1 September 1938. During the planning stage it was decided that RAF St Athan would be a maintenance base for aircraft with ample storage facilities, as well as a training establishment, something the RAF urgently needed. Initially the base was to have one concrete runway, but in 1939 work began on a second, which was completed in early 1940. Both runways were lengthened in

Ground plan of St Athan, 1990s.

1944 to accommodate the large four-engined bombers.

The first RAF element to arrive at the base was an advanced party of twenty-six airmen which were billeted at East Camp. Over the next few weeks a further 1,500 staff and trainees arrived at what was designated N° 4 School of Technical Training. By the outbreak of the war this figure had doubled. The first maintenance unit to be formed at the station was the civilian manned N° 19 MU, an aircraft storage unit, responsible of storing and keeping the aircraft in operational order until required by service squadrons. During most of 1939 aircraft were flown direct from the manufacturers to St Athan for storage, and by early 1940 there were 280 Fairey Battles and Hurricanes stored here. From May, these were joined by Bristol Blenheims, Bristol Beaufighter Is, Westland Lysanders and Boulton Paul Defiant Is & IIs, bringing the total of aircraft to well over 700 by September. From 1940 onwards, a variety of other aircraft types, including Spitfires, Whitleys, Wellingtons, Lancasters and Mosquitoes were in storage here.

Even with a large number of hangars, storage space at the airfield was at a premium, so the nearby airfield at RAF Llandow was used for additional storage. According to some sources, aircraft could be taxied from Llandow direct to St Athan via a series of taxiways and minor public roads.

By 1945, the main type of aircraft stored were the latter variants of Beaufighters, Mosquitoes and the new Bristol Buckmasters that were then entering service. In addition, hundreds of the older types still remained in storage awaiting disposal instructions. Every year since the base was opened, additional hangars had been built, some within the airfield perimeter, others on nearby requisitioned land. By November 1944 there were a total of 56 hangars sprawling around the airfield including twenty Bellmans, two 'D' types, six earth covered 'E' types, four large 'C' types and at least twenty Robin and Super Robin hangars. There were four large hangar type workshops used by N° 32 MU and N° 4 STT plus a number of blister type hangars.

St Athan had also became the home of N° 32 Maintenance Unit in 1939, which was mostly involved with the fitting of special electronics to various aircraft specializing in the installation of ASV, IFF and AI radars to aircraft, including Catalinas at Pembroke Dock (later became the responsibility of N° 78 MU at the flying-boat base). The MU also specialized in major repairs, even a complete rebuild of any aircraft in service. The unit was also responsible for various modifications, as manufacturers usually concentrated on the production of new aircraft. The unit also became renowned for rebuilding crashed enemy aircraft for displays throughout the country. Throughout the early part of 1944 the unit was busy with the modification of the North American Mustang fighter and preparing sixty Mk 1s for the Normandy invasion.

Avro Anson of N° 7 OTU, St Athan.

As the war in Europe drew to an end the MU began converting Lancaster bombers for the Tiger Force that was to bomb the Japanese mainland from the re-captured bases in Hong Kong and elsewhere. Work involved modifying the Merlin engine for the Far East, installing additional fuselage fuel tanks, fitting 20mm cannons instead of the .303 machine-guns and fitting American R/T systems. However, with the dropping of the A-bomb on two Japanese cities, Japan surrendered and Tiger Force was not required. Some of the Lancasters did serve with the RAF in the post-war Far East, but the rest remained at St Athan until sold to other air forces.

As well as being a major maintenance unit, St Athan was also a base for a number of minor units. The first of these comprised six Hawker Hurricane Is of N° 11 Group Fighter Pool which arrived at station on 27 June 1939. They became the only air defence for the airfield and surrounding areas for the next nine months. In April 1940 a School of Air Navigation (N° 12 Radio School) moved to the airfield from RAF Manston, equipped with Avro Ansons, but was transferred to Canada in September. The next unit to be based at the airfield was N° 12 Radio School, which was formed at St Athan on 1 September 1943, although it did not receive its first aircraft until December, when Avro Ansons of 'O' Flight of N° 7 OTU were transferred to the new unit, followed by ten new Airspeed Oxfords in January 1944, plus five surplus Ansons in March from N° 3 OTU at Haverfordwest. The unit trained wireless operators for the RAF until closed on 31 May 1944 when most of the aircraft went into storage at the MU.

Like most RAF stations built in the thirties, St Athan was known to the German planners and therefore became a target for their bombers. During 1940 there was a considerable amount of enemy activity in the area. On 15 July 1940 a Hurricane, while on a test flight for the MU, came into contact with enemy

Airspeed Oxford Is of Nº 12 Radio School. Together with the Avro Anson, this was the RAF's main twin-engined trainer.

bombers just after they had bombed Barry Docks. With no ammunition the frustrated pilot made several dummy attacks on the enemy aircraft, forcing them to abort their tight formation and head out to sea. After the encounter the MU unofficially kept at least two fighters armed and ready to go.

The first raid on the airfield took place in August 1940 when some bombs fell on the grassed area of the airfield, causing no damage other than a few craters. However, on 29 April 1941 at least twelve Ju88s dropped a cluster of incendiaries and high-explosive bombs on some of the hangars. Damage was minimal as only three Hurricanes were destroyed, whilst nine other types received minor damage which was quickly repaired. Some of the 'E' type hangars were covered with earth to absorb any damage, therefore the incendiaries that landed on the hangar just burned themselves out without causing any damage. The next attack was on 11 May, causing three fatalities and damaging two more hangars. As the result of these raids, SLGs were opened at St Brides and at Chepstow racecourse, as well as obtaining additional space at Llandow.

There was no more air attacks on the airfield as fighters from Fairwood Common had arranged an air defence umbrella for the area. But, on 3 February 1944 there was a serious fire in a 'E' type hangar at the Picketston site, in which ten Beaufighters and a Mustang were destroyed. The ensuing investigation reported that it had been caused by petrol, which was being drained from one of the aircraft, being ignited by faulty electrical leads; as the hangar's doors were wide opened a draught helped to spread the fire. Fortunately no personnel were hurt as they were able to quickly escape through the open hangar doors.

When the war ended both MUs and the STT remained at St Athan which had become an important support, repair and storage facility in the RAF. Since 1945, most of the RAF's front-line aircraft have passed through the maintenance and storage facilities here including all major servicing on Lincolns, Meteors, Canberras, Javelins, Hunters, Lightings and the three 'V' bombers. As the RAF Centre of Engineering, St Athan has handled all current RAF aircraft, including Dominies, Tristars, VC 10s, Hawks, Jaguars, Harriers and Tornadoes. The MU has also been the 'breakers yard' for a number of aircraft withdrawn from operational use. Most of the Valiant, Vulcan and Victor bombers were broken up at the station. More recently some VC 10s have been broken up for spares.

On 1 April 1999, the base changed its name to DARA St Athan, with the introduction of the Defence Aviation Repair Agency, but remained an RAF airfield supported by RAF personnel. The function of the station is more or less the same i.e. the repair, overhaul and storage of both RAF and RN aircraft. At the time of writing there are only a few aircraft permanently based at St Athan including the station's own flight with two Tucanos and the University of Wales Air Squadron's four Grob 115 gliders. Also based at St Athan is N° 634 Volunteer Gliding School equipped with two Grob Viking gliders. Visiting Hawks from Valley use the airfield while using the firing range at Pembrey. There is also an RAF Mountain Rescue Unit based at the airfield.

Today RAF St Athan is more or less the same as it was in the 1940s; many of the original wartime buildings and hangars are still in use, although most of the Robin hangars have been replaced. In March 2002 the Ministry of Defence announced future reorganisation plans for the station. DERA would relocate its engineering and repair facilities in one area of the base, with the prospect of a new engineering centre, capable of repairing all future British and NATO aircraft, being built. The remaining areas of the station would be allocated to various army units.

The first army unit to move in, was a battalion of the Welsh Guards from Aldershot, the first time that the Welsh Guards have ever been based on Welsh soil. There are also plans to move other army units to St Athan, taking full advantage of the vast hangar space available at the camp.

Unloading an RAF Tornado from a Hercules transport aircraft. [DERA]

The best viewing area for spectators and enthusiasts are from the coastal road, which has a few lay-bys and is usually not very busy.

31. St Bride's
Pembrokeshire

This airfield was situated south of the village of St Bride's Major, just off the B4265 road. The base was allotted to N° 19 Maintenance Unit (MU) at St Athan as N° 6 SLG (Satellite Landing Ground) which comprised of two separate units, St Brides East and St Brides West, joined together by a trackway through some fields.

From the beginning of the war it was felt that the airfield at St Athan would be a prime target for enemy bombers and therefore several SLGs were built for aircraft storage and dispersal. Work began on the site early in 1940 and was intended to be completed by December but, during an inspection, it was decided that several alterations were required, including a more adequate drainage system, and the base was not declared operational until 3 April 1941.

The first aircraft to be stored at the base were seventeen Hawker Hurricane IIs, followed by twelve Beaufighters Ics and some Bristol Beauforts. Over the next few months several other types were seen parked around the field and at times parking became a problem as in June 1943 there were fifty-five aircraft stored at the base, nearly double the number it was originally planned to accommodate.

Originally there were no plans to build any sort of permanent buildings as all the aircraft were to be stored in the open and personnel were to be accommodated in tents. In order to provide some degree of comfort for the base personnel a Nashcrete canteen building was constructed in October 1943, but it was not until May 1944 that a Robin hangar was constructed for minor maintenance on the aircraft.

St Brides was also used as an emergency landing ground by several of the nearby bases. On 10 June 1942, a Spitfire of N° 53 OTU decided to make an unscheduled landing here but, due to the nature of the ground, the pilot crash-landed on the NW/SE runway but managed to get out of the aircraft with just minor injuries. Shortly after this incident it was decided that the strip was not suitable for Spitfires, mostly because of their angle of approach and the delicacy of their undercarriage.

By 1945, as enemy air activity in the area had stopped, the importance of St Brides had diminished and plans were made to close the airfield. It was de-requisitioned in July (except for a small area around the Robin hangar which was used for breaking up some Hawker Henleys and Beaufighter IFs by the Bristol Aircraft Company). All activity on the airfield had ceased by August and the base

Aerial view of St Bride's in 1960. The dotted lines indicate the location of the landing strips.

was finally closed on 26 September 1945.

The whole area has reverted back to farming and there are no signs whatsoever that an airfield ever existed here.

32. St David's

Pembrokeshire

The airfield of St Davids is situated just off the A487 Haverfordwest to St David's road, a mile from the little fishing village of Solva. It is only about three and a half miles from Brawdy. Main access to the airfield is off the A487 road, but there are other entrances adjacent to some minor roads. Up until the closure of RAF Brawdy, St Davids was used as a relief landing ground.

The airfield had three 150 foot-wide tarmac runways. The main runway 08/26 was 5,910 ft, the two secondary ones, 04/22 were 3,200 feet and 13/31 3,570 feet respectively. Along with a perimeter track, there were thirty diamond-shaped hard standings in clusters of five. To the south of the runways was the main site with its control tower, two type T2 hangars, living quarters and various maintenance sheds. To the east of the airfield, situated between the approach of runways 13/31 and 08/26, was the other T2 hangar together with its associated workshops. Initially the airfield was to have four T2 hangars and a number of the

Ground plan of St David's, 1944.

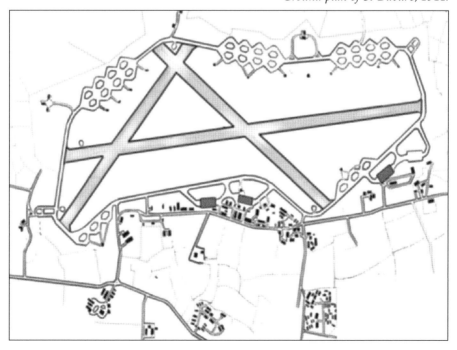

blister type but only three of the former were built, although a base for the fourth was put down, but was only used for parking and open air servicing. Three blister type hangars were built but were only used for vehicle parking and for the resident station communication aircraft. To the north, well away from the airfield, in a marshy ground, were the station bomb and fuel dumps. All the building on the airfield were either of the Nissen or Maycrete types.

Today, nearly all the buildings, and especially the T2 hangars, have been completely cleared. The main runways and the perimeter track with its hard standings can still be seen, although some parts are overgrown. While in use as a relief landing ground the main runway and part of the taxiway was kept operational by RAF Brawdy and therefore that part of the airfield is in a better condition. There are still some of the Maycrete huts in use by local farmers. The general layout of the airfield can be easily seen and one can easily imagine a fully operational wartime airfield.

The airfield was open in September 1943 as part of chain of coastal airfields for RAF Coastal Command. The proposed plan for this, the most westerly airfield in Wales, was to house a US Navy unit, equipped with Consolidated PBY4Y Liberators. However the Americans went to Dunkswell and RAF Coastal Command took over the airfield. The first RAF aircraft to occupy the new airfield was a detachment of Boeing B-17 Flying Fortresses from N°s 260 and 220 Squadrons, based at Thorney Island. The RAF Fortresses were never quite as successful in the role of day bombers as the service had hoped and, as Coastal Command had a shortage of long-range land-based aircraft, the Fortresses filled a gap until replaced by the Consolidated Liberator.

The detachments arrived at St Davids in December 1943 and remained until the end of the following year. However N° 220 Squadron returned to the west Wales base in June 1945 equipped with Liberator Vs, VIs and VIIs. This was just a short stay as the squadron left St Davids in September, to be fitted with Leigh Lights. The squadron's Liberator VIIs were converted to long-range transport aircraft due to a shortage of such aircraft in RAF Transport Command.

On 26 November 1943, two four-engined Handley Page Halifax bombers of N° 517 Meteorological Squadron moved in to their new base, followed on 11 December by Halifax IIs and IIIs of N°s 58 and 502 Squadrons. The squadrons were not declared operational until January 1944 when all the personnel had arrived. The Halifax was the second of the four-engined heavy bombers to enter service with the RAF. Nine squadrons were transferred to Coastal Command for anti-submarine, meteorological and shipping patrols, the aircraft being converted from BI and BIIs to GRII and GRVs (Specials). These versions were powered by four Rolls Royce Merlin XX engines of 1,390 hp, giving a top speed of 265 mph and a range of 2,500 miles.

Handley Page Halifax GRII prior to being painted in Coastal Command colours.

N° 502 Squadron, under the command of W/Cdr Bayliss came to St Davids from RAF Holmesley South and remained at the Pembrokeshire base until September 1944 when it was posted to RAF Stornaway in Scotland. From the offset, the squadron, together with N° 58, was involved with anti-ship and anti-submarine duties. In January 1944, four U-boats were attacked and depth charged, two in the same day. During another patrol, on 14 January, one E-boat and a cargo ship were sunk. On 25 April 1944, F/Lt Hoderness sank a U-boat in what was a classic Coastal Command Halifax night attack. After hours of patient patrolling, usually without any contact, a blip appeared on the radar screen. Flares were dropped on the contact, illuminating a U-boat and the Halifax dived on the target, dropping its bombs. Most missed but one found its mark and the submarine was cut in half. The Halifax returned to St Davids with only a 37mm cannon shell hole in its wing.

The Channel Islands ports became an ideal shelter for enemy submarines, but they also became a graveyard for many. On 3 June, a U-boat was attacked and badly damaged while it was sheltering in Guernsey harbour and on 22 June, Halifax 'T' for Tommy of N° 58 Squadron, sank a U-boat in Alderney harbour.

On 8 June, Halifax 'F' for Freddie sighted and attacked U-413. The aircraft made its run in on the target and, despite very accurate flak from the submarine, dropped four 600lbs anti-submarine bombs. Three missed the submarine, but the fourth seriously damaged the conning tower. The Halifax made four more machine-gun attacks on the U-boat but, on the fifth, received a direct hit on its port engine and had to break off the engagement.

On 4 July four U-boats were attacked and sunk, as well as seven surface vessels which were attacked off the north-west coast of France by aircraft from St Davids. During one of these attacks a Halifax, piloted by W/Cdr Grant, commanding officer of N° 58 Squadron, was shot down. The crew managed to get to the dinghy but two died from their injuries. A Canadian frigate picked up the survivors.

In February 1944 a Halifax, returning to base after a patrol in the Bay of Biscay, was attacked by a Junkers Ju88 causing the aircraft to crash into St Brides Bay with no survivors. Another Halifax was attacked but managed to limp home.

By February 1944, St Davids airfield had become quite over-crowded so, when its satellite at nearby Brawdy was opened on 2 February, N° 517 Squadron moved to the new base.

St Davids was never really suited for Halifax operations due to the alignment of the runways with the prevailing winds. On many occasions, it was found that a Halifax could not take off fully loaded. So the bombers would take off with a light fuel load, land at nearby Brawdy to top up the fuel tanks and then take off for a patrol. This was a serious drawback and the reason why Brawdy became the main base, with St Davids eventually being relegated to the role of a satellite airfield. The crosswinds caused several mishaps during take off and landing. In June 1944, the winds caused Halifax 'F' for Freddie (HX177), belonging to N° 517 Squadron, to crash on landing, skid across the grass and hit the control tower. The aircraft broke in half but, fortunately, there were no serious injuries to personnel.

As the Allied armies advanced across Europe, Coastal Command decided to reduce the number of bases that were used for anti-shipping and anti-submarine patrols to those located on the south coast of England and established bases such as Pembroke Dock. The importance of St David's then diminished and the base was gradually run down.

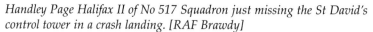

Handley Page Halifax II of No 517 Squadron just missing the St David's control tower in a crash landing. [RAF Brawdy]

Aerial view of DH Sea Venoms parked in front of the T2 hangars, 1950s.
[S. Broomfield]

The first squadron to leave was N° 58 in August 1944, which departed for RAF Stornaway in Scotland, followed a month later by the Halifaxes of N° 502 Squadron. For the next few months the airfield remained quiet except for a few visits from Halifaxes of N° 517 Squadron from nearby Brawdy. In June 1945 the airfield became the base for Liberators VIs and VIIIs of N° 53 Squadron, under the command of W/Cdr D. McKenzie, which came from Reykjavik in Iceland. The same month, St David's became the base for the Liberators of N° 220 Squadron. Both squadrons left their west Wales base on 17 September 1945.

With a modern airfield, perhaps not so much suited to the heavier types, it was decided that the N° 4 APC (Armament Practie Camp) located at RAF Talbenny should move to the airfield but, at the last minute, the scheme was dropped.

On 1 November 1945, the station headquarters sick bay, all administrative and most of its workshop facilities were moved to RAF Brawdy and St Davids was put on care and maintenance. The airfield remained on care and maintenance until 1 January 1946, when both airfields were taken over by the Admiralty for the Fleet Air Arm with St Davids acting as a relief landing ground for the main base at Brawdy.

During September 1955, while Brawdy was being modernised to be able to operate modern jet aircraft that were being introduced into service, the Fleet Requirement Unit took up residence at St David's. Operated by Airwork Limited, the FRU was equipped with various naval aircraft, ranging from Sea Hornets NF21s to De Havilland Mosquitoes T33s and eventually Gloster Meteor T7s (for

*The Fleet Air Arm used St David's to store aircraft such as these
Supermarine Attackers which were awaiting disposal.*

jet conversion training) and remained at St David's until Brawdy became fully
operational in October 1958. Also during this period a detachment of
Supermarine Attacker FB1s of N° 787 Squadron, Fleet Air Arm, was based at St
Davids from 22 April – 24 July 1952.

With the advent of faster and heavier jets St David's was used less often but
retained as a relief landing ground. Over the years, most of the buildings, and
especially the 'T2' hangars, disappeared from the skyline. One of the runways
was resurfaced for 'touch and go' flights, but, by today, even that is breaking up
and before long the whole area will be reclaimed by nature and used for farming.

In 2002 the airfield was used as the site for the National Eisteddfod of Wales,
when the cathedral city of St David's played host.

*A lone Maycrete building
at St David's in June
1961.*

33. Sealand (Shotwick)
Flintshire

Sealand airfield has its origins during the First World War. It was a very unique site as it occupied two strips of land on either side of a mainline railway and, as a consequence, two airfields developed separately, Shotwick as a training station and Queensferry as an Aircraft Acceptance Park. The Queensferry site on the southern side was not developed as quickly as the Shotwick site and the war ended before it became fully functional. However, the site remained under the control of the Air Ministry.

The main site at the time (North Camp) was called Shotwick and this was where most of the flying activities took place. This became the base for N[os] 95 and 96 Squadrons, equipped with a variety of standard Royal Flying Corps fighters e.g. Camels, Pups, Dolphins, Salamanders, Martinsydes and Avro 504s for training. N° 95 arrived at Shotwick from Tern Hill on 30 October 1917, and was followed a few days later by N° 96 Squadron from South Carlton. Both units remained at the airfield until April 1918.

In November 1917, N° 90 Squadron, under the command of Major Blackwood, arrived at Shotwick from Shawbury with more Avro 504s and Sopwith Dolphins, as a result of which more land had to be requisitioned and additional hangars constructed.

Another fighter squadron, N° 61, equipped with Camels, Pups and an Avro 504 arrived from Shawbury on 1 April 1918.

While awaiting postings to France in April, N[os] 95 and 96 Squadrons were disbanded and their pilots and aircraft were dispersed to other squadrons in the UK and France. This greatly relieved the parking problems at the airfield.

N° 90 Squadron with its

Ground plan of Sealand, 1918.

Sopwith Camels served with N°s 90, 95 and 96 Squadrons at Shotwick in 1917.

Camels and Pups was the next to go. The unit moved to RAF Brockworth on 18 July 1918 where it was disbanded shortly afterwards.

Initially, the base was intended to be used for training so, with the impending departure of these three squadrons, the airfield became a training base with the arrival on 1 April 1918 of N° 55 Squadron from RAF Lilbourne and N° 67 TS from RAF Shawbury, equipped with Camels, SE5s and Avro 504s. Together these two units formed N° 51 Training Depôt Station. By this time there was some standardization in the training of pilots and observers and N° 51 TDS became a three-unit, day-fighter training establishment with a compliment of 36 Avro 504s and 36 Dolphins, the RAF's standard trainers. However, due to the shortage of aircraft, a third flight was never formed.

After the Armistice there was a drastic reduction in all sections of the RAF and

A line up of Avro 504s of N° 67 Training Squadron.

a large number of aircraft were disposed of. The need for pilots and crews no longer existed and therefore training was given a low priority. Several squadrons were disbanded at Shotwick, including N°s 27, 98, 103 and 55. The latter, equipped with DH9s, was the last to be disbanded when the axe fell on 22 January 1920.

By the summer of 1918 construction work at the airfields was more or less complete and on 2 August the site at Shotwick was designated North Shotwick, whilst the Queensferry site was known as South Shotwick.

On 1 April 1920, N° 51 TDS was absorbed with other air training units to become N° 5 FTS equipped only with the Avro 504, which had become the service's main basic trainer. This was a time of peace and therefore training took place at a leisurely pace. It was also a time when redevelopment occurred at the airfield. More permanent buildings, including new hangars, brick built mess halls and classrooms were constructed for the trainee pilots.

The name RAF Shotwick had caused a number of problems for suppliers, the postal service and even the Air Ministry, as the name sounded, and looked, very similar to the Lincolnshire airfield of RAF Scopwick, so it was decided to rename the airfield RAF Sealand.

Throughout the 1920s the main activity of the airfield was the training of pilots for the RAF. An airman based at Sealand made a name for himself on 17 June 1926 when he made the first parachute escape from an aircraft. P/O Eric Pentland, while on a training flight over the Wirral in his Avro 504, went out of control while practising spins. There was no alternative other than to use the

RAF Shotwick, an aerial photograph taken from a south-easterly direction, 1920s.

Aerial view of the two camps in 1920. [Air Heritage]

escape chute, which actually worked and he was able to tell the tale. Up until then there were no records of any pilot using a parachute to safely escape from an aeroplane. All previous parachute escapes had been from observation balloons.

On 23 May 1929 the RAF Packing Depôt moved from Ascot to Sealand. The unit was responsible for the crating of aircraft that were to be sent overseas, a speciality that Sealand became renowned for both before and during the Second World War.

Distinguished visitors also passed through RAF Sealand — on 24 June 1931, the American aviators, Harold Gatty and Wiley Post made a refuelling stop in their Lockheed Vega while attempting a round the world flight and on 24 November 1936 the famous aviator Charles Lindbergh made a forced landing at Sealand.

In the early 1930s all basic and primary training was completed in an Avro Tutor aircraft before the pilot moved on to the Hawker Hart or Hawker Audax for advanced training. All three type were on N° 5 FTS's inventory which totalled sixty-five training aircraft, as well as a few ageing Avro 504s.

The next unit to be formed at Sealand was N° 3 Aircraft Storage Unit which was established on the South Camp on 2 December 1935, where a new area was laid out and several new buildings were constructed just east of the A550 road.

Unlike most airfields built in the 1930s which had a distinguished standard pattern, Sealand was completely different. It had several Air Ministry pattern buildings but also had buildings that were unique, such as the three-storey accommodation block. Even the station layout was different — on the South Camp there were nine Belfast type hangars, two large 'C' types and two 'L' types. A 'C' type was also built on the North Camp. All the hangars are still to be seen today. During the Second World War up to 18 blister type hangars, of various sizes were built, mostly on the North Camp. However, by today, all the blister hangars have been demolished.

With the declaration of war in 1939, there was an acute shortage of trained pilots. To cope with this shortfall, courses were reduced to sixteen weeks with only 100 flying hours per pupil. At one point, the shortage of trained pilots became so acute that great concerns was expressed throughout the RAF and the government. As a consequence, a whole new concept was implemented with the introduction of the OTUs in July 1940 which provided specialized training for pupil pilots before they were posted to their operational units. Over the years this training procedure was improved and modified, and by the end of the war the RAF training scheme was possibly the best in the world.

The Airspeed Oxford trainers had been replaced during the 1940s by single-engined Miles Master Is & IIs, some of which were fitted with six machine-guns as a stop-gap fighter until Spitfires became available. These armed Masters were kept at readiness for the air defence of the north-west although there is no doubt that the Masters would have been no match for the Me109s of the *Luftwaffe*.

On 14 August 1940, RAF Sealand suffered its first bombing raid, when a He111 dropped its bomb load on the barrack block killing and injuring a number of airmen. The Masters could not be scrambled, but a Spitfire Battle Flight from RAF

Sealand Empire Day, 1938, Hawker Harts lined up on display. [RAF Sealand Museum]

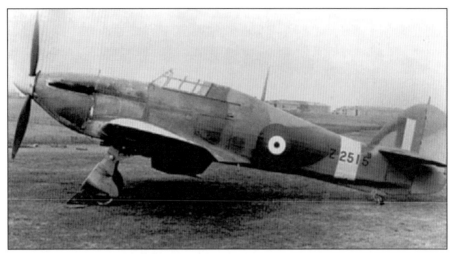

Hawker Hurricane at Sealand, early 1940.

Hawarden arrived on the scene and shot down the enemy aircraft.

As the United States had not entered the war, a number of volunteer civilian pilots came to Britain to fly with the RAF. Many passed through Sealand where a flight was formed, that eventually became the nucleus of the RAF's famous Eagle Squadrons.

As with most airfields in wartime, space became a problem. N° 30 MU, which had been formed at Sealand on 28 July 1939, urgently required additional hangar space. To ease the situation N° 5 FTS moved to RAF Tern Hill. In the early 1940s a new East Camp was built, with additional barrack blocks and officers and NCOs' messes. Storage sheds and various workshops were added later.

N° 30 MU was responsible for fitting electronic equipment into various types of aircraft, initially AI radar into Beaufighters. This was followed by the conversion of seventy Douglas Havoc light bombers into Turbinlite aircraft for night fighting i.e. the installation of a floodlight onto a Havoc, which would be used to illuminate an enemy aircraft for an accompanying Hurricane fighter to attack. Like so many interesting ideas that came about during the war it was dropped in favour of the AI radar. All Turbinlite squadrons were therefore disbanded in January 1943 and the Havoc were converted for training and target towing duties.

Another experiment that was carried out at Sealand in 1942 was a Hurricane fitted with an extra wing over the fuselage, resembling a biplane. This provided an additional fuel tank for the aircraft, giving it twice the range and endurance of a standard Hurricane. When the tank was empty it was jettisoned. This idea was also abandoned.

N° 34 MU was re-numbered to N° 47 MU and during February 1941 the unit

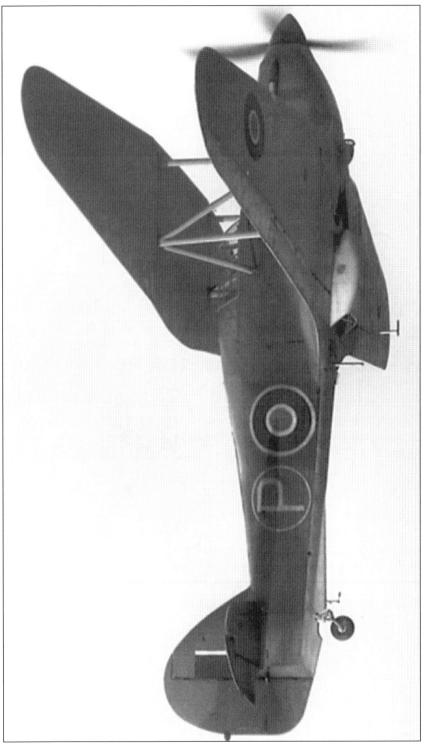

Hawker Hurricane prototype with a slip wing, based at Sealand, 1942.

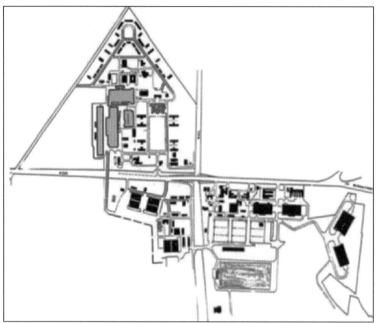

Sealand ground plan, 1970s.

crated a record number of aircraft (715), including a staggering total of 329 Fairey Battles destined for Canada.

With the reorganisation of RAF training, flying training at Sealand resumed on 21 June 1941 with N° 19 EFTS. By the time the unit was disbanded on 31 December 1941 it had trained 740 pupils on Tiger Moths.

Another training unit based at the airfield from March 1941 was N° 6 AACU, equipped with Lysanders, Leopard Moths, Dragons and Dominies. The unit was responsible for training army and navy units in the north-west.

N° 24 EFTS arrived at Sealand from Luton in February 1942 to train Royal Navy pilots. From August 1943 the EFTS concentrated on training only RAF pilots until it left for Rochester on 7 March 1945.

Due to the high number of aircraft movements at Sealand, it was decided to build a single concrete runway to replace the grass strip which was causing continuous problems. This also gave the station additional space for constructing of hangars.

By now N° 30 MU's major workload was the modification and repair of Mosquitoes, Wellingtons and the four-engined Lancaster bombers. N° 47 MU still had its parking space problems even after acquiring an additional hangar.

When N° 6 AACU was disbanded in 1943 the nucleus of Polish airmen were posted to Castle Bromwich to form N° 577 Squadron. A detachment of six Oxfords and three Hurricanes remained at Sealand until November 1944 when the flight moved to Woodvale to relieve the congestion at the airfield. When the EFTS left in March 1945, all flying training ceased at Sealand. The only flying at the airfield after this date was by aircraft being delivered to Nº 47 MU, or aircraft involved in Nº 30 MU trials and within a short period all the activity at the station was the preparing and packing of aircraft.

In the early 1950s the US Air Force took over Sealand as a supply and support unit for their base at RAF Burtonwood, which was being redeveloped. The RAF MU moved out to other stations as their work had diminished, whilst the USAF used the hangars for the storage of equipment, vehicles and spare aircraft. The base was handed over to the US 3rd Air Force on 15 March 1951 which coincided with the arrival of the 30th Air Depôt which was initially transferred from Kelly Air Force Base in the USA to RAF Burtonwood but, within a week, was moved to Sealand until work at Burtonwood was completed. In January 1952 the unit left for RAF Brize Norton and was replaced by creating a new supply unit the 7558th Air Depôt Group, which comprised of a re-training supply flight, the 59th Medical Material Squadron, the 7557 Supply Squadron, the 3rd Motor Transport Squadron and the 7552nd Supply Squadron. In the meantime additional hangars and storage sheds were built at Burtonwood and other American bases in the UK.

In August 1957 Sealand returned to RAF control and for the next few years there was an extensive refitting and modernisation programme carried out at the airfield as modern electronic equipment and radar required special storage facilities.

Nº 30 MU was reformed at the airfield on 1 February 1959 since when, RAF Sealand has become the main military avionics base in the country, specialising in the servicing of all aircraft avionic equipment in use by the RAF. In the early 1980s a new £5.1 million avionic workshop, with a floor space of 80,000 square feet, was built for use by the three services. It included a new storage and testing facilities for Tornado instruments as well as the instruments of any aircraft entering service in the future. At the time of writing it was being extended for the European Typhoon fighter avionics. The facilities were shared by all three services and DERA, under the control of the RAF, but as from 2002 DERA is going to take full control of the MU. In April 2004 it was announced that RAF Sealand (service side) would close at the end of the year or early in 2005. The RAF element would move to RAF Scampton after 90 years at Sealand. DERA would remain at the base for the foreseeable future.

Today, the only flying taking place at Sealand is by Nº 631 Volunteer Gliding School with its Viking gliders, although various military helicopters are regular visitors. The station is now quite different from its 1918 plan. Shotwick (North Shotwick) is a trading estate, whilst South Shotwick (Queensferry) camp is still part of the RAF Sealand complex. The main camp, known as east camp built in the 1940s, with its new storage facilities, is situated across the A550 road. On the trading estate there are still interesting remnants of the old camp, including several 1918 hangars, some 'C' type, a 1940s guard room and other wartime architectural gems. The airfield's only concrete runway is now part of a public road.

RAF Puma helicopter over-flying Sealand South Camp, 1980s. [RAF Sealand]

34. Stormy Down
Vale of Glamorgan

RAF Stormy Down was situated about two miles north-east of the seaside town of Porthcawl in south Glamorgan. The site was initially surveyed in early 1934 as a possible site for a future military aerodrome. As the threat of conflict in Europe became more real, land was required for a RAF training camp in the Porthcawl area and plans for the airfield were drawn up in 1937. Work began in March 1938 and the station was more or less completed early the following year and was officially opened on 1 June by the commanding officer W/Cdr J. C. P. Wood. The airfield was originally designated as the base for N° 9 Armament Training Station, but was reclassified as an Air Observer School on 1 September, two days before the outbreak of war. As with many Welsh airfields there was confusion and miss-pronunciation of place names and the original name, RAF Newton Downs, was renamed RAF Porthcawl in February 1940 to avoid confusion with RAF Newton

in England. It was officially renamed again in November 1940, becoming RAF Stormy Down as, according to an airman who served there, getting the right supplies was a nightmare as often urgent spares would end up travelling around the UK before eventually arriving at Stormy Down. One such order, spare windscreens for Avro Ansons, requested mid-1942, had still not been delivered when the airfield closed.

Initially, the station

Ground plan of Stormy Down, 1943.

Aerial view of Stormy Down, 1946. [National Assembly for Wales]

Westland Wallace of Nº 9 ATS at Stormy Down. Note the attempts to obliterate the squadron identification letters on the fuselage.

Hawker Henley of N° 631 Squadron at Stormy Down.

consisted of an assortment of wooden buildings for accommodation, administration, sick quarters and workshops. A VR type hangar and some concrete buildings were added in 1939/40. It consisted of a grass strip, which due to poor drainage, regularly became waterlogged. A concrete runway was requested in 1942, but due to the extra cost involved, and the nearness of other airfields at St Athan and Rhoose, it was turned down. Matters were made worse by the airfield's unique convex surface. The flooding and subsequent subsidence caused hidden cavities in the broken rock underneath the topsoil, resulting in the surface caving in under the weight of aircraft passing over it resulting in several aircraft sustaining severely damaged undercarriages. However, in 1944, the ground was levelled and properly drained, and pierced steel planking laid, which improved the situation. Some aircraft hard standing areas were included (previously the only hard standing at the airfield had been in front of the hangar).

The first unit to be based at Stormy Down was N° 7 Bombing and Gunnery School in November 1939, equipped with Armstrong Whitworth Whitleys and

Stormy Down VR hangar, photographed in the 1980s.

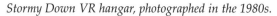

Miles Martinet II of Nº 7 AGS based at Stormy Down.

Fairey Battles. The unit changed its name to Nº 7 Gunnery School in early 1940 and, by early 1942, had been re-equipped with Avro Ansons; obtaining spares for the Whitleys and Battles was becoming a problem and the Anson was fitted with an upper gun turret, which made it an ideal training platform for air gunners. One of the first Officers Commanding Flying was the Welsh First World War ace, W/Cdr Ira 'Taffy' Jones, who, on one occasion, chased a Ju88 over Swansea in an unarmed Hawker Henley. While on a training flight, Jones spotted the Ju88 and, without any hesitation, dived out of the sun on the enemy aircraft, firing a Very pistol at it. This no doubt frightened the enemy pilot who headed for cloud cover over Mumbles Head. Jones continued with the pursuit but, when the enemy gunner fired back at him, decided it was better to head for home. He landed at Stormy Down with a bullet hole in the Henley's wing.

Whenever possible, the RAF provided aircraft for air displays, especially in aid of the Wings for Victory Weeks. On 3 April 1943 five Lysanders from Stormy Down provided a display for the people of Mountain Ash followed, on 15 May, by a display over the Rhondda by four Martinets. One of the Whitleys that had been parked on the side of the airfield since 1942 was given to the Air Training Corps at RAF Fairwood for use in training.

On 30 May 1943, a U-boat was sighted six miles west of the Scarweather lightship in the Bristol Channel. An Anson from Stormy Down was sent to the scene to investigate but, after hours of searching, found nothing and returned to base. On other occasions an Anson was often requested to chase and shoot down broken away barrage balloons, providing the gunners with very unusual targets.

During the latter part of 1943, two Piper Cubs, belonging to a US Army brigade based at Porthcawl, were temporarily accommodated at the airfield. Also, in November 1943, a special ciné-gun flight was formed at the airfield equipped with Martinets. The idea of the unit was to teach the students curve-of-pursuit attacks using an Anson as the target. It is not known if the technique was useful or not.

Landings and take offs had been a problem at Stormy Down due to the convex nature of the ground. In December 1943 a new flying control standardisation was introduced to try and solve the problem. This required a runway caravan equipped with a radio transmitter which could communicate with the aircraft. However, it was also necessary to position a look out in the watchtower, also equipped with a radio transmitter, to report of any unseen traffic to the caravan.

By October 1943, the Vickers Wellington was being replaced in front line service by the new four-engined bombers and, two aircraft were delivered to Stormy Down to assist with the air gunnery course, for a five-week trial session. However, due to the state of the landing strip, the two aircraft were redirected to RAF Llandow, where they remained for the entire five-week period.

On 8 February 1944, RAF Rhoose became N° 7 AGS's satellite airfield and, within days of opening, the unit's 33 Ansons, 20 Martinets and nearly 50 pilots took residence there. With the absence of any aircraft, major repair work on the airfield took place, including the lying of a PSP strip. While the work was being carried out a USAAF Cessna Crane overshot the field and crashed into a mound of earth. On another occasion, a Beaufighter crash-landed after under-shooting on approach in a gusty wind conditions. By 2 August the repair work was completed and N° 7 AGS returned from Rhoose only to be disbanded on 21 August. Since its formation, the AGS had trained at least 140 air gunners for the RAF, mostly for Bomber Command.

The next unit, N° 40 Initial Training Wing, arrived at the base from RAF Newton on 1 September. This was set up to train French airmen but, within a month, was stood down and, for the next few months, the airfield remained dormant and was officially closed in July 1945. It remained under Air Ministry control until 1946, when it was handed over for public use. However, due to its subsidence problems, it never was used for private flying and the land was used for light industry and storage.

Most of the wartime buildings still exist and for a number of years have been used as a Rehabilitation Centre by the local employment office. The 'VR' hangar remains and is used for storage, but at the time of writing is in need of extensive repairs and a coat of paint.

35. Talbenny

Pembrokeshire

If one proceeds on the B4327, the Haverfordwest to Dale road, for approximately eight miles, to one's right is the minor road that leads to the small village of Talbenny with its wartime airfield situated on an escarpment overlooking St Brides Bay, about three miles from Dale airfield. Today there are only a few Maycrete and Nissen huts scattered around the remains of this once busy airfield and most of these are crumbling away fast, with the exception of those being utilised by local farmers. The runways are more or less intact, but they too are overgrown and slowly breaking up.

It is hard to imagine when standing in the middle of the airfield that during the war it had three reasonable length runways capable of operating the heaviest of RAF aircraft. The runways had a central intersection; two had sea approaches from the direction of Ticklas Point and Borough Head, while the third had an

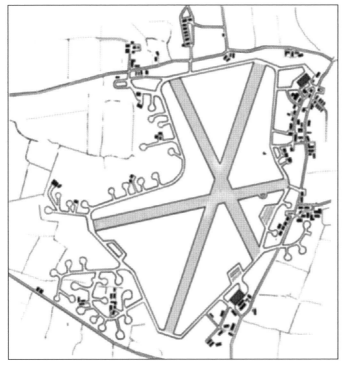

Layout of Talbenny airfield, 1945.

overland approach, from the direction of the village of St Brides. The landward approaches of the runways were from the direction of Dale, Herbrandston and Walton West. The airfield had a staggering thirty-six 'Frying Pan' hard standings, sufficient for the parking of two squadrons. During the latter part of the war, the airfield was taken over by RAF Transport Command necessitating the building of a new concrete apron to accommodate at least twenty-two aircraft. Initially four 'T2' hangars were planned for the airfield but only two were actually constructed and used for maintenance. A number of blister hangars were added later.

RAF Talbenny officially came into existence on 1 May 1942 under N° 19 Group Coastal Command, with RAF Dale to the south as its satellite station. Ironically, Dale remained operational well after Talbenny closed. For the first few weeks Talbenny was used for touch and go training flights by various squadrons and the first full squadron to be based here was N° 311 Squadron, a Czech bomber squadron, which arrived on 12 June 1942 from Aldergrove in Northern Ireland. The squadron remained at Talbenny until May 1943, when it was posted to Beaulieu and returned to the control of Bomber Command. Its sister squadron, N° 304 (Polish), was intended to go to Dale but, as that airfield was not fully operational, the squadron joined N° 311 at Talbenny in November 1942, but only remained for a month, both squadrons having transferred from Bomber Command for anti-ship and anti-submarine sweeps in the Bay of Biscay and the Western Approaches. They were equipped with Vickers Wellington Ic bombers,

Aerial view of Talbenny, 1944.

Mechanics working on a Wellington of Nº 311 Squadron.

which was the only aircraft available in sufficient numbers at the time.

On one patrol on 6 August, an aircraft from Nº 311 Squadron, Wellington 'P' for Papa, after hours of patient patrol work, sighted a U-boat, which it attacked with .303 machine-gun fire from the front turret and depth charge bombs, but its destruction was unconfirmed. Another notable operation took place on 25 August when all available aircraft of Nº 311 Squadron and Nº 304 Squadron (from Dale) made a high level bombing attack on German tankers and harbour installation in La Pallice. All aircraft returned safely to their bases. In November 1942 the squadrons were involved with anti-shipping strikes off the Gironde Estuary which were a success, as several enemy ships were damaged and had to return to port for protection.

Nº 311 Squadron did have its casualties — in early September, 'A' for Alpha was attacked by two enemy Arado 196 floatplanes. The Wellington was badly shot up but because of its unique construction managed to limp back to Talbenny with a badly wounded rear gunner.

In late August 1942, Nº 311 Squadron celebrated its second anniversary as a RAF squadron and, to commemorate the event, was inspected by members of the exiled Czech government including the Minister of National Defence, Mr Masaryk, the Foreign Minister and the Czech Deputy Prime Minister who had flown to the airfield in an Anson the previous day.

Due to the constant threat of attacks by enemy aircraft on the squadron's aircraft, in Janaury/February 1943 Coastal Command posted detachments from Nᵒˢ 235 and 248 Squadrons, equipped with Bristol Beaufighters. They were to fly escort duties for the Wellington strikes into enemy territory and for the next few months N° 311 Squadron had fighter escorts on all their operations which deterred any enemy aerial action. The Beaufighter was a formidable fighter bomber as it was armed with four forward firing 20mm cannons in the nose plus six .303 machine-guns in the wings, as well as one .303 machine-gun in the rear canopy. In the past, enemy fighters had the misfortune to mistake the aircraft for a defenceless bomber.

The shipping strikes came to an end and, in May 1943, N° 311 Squadron was returned to Bomber Command, the aircraft being required for raids on Germany.

In March 1943, N° 303 Ferry Training Unit moved to the west Wales airfield from Stornaway in Scotland, equipped initially with Vickers Wellingtons, but as the months progressed, they were joined by the larger Warwick bombers and some Lockheed Venturas. The unit's task was to prepare aircraft for overseas ferrying and briefing the crews for these flights. The preparation courses became shorter and shorter as the months went by and there was a fast turnover of both aircraft and crews. The unit despatched a total of 101 Wellingtons and their crews in one month.

The Ferry Training Unit was joined by N° 3 OADU (Overseas Aircraft Dispatch Unit) from Hurn airfield, Bournemouth on 26 July 1944. N° 3 OADU was taken over by N° 11 Ferry Unit on 8 September 1944 which was formed to collect aircraft from various Preparation Units and despatch them abroad. The unit was also involved with crew familiarisation on the various types of aircraft, including Spitfires, Ansons, Wellingtons and Warwicks. The unit left Talbenny in August 1945 for RAF Dunkwell.

Bristol Beaufighter of No 235 Squadron over the Pembrokeshire coast. [RAF Museum]

Mess hall at Talbenny, 1970s.

On Sunday 3 January 1943, eight Liberator bombers, belonging to the 44th Bomber Group, 8th USAAF, was returning from a daylight-bombing raid on the U-boat pens at St Nazaire. Running short of fuel as a result of several encounters with German fighters, the crews found themselves well off course for their home bases in East Anglia and headed for the Pembrokeshire coast and Talbenny airfield, which was used as an emergency and diversion airfield. Of the eight aircraft, only five made a safe landing. One crew misjudged the length of the runway, overshot and came to rest on the airfield's perimeter. Two others crashed having run out of fuel, one coming down near Haverfordwest, some three miles from the site of Withybush airfield, and the other on farmland south of the village of Puncheston. Tragically five airmen died in the three accidents.

In June 1943 the RAF wanted to exchange Talbenny for the RNAS base at St Merryns, which would be used for maintenance of RAF Liberators at nearby St Eval. The Admiralty declined the request, and the RAF was obliged to find another role for the airfield. On 11 October 1943 the airfield was handed over to RAF Transport Command which operated the airfield until it was closed in December 1946. The first unit to move in was Nᵒ16 Flight, equipped with a variety of aircraft —three Halifax IIs (transport), two Douglas C-47 Dakotas, three Vickers Warwicks, three Airspeed Oxfords and three Avro Ansons. This Flight was responsible for flying VIPs and its aircraft were seen at most airfields, while the heavier types were involved with flying cargo and personnel throughout Britain and mainland Europe (particularly after D-Day). The unit remained at Talbenny until 6 August 1945.

Even before Transport Command took control of the airfield, Talbenny, because of its location, had a secondary roll as a weather diversionary airfield, especially for flights from the United States. Notable visiting aircraft during 1943 were a civilian BOAC Liberator (G-AGFO) on 15 January 1943, a Boeing B-17 belonging to a US Weather Squadron based at RAF Watton on 16 January, USAAF Liberator in the same month, a Dakota from Marakesh on 12 December 1943, as well as a number of smaller types.

One unit that was resident at Talbenny from the beginning was N° 4 Armament Practice Camp, which was responsible for training in anti-submarine bombing, air–air gunnery and air–surface firing. The unit was part of the N° 19 Group, RAF Coastal Command.

After August 1945, the airfield was put on care and maintenance under the command of RAF Pembroke Dock. A skeleton staff remained at the base until the following year as it was still used for exercises and designated as an emergency airfield for trans-Atlantic flights, although it was never used. RAF Talbenny was finally closed on 23 December 1946 and all equipment was removed, leaving the empty skeletons of buildings. One unique feature still survives today, two brick ovens, situated just off the perimeter track, which were part of an emergency kitchen.

There is a Roll of Honour in Talbenny church for all those who lost their lives flying from the airfield.

36. Templeton
Pembrokeshire

Templeton airfield lies close to Templeton village, which is situated on the A478 Narberth to Tenby road. The airfield itself is wedged in between the A4115 and the B4315 roads. From Haverfordwest, one takes the A40 to Canaston Bridge, then the A4075 to Cross Hands then on to the A4115 road to the village of Templeton. Access to the airfield is on this road, about a mile from the village. The first question one asks on arrival is why was an airfield built on such terrain?

Although in its heyday various types of aircraft used its runways, being a satellite it never had the recognition afforded to so many other Pembrokeshire airfields. The site chosen was perhaps the most unsuitable in the county and was built with a hill in the middle of the triangular runway layout, resulting in an obscured all-round view. This caused concern and danger to aircraft taxiing and using the runways. One solution that was often used was a lookout posted, usually on the hill, using signal flags to warn of aircraft movements. Remarkably, accidents were few and far between.

Ground plan of Templeton, 1945.

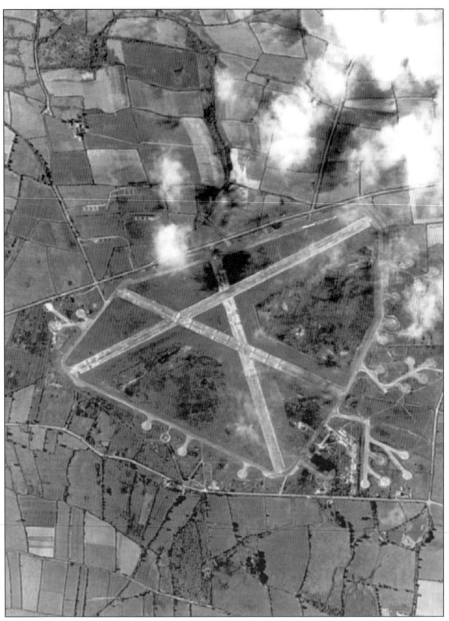

Aerial photograph of Templeton taken by N° 540 Squadron, July 1946.
[National Assembly for Wales]

Templeton airfield was constructed in late 1942 and early 1943, but was a low priority. It was offered to the various RAF Commands, but none were interested. At one stage, construction was abandoned however, at the last moment , it was decided that Templeton would become a satellite of RAF Withybush and, on 28

Bristol Beaufort of Nº 306 Ferry Training Unit, Templeton.

December 1942, the first aircraft, an Avro Anson with engine failure, was the first to land here.

The first unit to occupy the airfield was the administration section of N° 306 Ferry Training Unit which arrived, minus its aircraft, on 3 January 1943. The purpose of the unit was the training and preparation of crew for long-distance ferry flights. It was not until 24 February that the first aircraft arrived, an early mark of the Bristol Beaufort. Later models were received directly from the manufacturers' assembly lines in March and April. Surprisingly, two crews were fully trained within a month, and on 13 April flew two aircraft to Portreath and, eventually, to Egypt. The Bristol Beaufort was a torpedo bomber version of the famous Blenheim bomber and was mainly used by RAF Coastal Command for shipping strikes in every theatre of operations, but especially the Mediterranean, causing a great many problems for the Axis forces. The Beaufort was powered by two 1,130 hp Bristol Taurus engines, giving the aircraft a maximum speed of 260 mph and a range of 1,600 miles. Its endurance of 6 hours made it ideal for the training of ferry pilots. In March 1942, Coastal Command chose the faster and more potent Bristol Beaufighter to replace the Beaufort operationally. However, the latter remained in service in a training role until the end of the war. The unit only stayed at Templeton for a few months before moving to Northern Ireland in June.

The next occupant of the airfield was 'O' Flight of N° 3 OTU from Haverfordwest, equipped with 14 Avro Ansons; Haverforwest had for some time suffered acute problems with inadequate parking space for its Whitley and Wellington bombers. N° 3 OTU was a training unit within N° 19 Group Coastal Command, whose responsibility was the training of aircrews for the Command's heavier type of aircraft such as the maritime versions of the Whitley, Wellington and Warwick bombers. The unit remained at Templeton until December 1943 when they left for St Athan where it was renamed N° 12 Radio School. N° 3 OTU was a training unit within N° 19 Group Coastal Command, training aircrew for the command's heavier type of aircraft such as the maritime versions of the Whitley, Wellington, Warwick and Halifax bombers. Most of the training was conducted over water so that crews could familiarise themselves with navigating, bomb aiming, observing and flying over the sea.

After the departure of 'O' Flight, the airfield was left relatively idle for some months, manned only by a skeleton staff from Haverfordwest, it only aerial visitors being training flights from Carew and Haverfordwest, using the runways for touch and go exercises.

On several occasions aircraft were diverted to Templeton due to bad weather. One such diversion occurred on 17 January 1943 when a USAAF B-17 Flying Fortress, which had lost its bearings, made an emergency landing. After refuelling, the crew were allowed a rest and took off the following morning for their East Anglian destination. Fortunately, the emergency service was fully manned at this time.

With the introduction of towed, winged glider targets at the School of Anti-Aircraft at nearby Manorbier, it was felt that Templeton, with its concrete runways, was more suitable for aircraft towing targets than the grass strip at the school. The glider targets had a wingspan of either eight or sixteen feet and were more suitable for towing on a firm surface. They had a tendency of flipping over on a grass strip, particularly a waterlogged grass strip, and often flipped the towing aircraft as well. The gliders were experimented with at RAF Aberporth, using Tiger Moths and Henley towing aircraft but, from January 1944, the RAF re-equipped N° 595 Squadron, initially with Hawker Henleys, then later in the year, with the more capable Miles Martinet TT1 which had been used for some years in the training role but, by 1944, was mostly used as a target-tug. However, after a series of accidents, particularly during take off and landings with towed targets, the Martinet was replaced by early marks of Spitfire. These were found to be more suitable for the task, and were faster and more manoeuvrable, and therefore better able keep up with most aircraft. N° 595 Squadron received its first Spitfire in July 1944, so the sound of Merlin engines were heard across the Pembrokeshire countryside.

The first official towed glider trials by the squadron at Templeton took place on 17 August 1944. Initially the trials were not very successful and several gliders crashed on landing, resulting in a number of modifications to both gliders and the towing aircraft. The School of Anti Aircraft had twice successfully used gliders towed by N° 595's modified Martinets, resulting in several hits on the target, with both aircraft and target returning safely to Templeton. However, the second target made a successful landing but swung off the runway and was slightly damaged. Further trials continued until the squadron returned to Aberporth on 24 February 1945.

A small engineering section which remained at Templeton airfield from February to June 1945, utilising the 'T-2' hangar, was responsible for the repair and maintenance of N° 8 OTU's Spitfires and Mosquitoes based at Haverfordwest. When the OTU moved to RAF Benson in June 1945, all activities at Templeton were wound up and the airfield was officially closed in July/August 1945 and put on care and maintenance until December when it was declared to be surplus to requirements and put on the disposal list. However, for a brief period, the airfield, under the control of Haverfordwest, was used for the storage of aircraft awaiting disposal.

During the 1950s, the airfield was occasionally used in an emergency. On 3

July 1951, a Fleet Air Arm Tiger Moth, while on a training flight, had to make an unscheduled stop at Templeton to get its bearings by telephoning Brawdy to ask for directions. On 10 December 1952 a Hawker Tempest TT5 (NV965) of N° 233 OCU, piloted by F/Sgt Piatkowski made a forced landing at the disused airfield after an engine failure. After getting in touch with his base at RAF Pembrey, technicians came out and repaired the aircraft, which flew back to its base two days later.

Templeton airfield remained the property of the Ministry of Defence until the 1960s when it was eventually sold. Most of the wartime buildings had been demolished in the 1950s and, today, there is little evidence remaining of Templeton's wartime service. The firing butts, some of the garages and few Nissen huts have survived and are now used by local farmers. Sections of the three runways and perimeter track are still visible but, like the other buildings, are gradually crumbling away. Gone is the airfield's sole T-type hangar, the standard RAF watchtower and the accommodation huts that dotted the aerodrome.

Today, the airfield is being leased back to the Ministry of Defence for army training.

37. Towyn
Gwynedd

RAF Towyn was situated on a peninsula, just off the A493 coast road, overlooking the inlet of Aber Dysyni, about half-a-mile north of the town of Tywyn. For many years the town's name was written as 'Towyn', but, in recent years, it has reverted to the original Welsh spelling of Tywyn.

The airfield was opened on 8 September 1940 as a support base, providing air target facilities for the Royal Artillery Anti-Aircraft Practice Camp at Ton Fanau, on the opposite side of the estuary. During the opening ceremony a Miles Magister trainer aircraft flew down from RAF Penrhos warning of an enemy invasion — one of the many alerts that occurred during 1940. As instructed, all secret and confidential documents were prepared for destruction but, in the nick of time, a counter order was received. RAF Towyn came under the command of N° 70 Group Army Co-operation Command, which had only been formed in August 1940. The airfield's first commanding officer was the newly appointed S/Ldr Irens.

The airfield consisted of a grass landing area, Nissen and Maycrete type buildings, two Bellman hangars, two blister hangars, all with concrete bases and aprons, and two canvas Besonneau hangars, which were the first to be built. Initially, the base was only used for light transport and as an emergency field for aircraft based around Cardigan Bay area, as it was the only airfield on the west Wales coast between Aberporth and Penrhos. The first emergency occurred on 11 November 1940 when a Bristol Beaufort of N° 217 Squadron, on a flight from its base at St Eval to Abbotsinch, landed with engine trouble. On 3 June 1941 the pilot of a Henley trainer was unable to reach the airfield and crashed half-a-mile from Towyn.

On 16 December 1943, twelve P-38 Lightnings of the USAAF 97th Fighter Squadron were forced to make an emergency landing while on a flight from Northern Ireland to join the 12th Air Force in North Africa. At the time, parts of the airfield were flooded which made the landing dangerous. Causing one Lightning to skid across the grass and crash into a gun post on the boundary. The squadron remained at Towyn for two days until the airfield was declared operational. On the morning of 19 December the unit, minus the damaged aircraft, took off for St Eval and eventually onward to their new base in North Africa.

Aerial view of Towyn, 1945.

The most dramatic emergency landing took place on 8 July 1944, when a Boeing B-17 Flying Fortress (942.31321 CC-M) made a forced landing at the tiny airfield. The bomber belonged to 569th USAAF Bomber Squadron based at Framlingham in Suffolk. The aircraft is believed to be one that was on detachment to Russia during June 1944, flying shuttle missions to Italy and North Africa. The mishap occurred during its return flight to the UK when, because of poor weather, poor map reading and fuel running low, it flew up the Welsh coast looking for RAF Llanbedr, but could only make it as far as Towyn. With great skill the pilot landed the aircraft safely but, as the runway was far too short for such a large aeroplane, it continued across the railway line and eventually hit an air raid shelter. A small fire which appeared in the wing root was extinguished by the station fire service with the help of the town fire brigade. All fifteen-crew members had managed to scramble clear before the fire began. For weeks afterwards the crashed bomber became an attraction for local people, before it was eventually removed. Most of the other emergencies that used the airfield were aircraft flying from Aberporth, Llanbedr and Penrhos.

The first unit to be stationed at Towyn airfield was 'U' Flight of N° 1 AACU equipped with Queen Bee target aircraft which arrived during October and November 1940. Also 'C' Flight with its Hawker Henley aircraft from Penrhos arrived to provide target towing facilities. As the result of reorganisation, on 1 October 1943, 'C' Flight became 1605 Flight and was later joined by 1628 Flight which became N° 631 Squadron on 1 December 1943. The squadron was the last RAF unit to use the Hawker Henley, the last of which were replaced by Martinets in February 1945.

*Hawker Henley which was used by N° 1 AACU and
N° 631 Squadron at Towyn. [MAP]*

As with most secondary units, N° 631 did have its share of accidents the majority of which were caused by the condition of the landing strip itself. In October 1944, after a spell of wet weather, the airfield became water-logged and the squadron was transferred to Llanbedr. During this period some aircraft did attempt to land on the strip and became bogged down.

On 15 October 1944 a Hawker Henley (L3296) made a wheels-up landing on the soft ground; the pilot was unhurt but the aircraft had to be written off. There were also several pilot errors and mechanical failures such as the incident on 28 February 1945 when the squadron lost two aircraft piloted by the same person, P/O H. H. Russell. During the morning his Hurricane overshot the landing strip and ended up on the railway line then, in the afternoon, his Henley crashed in the Dysyni estuary. Tragically, P/O Russell was killed in the second crash.

N° 631 Squadron left Towyn on 10 May 1945 and the base was transferred to N° 22 Group, Technical Training Command. Few new personnel moved in but the unit was short lived and the base was closed on 25 July 1945. Of interest is the fact that the airfield supplied rescue and medical back-up to the emergency services dealing with aircraft crashes in the north-west Wales area.

Post war, the airfield was used as an army camp (Morfa Camp) with frequent visits by the Army Air Corp's DHC Beaver aircraft and various helicopters before becoming an outward bound school, using some of the wartime buildings for accommodation and the grass landing strip as a sports field.

Most of the war time buildings, including the hangars, have been demolished and only certain parts of the concrete apron remain.

38. Valley
Gwynedd

RAF Valley is situated on a minor road, off the A5 trunk road, close to the small village of Caergeilog, a mile from the village of Valley. It was planned and built during the early years of the Second World War and, due to its prominent position, it was decided from the beginning that it would be allocated to RAF Fighter Command for the protection of Liverpool, the industrial north-west of England and shipping in the Irish Sea, especially the sea-lane from the Atlantic to

Ground plan of Valley, 1990s.

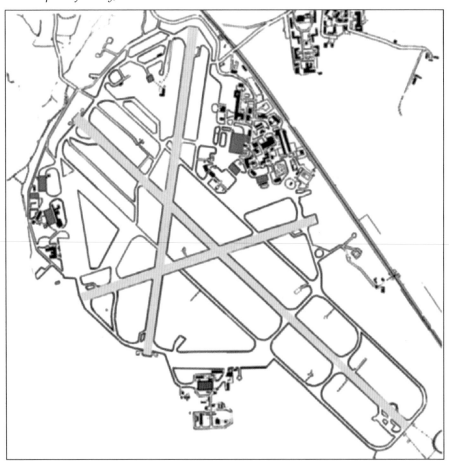

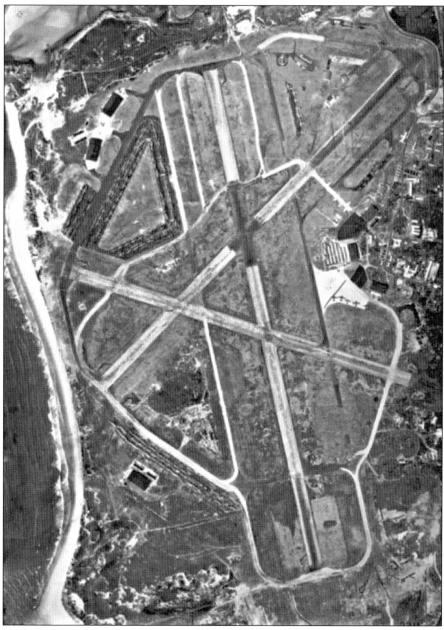

Aerial photograph of Valley, 1945. Large numbers of USAAF aeroplanes (including Liberators, Bostons and Dakotas) are parked around the airfield.

the Mersey estuary. The airfield was built in a lightly populated area of north-west Anglesey, among the wind-swept sand dunes, a bleak location that was not a popular posting with airmen, especially when the south-westerly winds blew in from the direction of Cardigan Bay.

The airfield was opened on 1 February 1941 as a Fighter Sector Station under the control of N° 9 Group whose responsibility was the Merseyside area. Its original name was RAF Rhosneigr but, due to pronunciation problems, was changed to RAF Valley on 5 April 1941. The airfield's first commanding officer was W/Cdr J. C. W. Oliver, DSO, DFC.

The first unit to be based at Valley was a detachment of Hawker Hurricane Is of N° 312 (Czech) Squadron from Speke, Liverpool which arrived on 3 March 1941, remaining only until 25 April when they left for Jurby on the Isle of Man. N° 615 Squadron, also equipped with various marks of Hurricane, arrived from Kenley on 21 April and remained at Valley until 10 September, during which period it was involved in four combats while on convoy patrols.

Typical of sorties undertaken by the squadron was one on 4 May when a Ju88 was damaged off the coast near Holyhead. Then, on 7 May, another Ju88 was attacked over Snowdonia. On 2 June, two Hurricanes attacked and seriously damaged a Ju88 west of Holyhead. The squadron's first confirmed kill occurred on 26 August, when a Ju88 had to make a crash landing in Eire after a skirmish with N° 615's Hurricanes over Cardigan Bay.

To cope with enemy night bombing runs, 'A' Flight of RAF Tangmere's N° 219 Squadron, equipped with Bristol Beaufighter IFs (fitted with AI radar), was posted to Valley on 10 May 1941. When the flight returned to Tangmere they were replaced on 28 June by another Beaufighter unit, N° 68 Squadron from RAF High

Avro Anson of the RAF Valley Communication Flight.

*Two Spitfire IIs of N° 350 (Belgian) Squadron, landing at RAF Valley,
November 1942.*

Ercall. An aircraft from this flight destroyed a Heinkel 111 near Gwlachmai in
November 1941.

It was N° 219 Squadron that, on 1 June, claimed the first night kill when a
Beaufighter shot down an enemy bomber off the coast of Aberystwyth.

On 30 June 1941 N° 456 Squadron (RAAF) was formed at Valley, initially
equipped with the Defiant I, but later re-equipping with Beaufighter IIFs and
VIFs. This night fighter squadron had one of the longest associations with the
airfield, as it remained at Valley until 30 March 1943. The squadron achieved its
first kill on January 11 1942, when all of N° 9 Group airfields, except Valley, were
shut because of bad weather. The Beaufighter chased a Do217 across Wales and
most of the Midlands before shooting it down near Nuneaton.

Another unit that had a long association with Valley was N° 275 Squadron, an
air-sea rescue unit, which was formed at the base. It came into being as a result of
the numerous training accidents in the sea around the island. The unit was
formed on 15 October 1941, equipped with various types of aircraft, Lysander IIIs,
Walrus Is & IIs, Defiant Is & Ics, Anson Is and Spitfire Vbs. The usual rescue
procedure was, once an aircraft was reported missing or down, a Spitfire a
Defiant and an Anson would carry out the search with a Walrus picking up the
crew from the sea and the Lysander on land.

With the airfield only few years old, alterations were put forward to develop
the base as a future trans-Atlantic ferry airfield as the lend-lease agreement was
beginning to take shape, the most noticeable being the lengthening of the main
runway by nearly 1,000 yards.

Throughout 1941/42 several squadrons made brief visits to Valley: N°ˢ 42, 242

Walrus of Nº 275 Air-Sea Rescue Squadron outside its blister hangar at Valley.

and 350 (Belgian) and a detachment of Nº 131 Squadron from RAF Llanbedr. Nº 242 Squadron, equipped with Hawker Hurricane IIBs, left for Palemburg in the Far East in November 1941 and Nº 350 Squadron was formed at Valley on 13 November, equipped with Spitfire IICs. This squadron consisted mostly of Belgian airmen who had escaped from occupied Belgium the previous year and had formed two flights of Nº 131 Squadron. The two flights were based at Valley mounting convoy patrols between 10 March to 14 May 1942. On one such patrol F/Lt Ray H. Harries and Sergeant Vilboux made contact with a Ju88 about thirty miles south-west of Holyhead. They attacked, setting one of the enemy aircraft's engines on fire, and the aircraft was seen crashing into the sea.

As the squadron was parked close to the sand dunes and the sea, they had great difficulty in keeping the aircraft serviceable as the fine sand blowing across that part of the

W/Cmdr Raymond Hiley Harries, DSO and Bar, DFC and Bar, Croix de Guerre (France), Croix de Guerre (Belgium), With over 20 confirmed victories he was the top Welsh fighter pilot of the Second World War. He was killed in a flying accident in May 1950.
[W Alister Williams via Chaz Bowyer]

airfield went into the Spitfire engines and cannons. As a result, the unit returned to Llanbedr on 14 May 1942, leaving N° 456 Squadron as the sole fighter unit at Valley, having to mount both day and night patrols. Their Beaufighters were best suited for the various roles the squadron was required to perform, particularly convoy patrols, as it had exceptionally long range and it was a match for any German bombers with its four 20 mm cannons and up to six .303 machine-guns. On 18 May, a Beaufighter escorting a convoy off Carnsore Point spotted a Ju88 which it then attacked and the German aircraft disappeared into the clouds with smoke billowing from its engines. Two days later the Ju88 crew was picked up from the sea by a fishing boat and what had been a 'probable' was claimed as a confirmed kill.

An aircraft from N° 456 was again in action on 30 July, when W/Cdr Wolfe shot down a He111 over Pwllheli. In early March 1943 the squadron was re-equipped with De Havilland Mosquito IIs, but did not take part in any further action and left for RAF Middle Wallop on 30 March.

A detachment of N° 315 Squadron (Polish) Spitfires was based at Valley for a short period on May 1942. During one of its patrols contact was made with a Ju88 just off the coast near Dublin. After a short skirmish, the Spitfire was damaged and had to make a forced landing just outside the Irish capital. Unfortunately, the pilot died from his injuries but it was later confirmed that the Ju88 had crash landed near Wexford.

Impressed with Valley's record in night fighting, on 1 May 1943 the USAAF sent the 414th Night Fighter Squadron, also equipped with Beaufighter VIFs, to work with, and hopefully gain benefit from, N° 406 Squadron which was the resident night fighter unit at Valley at the time.

In 1942 Valley was selected to be the British terminal for USAAF heavy

Gaydon hangar at Valley.

bombers that were due to come over to join in the European conflict. As the airfield was to remain under the control of Nº 9 Group (it still played an important role in the protection of the north-west of England), it was decided that Ferry Command would only be a lodger unit. To cope with a large influx of personnel and large quantities of aircraft, the runways were extended, new taxiways were constructed as well as fifty hard-standing parking areas. An American radio range for homing and instrument landing was installed in March. In May 1943, an USAAF Support Unit arrived, with responsiblity for the handling of American personnel and the large influx of aircraft that was due to arrive.

The first aircraft to benefit from the new set up at Valley were six Lancaster bombers returning from a raid over France. They were diverted to Anglesey because most of the airfields in the UK were blanked over with fog.

There were a further developments at the airfield, in particular a further extension of the runways, to comply with the USAAF safety policy of having longer runways.

On 19 June 1943 the USAAF Ferry Terminal became operational and from then on American aircraft began to filter through. The first to arrive through Valley were B-17s from Iceland on 28 July, followed on 11 August by eleven B-24 Liberators. Over the next few weeks there was a steady trickle of both heavy and medium bombers, with the occasional transport passing through Valley.

The RAF Fighter Sector closed on 1 November 1943 and all operations moved to RAF Woodvale, leaving Nº 275 Squadron (ASR) and Nº 125 Squadron (from November 1943, equipped with Beaufighter VIFs) for air defence and the protection of incoming American aircraft. These resident RAF squadrons were also used to act as 'shepherds' to incoming American aircraft that were lost or in trouble.

Nº 125 Squadron's first call came on 18 November, when two Beaufighters were scrambled to go to the assistance of a crippled Liberator which had been attacked by a Ju88 over the Bay of Biscay. Unfortunately the enemy aircraft had disappeared by the time the Beaufighters arrived, but the Liberator was escorted to Valley and landed safely.

On 19 December, a total of thirty-eight aircraft managed to reach the safety of RAF Valley, some escorted by the Beaufighters. There was an Aircobra, four Lightings, six Thunderbolts, a C-54 from Iceland, a Hudson from Wick, as well as a number of inbound USAAF bombers. The same month, aircraft from Valley had to search for a flight of incoming USAAF B-17s which were lost and flying in circles around Cardigan Bay. Eventually the flight were found and escorted to the airfield. On 18 February 1944, sixty-two Douglas C-47s flew into Valley from North Africa.

While at Valley Nº 125 Squadron was re-equipped with the more agile multi-role aircraft, the Merlin powered DH Mosquito XVI in early 1944, but then left for Hurn, Bournemouth, on 24 March.

By the end of May there was a daily transatlantic C-54 Skymaster service via Stephenville. On one such flight on 9 June, the Chiefs of Staff of the US Army, Navy and Air Force flew in for a meeting with General Eisenhower and the British Chiefs of Staff. The onward journey to London was by train from Holyhead as the top brass had had enough of flying for awhile.

From June 1944, Valley was more or less only involved with recovering incoming flights from the States and became designated USAAF Station 508. The USAAF Movement Section, under the ATC, handled all American aircraft, whilst the RAF handled all other diverted British aircraft and the general running of the station.

The busiest day in Valley occurred on 17 September 1944 when 99 Boeing B-17 Flying Fortresses and Consolidated B-24 Liberators flew in from Iceland. Similar aircraft movements continued right up to the end of the war in 1945.

When the war in Europe ended, Valley became a transit airfield for aircraft returning to the States. Over 2,600 USAAF bombers of all descriptions passed through the airfield, each carrying up to 20 passengers returning home. The USAAF Movement Section closed in September 1945 and Valley was returned to full RAF control.

On 1 November 1944 N° 1528 BAT Flight, equipped with Oxfords, was formed at Valley. It was renamed N° 1528 Radio Aids (Range) Training Flight, with the responsibility for training RAF Transport Command pilots in American radio range let-down techniques. The unit remained at Valley until 17 December 1945 when it left for Blakenhill Farm, Oxfordshire.

Throughout 1946 the airfield was gradually run down and was used only to provide additional space for other congested airfields and the occasional exercise.

In February 1951, RAF Valley was granted a very distinguished station badge, depicting a Welsh Dragon holding a portcullis, indicating the ever-open gates of the base had during the years when it was a Master Diversion Airfield. Its motto is '*In adversis perfugium*' meaning 'Refuge in Adversity'.

RAF Valley was transferred to Flying Command as from 29 July 1946 and was officially designated a Master Diversionary Airfield from 1947, although it was very rarely used. From June 1947 to 1951 the airfield was put on care and maintenance, but still was used as a diversionary airfield during which time it was decided that the airfield should be reopened as an operational base for the RAF. A number of improvements were made to the airfield, including new brick buildings, renovated hangars, the wartime Blister hangars were replaced and taxiways were resurfaced. The RAF Valley Mountain Rescue Team, which was formed in August 1943, was joined in 1949 by the team from RAF Llanbedr. Only

Hawker Hunter trainers at Valley, 1950s.

one unit operated from Valley during the building programme and that was Nº 20 (ACC) Squadron, which arrived from Llanbedr with various training and target tug aircraft. It remained at Valley until being disbanded on 16 October 1951.

The first training unit under Flying Training Command was Nº 202 Advanced Flying School, which was formed at Valley in March 1951 with DH Vampire FIs, FB5s, TIIs and Gloster Meteor T7s. The AFS continued until March 1954, when it, and Nº 206 AFS, which had arrived from Oakington in January, were re-numbered Nº 7 Flying Training School. However, during another reorganisation, Nº 7 FTS was renumbered to Nº 4 FTS on 15 August 1960 and was initially equipped with Vampire T11s, then Gnat T1s, Hunter F6s, Vickers Varsity T1s and, today, the BAe Hawk T1s which arrived at Valley in October 1976 and within three years had completely replaced its predecessors in Flying Command.

The school is responsible for the advance flying and tactical training for both RAF and Royal Navy jet pilots. It also trains qualified flying instructors, qualified

DH Vampire T2 gate guardian at RAF Valley, 1962.

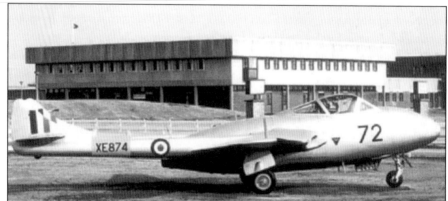

tactics instructors and qualified weapons instructors as well as providing training for other NATO forces.

On 1 January 1959, Nº 1 Guided Weapons Development Squadron was formed at Valley, although the unit had been at the airfield since June 1957. The squadron was equipped with Supermarine Swift F7s and Gloster Javelin FAW7s and was involved in guided missile testing and conversion. In May 1962 the squadron was disbanded and replaced by the Fighter Command Missile Practice Camp, which was renamed again in April 1968 to Strike Command Missile Practice Camp. Today the unit is known as Strike Command Air–Air Missile Establishment, and currently provides pilots who carry out live missile firings over Cardigan Bay. The target drones were provided by DERA at Llanbedr, which are either unmanned aircraft, specially built drones like the Jindiviks, or the supersonic Stiletto target.

RAF Valley has always been at the forefront of air sea rescue operations. Today the task is provided by 'C' Flight of Nº 22 Squadron operating the Westland Sea King Mk III, one of the busiest operational search and rescue flights in the country. The unit was formed at Valley in May 1955 to provide search and rescue facilities in the north-west sector. It also works closely with the mountain rescue teams based at the camp and in the Snowdonia and Lake District areas. Also based at the airfield is the Defence Helicopter Flying School with a Griffin HTI which trains crews for the RAF air sea rescue units.

The wartime airfield no longer exists as Valley has been completely modernized but there are still some traces of the past to be seen.

At the time of writing, plans were being drawn up to use Valley for scheduled civilian flights. During the 2004 Aviation Review it was decided that Wales, because of its poor transport infrastructure, was in need of a flexible air service. Plans proposed an air link between north and south Wales and east and west Wales. Initially, it was felt that Valley would be best choice as it was near to the A55 Expressway and close enough to the towns of north Wales. Part of the airfield has been allocated as a site for a small terminal and car park. Talks are in progress between the Ministry of Defence, the local authorities and airlines, who it is hoped will operate a twice daily service to Cardiff, reducing a five-hour journey to the south to a 40 minute flight.

Summary of the Units Based at RAF Valley From 1941 to Present Day
Nº 312 (Czech) Squadron from Speke 3 March 1941 with the Hurricane I. Departed for Jurby 25 April 1941.
Nº 615 Squadron from Kenley 21 April 1941 with the Hurricane I, IIa, IIb and IIc. Left for Manston 10 September 1941.
Nº 219 Squadron 'A' Flight, from Tangmere on 10 May 1941 equipped with the

Three BAe Hawk T1As over RAF Valley.

Beaufighter If. Left for Tangmere 30 June 1941.

N° 302 (Polish) Squadron from Jurby on 20 June 1941 to 11 July 1941 equipped with the Hurricane IIb.

N° 68 Squadron (a section) from June 28 1941 to July 18 1941 equipped with the Beaufighter 1f. The squadron came from and returned to High Ercall.

N° 456 (RAAF) Squadron was formed at Valley 30 June 1941 and left for Middle Wallop 30 March 1943. Initially the squadron was equipped with the Defiant I, but was re-equipped with the Beaufighter IIf and VIf.

N° 605 Squadron (one Flight) for three days from 6 August 1941 equipped with the Hurricane IIa. Squadron came from, and returned to, Baginton.

N° 275 (ASR) Squadron was formed at Valley 15 October 1941 and left for Warmwell 25 May 1944. Aircraft included the Lysander IIIa, Walrus I & II, Defiant I & Ic, Anson I and Spitfire Vb.

N° 43 Squadron from Drem 11 September 1941. Departed for Drem 17 September 1941 equipped with the Hurricane IIb.

N° 242 Squadron from Manston 16 September 1941, equipped with the Hurricane IIb. Left for Palemburg in the Far East 6 November 1941.

N° 350 (Belgian) Squadron was formed at Valley 13 November 1941 equipped with the Spitfire IIc. Left for Atcham 19 February 1942.

N° 131 Squadron, from 10 March 1942 to 14 May 1942 equipped with the Spitfire Vb. Came from, and returned to, Llanbedr.

N° 452 (RAAF) from Andreas 15 April 1942 equipped with the Spitfire Vc.

N° 247 Squadron, a detachment only, from High Ercall during April 1942, equipped with the Hurricane IIc & IIc.

N° 315 (Polish) Squadron, a detachment only, visited the base for one day 23 May 1942, from Woodvale, equipped with the Spitfire Vb.

N° 281 (ASR) Squadron from November 1942 to May 1943, equipped with Lysanders and Defiants. The unit came from, and returned to, RAF Ouston.

N° 23 OTU (Detachment) from Pershore for two weeks in December 1942, equipped with the Vickers Wellington Ic and II.

N° 406 (RCAF) Squadron arrived from Middle Wallop in May 1943 and departed for Exeter in November 1943. Equipped with the Beaufighter VIf.

N° 195 Squadron, a detachment only, arrived from Woodvale for one day 3 April 1943, equipped with the Hawker Typhoon Ib.

N° 285 (AAC) Squadron, a detachment only (from RAF Wrexham) during May 1943, equipped the with Martinet TT1.

N° 414 (USAAF) Squadron from 1 May to 11 May 1943, equipped with the Bristol Beaufighter If.

N° 125 Squadron arrived from Exeter 14 November 1943, equipped with the Beaufighter VIf. The unit left for RAF Hurn 24 March 1944. Whilst at Valley, it was re-equipped with the Mosquito NF XVII.

N° 157 Squadron from RAF Predannack, 26 March 1944 until 4 May 1944, equipped with the Mosquito NFII.

N° 1528 BAT Flight was formed at Valley on 1 November 1944, equipped with the Oxford I & II. Left for Blakenhill Farm, 17 December 1945.

N° 20 (AAC) Squadron arrived from RAF Llanbedr 19 July 1949, equipped with Beaufighters, Martinets, Spitfires, Havards, Oxfords and the Vampire F1 & F3. The unit was disbanded at Valley, 16 October 1951.

N° 202 AFS was formed at Valley in March 1951, equipped with the Vampire F1,

BAe Hawk T1 of N° 4 Flying Training School, RAF Valley.

BAe Hawk T1s overfly the airfield at Valley.

FB5, T11 and Meteor T7. The unit was renumbered on 24 March 1954 as N° 7 FTS and was disbanded on 14 August 1960 to be reformed as N° 4 FTS on the 15 August and remains at Valley to the present day. The Vampires were replaced by the Gnat T1 and the Hunter F6 and T7, as well as a number of Varsities T1s. From 1976, the BAe Hawk T1 was introduced into the service and by 1979 the type had became the standard RAF trainer. N° 4 FTS comprises of N°ˢ 19 and 208 Squadrons operating Hawk T1/1A training aircraft. N° 208 is responsible for advance flying training and N° 19 Squadron provides tactics and weapon training.

N° 22 Squadron ('C' Flight) air sea rescue unit established at RAF Valley during May 1955 and has remained at the airfield until the present day. It has been equipped with the Whirlwind HAR2 and HAR10, the Wessex HAR2 and today, the Westland Sea King Mk 3.

N° 1 GWDS, from 1 June 1957 to 31 December 1959, equipped with the Supermarine Swift F7 and 9 (Fireflash trials).

N° 1 GWTS from 1 January 1 1959 to 1 June 1962, equipped with the Gloster Javelin FAW7 (Firestreak and Redtop trials).

Newborough Warren

This was a decoy airfield, or 'Q' site as they were known, built as a decoy for the night fighter station at Valley. The purpose of these were to confuse enemy bombers as, during night time, they would be lit up to attract the bombers from the main airfield.

Newborough Warren was sited on some sand dunes in the south-west corner of Anglesey and came into use in 1941. The site consisted of only one enlarged Anderson shelter for the four-man team which was billeted in nearby Newborough. Standard Drem lights were used to mark out a dummy runway and were lit every night by the duty airman. The decoy field remained in use until 1943, until the threat of air raids had diminished and the site was abandoned. The Anderson shelter remained but has now been covered by sand and the area has been taken over by the Forestry Commission.

There is no record that the decoy deceived any enemy aircraft, although two bombers heading in its direction were intercepted by Spitfires of N° 41 Squadron from Llanbedr in 1942. Both bombers were driven away.

On 8 October 1942, Beaufighter Mk VIF (X8190) of N° 456 Squadron, RAAF, piloted by Sergeant R. Scott, and crewed by Sergeant C. A. Woods, was on night patrol when their starboard engine failed. Scott decided to return to their base at Valley but, while returning, flew into some low clouds and lost his direction. When the aircraft emerged from the clouds the pilot saw Newborough Drem lights burning bright and assumed it was Valley. The duty airmen did their best to warn the Beaufighter as it approached, but the aircraft hit the sand dunes and burst into flames. Both Sergeants Scott and Wood were killed in the crash.

39. Wrexham
Wrexham

RAF Wrexham was situated on a plateau, on the outskirts of the town, in an area known as Borras, which is just off the A534 road and about three miles north-east of the town centre. Work started on the airfield on 16 December 1940 and it was constructed by the local firm of Sir Alfred McAlpine Ltd. which had major government contracts at the time. It was built to the Air Ministry's pre-war plan and from the outset had three concrete runways. The airfield was officially known as RAF Wrexham, but local people always refer to it as Borras Airfield. It was initially intended that the airfield would house a fighter squadron (hence the concrete runways), as Wrexham was on the direct route of enemy bombers attacking the industrial areas of the north-west of England. It had one Bellman, three Super Robin and four blister type hangars.

RAF Wrexham was officially opened in June 1941, but the first unit to be based at the station was a N° 9 Group, Anti Aircraft Co-operation Flight, equipped with Blenheims and Lysanders, which arrived from Speke, Liverpool, on 10 August. The first fighter unit to move in was N° 96 Squadron (code letters ZJ) from RAF Carnage, the latter airfield often being waterlogged during the winter months. However, it took the squadron some months before fully completing the move. By 21 October 1941, the unit's fourteen Defiant Is and two Hurricane IIs had completed the move and while at Wrexham, during May 1942, was re-equipped with the Beaufighter II, with twin-engined conversion training done on three Oxfords borrowed from a neighbouring unit. The squadron retained the Defiant until July and the conversion was only marred by one accident, when aircraft T3414 failed to get airborne during a training exercise, left the runway and ran across a public road coming to rest in a small pond. The aircraft was totally destroyed by fire, but, due to the sturdy construction of the Beaufighter, the crew managed to scramble out safely.

Also in 1942, N° 285 Squadron became a lodger unit at the airfield. This was a co-operation squadron equipped with seven Lockheed Hudsons, four Blenheims, six Lysanders and four Defiants, used for target towing. Later the unit acquired some Airspeed Oxfords. On 29 October 1942, the squadron headquarters moved to RAF Honiley, but a detachment of one Oxford and four Defiants remained at Wrexham.

Aerial view of Wrexham, April 1946. [National Assembly for Wales]

The Duke of Kent inspected both Nos 96 and 285 Squadrons on his visit to the area on 5 May 1942. To show the RAF's appreciation of the Royal Observer Corps, a special air show was put on at the airfield on 17 May 1942 during which a variety of aircraft, including Beaufighters, Defiants, Hurricanes, Spitfires and a Mosquito from RAF Sealand, put on a demonstration for members of the Corps. A newly built Wellington from the Vickers factory at Broughton also made an appearance. Members of the ROC were also given the opportunity to experience a ten-minute flight in an Oxford.

Boulton Paul Defiants of Nº 96 Squadron at Wrexham. Another photograph where an attempt has been made to obliterate the squadron identification letters.

N° 96 Squadron's first Beaufighter patrol took place on 30 June 1942 and during the visit of the King and Queen to nearby RAF High Ercall, on 16 July 1942, the squadron's Beaufighters kept a standing patrol over Wrexham and the area. The squadron left Wrexham on 6 September 1942 bound for Honiley, to form part of the air defences of the Midlands.

For a period during the spring of 1943, USAAF C-47s became a regular visitors to the airfield, as their passengers investigated crashes in the nearby hills.

In February 1943 the airfield was transferred to Flying Training Command as a satellite airfield to nearby Carnage and on 1 March control passed on to N° 5 (P) AFU at RAF Tern Hill. However, on 4 May the unit was taken over by N° 17 (P) AFU and Wrexham became a satellite of RAF Calveley, which had 175 Miles Masters on its strength. When the unit had completed its task of training the allocated number of pilots, it was disbanded on 1 February 1944.

Wrexham remained Calveley's satellite airfield but, by now, N° 11 (P) AFU had became resident in the former airfield, operating Airspeed Oxford IIs. 'B' Flight, with forty-five aircraft, were allocated to Wrexham to relieve the situation at Calveley.

From the early 1930s the RAF's training policy had been in some disarray but, as the war progressed, some sort of strategic training policy emerged. In December 1944, N° 11 (P) AFU was converted to single engined trainers and Miles Masters returned to Wrexham but, by the end of the year, were replaced by the North American Harvard trainer. Eventually four flights were based at Wrexham, (E, F, G and H Flights) and the unit remained at the airfield until 21 June 21 when the OTU was finally disbanded.

Another lodger unit based at the airfield was N° 577 Squadron, equipped with

Line up of N° 577 Squadron personnel at Wrexham, 1944. [T. Bevin]

Oxford IIs and Spitfires, which moved in during the early part of 1943 and left for RAF Atcham in 1945.

After a brief period of hardly any activity, N° 5355 Airfield Construction Unit moved in to prepare plant equipment for shipment overseas.

When N° 577 Squadron left in July 1945, the airfield remained fairly quiet except for the occasional emergency landing and in September, was put on care and maintenance. Throughout the following year various airfield installations were removed.

In October 1959, the redundant and derelict airfield was auctioned off by the Air Ministry. The local council had expressed an interest in acquiring the airfield as a potential aerodrome for the town but the plans came to naught and the airfield was handed back to its original owner, Lord Kenyon, who offered it for sale. Alfred McAlpine Ltd, the same company that actually built RAF Wrexham, bought it and during the 1960s, two of the runways were broken up for hardcore for roadways, but the third was retained for flying during the 1960s and 1970s, being utilised by Sir Jimmy McAlpine's Beech Super King Air aircraft. Eventually, the company ceased all flying and the remaining runway disappeared as the site was excavated for gravel. The RAF accommodation area was built upon during the 1960s, becoming the Borras Park housing estate.

In 1977 National Eisteddfod of Wales was held on the airfield.